ALPHA BOUND

DAWN OF THE CURSE BOOK 2

LEISL LEIGHTON

Published by Leisl Leighton as Permien Press. For more information, email: leisl@leislleighton.com

Cover design – Samantha Marshall

Editor – Brooke Halliwell

eBook ISBN: 978-1-922836-21-2; Print ISBN: 978-1-922836-22-9

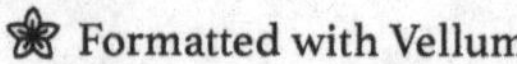 Formatted with Vellum

PRAISE FOR THE PACK BOUND SERIES

Wow! I have found a new author to read! Leisl Leighton has created a world full of intrigue and captivating characters that draw you into the story and hold readers hostage until the very end. I was certainly spellbound throughout.

— EVA MILLIEN - STORMY VIXEN'S BOOK REVIEWS

Leisl Leighton is an awesome story teller. This whole series so far has me wanting to keep finding out more about other characters and read her other books.

— JESSICA - GOODREADS REVIEWER

I was hooked!

— CYN - GOODREADS REVIEWER

Leisl has out done herself again ... Strong characters and a great story line that will keep you entertained ... I can't wait to read more of her work either too. I have come to love this series.

— KIM - GOODREADS REVIEWER

I found the premise very cool...I recommend to all shifter and witch fans because this is an intriguing story with tons going on and a new spin that you will love! I can't wait for the next book!

— CASSANDRA LOSKOT - CASSANDRA LOST IN BOOKS BLOG/BOOK REVIEWS

ALPHA BOUND

To my dad, who showed me what the best Alphas should be.
💕 Love you always 💕

1

'I willna change my mind,' Iain said to Dougal and the other lieutenants ranged in front of him on the other side of the long table. 'I dinna understand why ye bring this argument to me again today. I gave my answer yesterday, and I meant it.'

Dougal managed not to clench his jaw—or punch the table in front of him—even though his anger was a raw, wild thing inside him. Somehow he managed to say evenly, 'My Alpha, I beg that ye listen to what Cal has said.' He gestured to his second in command and oldest friend, who stood beside him, tension in every inch of his tall frame. 'The pack is unhappy about this ruling. They dinna think it is sufficient after the death, destruction and injury that Lachlan caused. If ye canna sentence him to immediate death by hanging, then his Packbond should be broken and he should be banished. It is the fitting punishment fer what was done.'

Iain's jaw squared dangerously and he thumped his hand down on the table in front of him. 'My son's punishment has been handed down. He will be put into the dreamless sleep by one of our Healer witches.'

'Neither Morghanna nor Abigail have the time or energy to do such a thing right now,' Cal said, standing firmly beside Dougal even while some of the others—including Cal's brother, Bram—took a step back.

'Then the other one ye have been sniffing around can do it,' Iain said briskly, blue eyes pinned on Dougal as he waved his hand in the direction of the Healer Hall. 'Although why ye show interest in such a mousy, scarred thing, Dougal, I dinna ken. A Were like ye needs to mate with another strong Were.'

Inside him, his wolf saw red—and he didn't blame him. How dare anyone, even their so-called Alpha, talk about their future mate in such a way. He wanted so badly to let his wolf have its way, to burst out of him and take the selfish, narcissistic Alpha by the throat, but that would create more chaos and right now, he was unlikely to win. Even with others by his side like Cal. Their Alpha was still too strong —something he was to blame for more than any other.

So, instead of attacking to avenge the slur on his future mate as every muscle and fibre inside him longed to do, Dougal viciously shoved his rage down, telling his wolf everything he had been telling himself this last month to try to make it remain calm. He clenched his hands at his sides, desperately trying to stop his claws from clicking out—at this point, even something so small would shout a challenge to the increasingly paranoid Iain. The pack desperately needed stability. He couldn't be the thing that tore it apart. Not during this difficult time.

Cal shifted, briefly bumping his shoulder, the touch offering his support physically as he sent it down the part of the Packbond that connected them to each other. At the same time he said, with a calm Dougal was striving to feel, 'I am certain ye are aware, my Alpha, that one doesna choose who the Fates deem ye are mated to.'

'Hmph.' Iain folded his arms across his chest before saying with a smirk, 'Shame. But I suppose it canna be helped if she is who ye want, Dougal. At least she is a strong witch despite her mousiness and the ugly burn scars on her face.'

Dougal just managed to tamp down his wolf again before it could burst out and take what was theirs. He didn't manage to cut off its growl, though he did manage to squelch it. Iain's brow rose—he'd heard it—and leaned forward, as if preparing for the challenge he was obviously trying to provoke.

Swallowing down hard on his fury, Dougal pushed his wolf back with as much force as he could, pleading with him just to hold it in. '*Fer the pack. And fer Leanna,*' he said inside his mind to his wolf. '*She doesna need the stress of our injury or death, especially now. We have to hold back on our challenge fer her.*'

His wolf subsided, but remained on high alert. As did he. It was hard not to be when the Were in front of him kept insulting his mate. She was so much more than those scars on her face. The thought helped him to keep it together and say in her defence, 'Leanna is stronger than she appears. Morghanna says she is the strongest Healer we have aside from Abigail, and soon will surpass her with a little more training.'

Iain's shit-eating grin widened as he waved his hand. 'Which is why I said she can take care of carrying out the sentence on my son.'

Dougal gritted his teeth aware now that Iain was definitely trying to bait him. How had he ever given all his loyalty to this Were? He was so uncaring of his people and what his decrees did to them. Despite the fact that Iain, being the Alpha, should already know it, Dougal pointed out, 'It will hurt her to do such a thing. Ye canna ask it of her.'

'I will do more than ask. I demand it.' Iain smacked his hand on the table once more, his eyes darting around, taking in who else was in the dining hall that was standing in as their temporary Alpha Hall after it was destroyed by Lachlan when he tried to take over the pack and falsely claim Morghanna as his. As his eyes landed on the dozen or so kitchen workers setting up for the midday repast, he straightened his shoulders and roared, 'All of ye, get out!'

The workers immediately dropped what they were doing and scurried out of the hall like a cur with its tail between its legs. Hating to see his packmates so cowed, Dougal said, 'My Alpha, they were only doing their jobs.'

Iain's gaze snapped back to Dougal, and he said with the full hardness of his Alpha voice, 'I remind ye, I am still Alpha of this pack. Unless ye or anyone else here has something to say about that?'

Those around Dougal lowered their gazes and Dougal had to force himself to do the same so their angry Alpha wouldn't take eye contact as a challenge. He needed time and a plan on how to cut off the flow of power between him, the lieutenants and senior soldiers, and the Alpha—especially important given too many of them were still blindly loyal. Until they'd stopped feeding Iain their power without giving their intent away, Iain would be strong enough to fatally wound him in a challenge even if Dougal could manage to take him down.

There was a tense silence as everyone waited to see which way Iain would go.

'Good,' Iain said finally. 'That is settled then. As is my decree. The scarred Healer will take care of putting my son into the deep sleep until the Healers find some way to fix him. Once asleep, he will be kept where I can visit him regularly. Those are the last words I will say on this matter.'

'Aye, my Alpha,' Dougal intoned along with the others, their words ringing in the empty hall. Hopefully it wouldn't be long until the pack's Alpha Hall was rebuilt, because having these meetings in such an open space where there was no true privacy was making it impossible to reason with Iain. He'd always been stubborn but now ...

He shoved that thought aside as it only made the anger inside him rise again. Something neither he nor his wolf needed more of right now. They needed clear-headed thinking. The timing for a challenge had to be right. Especially given too many of their people were still scared and hurting from the aftermath of Lachlan's attack. And unlike his Alpha, he wasn't going to be accused of putting anything before what he owed to his pack—except for his mate of course.

Mates were the only exception to the 'pack first' rule.

Not that Leanna was his mate yet. But she would be. Soon if he had his way. He'd been slowly bringing her around—a necessity given her past—and he wasn't about to hurry her along now. It must be her choice. Despite his and his wolf's need to hold her in their arms and claim her as theirs, they were both firm on this one point.

Leanna needed to choose them.

So he'd given her time and space and had gently courted, allowing her to get to know them. To trust them. He thought she was almost there. He just needed to—

'Well? What are ye waiting fer! I have given my final word. Go see it done!'

'Aye, my Alpha,' Dougal said, his bow deep and as subservient as he could make it. Then he backed up, Cal at his side, the others already making their way out of the door.

He couldn't believe he had let his mind wander like that while standing in front of his Alpha and the other lieutenants and senior soldiers. The degree of his distraction due to the unresolved nature of his mating was another reason why the time was not right to challenge for Alpha.

As he closed the door behind him, he straightened and let the life of the Pack Village surround him. He and his wolf needed the calm familiarity it always brought to stop him from turning around and going right back in that room.

The sound of construction filled the air, as did the sounds of pack and coven going about their work. The scent of freshly baked bread wafted out of the kitchens beside the hall, as did the smell of blood and viscera from the deer the Hunters had brought in this morning. The cooks planned to turn some into Iain's favourite venison stew and the rest would be salted and dried for use through the colder months when prey was scarce.

Hopefully the stew would be ready soon as he knew Leanna liked it and it would tempt her to leave her work to fill her stomach— something that was becoming increasingly difficult to do in the month since the attack. She lost herself too often in reading though the ancient grimoires and diaries Bridgette Cantrae and her mate, Malcolm, were sending back from their travels through Europa to continue to unite packs and covens. New packages arrived by magical means every week it seemed and Leanna was fascinated with them—

she said they were showing her how much had been lost through the centuries.

Cal cleared his throat, bringing Dougal's attention back to the present. He glanced at his friend who stood at the bottom of the stairs and saw that Cal was looking at him as if waiting for a response. 'I am sorry. I was lost in thought. What did ye say?' he asked as he jogged down the stairs.

'I can see ye are worried. So I was asking do ye wish me to go and tell Leanna?'

Dougal sighed heavily as he shook his head. 'Thank ye fer the offer but nae. It must come from me.'

'Ye are a good Were,' Cal said, slapping his shoulder as they began to walk towards the Healer Hall.

'I try to be,' he said softly. 'I dinna think I am doing much of a job of it right now though.'

'Hogshite. Ye are the only reason our pack is still as strong as it is.' Cal looked around as if checking to see who might be near, then leaned in and said quietly, 'Ye should be our Alpha now.'

'Cal,' Dougal said warningly.

'What? It was always meant to be ye when Iain was ready to stand down.'

'He doesna want to stand down yet though, does he?'

'Nae. More's the pity. He has let us down too often. And used us fer too long to strengthen himself. Now with this latest decree about Lachlan's punishment ... The pack are nae happy.'

'Whist,' Dougal whispered, leaning in close to Cal and speaking in an undertone no other Were should be able to hear, especially given there didn't seem to be anyone around. 'We canna talk like that —not yet.'

'But when?'

'As ye said, it would hurt the pack right now and I canna be responsible fer that.'

'Iain is hurting the pack with his selfishness.'

'Aye. But we need to be certain all the lieutenants and senior soldiers would back my challenge or we risk causing a schism we would struggle to rise from. I canna do that to the pack.'

'Most of the pack are ready fer ye to be leader.'

'That is an overstatement, Cal. There are still too many who dinna see him like we now see him.' He looked away, towards the mountain peaks across the loch. 'I am ashamed. I was so blindly loyal fer so long that I didna do aught even though deep down the wrongness of what he was doing was a bitter whisper inside me. That I let him weaken me to the point where I couldna stand against him with any certainty of winning ...' He sighed and shook his head heavily. 'I truly thought I was doing the right thing in following his lead, his instruction, so blindly. I am ashamed it took Lachlan trying to rape Morghanna to ken just how wrong Iain was in how he handled his son. And just how blindly loyal we all have been to go along with it.'

He looked back at Cal, the shame and anger—with himself as much as with Iain—swirling like nausea inside him. 'It is a struggle to do aught about it now, but it would be even more wrong to make a move when the pack needs stability. Even the stability of a leadership that does not place them first, as it should, is better than the trauma an Alpha challenge would bring right now.' He patted Cal on the shoulder. 'I am sorry to have to ask for ye to swallow yer anger and pride too, and continue to follow Iain's leadership, but if we care fer the pack, we canna do aught else. Do ye ken?'

'Aye. It goes against the grain, but I ken the need to wait. Especially with this latest decree causing so much difficulty fer ye with yer mate.'

'I thank ye, *mo bràthair*, fer yer concern. But I am not worried fer myself. I am more worried about her reaction when I ask this of Lele.'

'Will she refuse?'

'Nae. It isna in her to refuse to do something to help, even if it hurts her to do it.'

'How do ye cope with that? I would want to take my mate away from everything that caused her pain and never let her out of my embrace.'

Dougal chuckled wryly. 'It is a struggle for both sides of my nature not to do exactly that. But Le-le has been smothered and treated like she isna capable her entire life by people who should have known better. Morghanna told me some things ...' He shook his head, the words sticking in his throat because not only were they private things Le-le did not want to share with many people, but it was hard to think about how she was treated by her mama and other members of her family and former coven before coming here. He swallowed hard and looked down at the ground as Cal stood silent by his side, waiting for him to continue.

'She has been through so much. She simply needs trust and love and support from me and no more.'

2

ougal took a deep breath in and looked towards the Healer Hall where he could feel his future mate even now. Given they weren't mated, he should not feel so strongly and with such certainty where she was. Nor should he feel her emotions with such clarity as she went about the work of Healing that she loved. But it had been like this from the first moment he'd seen her when a small piece of the bond had snapped into place even though that shouldn't have been possible.

He shouldn't have been so surprised though given the strength of the pull that had drawn him towards the edge of the village that day when the caravan of travelling witches had arrived to be bonded by the Pact to Pack MacCrae. Leanna had been there among them, hiding in the back, and he'd instantly known it was she whom he had been drawn to see. He hadn't been able to take his eyes from her as Morghanna had taken her under her wing and ushered her away to the temporary bunkhouse that had been set up for the new arrivals.

He'd followed at a distance, not wishing to spook this witch who was going to be his mate. Even without that little thread of bond that improbably attached them upon the moment of seeing her, he could sense he needed to be careful with how he approached her.

Thankfully Morghanna, having seen him waiting outside the bunkhouse, had asked him to be her *Sgàth*, her Shadow, and oversee her safety. She hadn't said it then, but he knew now she meant to keep Lachlan far away from the shy and damaged witch. And as he'd gotten to know the gentle strength that was his mate, he understood exactly why the Fates had matched them as they had.

She was the other half of him, the part that reminded him why he should care for others, not just that it was his duty because he was Alpha born. Knowing her, working alongside her, had made him a much better Were and first lieutenant and had made him ready to see just how wrong he'd been in blindly following his Alpha, despite the fact he'd been brought up to believe that was his duty.

He understood now that the strength in other packs, like the McVale Pack, wasn't in the strength of their Alpha and his lieutenants, but in the way they worked together, in the way they didn't follow blindly, but questioned and pushed their leader to be better, to do better.

That's what he wanted for their pack.

And what they wouldn't have under Iain's leadership. Especially with him continuing to put his son first.

He sighed as his thoughts came back around to the main issue that plagued him. And the conversation ahead of him. He turned to Cal and said, 'Thank ye fer yer considerate offer, but I need to tell Le-le about Iain's decree and help her prepare for what she must do. But we will talk more about the issues plaguing our pack after Lachlan is taken care of and everyone has settled down to routine once more. I warn ye though, I willna make a move until the pack is more settled and ready fer such a change.'

Cal nodded. 'Aye. I agree. But do ye wish me to begin wording up some of the pack that see things as we do?'

'Nae. Not yet. We need to be more certain who is seeing the truth of the situation, especially among the lieutenants and senior soldiers.' He scrubbed his fingers against the roughness of whiskers that shadowed his chin and cheeks. 'Let us get through dealing with

Lachlan first. Then we will be more certain about who is with us and can talk about what needs to be done.'

'And hopefully by then ye will have the strength of a mating to a powerful witch behind ye.'

Dougal couldn't help the smile that quirked his mouth. 'Hopefully. But that is up to Le-le. Which, after asking her to do this today, I am uncertain she will be ready fer any time soon.'

Cal patted his shoulder and smiled knowingly. 'By the scent that surrounds her—yer scent—I ken that time is sooner than ye think.'

He didn't say anything to that because the hope for it was too tight in his chest. Instead, he nodded and said, 'Get on with yer assigned tasks then. I will get to mine.'

'Aye. I will go straight to the cabin and see Lachlan is properly secured. I will await yer's and Leanna's arrival.'

'Very good.'

He turned and continued on to the Healer Hall where he knew Le-le would be pouring over the old diaries or creating Healing potions and tisanes—one of her favourite things to do.

As he entered the hall, he couldn't help but think about how he was going to tell her what had been decided. He really didn't want her anywhere near Lachlan, but he couldn't protect her from this. She was the strongest Healer they had aside from Abigail and it was her duty to do this.

But truthfully, no Healer should be asked to do this. Even to stop such an evil from hurting the pack and coven again. The sentence for such an evil should be banishment if not death—a sentence Iain would have brought down without hesitation on anyone else had they done what Lachlan had.

Dougal sighed angrily and shook his hands out. He couldn't face Leanna with such anger and disappointment in his heart. Because she was too empathetic and would be unable to cope with such extreme emotion. Especially now when he was here to take her to do something he knew she would not want to do.

But there was nobody else who could do it. Even if Morghanna was as good at sleep spells as Leanna, she was too busy with her duties as head of their coven, not to mention helping her husband with his memory loss and retraining him in his powers—powers he'd used to save them all. And Abigail couldn't do it—the old witch's health had already been fading before Lachlan had tried to destroy the pack and coven, but since then, having given her all to Morghanna and Alistair in the fight, she really hadn't recovered.

Morghanna was afraid the old witch wouldn't be with them for much longer if she couldn't find some way to help rebuild her strength.

But that was a worry for another time. Today's worry was all centred on Leanna and getting her up to the prisoner cabin where Lachlan was being held. He had to support her in the difficult task ahead. And he couldn't do that if he showed up with this anger in his heart.

He took a moment to pace the space outside the door of the herbal stillroom, breathing slowly in and out to calm himself and his wolf. And only when he was certain he could face her with some semblance of calm, did he open the door.

She looked up immediately, not hiding the scars on her face behind her strawberry blonde hair like she used to do with him—and still did with most everyone else. It was as if she had known it would be him. But there was no sign of the shy smile she'd begun to give him every time she saw him. No sign of true welcome in her eyes.

She knew.

Of course she did. She would have been told of Iain's decree yesterday the same as everyone else. Undoubtedly Morghanna would have already spoken to her about it. Morghanna had told him earlier that he would not change Iain's mind—and she had been right, as she most often was about these things. By the looks of the shadows under Le-le's beautiful brown eyes, she'd had the conversation with her mentor last night.

He could wish Morghanna had kept the news to herself until this morn so that Le-le at least had a good night's sleep under her belt. Not that she wouldn't be capable of the magic required of her with no sleep—she was so strong and could go without sleep for days without faltering in her Healing duties. But the emotional toll of what was ahead would be better faced if she were well-rested.

'He said no to your request,' she said solemnly.

Dougal's brows rose. 'How did ye ken I asked Iain to rethink his decree?'

She tipped her head towards him, her plump lips twitching into something close to a smile. 'I have spent enough time around you, Dougal, to realise you would not agree with such a decree. But you should not have bothered. Iain will never change his mind where his son is concerned. And this is the best solution given everything.'

'Not fer ye, it isna. Ye ken ye are the one who will have to put him into the sleep?'

Leanna nodded briskly, her hands moving nervously over the herbs in front of her. 'I know. I knew as soon as I heard. I told Morghanna and Abigail I would do it.'

'Ye did?'

'Yes.' Her brows rose. 'You do not expect me to ask them to do it just to save me the difficulty of such a thing, do you?'

'Nae,' he said, smiling fondly at her. 'I didna expect any such thing.'

She tilted her head, her pointed chin lifted stubbornly and she pulled her shoulders back. 'Let us not dally then. It is best we simply get on with the task. The sooner done the sooner it will be over.'

'Very wise.'

Her eyes flashed with a little hit of temper. 'You are not laughing at me are you, Dougal MacCrae?'

'I dinna dare, Leanna Finnigan.'

'Good.' She took a deep breath and put the rosemary down she'd been running through her fingers. 'Well, let us go then.'

'Ye dinna need to take aught with ye?'

She looked around her as she shook her head. 'It is not that kind of spell. Although, maybe if we can get him to drink a calming tisane, it would make the entire process easier.'

'Given he has refused anything magical to help with his pain, I dinna think we will have any luck with that, but we can take some and try if ye wish.'

She paused for a moment, her gaze roving over the stills and jars in front of her, and then shook her head. 'No. Best I simply do the spell and put the poor Were to sleep.'

'Dinna feel sorry fer the bastard, Le-le. He doesna deserve yer sympathy.'

'No. Maybe not. But he will get it none-the-less. He is a lost soul who has been horribly affected by the Darkness. Despite what he has done, I will not allow my anger and hatred to override my ability to feel pity for such a retched creature. He will never know true happiness and for that reason alone, he has my sorrow.'

'Ye are a wonder, Le-le.' He had drawn close as she'd spoken and reached out to brush a lock of hair behind her ear, the silken strand like warmed sunlight against his skin. Her scent—like sun-warmed lavender and the sweet tang of a just-ripe apple—wove around him, making him want to stand there and simply breathe her in.

She looked up at him as his fingers grazed against her cheek, her skin pinking a little, the flecks of amber in her brown eyes glowing a little in the sunlight streaming through the window behind her. 'Dougal,' she breathed out.

He leaned in a little. 'Aye?'

Confusion and uncertainty swam through her brown eyes, the amber flecks in them flaring brighter for a moment before she swallowed hard and took a step back, embarrassment a flush over her skin.

He let his hand drop to his side even though he longed more than anything to reach for her again, to cup her face in his hands and take her mouth in the kiss he was certain she wanted as much as him. But she obviously wasn't quite ready for that, besides which, now wasn't the time. To cover up his obvious arousal, he stepped to the side and held out his arm. 'Shall we go?'

'Yes,' she said, her voice huskier than usual. He heard her swallow before she said, 'You will not leave my side, will you?'

'Never,' he said. 'Not unless ye wish me to.'

She nodded and said softly under her breath, 'I would never wish that.'

He wasn't certain if she'd meant him to hear that, so ignored it and gestured towards the door. 'Shall we?'

To her credit she lifted her head and marched steadily out the door at his side, never wavering as they headed up the hill towards the cabin in the woods where the pack's greatest enemy was being held.

3

Leanna was glad Dougal was at her side as she entered the cabin because the scene was confronting.

Lachlan was being held down by Callum and a number of other Were, his face red, spittle flying out his mouth as he swore at them and struggled against their hold.

She was sorry he had woken—or been woken—because this would have been so much easier if he'd remained asleep. He'd been asleep a lot in the weeks since the fight. She supposed it should be expected given what had happened to him. He, like so many others, had been weakened and made ill by the forces at play that horrible day.

A day that he had been completely responsible for.

Well, maybe not completely. The Darkness had been within him, changing him into the Beast and pushing him to do the things he'd done for its own machinations.

How much of that had been within Lachlan's control, they couldn't know. He had to have wanted some of it given the fact he'd invited the Darkness in. Or maybe the Darkness had never left him when the MacCraes were tied into the Pact. Maybe because of the way he was he ...

Dougal squeezed her hand that was lying in the crook of his arm. She looked up at him, into his dark blue eyes that had begun to shift into the lighter blue of an Alpha over the months she'd known him, her gaze running over the sharply masculine planes of his face, the glorious golden colour of his sun-kissed skin, and across the breadth of his chest and shoulders. His black wavy hair was in need of a cut and she longed to reach up and rake her hands through it, but she let go of his arm and clenched them at her sides instead. She took in a deep breath, breathing in his unique scent—a mix of the burst of citrus when you broke into an orange and the sun-warmed lavender in the fields.

She could stare at him—and breathe in that scent—for hours, but there wasn't time. Right now she had a job to do. A job she didn't want to do. But just looking at Dougal gave her strength and comfort, especially because of what she saw reflected in his eyes as he looked down at her.

Nobody looked at her like Dougal. He made her feel capable of being so strong, so sure. He trusted her like Morghanna and Abigail trusted her. He trusted in her powers as they did too. He had brought her here to do this job, not because she had to, but because he thought her capable of it.

She hated the necessity of this, but Morghanna was right. There was no alternative. Their Alpha had done nothing to curb his son, and this was the only way to ensure he could hurt no one else.

Still, it felt like a sacrilege to put another living being into what would become a permanent sleep. Iain's hope that Lachlan could be saved or changed was futile. There was no changing one such as he. The evil had got inside him too deeply and there was no carving it out magically or otherwise.

Even so, she couldn't escape the sensation crawling up her spine that told her no good could come of this.

But Morghanna and Dougal needed her to take care of it, and given only she or her elderly mentor, Abigail, could handle this spell being used in this way, it was up to her. She wouldn't ask the woman who was more a mother to her than her own mother had been to take on this burden. She was ill enough as it was. Keeping this spell alive might be the thing that would kill her.

Leanna couldn't live with herself if that were to happen.

So here she was doing this thing she knew was the only way, despite the voice deep in her mind warning her that something horrible would come out of it.

She just had to push that voice, that feeling, aside and do the job that was hers to do.

And she would do it with this strong, glorious Were standing by her side. Who was always standing by her side, more than a Were Shadow—a *Sgàth* in his language—was expected to do. Maybe he did feel some of what she was feeling. Maybe ...

Leanna shook that fanciful thought away. There was no way this Were could possibly feel what she felt for him. The bond between them was simple friendship amplified by the Packbond, that was all. It was silly for her to imagine it could be anything else. Especially now when they were here with this task before her.

She turned her attention back to Lachlan who was still struggling against the Were holding him down. Thankfully he was still too weak to truly hurt those he fought against. But she should act quickly before they hurt him.

She lifted her hands to cant the spell of sleeping. Blocking out his struggling and screaming, she called her magic to her, forming the words of the spell in her mind to bind the power into it.

She'd only just started when he managed to get a hand free, grabbing a mug on the bedside table and throwing it at her. She managed to stumble out of the way of the projectile as Dougal leapt forward and grabbed the Were's hands, pinning them down on the bed. Callum and the others followed his lead and held their prisoner down more firmly so he could barely move.

Dougal threw a look over his shoulder and said, 'Leanna. Now.'

As she lifted her hands again she saw a shadowed blackness swirling in Lachlan's eyes; an evil with no end.

She sucked in a shocked breath. The Darkness had been banished from Lachlan, so what was this? Did he still have some part of it inside him? Was he about to turn into the Beast again? It should be impossible, but after everything that had happened, much that she'd thought impossible had proved otherwise.

One thing was certain. There was still too much evil inside this Were, so she needed to do this quickly before it could infect or affect anyone else.

She pulled her power close, winding it around her, filling it with her intent. As she did so, Lachlan's venom- and hate-filled gaze raked over her, making her shiver.

Then, before she could cant the words of her spell, he shouted, 'I vow this night to seek my revenge. On Morghanna and her Alistair. On every pack member who brought me this low. May the dark Gods ken, my Were-vow never be forsworn, I will have my revenge.'

Outside, a roll of thunder rumbled across the sky, finishing with one knocking clap above the hut.

A flash of lightning and a crash of thunder quickly followed. The cabin trembled as the lightning struck close by, bits of plaster and dust raining down from the ceiling.

'What the—' Dougal let go of Lachlan to race across the small space to her, pulling her to his side and swinging them around so his large body was between her and Lachlan. She pushed at him—she couldn't do the spell if she couldn't see Lachlan. But before she could get the muscled Were to budge, another flash lit the sky.

The white flare hit the hut, sending wood and thatch and Were flying.

Including her and Dougal.

The last thing she saw before she was enveloped in Dougal's arms was Lachlan tossed into the air, through the large hole created by the lightning explosion, disappearing in the night black shadows between the trees. His expression was lit up by the fires caused by the explosion, and it was gleeful and yet somehow so full of menace.

Then she could see nothing as her face was pushed into the first lieutenant's muscled chest, his arms a band around her as he endeavoured to shield her from the explosion and the impact of their inevitable landing.

Branches of the trees that surrounded the cabin whipped against them. Dougal took most of the brunt the way he was wrapped around her. She tried to raise a shield around them as they flew through the air, but her magic was sluggish to her command. Having been drawn to create another, bigger spell, it was reluctant to be focused to another task. Damn it! Why did her magic have to do this now?

A shield sputtered into life, flickering as she tried to wrestle her power to change to a new intent, but before she could firm it into something that would protect them, they smacked hard onto the firm earth between the trees.

Even with the protection of Dougal's arms around her, the impact drove the breath from her lungs. Stars filled her sight as they rolled along the earth, crashing through underbrush to finally come to a bone-crunching stop against an ancient tree.

A cry of agony exploded out of Dougal and his arms loosened around her, falling to smack into the ground beside them.

She rolled off him, gasping for breath. The sudden stop had winded her. She rubbed her chest, her diaphragm, trying to ease the muscles so she could take a breath. Any moment she expected Dougal to appear in her line of sight, his handsome face creased into a worried frown as he tried to help her. But he didn't appear. In fact, she didn't hear him moving at all.

Worried, even as she gasped to breathe, she turned her head to the side to see what had happened to her *Sgàth*.

His eyes were closed, his leg and arm nearest the tree were obviously broken. A dark rivulet ran from the ear she could see, another from his nose and the edge of his mouth. But that wasn't the worst of it—he was lying with his back bent around the tree in a way it shouldn't.

Oh Goddess! Goddess. Was he dead? No, his chest was rising, but not in the way it should. Only one side was rising and he made a strange rattling sound.

His ribs were obviously broken and it was more than likely that the broken bone had punctured his lung.

She tried to move, to get up so she could go to him, start a Healing, but pain shot through her chest making it impossible to rise. She gasped, rubbing at the pain, at the tightened muscles that stopped her from breathing, but still, she couldn't catch her breath. She hadn't broken a rib—of that she was certain. She'd simply been winded badly.

The night darkened around her. Had the moon been hidden behind a cloud?

No, the darkness was edging in her eyes like a cloudy haze.

She was losing consciousness!

No. No. She couldn't fall into unconsciousness now. Dougal needed her. He needed her to Heal him. He needed her to save him. She had to stay awake. Had to find a way.

But if this was because of a head injury, there would be no fighting it off for long.

She touched her aching head, her fingers coming away sticky with her blood. She'd hit her head. But not badly enough to make her lose consciousness. She'd feel that kind of injury, she was certain. She tried to take a deep breath, to settle herself, but all she could do was gape and suck without the relief a breath would bring.

She was going to lose consciousness because she couldn't get a damned breath.

She couldn't lose consciousness. She had to help Dougal. The pack couldn't afford to lose him. *She* couldn't afford to lose him. His belief in her, his protection, had come to mean so much despite the fact she knew her feelings were one-sided, that he could never be with one such as her—he did nothing that wasn't for the good of the pack and so he must mate with a strong Were to preserve the line.

It wasn't his fault she couldn't manage her feelings or expectations.

Not that any of that mattered right now. Damn her stupid thoughts! Why could she never rope them in? Abigail had tried and tried to teach her, but to no avail. Nothing could ever calm her roiling mind, no matter how she managed to evince an air of calm for her patients in the past month. It's why she had never truly managed to get a handle on her powers. If she hadn't hesitated tonight, Lachlan would never have been able to do what he did.

How had he done it?

She shook her head before the question could take hold. No. No. She had to concentrate now. Had to get her breath back. If there was any time to rope her stupid unmanageable thoughts in, it was now.

But the night became darker as she gasped for breath, the lack of oxygen drawing the shadows around her faster and faster.

No! No!

She shot a look at Dougal. There seemed to be more blood and his breathing was increasingly laboured.

Goddess. Please. Help. If there was any time for you to hear me, it's now. Help. Help me save him.

But of course, her plea was met with nothing but silence. Not that she expected to hear her Goddess. But she had expected to feel her presence as everyone else seemed to be able to do, especially in times of great need. But she hadn't felt her since the magical explosion that had taken her parents and scarred her so terribly.

Another sign that there was something horribly wrong with her. Who had ever heard of a witch who couldn't commune with the Goddess?

Dougal made a rattling sound.

Tears streaming from her eyes, she made a last ditch attempt to hold onto consciousness and pull in a breath.

All she managed was a gasping wheeze.

4

Leanna tried to take another breath but nothing came. No, no, no!

If only she could use her Healing power on herself, but that was a skill seemingly forbidden to all Healers. They could only use their magic and powers on others, never on themselves. Which seemed stupid really. How could they help another if injury to themselves made it impossible?

Frustrated and angry—with the rules that governed Healers, with herself for not managing to take in a simple breath, and with the Goddess for remaining absent in this hour of need—she thumped her hands against her chest, her diaphragm, over and over trying to get them to respond.

Pain shot through her—she would be black and blue tomorrow— but she didn't care, kept repeating the action harder and harder, her anger rising, rising every moment she failed to take in a breath.

Orange power flared to life on her fingertips and shot into her.

Warmth filled her and her lungs expanded. She took in a loud gasp of breath. The shadows that had encroached her vision fled as sweet oxygen filled her lungs. She breathed in deeply, once, twice, then rolled to her side. Her chest protested, still aching from however long it had been without oxygen, but she didn't care. Didn't even care to think about how she'd managed to use her power on herself. All she could think about was getting to Dougal.

Helping Dougal.

Yea Gods. He was so pale; the blood running from his ears, nose and mouth black and glistening against his too pale skin. His mouth had fallen open as he gasped for breath, his chest barely moving now. The way he lay against the tree trunk, his legs caught in the underbrush on one side, made it difficult to take in visually the full extent of his injuries. But she didn't dare move him for fear of waking him from his unconscious state and causing him to register the pain he must be in.

Getting as close as she could, heedless of the sharp edges of broken branches and shrubbery digging into her knees, she lifted her hands and called her power to her once more.

It came more easily than when she'd tried to call the shield. It had been ready to be used in a Healing ritual and while this kind of Healing was different, it used the same pathways.

She closed her eyes, running her hands over him, touching his aura rather than his skin to get a full idea of his injuries.

By the Goddess ... so many broken bones. He'd taken the full brunt of the impact of the explosion that had sent them flying and then taken it again as they'd flown through the trees and landed, coming to a bone-breaking stop against this tree. That explosion must have been astonishingly powerful, because Dougal was one of the strongest Were she'd ever met; his bones shouldn't have broken so easily. And yet, they'd snapped like dried twigs.

Both legs were broken—one femur and one tibia. His arm was indeed broken—the edges of the break had torn through his skin. His collarbone had snapped under the impact of their landing and his opposite shoulder was dislocated—probably from the impact against the tree. Four ribs were broken on that side too, one of them having pierced his lung as she'd surmised. And there was bleeding internally in his stomach and a small bleed on his brain. His eardrums had also been damaged from the sound of the explosion.

But as she'd feared, none of that was the worst of the damage.

His spine was broken. Multiple places from halfway down.

Oh. She sucked in a sob as she felt the extent of the damage. The spinal column was completely severed. If it had been higher, it was doubtful he would have lived. But miraculously, the break wasn't life-threatening.

He would never walk again though. Possibly even have restricted use of his hands and arms if the spine severed higher up as it was close to doing.

She could mend the rest of his injuries over time, but as far as she was aware, no Healer had ever managed to mend a broken spine.

Maybe though, as a Were, he would be different. Maybe, after some time and many Healings, and changing into his wolf—for some reason the change helped the Were Heal faster—he would recover from this injury the same as he would the others.

Maybe, if she were a stronger Healer, if she could truly rope in the powers Abigail said would be hers if only she could manage to make herself concentrate and control them properly, she could give him the miracle that was his due.

She shook her head. Useless to make impossible wishes. Especially given if she didn't deal with the punctured lung and the internal bleeding in his stomach and in his head, he wouldn't have a chance to discover the Healer who could help him find his miracle.

Those were her first priorities before she even started on anything else.

He made a small sound, like a groan.

Her eyes snapped open, gaze going to his face. His eyes were still closed, but his brow was furrowed. He was lifting from his unconscious state, starting to feel the pain.

She couldn't allow that.

Touching his face lightly, she stroked her thumb across his closed lids and whispered, 'Sleep, Dougal. Sleep. Let me take care of you now as you have always taken care of me.' Then she loosed a variation of the spell she'd meant to use on Lachlan, ensuring Dougal would remain asleep while she set about Healing him as best she could. She had no idea when help may arrive or even if it would given how many Were must have been seriously injured by that explosion.

As the sleep spell took hold, his frown faded and his features slackened.

Unable to stop herself, she bent and placed a light kiss on his lips, breathing in the warmth of him, that citrus and sun-warmed lavender scent she so loved. Staring at his face, filling herself with her love for him, her need for him to be well, she whispered, 'Live, Dougal MacCrae. Heal.'

But as she whispered it, he made a gargling sound. Blood foamed on his lips and as it did, he stopped breathing.

Goddess, no. No! 'You have to live. You have to live!'

But shouting at him did nothing. Only she was capable of doing something to change what was happening to him. Despite the fact she had never been strong enough, never capable enough to grasp a hold of the full extent of her magics—as her mother was fond of telling her over and over before she died—she had to be right now.

For her *Sgàth*. For her Dougal.

She closed her eyes then, ignoring the tears that fell down her cheeks and onto his, and placed her hands over his chest. If he were to live he had to breathe.

Calling all her power to her, she channelled it into her hands and out. But even as she did it, she knew it wouldn't be enough. She could feel him fading from her, his aura darkening, his spirit starting to lift from his body to pass between the veils.

'No! No. I will not let you,' she screamed into the night. 'I will not let you go.'

Something deep inside her reared up in that moment, lashing out to grab a hold of the spark that was his soul that she could see lifting from his chest. She shouldn't have been able to see it like this, certainly shouldn't have been able to touch it, but tentacles of pale golden light wound around it, tentacles that came from deep inside her, and they filtered some of their light into the fading spark of his soul.

It flared in their grasp and as it did, the tentacles pushed it back into her *Sgàth's* chest where it seemed to have risen from. Dougal's body trembled and jerked and he took in a gargling breath once more.

But only one.

If she didn't do something to mend the damage to his ribs and lung, she would lose him again and she didn't know if she could do whatever she had just done to keep him here. The tentacles had disappeared and she couldn't feel their power at all or even figure out where from inside her they had come.

Not that she had time for that now. She had to act or it would all be for nought.

She closed her eyes again, grasping at her normal Healing powers. They seemed to be so much larger than they had ever been, so much stronger. She only hoped she could manage to wield them without either flaming out—which would be bad, because if she was to lose consciousness now or lose access to her powers for days, she would be unable to help him further. Of course, flaming out wasn't the only worry. She could explode with the enormity of these powers.

For they were enormous. Worryingly so.

But it didn't matter what happened to her. All that mattered was that she save this beautiful Were who she loved with everything in her. And if she felt like she was going to explode like her papa had done, she would get as far from Dougal as she possibly could.

She grabbed a hold of the powers, wielding them in the only way she knew how, pushing them through her hands and into Dougal's body.

Behind her lids, the black of the night brightened with a golden-orange glow the way they did when she looked at the sun. So much power—too much power? She didn't care. She could pay no heed to the beacon she created by her Healing. Everything she was in that moment had to focus on Healing her love—for she did love him. So much. She could admit that to herself if to nobody else.

The first order at hand was to keep his heart pumping as she put his ribs back into place and Healed the puncture in his lungs. She would then have to draw out the pool of blood and fluid that stopped him from taking a proper breath. It was a delicate task, for one wrong step and she could explode his heart or lungs. But she could do it.

She *would* do it.

And once she was done with this part, she would see to everything else.

Everything but his spine. Because even with this extraordinary power, she couldn't mend a break of that kind. It was beyond even the greatest Healer's powers.

'But then, so was using your power on yourself, and you just managed to do that.'

She jerked at the sound of the voice and almost faltered in her Healing. 'Focus, Le-le. You have to focus.'

She had to do this. Now. Before he stopped breathing again. He had only her. And she wouldn't let him down. She couldn't let him down.

Focusing as she'd never done before, she pushed her power into him, keeping his heart pumping as she Healed first his broken ribs. She then reversed the order of what she'd thought before, pushing the blood pooling in his lungs back through the severed vessels that carried the precious fluid through his body, before Healing the puncture. It was more difficult to do it this way, to push the blood back where it was supposed to be, but he had lost so much, she couldn't afford to waste any.

She was sweating by the time she finished the task—it was a Healing greater than any she had managed before—but still she didn't stop. There was too much to do. She turned her attention to the dangerous bleed on his brain. She had to stop it and then drain the fluid to relieve the pressure building there. Such pressure would cause death as certainly as the damage to his lungs had done—or so she'd read in a few of the ancient grimoires she'd been studying.

Goddess! It hurt so much to keep pushing her Healing energies into his body, to manipulate them to do the work that must be done. But she didn't stop. Couldn't stop.

She didn't stop when Morghanna and Alistair arrived, other senior pack members close behind them, the sound of them breaking through the agony cascading through her body. She didn't stop when they both kneeled beside her. 'His shoulder. His leg. His arm,' she managed to gasp, hoping they would start to Heal those to help her. To help him. Because he needed more than her to help him. This power she was suddenly wielding, it was strong but given the pain she was in, she wasn't certain she could hold on long enough to mend all his bones and stop the life-threatening bleeding in one sitting.

'Le-le, you have to stop. Your power usage is too great. You will flame-out or ... worse.'

She ignored Morghanna's plea though—and Alistair's when he joined with Morghanna's pleading. She couldn't stop. Even though her power was fluttering in her grasp, she couldn't stop. She almost had the bleed on his brain stopped and it was better if one Healer took care of one injury as their powers worked slightly differently and someone else might miss a sliver of bone or a bleeder that she could see so easily given she'd been working on this area already.

Of course, she wasn't surprised when Abigail arrived and tried to make her cease what she was doing. 'You have done a fine job, my girl. Let others take over now.'

Anger fluttered in her chest that they would bring the old witch out here to try to make her stop. But she didn't let that anger alter any of what she did. She didn't respond, just kept going, ignoring the pain that shuddered through her, the sweat that covered her body and ran, stinging, into her closed eyes.

'Lassie, you will flame-out if you do not take a break.'

She firmed her lips and kept going.

'Leanna Finnigan. You have to stop now. You will hurt yourself if you continue.'

She didn't care. Didn't care what happened to her.

All that could matter, all that *did* matter, was the Were she loved with everything in her who lay unconscious and injured in front of her. She needed to help him, to Heal him. Because, the horrible truth was, she simply couldn't live in a world that Dougal MacCrae wasn't alive in.

She kept at it, even as the dark shadows began to crowd her mind once more, even as her powers stuttered and became harder to manage. She had to keep going. Had to finish this. One last splinter of bone to remove from his brain that was causing the final bleed. She drew the blood and fluid up and out, turning it to vapour with her magic then encouraged the brain matter to return to its natural form while she stitched the torn flesh on his head back together and mended the fracture in his skull with the golden-orange of her magic.

As she put the final touch on Healing the dangerous wound on his head, he took a deeper breath and then another, and she knew he was finally out of danger.

And as that knowledge hit her, her power stuttered and died and the world around her became nothing but shadow as she was sucked into unconsciousness.

5

An angel hovered in the fog that was Dougal's vision, a halo of light expanding around her head, casting her face in shadow.

But he didn't need to see her face. He knew her.

He'd always know her.

His Le-le.

His mate.

Something was wrong though. He could feel her worries and doubts through their fledgling bond. As well as her harsh criticisms of herself.

He wished she wouldn't be so hard on herself. Wished he'd managed by now to make her see that she wasn't the flawed and weak witch she'd thought she was when she arrived to join their pack and coven. She had no idea just how strong she was. He'd vowed on their meeting, when she couldn't even look him in the eye, her head lowered, hair covering the scars on her face and neck, that he would do everything he could until he could no longer draw breath—and maybe even beyond that—to ensure she knew just how strong and special and good she was.

He would have done that for her even if she weren't his mate, because there was just something about her; something that called to him beyond the bond.

She was meant for bigger things. He and his wolf had known it from the first moment they'd seen her. They'd *known*.

'*She is ours.*'

'*Yes,*' he whispered back to his wolf. '*She is. Always and eternally ours.*'

It was a comfort, that fact.

Although, right now, he couldn't let it comfort him. Not truly. Not when she felt the way she did.

Why had she regressed so? He'd thought things were getting better. Had felt her confidence and courage growing in the last few months, especially since Lachlan's attack.

Lachlan!

Memories flashed before his eyes: of the cabin in the woods where they'd kept Lachlan; of Le-le raising her hands to do the spell as Lachlan spilled filth at her; of Lachlan's eyes turning dark before all hell broke loose.

An explosion.

Bodies flying through the air.

He'd grabbed Le-le, holding her close to protect her as the shock wave hit them and they'd ...

Pain. He remembered so much pain and then ... nothing.

There was nothing.

By the Moon! Was he dead? Was Le-le dead? Was that why she hovered over him, glowing like an angel?

Nae! Naaee!

He tried to sit up, but his angel leaned closer, the warmth of her hands pressing into his shoulders. 'No, Dougal. Do not. You must rest.'

Rest? What did he need of rest if they were dead?

'Le-le,' he managed to choke out. Hells—why did his throat feel as raw as if he'd drunk far too much mead and spent the night vomiting up his vittles and everything else besides?

'Shh.' She stroked his shoulders.

His wolf hummed his pleasure. He liked it when their mate petted him—she did it so rarely. In fact, she barely ever touched him. So why was she doing so now? 'Le-le—'

'No, my *Sgàth*. Do not try to talk. You are still too weak. Go back to sleep.'

'Weak?' he managed to ask. He was feeling so very weak—but why?

'You were … injured,' she said, voice thick. 'P-protecting me. You almost died.'

He had? He couldn't remember. Couldn't remember beyond grabbing her. And the pain. He didn't think he'd ever forget that pain as he'd protected her from the inevitable impact as they were thrown through the air.

Something wet plopped on his shoulder. Was she crying? 'Le-le—'

'No. Do not move. You must stay as still as possible so the Healings can do their work.'

She grabbed the hand he was trying to raise from the bed—although she needn't have bothered. He could barely lift it more than a finger-width from the furs. His entire arm felt very much like it was weighted down with a cart-load of rocks. Actually, his entire body felt that way. Except for his legs. He couldn't feel much down there at all.

'How … injured?'

'I …'

More wetness hit his shoulder. Hells. Was it that bad? He wished he could see her face, but it was still in shadow, the lantern behind her casting a light that haloed around her, but didn't let him see more than her outline. 'Le-le … d-dinna c-cry.'

'D-D-Dougal.' His name came out like a sob. 'I am so s-sorry.'

'Le-le. Dinna fash … yerself.' He swallowed hard. By Alpha Moon, even talking that small amount was sapping him of energy it seemed he didn't have. 'I ken ye did … all ye could. I am dying then?' He did not want to die. He had so much to live for in the woman standing before him.

'No. N-no. I w-would not l-let you. B-but I sh-should have done m-more. I w-would have tried i-if they had let m-me. Th-they only just l-let me come back to s-sit with you.' Her fingers slipped from his shoulders as she spoke.

He missed the warmth of her immediately, wanted her to touch him again, but even in the low light, he could see she wouldn't. She'd shoved her hands in her lap, her shoulders stiff as a board as she tried to keep herself together.

'*Strong. Our mate strong,*' his wolf said, pride glowing through them.

'*Aye.*' She was. Magnificent. And very upset because she thought she hadn't done enough to Heal him. But that was obviously rubbish —because nobody was as powerful as she was in the Healing arts; not Abigail because of her frailty, or their Morghanna, or their young Pack Healer, Sebastian. And no other gave themselves to their Healing as much as she did. So often since she had been bonded to his Pack, he and others had to pull her back from giving too much and flaming out. So he knew that she had done everything she could to Heal him; to pull him back from death by the sounds of things.

'I will ... be fine,' he croaked. 'W-with you ... taking care ... of me.' The last was said on a gasp as pain spasmed through him from the middle of his back, wrapping around his chest, squeezing so that he could barely draw breath.

'Dougal!' Her chair toppled to the floor with a loud clatter as she stood abruptly, leaning over him to run her hands over his chest, his stomach.

The Healing touch filled him with warmth, helping to dull the pain, to lessen the squeezing of his lungs. Breath shuddered into him, then out, and he almost sobbed at the relief. He wanted to thank her, but she moved further down the bed, her touch disappearing.

No! He wanted it back.

He tried to lift his head, managed to lift it enough to see that her hands were on his legs, running over them to his feet. Light touched the side of her face—a face that was too pale and marred by a deep frown of worry and concentration as she used her magic on his legs.

He lost sight of her as his head thunked weakly back on the pillow, sweat dripping from his skin at the effort of that one small movement, and the recent pain that had gripped him and almost carried him into unconsciousness once more.

'Nothing. Nothing,' she murmured.

'Le-le,' he managed to gasp.

'Dougal.' Her hands were back on his chest as she once again moved to stand beside his upper body. 'Are you better? Has that helped with the pain?'

'Aye.' He swallowed hard. 'Is good.'

Her sigh of relief brushed over his skin. 'Thank the Goddess. That was a bad one. I am glad I was here to deal with it.'

Bad one? What was she talking about?

She must have seen the question on his face. 'The spasm. From your injuries. The Healings are knitting things back together, but it is causing the damaged muscles to spasm as they mend. I am sorry. I wish there were something more I could do for you. T-to Heal you fully.'

Heal him fully?

Was that why she was so upset? Because there was something she couldn't Heal? She'd said he wouldn't die. But if his injuries wouldn't cause his death, then what else was there to worry about?

He swallowed hard, his head so heavy and filling with fog again. Exhaustion weighed down his limbs in a way that told him he needed to sleep. But not before he understood exactly why she was so upset.

'No run.'

He frowned at his wolf's strange words. No run? What did he mean? Obviously they weren't going to run anywhere right now.

'No run,' his wolf said again, then began to howl—a mournful sound of loss and sorrow.

'Dougal?' Leanna leaned closer as if listening. 'Why are you making that sound? Are you in pain again?'

She could hear that?

She gasped. 'Is that your wolf? Is he in pain?'

'N-nae.' At least not physically. But emotionally ...

He was devastated.

'*No run. No walk. No play.*'

'*What do you mean?*'

'*All gone. Life gone.*'

'*Le-le says we will live.*'

'*Nae.*' Then there was more howling.

What did his wolf know? Had Le-le lied to him? He didn't think she had it in her. She was so—

The image of her hands on his legs hit him at the same time the howling went up in pitch.

He hadn't felt her hands on his legs. He'd felt them on his shoulders, his chest, stomach, his hand. But not on his legs. Not anything below his lower hips.

The fog in his mind flew away as realisation hit.

He couldn't move his legs. Couldn't feel his legs.

He could feel everything else. Move everything else. Even though it was difficult, he'd been able to move his hand, his arm, his head.

But his legs ... It was like there was nothing to move; like they weren't even there.

Fuck!

His wolf was right. No run. No walk. No play. No life without them.

Because he was a senior lieutenant in one of the most powerful Were packs in Scotland, nae, in all of Britain. Second to his Alpha. Meant to be the next Alpha. He'd just been talking about the need to take the leadership from Iain with Cal before all this had happened.

But now ... He could be none of it, do none of it, if he could not stand and fight to protect his pack.

Nae. Nae. It couldn't be true. He had to be mistaken. Maybe they were immobilising him with magic to help his injuries mend faster. That was something he'd seen Healers do.

He had to ask. Had to be sure. He swallowed harshly and took a few goes before he managed to whisper, 'I canna ... feel my legs. Did ye ... do some magic to ... immobilise me?'

'Dougal ... please.'

Her voice ... her agony. It told him there was no magic involved in this. Which meant one thing ... 'I canna walk. Can I?'

'Dougal ... I ... l-let me go fetch Morghanna.'

She went to move away, but with the last bit of strength he had in him, he managed to grab her hand, stopping her from leaving him. Stopping her from going and leaving him alone with this knowledge and the need that was building inside him.

A need to go. To release them all from the burden of him. As was Pack Law with these kinds of injuries.

'Why d-did ye ... save me?' he gasped. 'Ye should have let me die ... r-rather than wake to th-this.'

Her eyes widened in shock. 'What are you talking about? Of course I saved you.' She gripped his hand again.

It felt so good.

He couldn't let it feel so good. But he couldn't pull his hand out of her tight grip. 'I am nought but ... a b-burden to ye ... to the pack ... now.'

'No. No. You are not. Never that.'

'Only that. N-now.' He could never be Alpha. Never save the pack from Iain's selfish leadership. Never—

Suddenly her hands were on his face, her eyes blazing with passionate certainty as her gaze bore into his. 'That is nothing but horseshit, Dougal MacCrae. Do not even think such a thing.'

The glory of her hands on his face, her lips so close to his as she spat words of anger, of anguish, at him, was magnificent. He wished he could sink into that sensation and never let go of it, but he had to. If he were to make her see sense. He'd had such plans and now none of them could come to fruition for him. He had to die to make way for Cal or one of the other strong soldiers to rise to be next Alpha. 'Ye ...' He swallowed hard, the words like ash in his mouth. 'Ye have to let me go. I canna live ... like this. No Were could. Dinna expect ... me to.'

'No! Do not say such a thing.' Her fingers moved over his face, into his hair, clenching, the flickering candlelight to the side of the bed exposing the anguish in her expression; the grief; the panic. 'You have to live, Dougal. I cannot do this without you.'

Her words ... Not so long ago he would have exulted over them. He would have grabbed her and kissed her and vowed to never let her go; to always be her rock, her mate, the one who would always remind her of just who she was and what she could do.

But now. Now they were like bitter death.

The mating bond. Even though she had not yet accepted it—didn't even know it existed—was inside her, those few threads that had joined them from the first. They made her feel him, made her think she needed him when she didn't. She never had.

But without it, she would stop trying to save him. She'd see him for the burden he now was—to her, to the pack.

Without the bond, he could do what must be done—his *bràthairs* would most certainly help him as they'd helped other like-injured Were before—and Le-le ... she would go on to do the great things he knew were in her future.

Before any of that could happen, though, he had to break the few threads of the mating bond already in place.

No easy thing to do in his state, but his wolf—who had stopped howling as he came to his realisation—was in agreement.

They had to let her go.

Then they had to go to their final freedom.

He never thought his death would come like this. He always thought he'd go in battle, fighting for his pack. It was what all warriors hoped for—before the Pact that was.

Since then, he'd started to believe his death would come when he was old and surrounded by his and Le-le's *bairns* and their *grand-bairns*, where he just fell into the final sleep, surrounded by all the love he thought once never to have.

But now, because of Lachlan, that newer, most precious of dreams, was being stolen away.

'L-let me g-go,' he said.

'No,' she said, her fingers tightening on his hair in a way that would once have made his cock thicken. 'No.'

'Then ... I must—'

He didn't finish. The words were too hard. So, with every bit of strength he had left in him, he wrapped his mental hands around the fledgling bond, his wolf gripping it in its jaws. Then, as his wolf bit down, tearing into the barely formed threads, he helped by yanking as hard as he could, trying to break it.

'Dougal!' Le-le's scream rent the air. 'Stop.'

But he couldn't. Because he was doing this for her. One day, she would understand ... and hopefully forgive him.

He pulled harder as his wolf bit down and began to shake his head from side-to-side, tearing at the precious threads. His wolf, while still inside him, might not hold physical form, but neither did the bond, both being something real but not real while in this place in his mind. But his wolf teeth in this non-physical form were as sharp as they were in his physical form, his jaw as strong, and slowly, with him pulling and the wolf tearing, the bond began to fray.

Le-le's screaming fell into the background as the pain of what they were doing threatened to overwhelm him.

But he couldn't fall into unconsciousness. Not yet. Not until he'd freed her from him.

Then, inexplicably, a warmth began to fill him. And as it did, non-corporeal hands—her magical hands—gripped the fraying bond and held it together.

'*Nae!*' he yelled in his mind, the pain of what he was trying to do making it impossible for him to move his mouth or make any sound. '*Let me go!*'

'Never. I will not let you go. Ever.'

'*Le-le—*'

'No! Your worth is more to me than your ability to walk. You will live. You must live!'

She gripped tighter. The warmth inside him became hotter until it almost felt like a burn. In his mind's eye, the bond glowed gold around where her hands gripped it, the glow brightening and brightening. Then he realised he wasn't just seeing that glow with his mind's eye. He was seeing it with his eyes. It filled the room, making his eyes water, sending a flood of warmth over his skin, from the middle of his chest where she'd placed her physical hands.

The glow pulsed over him, heated waves of Healer energy covering him, wrapping around him, lifting him up until he could no longer feel the furs beneath him. It was so strong, so powerful, he almost imagined he could feel it around his legs—an impossibility of course because no Healer had ever mended an injury such as his.

What she was doing though was Healing the bond he'd begun to tear.

Not just Healing it. She was strengthening it.

'Nae!' he managed to yell out loud as his wolf howled its distress inside him before returning to its efforts to tear the bond. He tried to help, gripping the thickening bond more tightly, pulling harder, with everything in him.

In one part of his mind, he became aware of others rushing into the room—Morghanna and Alistair, Cal hobbling with the help of a walking stick, one arm in a sling and Abigail bringing up the rear— their voices raised, shocked at first, then turning to pleading.

'Stop. Stop. He dinna want this, ye ken?' Cal's voice rose above the melee. 'I told ye, he wouldna want this. Ye have to stop, lass. Let him go.'

'No,' was all she said as she renewed her efforts.

'Leanna. Stop. You are going to flame-out. You'll lose consciousness. Lose access to your powers for days. Maybe worse.'

'No.'

Other powers began to light the room, to try to stop her from doing what she was doing. But she was too strong. Too powerful. She sent a pulse of warmth and light down the bond, almost like an electric shock. The others cried out briefly and then fell silent.

In his mind, his wolf's jaws went slack and his hands fell away from the threads of the bond. And as they did, it snapped viciously and fully into place as she finally accepted what she'd denied all this time.

Dooming them both to a life of misery.

'Nae!' he cried out before she used her powers to send him and his wolf to sleep.

Just before he lost consciousness, he heard her whisper, 'It is done,' then her slight weight landed on top of him as she flamed-out and lost consciousness with him.

And together, they tumbled into dreams.

6

L eanna knew that she'd been put in a long sleep to Heal and this was nothing but a dream, but she didn't care.

Dougal was kissing her. All. Over.

Again.

She'd been having these dreams, been calling them to her to fill her time while she was forced to rest by Morghanna, Abigail and Alistair ever since she'd fallen unconscious in her efforts to Heal Dougal.

But none of that mattered.

Not when Dougal was kissing her. Even though it was only a dream.

She never imagined kisses could be like this. She'd seen other people kiss on the lips—her parents included. She'd even caught them in numerous passionate kisses which, as a young girl, she didn't understand, and when she was a little older and understood the emotion and love behind what she saw, baffled her. How could her papa kiss her mama like that when they were so very different and disagreed about everything to do with her?

It also made her feel so alone. Like they were wrapped up in each other and had no room or need for her.

And they didn't. Not really. Well, at least her mama hadn't.

But no need to get lost in the sadness of that now because Dougal's lips moved to her breast, covering the rosy tip and did that thing with his tongue she was coming to realise she loved.

In fact, in all the dreams she'd winked in and out of since she'd fallen in to this long sleep, this was one of her favourite parts.

That and when he kissed her on her lips, his tongue stroking against hers. And when he kissed down her neck, nipping a little, his wolfish growl of pleasure vibrating against her skin. Oh, and when he continued kissing and nipping, licking and sucking, all the way down her body to her nethers and pressed his mouth and tongue against that most private—and sensitive—part of her. Oh how she loved that.

Because when he did that it made the tension and pulsing in her muscles rise and rise until she burst up into the air in waves of pleasure so deep and sweet she never wanted it to end.

Except it did.

And when it did, when she came back to herself, it was to find him hovering over her in this dreamscape, his beautiful eyes staring into hers as he slid into her in a glorious glide and started the mad, pulsing insanity of pleasure all over again until they exploded together.

Was intimacy like this with all males? She wasn't sure. But she was willing to give herself over to her imagination in these dreams. She'd never thought her imagination was quite this good—but she was glad it was.

Her back arched as he kissed his way from one breast to the other, licking around her nipple before sucking the tip between his teeth and biting ever so gently.

Goddess! The feel of his teeth grazing against her skin! She'd never imagined she'd love such a thing, but she did.

'More,' she gasped.

He raised his head to meet her gaze, his wolf clearly in his eyes as he growled, 'With pleasure.'

Then he went to work creating glorious sensations to spiral through her.

With his mouth he paid lavish attention to her breasts while his hands wandered over her body, stroking over-sensitised skin, down, down to her slick, throbbing core. And as his tongue flicked at her nipple, his finger slipped through her slit, up and down, up and down, pausing each time at that knot of nerves to press down on it in a way that made her gasp and quiver.

'Do ye want my lips down there?' he asked roughly as he licked between her breasts. 'My tongue?'

'Yes!' she breathed, the sound more of a sob than a word. 'Now.'

She could feel his smile against her skin. 'Demanding.'

'You love it,' she said, not understanding where this sassy side of herself came from, but enjoying the fact she could imagine she'd be like this with him.

Another smile against her skin then his hot gaze meeting hers again. 'Ye ken I do.' He started to make his way down her ribs to her stomach, but she grabbed his head, urging with her fingertips for him to look up at her again. 'Aye, *mo ghrádh*?'

She shivered delightfully at the sound of those words on his lips. There was a momentary stab of pain as the part of her still attached to reality reminded her they were words she would never hear from him in real life. But she quickly ignored it, determined to enjoy this slice of imagination her brain served up while she slept and her body and magic mended.

She smiled at him as he stared up at her, so much love in his eyes. 'Kiss me here first,' she said, placing her fingertips on her lips, needing his kiss in the way a dehydrated person needed water. 'Then kiss me down there.'

'As ye wish.' His smile turned lascivious as he prowled up her body, then his lips were on hers.

She sighed her pleasure into his mouth.

Their tongues met in a long, languorous kiss that heated up when he pulled back just enough to suck her bottom lip into his mouth. As he pulled away slowly—oh so deliciously slowly—she darted her tongue out to swipe across his lips in the way she knew drove him wild.

A low rumble of pleasure hummed in his chest and up his throat, a dual sound of man and wolf. 'Hello, beautiful boy,' she said on a groan and licked again before sucking his lower lip into her mouth to return the pleasure he'd just given her.

This side of herself—she enjoyed it so much! Why could she not be like this in her real life?

His fingers gripped her chin and he pulled away from her kiss to look in her eyes. 'Where did ye go, *mo ghrádh*?'

'Nowhere. I am here with you.' And she would be. If she could just stop thinking and questioning and let go.

'I ken what will keep you here with me and make ye let go.' He gave her one more long, luscious tongue-tangling kiss that made her mind spin, then he prowled back down her body. He trailed his hands over all the sensitive places as he kept eye contact with her. Then, finally nestled between her legs, he bent his head and licked right up the centre of her.

She gasped and shuddered.

'Sae my name.'

'No.' She had no idea why she denied him, but loved the way he looked when she did.

He smiled and then licked again, twining the hard tip of his tongue around the sensitive nub of nerves before licking again.

A long moan was torn out of her and her back arched as he repeated the action.

'Sae. My. Name,' he said between long, flat-tongued licks.

'No,' she panted, hands clawing at the sheets.

'So stubborn.'

'Want more.'

'So do I.'

He kept eye contact as he licked her again, following the action with his middle finger, sliding it up and down her cleft once, twice, then sliding it inside her in one, swift glide.

She groaned, long and loud. 'More.'

He licked and inserted a second finger. 'Sae my name.'

'Give me more,' she gasped through panted breaths.

He smiled at her as he pumped his fingers inside her, fast and hard, curling them on the upward stroke so his fingertips pressed against her internal muscles in a way that made her writhe and buck, her breath mere pants. But still she managed to demand, 'More!'

He inserted a third finger, widening them slightly to create more friction as he pumped them in and out of her tight, wet core.

'So hot. So wet,' he said before licking and licking, eating her up as he pumped his fingers in and out of her.

Oh Goddess! Goddess! 'I am going to come!'

'Not before ye sae my name,' he said roughly, while continuing to pump his fingers inside her.

'Then come inside me and I will scream it out to the heavens,' she managed to demand.

'Done!' And in one swift move he was aligned over her body, his thick, long member pushing inside her in one glorious glide until he was balls-deep, unable to go any deeper.

She wrapped her legs around his waist, opening herself up to him more, and held on to his shoulders as he pumped in and out of her, harder, faster until she screamed his name as promised.

'Dougal!'

'Leanna!' he cried, joining her as she catapulted over the edge of pleasure into a plane beyond it she'd never known possible.

Up and up and up and ...

Pop!

She jolted, the sensation pulling her out of her sensual dream and thrusting her into ...

She looked around her. She didn't know where. It was misty-grey and pulsing with something that was like life but not.

There was no sound here, no feeling.

She hated it. Particularly as it had somehow pulled her out of her dream, away from the pleasure of lying with Dougal afterwards cuddled against him.

She felt ... incomplete.

She shuddered, wrapping her arms around herself. Which was

when she realised there was some form of tether coming out of her chest. It pulsed with her life force and something else.

She looked closer.

No, it wasn't one tether but two. One angling down immediately below her and the other heading off in another direction. Both tethers were made up of sunset-coloured strands mixed with a brilliant silver, but in the one heading off into the misty-grey, there were also strong green threads that had no feel about her in them at all. They were familiar though. So familiar it felt like she'd known what they were all her life.

She began to follow those threads to see where they led.

'Ah-ah-ah!' a voice said behind her just as she felt a definite tug on the other tether, pulling her back. 'You are not ready for that yet.'

She knew that voice!

She spun and blinked, unable to believe what she saw before her.

'Hello, Rabbit.'

'Papa!'

She raced towards him as he held his arms out to her.

Oh, oh! The feel of his arms wrapping around her. It felt like it always had. And his scent. How did he still smell like woodsmoke and the tartness of the metal he used to forge into tools for the farmers in their village, and the swords and armour for the lord they owed allegiance to? And of course the special pieces he forged with his magic for their coven to help keep their secrets. That was where his true talents lay, although he was a strong Healer too. It was that dual strength of power that had in the end caused his death.

His death.

So this was his spirit.

Did that mean she was dead?

'No, Rabbit. You are still very much alive. We are in the astral. I needed to speak to you and so pulled you here from the dream bubble you created while you remained asleep to Heal.'

'I am so happy to see you.' She pulled back enough to look up at his handsomely rugged face with its nicks and scars he'd earned through plying his trade. 'But why are you here?' It was difficult for spirits to travel in the astral, and they must have great need to do so and maintain their physical form.

His expression was grave as he said, 'The ancestors and I are concerned with what you have done and where it might lead.'

Leanna frowned. 'What I have done?'

'Yes. In pulling on powers you should not have access to, to bring that Were back from death, and then to Heal the almost severed part of his spine as you did in that second Healing, you have drawn notice.'

Her frown deepened as she pulled away from him and wrapped her arms around her middle. 'I ... I had to help him. It is my calling as a Healer.'

'Yes. You more than other Healers are pulled to the calling in ways you are yet to understand.'

'What are you talking about?'

He shook his head, turning from her so she could read nothing on his face. 'I am forbidden to say more about your future and what awaits there.'

'Forbidden? By whom?'

'I am servant to the Goddess as I have always been. I am privy to things now that I have passed through to the Beyond, but I cannot share those things with those on the mortal plane for fear of what might overhear.'

'We are not on the mortal plane,' she said.

'No. But it is still too close. There are very few places the Darkness cannot infiltrate, either with pieces of itself or spies twisted into being his servants.'

'Like Lachlan.'

'Yes. Like the one who became the Beast. It is no coincidence that he injured your ma— The one called Dougal. The power behind him needed to get rid of the strongest Were. Because that Were is marked to turn the pack onto a path of light—one that will always lead towards the Goddess, now and in the future.'

'We still are on that path!' she objected.

'The coven is, yes. But some of the Were are being lured to a different path through the weakness of their Alpha.'

She turned from him, pain riding in her chest at his words. 'I need to warn them!' She reached for the tether that would lead back to her body and consciousness.

'No!' Papa pulled her back again, stopping her from touching the tether and following it to its source—her body. 'You are not ready. You used too much of yourself in bringing Dougal back and trying to Heal him fully.'

'Trying?' She hadn't succeeded? 'I thought you said I had Healed his spine.'

'You Healed the part higher up that was almost torn, but you did not Heal the full break lower down.'

'Oh, no.' Tears pricked her eyes.

Her papa put his hand on her shoulder, his features folding into lines of empathy. 'You brought him back from death but you had already given too much. Despite the power you called on, you do not have the knowledge or skill as yet to Heal such a terrible injury. You did more than anyone else ever could have though, Healing the part that was partly torn. You gave him full use of his upper body. So take comfort in that.'

'But Dougal—'

'Will survive for now. And you being who you are, will not give up on him when you wake.'

'Then I must wake.' She reached again for the tether.

He grabbed her hand, stopping her from touching it. 'Not yet. As I said, you need more time to recover. Your body and magic were drained to almost death trying to Heal that Were. I will not allow you to wake too early and hurt yourself further for him.'

'He is worth it!'

'Why?'

She stared at him, so many emotions working inside her, surging to come to the surface, to be heard. But fear kept them suppressed— fear to truly feel what she felt; that her dreams were truly delusions and she would forever be alone.

So instead of voicing any of her hopes, she said, 'As you said ... he is necessary to the future well-being of pack and coven.'

He stared at her for long moments before saying, 'Is that all?'

Could he see into her soul? Might he see the truth in her heart she dare not speak, particularly if he held her gaze for any longer?

She dropped her gaze and said, 'Yes, of course. What else could he be?'

He sighed and shook his head. 'As I said—you are not ready. You must stay in the astral or in the dream, using the protection of the long sleep to keep you safe and help you to Heal as much as possible before you wake.'

'And when will that be?'

'A week has already passed. I think another week will do.'

'It never takes that long for a witch to recover from a flame-out!'

'No. But what you did was not simply flame-out.'

'I do not understand.'

'No. You cannot. But you can listen from the astral. You can learn that which you are not ready to learn by yourself.'

'What are you talking about?'

He pointed down to the source of the tether. The misty-grey had cleared so that she could see her body now. See Morghanna sitting at her bedside, Abigail in a chair beside her.

She looked up at her papa—but he was fading away. 'Papa?'

'Listen. Heed. And try not to give in to the bonding dreams.'

'Bonding dreams?'

'The ones with Dougal.'

She blushed bright red—he knew about that? Mortifying! Her face was suddenly so hot—she'd had no idea one could blush in the astral.

He touched her shoulder, the sensation less than a whisper. 'Do not give in to the bonding dreams if you can help it. Stay strong for your own sake. Hard times are ahead and you cannot keep giving him more than you can afford to give.'

'I do not understand.'

He pointed down towards her body. 'Use the astral while you can.'

His voice was barely a whisper, his form wavering into whisper fog. But before he disappeared she heard in her mind, 'Watch. Listen. Heed.'

Then he was gone and she was alone.

She wanted to cry, to scream her need to see him again, but his final words echoed in her head, their urgency pushing her to overcome emotion and do as he bid.

So, she sank down closer to her body without following the tether the entire way, close enough do what he'd asked of her.

Watch. Listen. Heed.

7

'How is she?'

Morghanna looked up as Abigail, supported by Alistair, entered the room. 'What are you doing here? I thought I told you to rest after you finished the Healing on Cal and the others injured in the explosion—which, by the by, I am still angry with you about. I told you I would complete his Healing later.'

'You have enough to do,' Abigail said sternly. 'Besides, we need Cal and the others to guard the village now Iain has taken all the Hunters and soldiers with him.'

'Hmph,' Morghanna said then turned her scowl on Alistair. 'I know you cannot remember what happened before your illness, but I thought you had the sense not to let Abigail talk you into helping her walk all the way from her cabin to the Healer Hall.'

'I am sorry, my love. I ...' He looked between Morghanna and Abigail.

'You what?' Morghanna snapped. Leanna had never heard her so angry with anyone but Iain.

Abigail snorted. 'No use taking out your temper on dear Ali, Morghanna. I did not give him a choice. I was already dressed and halfway across the courtyard before he came upon me.' She shuffled forward, obviously leaning very heavily on Alistair, her face pale, lips tight with pain.

'You are nowhere close to recovered, Abigail.'

Leanna had to agree with her mentor. She half expected Morghanna to order Alistair to pick the old witch up and take her back to her bed. Instead, with a resigned sigh her mentor rose from her chair by Leanna's bed and, with Ali still taking most of the older witch's weight, helped Abigail to it.

The older witch sighed heavily as her bottom settled in the seat, then shivered.

'I will fetch a blanket,' Ali said before Morghanna even had a chance to ask.

Leanna frowned. They were so close even though, to Alistair, he'd only known Morghanna a few weeks. If she didn't know better, she would have called what they had a mating bond. But it couldn't be that—he was a warlock, not a Were.

Whatever it was, she longed to feel something like it in the future. Although, the male she wanted to feel it with could never feel the same about her. Maybe love like that simply wasn't written in the stars for someone like her.

'What are your frowning over, dear?'

Abigail's question broke into her thoughts and she returned her attention to what was going on around her body. Morghanna wasn't simply frowning. She had a curiously sad expression on her face as she stared down at Leanna's body.

Morghanna shrugged and gestured at Leanna. 'I am simply worried about Le-le.' She bent down and gripped Leanna's wrist in her fingers, checking her pulse. 'Her heart is beating as it should and yet, she is still unconscious. It has been a week already. Even with all the magic she used both times, she should have woken by now.' She rubbed her brow.

'Anna, are you unwell?' Alistair had returned with a blanket, which he draped over Abigail's legs. 'Is it the headache again?'

For a moment Morghanna looked like she would deny his question, but then she sighed and said, 'It is. The spirits are very restless, flitting around me constantly.' Her eyes roved around the room and stopped where Leanna was floating. For a moment Leanna thought her mentor could see her, but then she sighed again, rubbed her head and looked away. 'No matter how I try, not a one will tell me what is wrong.'

'Perhaps you should rest. I can remain here with Abigail.'

'No.' She rolled her shoulders. 'I cannot rest while Leanna is like this. I should never have left her alone with Dougal.'

'You could not have known she would try for a deeper Healing when she was barely recovered from the first flame-out.'

'She is his mate. I should have known she would try.'

What? Leanna jerked back, losing control over her astral spirit. For a moment, she spun around and around as if the shock had been an actual blow. But she had to regain control because she was missing something. Something important about her being Dougal's mate.

That couldn't be right. Could it?

She had to get back to Morghanna's side and listen to what was being said. With teeth-gritting control, she stopped the mad spinning and edged her way, hand over hand, down the bond to her body, stopping so that she hovered just out of range to it, and listened in to the conversation.

Morghanna was saying to Alistair, '... careful. So while she might not have accepted the bond as yet, it is there, making it impossible for her not to help him in every way she can. More than anyone, I should have known what she was capable of doing.'

'Why would you know that?' Alistair asked.

'Alistair is right,' Abigail said, staring at Morghanna as she paced back and forth beside the bed. 'You may be in love and with your soulmate, but you are not mated. You cannot be expected to know exactly how that would affect someone who is—or is slated to be mated.'

A strange expression of panic crossed Morghanna's face, but then she turned away, hand flapping as if to wipe the words aside. 'Bridgette has told me much. About how it is for her and Malcolm. I should have thought ... should have known.'

'Stop.' Alistair gripped her shoulders, stopping her pacing. He began to gently massage the muscles at the base of her neck as he said, 'You must stop blaming yourself. None of this is your fault. The blame lies squarely with others.'

He might not have said who, but by the tension in his voice Leanna knew where he thought the blame lay. As did everyone else in the room by the looks on their faces. But none of them spoke the names, just listened as Ali said, 'You have done all you can for Le-le.'

'Have I?' Morghanna screwed her mouth to the side as her gaze returned to the bed. 'I feel like I should be doing more to bring her back to us. There has to be something in the diaries or grimoires about major flame-outs and how to treat them. I—'

'Maybe there is more, but unfortunately, we are walking a new path,' Abigail said, interrupting her. 'Until the Pact, nobody who used that amount of power at any one time ever survived. Pulling on that amount of power always led to magic-fuelled explosions. So there is nothing passed down from our forebears that will help with this kind of thing. You know this as well as I.'

Morghanna made a sound of frustration. 'But ... when we fought Lachlan, we all used more power than had ever been used by anyone before, except Bridgette when she created the Pact. All of us flamed-out and yet we awoke after a few days at most. What is different now?'

'According to you, we channelled Goddess energy, as did Bridgette,' Alistair said. 'Perhaps that is the difference here.'

Abigail nodded slowly. 'Your soulmate is correct, Morghanna. While we do not know exactly what Leanna did, we do know she pulled the power only from herself. There was no sign at all of any God or Goddess influence on either her or Dougal.'

Morghanna hissed in frustration. 'We should know more. I know that you are right. We are paving new ground with this Pact of Bridgette's.'

'Yours and Bridgette's,' Ali said firmly, making Leanna smile. Before he lost his memory he had always made certain his love take credit for her part in the wonder of the life they were now all living. It appeared the need to protect Morghanna hadn't been lost to him with his memory.

Morghanna waved away his words and pulled from his gently massaging grip to take her place again beside the bed. 'I know there is bound to be many things we do not know and will have to learn in the years ahead.'

'Including figuring out what to do for someone who used power like Le-le did,' Abigail said.

'Yes.' Morghanna bit her lip as she leaned forward to brush a lock of hair from Leanna's brow. 'I hate seeing her like this. After everything she has been through ...' She swallowed hard. 'It is not right. She deserves so much more than what the Fates have woven for her. I want her to have the happiness that she was robbed of when she was but a child. I want—' She blinked rapidly, obviously fighting tears.

Abigail took her hand and gave it a squeeze, tears leaving her eyes to run down her wrinkled cheeks. Despite her distress though, she managed to say, 'I know.'

Leanna wanted to reach out and hug them both, but that was impossible right now. Instead, she had to float here and watch these two women who meant so much to her suffer in this way. Because of her.

It wasn't fair. But she had to do as her papa had bid.

Morghanna—with a strength that Leanna never ceased to admire —visibly pulled herself together and met the older witch's gaze. She took in a deep, shuddering breath, then said, 'We need her. I need her. She is stronger than me. In so many ways, she is stronger.'

Leanna snorted at the ridiculousness of that statement. She wasn't surprised at all when Abigail said, 'Not stronger. Her powers simply lie along a different path to yours. But I know you did not simply mean her magics are stronger. You still—' She began to cough.

Leanna reached out to her, but her hands went right through the elderly witch.

'Are you all right?'

'Water. Please.'

Morghanna rushed to the far side of the room where a jug was kept full of drinking water, poured a mug and brought it back to her mentor's side. She hovered, hands out as if she worried the elderly witch would drop the mug, while Alistair rubbed Abigail's back.

Abigail swallowed the water down, the wrinkled, paper-thin skin of her neck moving convulsively.

'Honestly, Abigail. You should not have come here,' Morghanna said tightly. 'Ali, can you please help her back to her cottage and stay with her while she rests?'

Abigail flapped her free hand at both of them, then after she'd finished swallowing the mouthful of water, said, 'I wish to be here. I have a feeling it is important that we be here.'

'What do you mean?' Alistair asked.

Good question, Leanna thought. Was this what her papa wanted her to watch and heed? Or was it something else. She had a feeling something had been said about her and Dougal, but for the life of her she couldn't remember it. Maybe it was unimportant. Although, she had a feeling it wasn't.

But then Abigail began to speak and she had to concentrate again on what was being said.

'I am not quite certain what I mean. All I know is that I felt drawn here today. It was almost as if I could hear Le-le in my mind, asking me to come and be by her side. Even though you were already here and she was well-cared for. It is as if—' Her eyes widened. 'Oh. I had not thought of that.'

'What? Had not thought of what?'

Abigail didn't answer, but simply mumbled, 'I wonder if I ...'

'Wonder if you ... what?' Morghanna asked, kneeling down at Abigail's side and clasping the wrinkled hands in hers.

Abigail's gaze was distant, her power a prickle on the air as she did something that Leanna couldn't quite catch—some form of Healing she was not adept at perhaps? Although, that encompassed many things given how far down the path of learning she still had to go.

'What are you doing?' Alistair asked wonderingly. Maybe he could feel what she could feel.

'Your hands are shaking uncontrollably,' Morghanna said. 'Stop whatever you are doing. Or I will stop it for you before you kill yourself.'

'No.' Ali's hand on Morghanna's stopped the magics she was calling on to block whatever Abigail was doing. 'I see what she is working.' He put his other hand on Abigail's frail shoulder, his gaze unfocused as he joined his magic to Abigail's, helping her.

Leanna couldn't believe how powerful he was already, how in control of his magics he was given he had so little training before coming here—and now couldn't remember any of what he had learned. Even untrained, he could do things instinctively that no witch or warlock had done in living memory. Leanna wished she had a little of what he had.

Morghanna didn't argue with him, but trusted her love in a way that made Leanna's throat thicken. She pulled her magic back at his behest and let him do what he must to help Abigail.

The paleness in Abigail's cheeks gained a light blush of colour and the slight milkiness in her eyes that worsened with the passing of each new moon, faded until her brown eyes were brighter than Leanna had ever seen them.

Then she focused her gaze on Leanna's body.

Morghanna looked between Abigail and Alistair then her gaze roved over Leanna's body in the bed which was as still and pale and almost lifeless as before. 'Whatever you are doing, it is not working,' she said softly.

Alistair didn't stop what he was doing with Abigail as he said, 'We are not helping Le-le. We are checking something.'

'Checking what?'

'Her bond. Abigail thinks maybe that is what is keeping her in this state. I think she is right. It is ...' He frowned. 'I am not certain how I know this, but it is thicker than any fledgling mating bond should be. But wrong somehow. Like it is being pulled too tight and is about to break. And ...' He sucked in a sharp breath. 'Leanna is feeding power into it to keep it strong.'

What? Fledgling mating bond? What was he talking about? Mated to whom?

A memory fluttered in her mind, of her grabbing a hold of something that lived deep inside Dougal and pulling on it, attaching herself to it when she was trying to Heal him.

The mating bond? Was she mated to Dougal? How come she couldn't remember it? Surely that would be something she'd remember?

'What?' Morghanna's abrupt shout caught her spiralling thoughts and pulled her attention back to what was going on before her. 'As far as I know, the bond is purely one-sided. She has not accepted it yet. Iain has said nothing about feeling it through the Packbond. And there is nothing—'

'It is because Dougal is fighting her,' Abigail said, coming out of the trance she'd been in. She sighed deeply and rubbed her brow. 'What a fix this is. The Were has been trying to get her to mate with him all these months, and now he has been injured like this, he is trying to reject the mating. It is that which is keeping her in this state.'

They were mated? And Dougal was fighting the mating bond? But why? The pain of that stabbed over and over deep inside her. Is this what they had said before? Then why could she not remember it?

'How do we fix it?'

No. No. That wasn't the question she wanted asked and answered. But there was no way to make them hear her while she was like this, and she obviously couldn't enter her body because if she were giving over her energy to Dougal to stop him from dying, she had to remain asleep to do so.

Abigail shrugged. 'I cannot believe I am saying this, but I wish Iain were here rather than gadding about looking for Lachlan. An Alpha command would stop Dougal from doing what he is doing.'

Unsaid was that he'd taken with him the remaining lieutenants and soldiers who survived or were uninjured in both of Lachlan's attacks. Another breach of the Pact, if not of his duty to the rest of his pack. It was wrong that he left his coven, the children and non-fighting Were, not to mention the injured and recovering, to fend for themselves while he took the strongest of them to support him in trying to find and bring in his son. He should have increased security here and given his energy over to helping their young Pack Healer and the witches tend to the injured. He should have been here giving comfort and support.

'No,' Alistair said shortly. 'Iain would not be able to do as you asked even if he were here. He is not stronger than Dougal—Dougal is the real Alpha, and we all know it.' He shook his head. 'We need to tell Dougal what his actions are doing to Le-le.'

'Good idea,' Abigail said. 'He will not wish to hurt the lass, even if he no longer wishes to be mated to her.'

No, no, no. That couldn't be true. Her thoughts spun and she struggled to continue to stay where she was, doing as Papa bid.

As if from a distance she heard their conversation continue ...

'I also think he needs to be brought here.'

'He should not be moved,' Abigail said.

'How will moving him affect him?' Alistair asked.

'His injuries could worsen. He could die.'

What? Her mind stopped spinning and she focused back in on the conversation like a whiplash.

'The worst has already happened, as far as he and the other Were are concerned,' Ali said grimly. 'Despite the fact Leanna Healed Dougal's upper spinal injury in that latest Healing, the lower spine is severed. Given that, many of them, Dougal included, would be relieved if he were to die now he is ... unable to be who he has been.'

Abigail tsked. 'A short-sighted attitude. Dougal's worth is not contingent on him being able to walk.'

Exactly right!

Morghanna held up her hand. 'You are arguing your point with the wrong person, Abigail. Ali and I agree with you. But I think Ali's point was, nobody would stop us from moving Dougal here given his survival is thought a burden by many. And if Ali thinks putting them together would help this horrific situation, then we should seriously consider it.'

'Why? Why would putting them together make any difference?' Abigail asked just as Leanna thought the same question. 'Dougal's attitude will not change. He is practically willing himself to die as we speak.'

Oh no. How could he do that? He had to stop. He had to. They had to make him stop. She stared at them, willing them to feel her need. Her desperation.

'The separation from his mate,' Ali said steadily, 'is helping him to deny their bond. To him, it feels like he has nothing to live for. However, if we bring him here, or take Le-le to him, having her right there beside him will make it so much harder for him and his wolf to deny her and the bond and continue down the path he thinks he wants right now. Her presence will make him want to live.'

'How do you know that for certain? It could simply make things worse for Le-le,' Abigail said.

Morghanna's eyes flared wide, panic in them—was she feeling Leanna's panic—as Alistair frowned, rubbing his chest with his knuckles as if rubbing away a nagging pain.

He stopped rubbing and shrugged. 'I am uncertain how I know. I simply do. Maybe I have lived with Were before and have learned this from them.' He made a hissing sound of frustration. 'I truly wish I could remember my past so I could tell you why I feel this is so important, but all I have is the memories since I awoke and the absolute certainty that I am right.' He glanced at Morghanna and she gave him an encouraging smile, the panic gone as fast as it had come.

'I am certain you are correct,' Morghanna said. 'But why would none of the Were have suggested this? Surely they are aware of the fledgling bond—they would feel it in a way I could not.'

Alistair shrugged again. 'They probably think it a kindness that she be kept from him to minimise the damage to her and encourage his fading into death.'

'Stupidity,' Abigail muttered.

Morghanna patted her on the shoulder. 'It is simply one more attitude we must change.'

'Maybe there is information in those ancient Pack Diaries the cubs found yesterday in that cave that was exposed by the explosion,' Alistair said. 'I think we all should start reading through them.'

'Aye, you are right,' Abigail said. 'We might find things that have been lost to them like we have been finding information lost to us in the grimoires Bridgette has been sending to us.'

Morghanna frowned and rubbed her forehead again. 'Even if we do find something, it might not be soon enough to get through to Dougal and help Le-le.'

'Aye. It is paramount that we make him stop trying to break the bond,' Abigail said. 'Leanna is weakening by the second.'

Bond? What bond? What were they talking about? Whispers of memory came to her but she couldn't grasp at them. Why? What had she forgotten? Something important. Something ...

'I will go right now,' Morghanna said, then turned to Ali. 'Stay here with Abigail and watch over Leanna until I return.'

He nodded and kissed her. 'Be quick. She cannot fight him for much longer.'

Fight who? Was this why she felt so weak? Why it was beginning to be so hard to remain in the astral so she could keep watching, listening and heeding? She tried to move, to follow Morghanna, to try to figure out what she couldn't remember, but the pulling she'd been ignoring suddenly became so great. She lost control of her astral self and spiralled down the bond to her body, sucked into it with a suddenness that took her breath and had every muscle and sinew spasming in pain.

Somewhere in the distance, she heard someone cry out her name. Then she was sucked into unconsciousness.

8

uck! He hurt.

In so many ways he hurt.

Why did it feel like this? Having a broken back with no feeling below his pelvic region should be painless. Given he felt no pain down there.

Except, he kind of did. Although what he could feel where his legs were wasn't like pain as he knew it. It was loss. Grief. And pulsing sparks without any consistency.

He'd heard those who had lost a limb felt ghost pains for years after, but this didn't feel like what he imagined that to be.

It was less. And yet, so much more than ghostly.

Then there was the pain everywhere else. From the injury up, his body was screaming, his back muscles twisting in agony.

And that didn't seem right given Le-le had done two huge Healings on him before they'd both passed out. Not to mention the multiple Healings Morghanna and Alistair had done on him before Sebastian and the McVale Pack Healers had arrived a few days ago. Morghanna had put out a call to them to bring back the young Pack Healer they were training now the previous MacCrae Pack Healer was dead. They had not wanted to touch Dougal given the Were's attitude to an injury such as his—they rightly thought he should be encouraged into death. But Morghanna had insisted they help.

Such a stupid, wasteful use of their power and effort. For the minute Iain returned from the hunt, his life would be counted in seconds.

No Alpha worth his weight would allow a member to be a drain on the pack like Dougal now was. If Dougal wasn't capable of killing himself, Iain would do it.

Scrap that—he'd probably order one of the Hunters to do it. He never liked to get his hands dirty after all.

Dougal had once thought that was a sign of a good leader to trust in others to do important tasks, but after Lachlan had given in to the Darkness and become the Beast and Iain had looked to others to clean up his mess, he knew it was a sign of weakness. His Alpha had been more concerned with what would happen to his son and had pulled more strength and power from Dougal and the other lieu-tenants and senior soldiers to bolster himself so he could protect his son from the retribution of angry members of the pack.

Now he would have to leave dealing with Iain to someone else. With him gone, Cal most likely would rise to be Alpha. He had always had the hint of Alpha about him even though it had always been secondary to the power that was in Dougal. But now that power was gone, Cal could come into his own. And he was happy for his friend in that.

To that end, for the good of the pack, he had to talk to Morghanna and Alistair and get them onside—and have them stand behind his choice of death and his choice of successor.

He would have to get them to support Leanna as well. Because when he cut the threads of bond it would hurt her.

But not anywhere near as much as if he allowed the mating to come to completion and then died.

That could destroy her; break her mind, if it didn't break her body and kill her.

His wolf made a sound, more a scream than a howl, pulsing in his throat, aching to push its way out.

The thought of them being responsible for hurting her or causing her death was unbearable. It squeezed his chest, choking his breath in his throat.

This terror, it added to the pain of blocking the fledgling bond, causing agony.

Sweat poured down his face, his chest and limbs, wetting the linen night-shirt someone had dressed him in while he'd been unconscious. He trembled with the force of his wolf's anguish, anguish he shared in full.

But he couldn't stop. Couldn't stop trying to save their mate pain and anguish. Couldn't stop not only trying to block the bond, but to break what had formed from his side before Iain returned.

Morghanna, Alistair and Abigail would ensure she didn't grieve for too long; they'd make certain she moved on and lived the life she deserved. And she could be happy because she wouldn't really know what she had lost; he was certain she did not know what they could have been to each other.

That had to be enough. It had to give him the strength to do what must be done.

His wolf quieted inside him as it too came to terms with what they must do.

Panting and still trembling, he closed his eyes and shoved down the anguish, blocked himself to all the different types of pain racking his body, his heart, his soul. They wouldn't quiet completely, but he got them to a point where he could concentrate on what he must do to break the fledgling bond.

He sought that part of his mind that could not only feel the bond but see it and settled into it with a little whoosh and a soothing sensation like coming home.

In his mind he opened his eyes, expecting to see some muted strands pulsing in the dark.

Instead his mental eyes squinted against the brightness there. The orange and yellow and silvery glow that was coming from the bond—a bond that was far thicker and more stable than it should be.

No!

No!

How could this be?

But as he asked the question, memories of what had happened flooded his mind.

She'd seen the potential power in the bond when she Healed him and grabbed it, using it, strengthening it ...

Accepting it.

No! No, no, no, no, no!

Why had he not remembered this until now? And why the fuck hadn't he done more to stop her?

He had tried. By the Moon he had tried. But she was so strong. Stronger than he'd known she was. And she'd held on. Despite the fact he'd pushed at her, tried to deny her, screamed at her that he didn't want this.

But she hadn't cared. Or maybe she hadn't truly known what she was doing. She simply saw that it would save him, that there was power there that could hold him to this life while she Healed him. She'd held out against him, had proved the strength of her will.

He would never wish that strength away, but by all that was good and holy, he wished it hadn't shown itself at that moment.

But it had and the bond was ...

He stared at it hard, noting that it wasn't as thick or rope-like as a fully formed mating bond should be. He'd seen the mating bond between his parents: multiple glowing strands of two colours winding around each other to create a thick rope that was both flexible and stronger than the strongest thing anyone knew of. Nothing could break a fully formed and healthy mating bond except death. Some said not even then as some souls found each other again and again through various lifetimes.

This was not that.

Yes, it was bright—but that brightness was not caused by the usual two colours. There was a dark, slightly sickly looking green he assumed was him. But then where Leanna should be represented by one colour, there were multiple strands that looked like a sunrise, the colours ranging the light spectrum between light gold to burnt orange with an astonishing bright silver strand that looked like the rays of the moon in a darkened forest—one of his and his wolf's favourite sights to see when running in the woods.

And while this confirmed that his Le-le was as remarkable as he knew her to be, there was something not right about those strands. The brightness fluctuated, like it wasn't settled or set, and they didn't wrap around each other tightly as they should but lay loosely next to each other so he could see between them.

And while they wound around his plait of strands, they didn't touch it—which was why he hadn't noticed this until now, particularly as he had been blocking it until he had the wherewithal to deal with it.

But why weren't her strands touching his?

It was like she'd accepted it but not really. Like she didn't know.

She didn't know!

His heart beat loudly in his chest. Not from stress, guilt or pain. But from hope. Because if she truly didn't know, if she didn't realise what they were to each other—what she meant to him—then maybe he could break it still even though it had gone further than he'd wanted it to.

Or maybe he could make her let go by not wanting him. He could make her refute him!

His wolf whimpered at the thought of being short with her, of doing things to push her away, but it understood the necessity.

A few moments of discomfort to save her from a lifetime of pain and grief.

He could try to tear at the strands from the inside until they weakened so much they broke. Just like he'd tried to do before.

He pushed into the space where he could see the bond and reached for her strands.

The moment his mental hand grasped them, he froze.

By the Moon—he'd never felt anything like it. It was the essence of his Le-le—like he'd always imagined she'd feel but better. So much goodness and kindness and endless empathy—she felt not just for others but *with* others. And yet, she still used her powers to Heal even though it could hurt her too.

Despite all the power and strength there, doubt resonated among the strands—he'd hoped she no longer felt doubt about herself—alongside worry and pain.

She was in pain!

He jerked upright—at least he tried, but nothing worked as it should. Pain spiked through him so badly he cried out. His chest constricted and he could barely breathe.

He grabbed at it, at his neck, mouth gaping as he tried to pull in a breath to lungs that suddenly weren't working properly. Black stars sparked in his vision and began to swing wildly around, growing, growing—

'Dougal!'

With the sliver of vision he still had he saw Morghanna rushing across the room to him. She was shouting at someone behind her but it was like hearing under water. And his vision had closed down so much he could barely see her now, even though she was beside his bed.

She put her hands on him, her lips moving as she looked him in the eyes—she was probably asking him where the pain was or saying it would be okay, but he couldn't understand, couldn't answer, didn't care.

All that mattered was that he felt like he was going to die and Le-le was bonded to him, no matter that it was not right, and she would feel his death like it was her own.

He couldn't go yet. Not until he'd broken the bond.

'Save me,' he gasped. 'For Le-le.'

Her mouth moved again and she nodded. Then his vision went to black just as the warmth of Healing began to rush through him.

The black began to recede as the golden warmth filled his muscles, relaxing the cramping tension, pushing away the pain. And suddenly the crushing sensation around his lungs lifted and he drew in a huge shuddering breath.

Hearing rushed back with the oxygen as Morghanna said, 'You

are not going to die. We need you, Dougal. But most of all, Le-le needs you. She needs you to stay. She needs you to accept.'

His head swam with her words, the implications making him dizzy.

They knew? They knew she'd mated to him? But how when he'd only just discovered it himself?

He tried to ask but words were still beyond him.

'Do not try to talk, you stubborn Were. Just let me do the Healing and take your pain. Then you must rest. Later we can discuss what needs to be done about Le-le.'

What needed to be done? 'Save her,' he said, his voice a croaky gasp. 'From me.'

'You are determined to hash this out now?' He nodded. She tsked. 'Well, I will say this much, you have to stop fighting her. You are hurting her.'

What? Nae! He had to have heard wrong. 'I am not fighting her,' he managed to say. Except, it wasn't true. He was fighting her by blocking the bond, by trying to stop the bond from being.

'You are. You are fighting the mating bond. And you cannot do that anymore. She is expending too much energy trying to reach you through it. It is why she is still unconscious. You must stop fighting her for now. I understand why you might not want it, but it has already happened and you need to accept it. If not for yourself, for Le-le.'

'I will hurt her.'

'You *are* hurting her. If you continue, she will die.'

'Nae!' he shouted, then coughed and cried out in pain as the effort made his muscles spasm again.

'See, I told you not to talk. We can finish this discussion after you have rested.'

'I dinna want to rest.'

She swore under her breath and then said over her shoulder, 'Ali. Please make him sleep.'

A shadow appeared on the other side of the bed, and before he could protest, the warlock had put his hands on Dougal's head and intoned the spell for sleep.

The dream state folded over him, taking him down-down into a world free of pain and full of bliss because Le-le waited there for him, her strawberry blonde hair glowing in the light of the moon, a smile on her face—the smile she only shared with him.

He'd had these dreams many times since the accident. Had lost himself in them for what seemed an endless time after Le-le had tried to Heal him. They'd been all he had of the life that was now beyond his grasp.

And even though he knew he shouldn't lose himself to them again, he couldn't help but give in to the need inside him that would never die. For her.

For his Le-le.

In dreams was the only way he would ever have her. So in dreams he would have her even as he worked outside the dream to destroy their bond. For Morghanna was wrong. The only way to save Le-le was to break what tied them together.

He thrust that depressing thought aside as Le-le walked towards him. Arms opened wide, she said, 'Finally, my love. You are here. Take me to bed and make me scream your name over and over.'

'With pleasure, *mo ghrádh*,' he growled, sweeping her off her feet and into his arms as he headed to their big bed. Then laying her down on it, he stripped her bare, kissing every part of her before ravaging her mouth with a passionate kiss.

As she moaned into his mouth, he nudged her legs aside and pushed into the welcoming warmth of her pussy, stroking her tongue with his as he stroked his cock in and out of her wet centre. Faster and faster and harder and harder at her urging. Then, delighting him, she used her power to flip him so he was on the bottom and she was riding him. He cupped her breast with one hand as she rode him hard, and moved his other to play with the little nub at the top of her slit, until she screamed his name. He came with a roar of her name full of the love he felt inside for her.

Finally they came back down, the weight of her pinning him to the bed.

He wrapped his arms around her …

Except, it wasn't her he held, but the heavy blankets Morghanna had placed over him that weighted him down.

He opened his eyes, desperate sadness enveloping him.

It had been a dream.

A dream that could never be brought to reality. Not in the life he now had.

He could never let the mating complete. Even if by some miracle he was fated to live—which was very unlikely given who his Alpha was—Le-le deserved more than a husk of a man who might never be able to sweep her off her feet and fulfil her in ways she deserved.

She deserved everything.

And he could no longer give her that.

By the Moon, that thought made him want to die.

But not yet. Not until he'd made sure she was free and clear of him. Not until he was certain she wouldn't want to die with him.

But Morghanna was right. For now, he had to stop fighting her so she would stop doing whatever she was doing to give him the energy and strength she could ill afford to give.

He would give in, momentarily, until she was up and recovering again.

Once he was assured of her good health, he would start to cut the bond that tied them together.

It was the right thing to do. It was the only way.

9

'L e-Le. What are you doing out of bed?'

Leanna whipped around and almost fell over. Curse this weakness and dizziness that had been plaguing her ever since she'd woken from trying to Heal Dougal that second time! She had things to do. Things that were the only value she had to this coven and pack that had taken her in after she'd lost everything.

Her talents with Healing and her craft were needed and valued. It was still difficult to believe that she was good at anything at all, her magic always having been difficult to harness and a bit of a disaster to be frank—or so her mama had said. Even though Abigail was certain she was holding something back, under her and Morghanna's steady tutelage, she had become quite proficient.

But not proficient enough to finish mending Dougal's broken back.

Which was the reason she was up now—the only reason she hadn't sunk back into that glorious, sexy dream she'd woken from fully sated. She'd had other dreams too where her papa had come to her, but she couldn't remember anything from those except for his warm and comforting presence—just like when he'd been alive.

The dreams about Dougal though ... She fanned her face. She'd had those dreams every night since she'd Healed Dougal. She would happily spend her life in those dreams, but ...

Dougal's back would remain broken unless she found a way to mend it. And the only way she could do that was to read through all the coven diaries and grimoires to see if one of the ancient witches knew something that had been lost to them.

That maybe they knew how to give Dougal the use of his legs.

'Le-Le,' Alistair said as he crossed the room to her. 'Let me help you back to bed.'

He put his arm around her in that brotherly way he had that made her feel safe with him. It was quite lovely, particularly as she felt safe with so few people. Except, she didn't want to be herded back to bed and coddled.

So she surprised herself by pushing his arm away and meeting his gaze.

The entire standing-up-for-herself thing was ruined by the fact she stumbled and he had to grab her so she didn't fall.

'Le-Le,' he said softly, his deep French-accented voice soothing and gentle, his touch calming as he slipped his hands down her arms to take her hands.

A calm that belied the raw emptiness she felt inside him, like something essential had been torn from him.

It was probably the loss of his family years ago—a loss, Morghanna said, that had set him on his path to find her. Except ... this loss, this emptiness, slashed at her with surprisingly fresh pain. Strong enough to make her gasp and pull back from him.

'Le-Le? What is wrong?' he asked, reaching to steady her again.

She held up her hands, warding him off, not wanting to feel that raw emptiness inside him again. Not right now at least. Not when she was trying to be strong enough to do what she wanted to do. What she must do.

Heal Dougal.

So, despite every instinct inside urging her to back down, to do as Alistair wished and rest, she straightened her spine and met his gaze. 'Nothing is wrong, Alistair. And no, I do not want to go back to bed.'

He sighed and looked at her with consternation—her standing up to him was unusual. But despite trembling in every limb with the desire to drop her gaze and hide behind her long, lack-lustre hair—with its strange colour that was neither blonde, red or brown—and give in to any will except her own, she stayed strong. 'Truly. I need to be up and doing something. Anything that is not lying around and being with my thoughts.' Given his recent illness, she knew he understood that. And despite his lack of memory, she knew he understood her dark history in a way many others didn't. It was the reason she found his presence a comfort in ways she never did with others.

Except for Dougal. But that was a different kind of comfort. An edgy, skin-prickling warmth running through her like wildfire kind of comfort. She drowned a little in it. Willingly. Strange that she thought of it as comforting at all, but it was. A comfort that made her feel like she had her own special sun inside lighting her up. It made her feel ever so slightly like there was a path out of the bleakness she'd been travelling in for so long.

And she'd almost lost him. Might still if she didn't find a way to make him realise his life was important.

Another dark thought she really wanted to push aside. But only if she could do something useful. And the best way to do that was figure out how to mend his back. 'Please. I need to do something.'

Alistair sighed gently again. 'You know Morghanna will have my guts for garters if I let you overextend yourself.'

She giggled at his exaggeration. Morghanna would never hurt a hair on her lover's head. She would tear anyone else apart who tried to hurt him—a fact that was well known after what she did to Lachlan. But her lover was precious to her.

So very precious it almost hurt Leanna to witness it.

Because it was something she could never have for herself. No matter how she longed to be mated to Dougal, she never could be. She would never be what Dougal needed. Not with how damaged she was both inside and out.

But that was one of the dark thoughts she was trying to escape, so she thrust it far back into the recesses of her mind and tried a smile. It still felt strange to smile, the scars on her face stretching in ways that made it feel unnatural, but Abigail said it would be helpful for her to move the muscles under the skin if there was a hope of smoothing out the minor scars and lessen the red rope-like big ones even after all this time.

A big hope but one she clung to because there had been so little hope to cling to for so long.

'I promise I will not do more than go to the herbal stillroom to work on some concoctions to help with strengthening patients in their recovery.'

'No magic yet,' Alistair said, pointing a finger at her. The gesture would have had her skittering away not so long ago, but now she tried another smile, enjoying his responding smile—she must be doing it right. 'Both Abigail and Morghanna said that you need to rest your magical muscles for at least a few more days.'

She deflated a little—it would be so much better if she could use a little magic, but given she was still so weak—ridiculously so—and her magic felt so sluggish, she probably couldn't use it even if she wanted to. 'Fine,' she said, looking down at her hands for the first time. 'No magic.' Some little spark of what her grammy had called 'the devil' suddenly flared to life inside her and she peered up through her dark lashes and said, 'But maybe you could use a bit of your magic to help me out.'

He laughed. '*Certainement*. You will have to instruct me. Herbal medications are not my forte.'

She preened a little. He was such a powerful warlock ... it was amazing that he would take instruction from her. 'I will try to be a good teacher.'

'Given your expertise I am certain I will learn much.' He clapped his hands together and then said, 'So, shall we go now? Or would you like to go by the kitchens for some lunch first. Sally mentioned you did not eat much of your breakfast again.'

He gave her that look they'd all been giving her this last week since she'd awoken from her long sleep. The look that said they didn't think she was looking after herself. That they were afraid she was slipping back into old self-destructive ways. But she wasn't. She had things to live for now. And she was trying to eat except ... 'I am not hungry because I have been doing nothing to make me hungry. However, if it will make you feel better, we can stop by the kitchen and get some of those fruit buns I know you made this morning.' She sniffed loudly. 'I can smell them on you.'

He laughed and clapped his hands again. 'Oh-la. You would be right. And I made an extra batch and put them aside for Morghanna for later. So there will be some left.'

'I do not want to take Morghanna's treat.'

'I put aside more than she would ever eat. There will be plenty enough for us to take a few. Besides which, she would take more pleasure in seeing you eat them than eating them herself.'

'I doubt that. There is nothing quite like your fruit buns.'

He had turned out to be an amazing cook and baker and had been working many shifts in the kitchens, learning their methods—Were had a whole thing about scents and tastes and always had amazing cooks among their packs. Alistair for his part was teaching them French recipes and techniques that he thought he might have learned from his parents—although he still couldn't remember them.

He waved his hand in that French way of his, and said, 'Enough flattery. Let us fetch those buns and then I will accompany you to the herbal stillroom so you can teach me some of what you know.'

She nodded and took his arm for support—there was no way she'd make it to the kitchen and then the herbal stillroom without it. No amount of stubborn determination or need to be busy would give her the energy to do that all in one go. Particularly if she meant to work at the end of it. Even walking that distance might take too much out of her, leaving her with no energy to create her medicinals.

After a few steps she looked up at him and asked shyly, 'Would you mind carrying me very much as you have done other days?' He was the only one she'd been comfortable with doing that, allowing him to carry her to the bathing rooms when she'd finally been allowed to go, with Morghanna to help her once there of course.

He nodded and without saying anything, scooped her gently into his arms. As they went out the door she said, 'And if it would not be too much trouble, can we drop by the library on the way? There are some grimoires I would like to take with us.'

'Well, now you are asking for too much.'

She was about to apologise when she realised he was joking with her. She smiled shyly and said, 'Thank you.'

'My pleasure.' He smiled down at her then looked back to where they were going. 'But I think we might be held up on the way.'

'What? Why?'

He nodded towards the heart of the Pack Village. People—both Were and coven—had noticed them and were waving at her, calling out greetings, some of them making their way over. She thought at first they simply wished to talk to Alistair—he might not remember all of them, but they remembered him and what he'd done—but they all seemed to want to speak to her; to find out how she was faring; to say how happy they were to see her in their midst again and hoped to see her every day.

By the time they were halfway to the kitchens, it seemed half the village had either called their greetings or come over to say hello. It was a little overwhelming to someone who had tried her best to be invisible for so long. And had thought that barely anyone here—particularly the Were—knew who she was or that she even existed.

Their concern and happiness to see her though was genuine.

Unfortunately, all the attention tired her out. By the time they'd collected the buns and some refreshing cold ginger tea—the root was a luxury the McVales brought in from overseas and traded with the other packs in Scotland—grabbed the grimoires from the library and made it to the herbal stillroom, she could barely sit upright let alone stand at the bench to do her work.

Tears of frustration sparked in her eyes as she collapsed in the chair against the wall.

'Should I fetch Morghanna?' Alistair asked, coming down by her side.

She shook her head miserably. 'No. I do not wish to worry her.'

'Morghanna worries whether you wish it or not.'

'I *should* be able to do this!' she said, tying knots with her fingers in her lap, barely able to see them for the tears filling her eyes. By the Goddess, she didn't want to cry in front of him. What he must think of her! Weak. Foolish. Ruined.

'Perhaps I should take you back to your cottage to rest.'

'I do not want to go back there. Staring at those walls is driving me insane.'

'I understand that, Le-le. Believe me, I do.'

She glanced up at him, sorry for her lash of temper. 'I am sorry. I do not wish to remind you of your illness.'

'There is not much to remind me of as I remember very little. But after I awoke and felt fine, people still treated me like an invalid, and it was very frustrating. They would not let me do much of anything for days until they realised I was indeed fine.'

His understanding was wonderful but it didn't give her more energy in this moment; energy she desperately needed and would get no other way than lying down and having a sleep. 'I feel so useless.'

He huffed out a sigh and she felt him shift as if looking around but she didn't look up to see because she was hiding behind her long thick hair, trying desperately to hold back the tears.

After a moment he stood and she braced, ready for him to pick her up and take her back to that room she had started to hate.

But he didn't do that. Instead he said, 'How about I carry a cot in here for you? There is room over by the back wall if I move that bench into the corner. You could rest here and then when you are feeling better, you can get right back up and start your work without expending all the energy you did getting here.'

Tears were streaming down her face by the time he finished speaking. 'You would do that for me?'

'Of course. It is no trouble. And perhaps we can make a daily thing of it. I could bring you here every morning after you have broken your fast and you can work until you need to rest and then work again after that. How does that sound?'

'It sounds ...' Blissful. Remarkable. Wonderful. 'Perfect.'

'*Merveilleuse*. Well, it is a plan. And I can fetch more grimoires as you need them—I expect you want to research different kinds of Healing in the older ones that have not been looked at for years. Maybe there could be things in the Pack Diaries too.'

'I ... I ... But what will Morghanna say?' Her mentor was amazing and kind, but she was fiercely protective of those she particularly thought of as being in her care, and Leanna had become aware over the last months that, no matter how unbelievable it was, she was one of those people.

'I am certain she will be all for it when I explain how you feel. Although, given it is Morghanna, there will be rules.'

She snorted out a laugh. 'I can deal with rules.'

'*Bon*. I better talk to Morghanna and secure her agreement first— and do not worry, she will agree. Then I will fetch the cot and some bedding and get you settled. Will you be fine for a few minutes?'

'I will.'

He quickly left the room and she held onto the chair as if her life depended on it—because in a way it did. At least her sanity did. For if she collapsed off the chair and onto the floor, she wouldn't be able to get herself back up. And if Morghanna came back with Alistair as she undoubtedly would, and found her sprawled on the floor without the energy to get up, she would not only refuse Alistair's idea to take place, she would probably make Leanna stay in bed in her cottage for even longer.

Which would well and truly crack her sanity in two. And then she would not be able to do what she had to do. Needed to do.

Heal Dougal so that he could be happy again.

Nothing was more important to her than that.

Leanna swore as the potion she was making fizzled rather than popped then turned into sludge, the constant ache inside her increasing with her failure.

Why wasn't this working?

She glanced over the instructions in the ancient grimoire propped in the middle of the work table. She'd followed them exactly.

So why was the potion a dull green-grey sludge and not the vibrant spring green viscous fluid that it was meant to be? If she couldn't get this right, how was she supposed to figure out how to change it to do something the original witch who created it never thought it could do?

At its heart it was a simple salve used to repair damaged muscle and tendon when a witch Healer wasn't available. It had been lost to them when the coven responsible for its making were all slaughtered by a raiding party of soldiers sent by the local lord in the middle of the night for reasons nobody knew. All their grimoires had been lost to the fires the soldiers set—at least that was what had been supposed. But then Bridgette and Malcolm had found them in an abandoned *Chiesa* outside *Firenze*—their power had called to Bridgette. And since then, as well as travelling to bring more covens and packs into the Pact, Bridgette and Malcolm searched for grimoires thought lost to time and sent them back to Morghanna for cataloguing.

Leanna had been thrilled when Morghanna asked her to help in this task. And she'd been doing so well working through them—even, thanks to a quirk in her powers, being able to translate the ones in different languages. But now, given her lack of energy, it was taking so much longer. She'd barely got through two and had only found this one possibly useful salve.

Useful if only she could make it work!

She had no idea why it was taking so long for her to recover. She should be getting better by now. Okay, she'd been pushing herself a little, but mostly she'd been doing everything she'd promised Alistair and Morghanna she would when Alistair had come up with his solution to her boredom and frustration.

Those first few days after she'd been allowed to work and research had been wonderful. Hope and enthusiasm had filled her. She'd always loved working in the herbal stillroom, creating something from a scattering of ingredients that by themselves did little, but with the right combinations and amounts—and magic—could be used to help people in so many ways.

It hadn't even bothered her that she had to nap regularly when she ran out of energy—which was far too often—because being able to stay-put, knowing when she awoke she could get back into her work, made it, if not all right, at least acceptable. She had felt useful once again. Less of a burden.

It had been marvellous to hear that she'd managed to mend his upper spine with that last Healing, but that hadn't been completely severed like his lower spine which was an entirely different matter. It would need so much more power than she had. Or feared she would ever have again.

She sighed heavily. Her continued weakness and lack of energy was starting to wear on her, especially because she still hadn't come up with anything to truly help Dougal. And the fact she wasn't allowed to see him wasn't helping either. They were apparently worried that if she saw him she wouldn't be able to help herself and would try to do a big Healing again.

Maybe they were right. She probably would if given the chance. But given she barely had any access to her power at all, there really was nothing to worry about. Morghanna however was not moved by her request to be allowed to help nurse Dougal.

That was when she found out Dougal had said he didn't want to see her. Well, not her specifically. She was probably not much in his thoughts at all. He didn't want to see anyone bar Morghanna, Abigail, Alistair and Cal, his best friend—who was on their side despite pack sentiment. Given that, she tried not to feel badly, but it was difficult not to feel rejected somewhat.

It had given her time though to concentrate on reading through the grimoires and diaries. Although, she'd had no luck with them until she'd had another one of those strange dreams where her papa came to her and she woke from that dream with the memory of reading about a spell a few months ago that could enhance a Healing potion.

It had taken her days to track it down but it had felt worth it, because when she finally read it she knew she was on the right track.

Together, the salve and spell could ready Dougal's body for a greater working. A working she still hadn't figured out how to do, but that was a problem for later.

This salve, with the spell's help, should give him back some sensation in his lower body at least. Which would help with so many issues they faced—namely him giving up hope and wanting to die.

She pressed her knuckles against the tightness in her chest that thought brought on. Dougal had already tried to die. He'd tried to make her let him go when she was holding on so tightly to keep him with her. But for the first time in her life she hadn't given in; hadn't given up. She had ignored him and held him here. With her.

Maybe it had been selfish in that moment, but she didn't care. She couldn't imagine life without him a part of it. He may never be hers but that didn't matter. All that mattered was that he lived.

In all the histories, so the Pack Librarian had told them, any Were who broke their back and survived to live long enough for it to be confirmed they would never walk again, lived very few days after. It was accepted—and encouraged—for the injured to kill themselves so they were not a burden on the pack or made it weak. And if they were unable to do the deed themselves, the Alpha would do it for them.

Such outdated thinking. So much unnecessary loss.

Morghanna was afraid Dougal would be made to do the same when Iain returned. If he hadn't already done it before then.

The thought squeezed at her chest, making her gasp for breath. She sat down with a plop on the stool behind her and held onto the bench, trying to breathe normally.

Morghanna and Abigail were doing all they could to fight against anyone who so much as suggested Dougal should die—which was another reason they'd given her for why they were happy to acquiesce to Dougal's request not to see anyone. They were happy to be the only ones to talk to him to make him see that all was not lost—and they didn't need her help with that.

Their argument to Dougal and the pack was a sound one—that now the Were had access to magic, there were many things that could be done to help Dougal get around. They thought maybe they were getting through, but they needed some progress to show soon.

Which was why she needed this to work. Why she'd been working so hard on it and hadn't argued much about not being allowed to see Dougal—because finding and working this potion was so much more important than her need to see him.

If only she could make it work!

The only real use she had to him was to find a way to give him back some feeling—hopefully more—and she was failing abysmally at it.

The sense of helplessness and futility that had been wavering on the horizon ever since she'd woken from unconsciousness crept closer. Panic rose in her chest and she wanted to give in to it. Give in to what her mother had always told her—that she had always been useless and always would be.

But no!

Dougal needed her. She couldn't forget that. He *needed* her. And even if she gave up on herself, she wouldn't give up on him!

She pushed the small cauldron with the sludge away—nothing would save it now, especially given she had very little access to her magic yet—and pulled the mortar and pestle back in front of her. She'd have to start again.

'That was a big sigh.'

She snapped around to see Alistair standing at the door with a tray of food and another grimoire under his arm. 'I am not hungry.'

'I think that hardly matters,' he said, kicking the door shut and walking over to the small table he'd cleared at the start of the week for them to eat at. 'I am hungry and I would like your company while I eat. You do not want me to go to Morghanna and tell her I need a lunch companion because my regular one is not eating as she promised to.'

Leanna glared at him as he set the table and then blew a raspberry when he turned around and smiled at her.

He laughed. Which got him another raspberry. And then a smile when he said, 'I brought you a piece of rhubarb tart and fresh cream.'

Yum! She could eat his rhubarb tart even if she wasn't hungry. 'May I eat it first?'

'Of course.' He sauntered back to where she sat and held out his hand to her. 'But you also have to eat at least one piece of bread and cheese.'

Given she had a weakness for the tasty cheese the pack specialised in making—tart and yet creamy—when paired with the crusty bread, it wasn't much of a hardship to agree. Which he knew. 'You do not play fair.'

'When it comes to our most stubborn patient, playing fair does not work.'

'I am hardly your most stubborn patient.' She put her hand in his and allowed him to help her up. 'If anything, I am known for my lack of stubbornness.'

He snorted as he escorted her to her seat. 'You are one of the most stubborn people I have ever met.'

'You do not remember anyone except those who live here.'

'True. However, the Were here are incredibly stubborn and yet you give each of them a run for their money.'

'I do not believe that is true. I cannot stand up to anyone.'

'You do fine standing up to me and everyone else who has wanted you to look after yourself since the explosion. Case in point ...' He gestured around them at her work.

'You know I need to help.'

'Yes and that need is part of your stubbornness; to look after everyone else even over your own well-being.' He began to divvy up the bread and cheese on two plates adding a big dollop of the fig jam that went perfectly with the cheese.

'I am a Healer. It is my Goddess-given mandate to Heal and see to the well-being of others before my own.'

He sighed. 'You sound like Morghanna.'

'Thank you.'

A generous piece of tart was added to each plate. 'It was not a compliment. She spouts the same stubborn-headed idiot nonsense you just did.'

She gaped at him before spluttering, 'I hope you do not say that to her.'

'*Mais bien sûr.* Because how else can I make you both see how ridiculous you are when you refuse to do what is best for your patient—'

'I do do what is best for my patient!'

He ignored her as if she'd not spoken, finishing as he plopped clotted cream on top of each piece of tart, '—which is look after yourself. After all, what good are you to your patient if you are flamed-out or dead?'

He picked up one of the plates and held it out to her, his brows raised as if to say, 'Argue with that, if you dare!'

The problem was, she couldn't.

So she frowned at him and took the plate.

Now she was sitting at the table with the scent of fresh baked crusty bread, tangy cheese and the sweetness of the tart rising to greet her, her mouth watered and her stomach growled. Which annoyed her because it proved his point—if he hadn't come in with lunch she wouldn't have thought to eat, which was stupid. Starving herself would not help with her recovery.

So she reached for the bread and cheese first even though the tart was calling to her.

They ate in silence for a few minutes—the cheese, bread and fig jam were so good she had started on a second piece when Alistair broke the companionable silence.

'So why the big sigh when I came in?'

She swallowed her mouthful and took a big gulp of the fresh water he'd poured for her, before answering. 'I mucked up the potion.' She sighed, staring glumly at the tart on her plate. 'I do not know why it did not work. Unless it is because I cannot give it enough of my magic. Which is entirely possible given it is sporadic and weak at best.'

He put down the mug he'd just picked up with a loud clack on the wooden table. 'Do not tell me you have been trying to use your magic. I thought we had agreed you would call me for any magical work.'

She glanced up at him, guilt stabbing at her so hard she knew it showed on her face. 'And I did.' His eyes narrowed—she hated the distrust on the face of this man she now thought of as a friend. 'I promise. I always called you for the potion work where a spell was needed.'

'So, then tell me how you know,' he said evenly, 'that the problem that caused that cauldron of sludge is your magic?'

She glanced back down at her plate, certain now she was never going to be able to eat any of his delicious tart—a tragedy. 'Well ...' She twisted her hands together in her lap wishing she could find some way to get out of telling him but knowing it was useless. She'd already said enough to incriminate herself so she might as well save herself the anguish of trying to be clever or a liar when she was neither of those things. 'I was going to call you but the potion instructions asked for such a small amount of magic—simply to bind ingredients together that normally do not bind and enliven certain elements more than others—that I thought I could manage it. After all, it has been more than three weeks since I flamed-out, well beyond the usual requirement to rest and not use magic.'

His fingers had started to drum on the table as she spoke but as she finished, he ceased all movement and the room fell ominously quiet.

She drew the courage—she wasn't sure where from—to glance up at him through the hair that had fallen to cover her face, and was surprised to see he didn't look angry or annoyed. In fact he was smiling a little, almost as if he were impressed.

He noticed her peering at him, and his smile widened as he shook his head a little. 'We are all so very glad you are finally stepping into who you truly are.' His smile faded a little. 'But using your magic when you have been instructed not to is not the stubborn spear you want to impale yourself on.'

'I am not impaling anything!' she said, head snapping up so she could meet his gaze fully. 'I mean ... you know what I mean.'

He chuckled and said, 'I do. But still, you promised.'

She pouted at him and started picking at the piece of bread on her plate rather than the torn skin around her fingernails. 'I promised when I thought there might still be danger. But honestly, it should have been safe to use my magic days ago. So there was no reason I could think of for me not to use my magic in small doses except for the fact you all seem to want to cosset me more than usual.'

'That is because you used and channelled more magic than has been used by any Healer ever recorded and you pushed beyond normal levels that would cause flame-out. Morghanna, Abigail ... they have never seen anything like it before. Not even when Bridgette channelled the Goddess to create the Pact.'

'I did not ... that is not ...' She shook her head unable to accept what he said. 'I ... I used a lot of power but not more than anyone else would or could.'

He frowned. 'That is not true. We all felt it. It knocked all of us off our feet. That amount of magic ... You should be dead and yet you are not. So forgive us all for being overly cautious with your recovery and with when and how you use your magic again.' He reached across the table to grip her hand and the look on his face!

Goddess!

That look hurt her heart.

'I did not mean ... I ...' She could barely speak because that look put a lump in her throat it was hard to form words around.

'We cannot lose you, Le-le. Not just because you are a remarkable witch and Healer and a boon to this pack and coven, but because you are our friend. Our family. Morghanna has already lost her parents and her sister has gone missing. Do not do something that means she will lose you too.'

11

Leanna's vision starred, tears tumbling down her cheeks. She should be embarrassed for crying like this—her mother would have scolded her for a fool—but his words ...

They were something to cry over. She'd longed to hear words like that from more than just Papa for her entire life but had never thought she would—especially given how damaged and scarred she was now.

'I can see by your face you do not yet understand how important you are to us,' Alistair said firmly. 'But if you cannot believe my words then believe our actions. Believe how worried we are about you. Believe that we are overprotective for good reason.'

'Which is?' she somehow managed to ask.

'Because we love you. We want you to flourish and we want to see you happy. We do not wish to see you use yourself up until you die.'

'I am not doing that!'

'It feels like you are when you take such little care of yourself and ignore the advice of your mentors.' He held his hand up to stop her from responding—not that she really had words to respond because what he was saying was so incredibly wonderful and totally unbelievable. 'I ask one thing—that even if you do not believe what I say is true, believe that we do not want you to hurt yourself again. And we most definitely do not want you to work yourself to the bone until you are virtually a wraith or dead. This coven has suffered enough.'

She swallowed hard. She'd had no idea they thought she was hurting herself because she didn't care about herself. 'I do not want to die. I want to help.'

'You cannot help if you are not strong enough. You cannot help if you keep trying to use your magic before it is ready to be used.'

'And you do not believe I am strong enough to be able to use my magic again.'

He sighed and rolled his eyes. '*Sacre bleu*. It is so aggravating talking to you when you keep twisting my words to make it sound like I think you weak and stupid. I think neither of those things. I do think you are whip-smart, extraordinarily talented and stronger than every witch here aside from Morghanna.'

'You are as strong as her.'

He waved that statement away. 'We are not talking about me. We talk about you.'

'If I am so strong, then why can I not use my magic yet?'

'Because of what you did. The extraordinary power you pulled in and used. I was not overstating things when I said nobody in this coven or those Morghanna has reached out to, has ever seen its like.'

'Then why did it not work? Why can he not walk?' Her chin trembled and more tears slipped from her eyes. She brushed them away impatiently. 'Why is his back still broken?'

He reached out again, taking her hands in both of his and holding them firmly as he looked directly in her eyes. 'Leanna, do you not know what you did?'

She shook her head. 'I did not finish the job. I was too weak to complete the Healing.' She hated the wobble in her voice and the tears starring her eyes making it difficult to see.

He gripped her hands a little tighter. '*Non*. Do not do that to yourself.'

'Why not? It is true.'

'It is so far from the truth it is laughable. You did something no Healer has done before. You brought Dougal back from death.'

Leanna blinked at him for long, slow seconds. Maybe minutes. She couldn't be sure because time seemed to stop when he uttered those words. Because ... 'Nobody can bring another back from the dead.'

'You did.' He sounded so definite. 'We all felt it. Felt that moment when you pulled his soul back and restarted his heart.'

She remembered now ... for some reason she'd forgotten so much of what had happened between the explosion and waking the second time. But now that moment when she thought he had slipped away came crashing back—she'd grabbed at him in desperation with everything in her.

Had she actually done then what Alistair said she had? 'It seems ... too impossible.'

'We thought it was. But then you did it. And if that was not extraordinary enough, you continued the Healing until you ran out of all the magic you had pulled on to do such an astonishing feat. That is why you are still so tired and weak. That is the reason you struggle to harness even a little bit of your magic and use it in a steady way. All your magical pathways were completely overwhelmed and it is going to take some time for them to recover.'

'How long?' Really, that answer was all that mattered now. She couldn't let herself think about what they said she'd done. Could only let herself think about what was still to be done. And without the ability to use her magic, it would be impossible even with Alistair's help.

He shrugged and squeezed her hand again. 'Given this is a first, Abigail is uncertain. However, given your magic has only just started filtering back in through pathways that are still overly raw, it is going to take another week at least. Probably two.'

'But ... I cannot wait that long! Dougal cannot wait that long. Even if Morghanna and you and Abigail can keep him from willing himself to death, Iain will be back soon. He has already been gone for a month. He cannot be away from the pack another moon. We all know he will command Dougal to die the moment he returns. So things need to be done before then if we ever have a chance of making a significant enough change to make them all see he must live.'

He let go of her hands and sat back abruptly. 'You think you can Heal his broken back?'

She picked at the edge of the tart. 'I am hopeful of at least giving him back some movement and sensation. But ...' She peered up at him. 'It would be easier to figure out what needs to be done if I could see Dougal. I need to read his aura and feel with my Healing ability where the biggest issues are and how deep they go so I can figure out the best way ahead. I am guessing with this potion. I mean, it should help to do some repair on the damaged muscle and ligaments and enliven them, but I do not truly know. And I really need to know.'

'But ... Abigail and Morghanna say no witch or Pack Healer has ever Healed a completely severed spine. It is simply not possible.'

'Neither is bringing back someone from the dead.' The smugness in her voice surprised her because she doubted she'd done exactly that—they must have been mistaken in what they'd felt her do. Dougal had been near death, certainly, but he had not crossed that threshold. However ... 'If you believe one impossible magic is possible, there is no reason not to try something else deemed impossible.'

He was suddenly on his feet and around the table to kneel in front of her, his hands on her shoulders, gripping them in what she could only read as panic. 'Surely you jest? Tell me you jest. That you know it is lucky you survived the first time. That you cannot try such a feat of magic again for it will surely kill you this time.'

'How do you know?'

He shook her a little. 'Have you forgotten the first rule of magic? That the Gods are jealous beings and those who try to use power to rival theirs never last for long past the trying. And that magic you used ... it was like that to rival a God's. You got away with using it once. We all believe you would not be so lucky again.'

She shivered at his words, but still couldn't let it go. 'How can you know for certain? If I think it's worth it to try, why not allow me to take the risk? Especially given Dougal would be able to walk again and do what he was always meant to do: save this pack and coven from Iain and his sycophants. So the end justifies the means.'

'The end never justifies the means. Especially if it means taking a life to give a life. The sum is not equal. And if you asked Dougal, he would agree with me.'

'Well we cannot ask Dougal, can we? Because I am not allowed in to see him.'

'Apparently for good reason, given what you have just told me.' He let her go and sat back on his heels. 'But I can ask him when Abigail next wakes him to check his pain.'

'You cannot do that!' She leaned forward, grabbing his arm before he could stand.

He gave her a self-satisfied look. 'Because you know he would not agree to you hurting—or most likely killing—yourself if he was told doing so would give him back the use of his legs. He would do every-thing in his power to stop you.'

'But he will try to kill himself if we do not find a way to mend his broken back. And if he does not, Iain will.'

'We are working on that problem as you well know.'

'Yes, but it is by no means a definite.'

'Neither is your plan.' He gestured at all the grimoires spread across the room. 'Have you found anything to indicate such a Healing is possible?'

'I ... well ... no. But I have barely started my research of the old grimoires. And Bridgette sends more to us all the time. I could find something any day.'

'You will not.'

'Thank you for your positivity.'

His lips pressed together in a thin line as his gaze swept over her face. 'I will never feel positive about my friend trying to find a spell that would allow her to kill herself. That I will *never* encourage. And if I knew that was what you were truly up to here, I would never have brought you the grimoires. In fact, I will remove them so you do not continue to be tempted.' He rose swiftly to his feet and moved towards the nearest pile.

'No!' She jumped to her feet to grab at him. 'You cannot take them! I need them. Dougal needs them.'

'Not for what you intend.'

'No! Not just that. You are right. I will probably never find anything about mending a broken back. If a witch or warlock managed it the Gods would never have allowed them to write it down so that another could follow in their footsteps, for that kind of Healing is theirs and theirs alone.'

'*Enfin*, she shows some sense!' Even so, he continued to pick up the grimoires.

She grabbed his arm, the exertion, sudden movement and her distress making her dizzy so her grab was more like a slip and stumble into the edge of the bench.

'Are you hurt?' He dropped the grimoires to steady her.

'I am fine,' she lied—her hip stung where it had hit the edge of the bench but she was used to pain and shoved the sensation away. She turned away from him. 'But I will not be if you take the grimoires away.' She reached for the ones he'd just dropped, but he grabbed them out of her reach. Glowering at him she said, 'Reading them, learning from them, discovering the odd lost potion and spell to help muscle and ligament issues—like the salve I have been trying to make today—is the only thing keeping me sane. The only thing keeping this ...' she gestured to her body, '... this feeling from taking over until I want to scream from the aching, itching pain of it.'

'What feeling?'

'This feeling,' she said, running her fingers over her chest, her abdomen, her shoulders, her arms. 'I woke from the sleep I was in after I tried to Heal Dougal and it was there inside me. A never ending ache. At first I thought it was just the pain of flaming out. But it didn't subside. It got worse as the days went by. Making me feel edgy and nervous and like I needed to do something; go somewhere. And all I could think of was Dougal. It must be because my Healing magic had not finished the job it started and all I need to do is find some way to finish it. Or help him.' He was staring at her as if she were telling him the worst thing ever. 'I told you I was feeling like restless madness was taking me over.'

'I thought that was because you never like to be still and needed something to do.'

'It was. In part. But it was mostly this. And when you organised for me to come here and actively try to find something to help Dougal it stopped aching and itching so much.' Her gaze darted around the space. 'But just now when you said you would take the grimoires away, it started hurting more, burning and pulling, like I was being rubbed red-raw on the inside. You cannot take this away. You cannot.' She grasped at her chest, clawing at her blouse. 'Please. I cannot stand it. It hurts. It hurts.'

Alistair dropped the grimoires and pulled her into a brotherly hug. '*Non*. Stop. I will not take the grimoires. You can study them, *n'est-ce pas vrai*? And I promise to help you with any magic you need like I did before. As long as you promise to give up thinking about finding a God spell to fix him. You can help him in smaller incre-ments, but not that. *D'accord*?'

She pulled back a little, aware her face was red and blotchy from crying, but she did not care. All she cared about was that with his words, the raw, pulsing, pulling ache lessened a little. 'So you mean it? Can I keep working?'

'Yes. But only on what we just agreed to. And either Abigail, Morghanna or I must approve the spell.'

'You do not trust me?'

He let out a shuddering sigh before setting her away from him to look down at her face, a look of consternation on his. 'I have a feeling that you would not be able to stop yourself if you came across a God spell to use. I also think that I need to have a talk with my Anna about letting you help look after Dougal.'

'Really?' Suddenly she could stand straighter, breathe easier, felt lighter. In fact everything suddenly looked brighter too, like more colour had washed over the room. 'I will be able to directly care for him?'

He held his finger up. 'I said I would talk to Anna about it. I think once she knows what you have told me today, she will acquiesce.'

'But what of Dougal? You all said he does not want anyone but you, Morghanna, Abigail and Cal to see him.'

'Morghanna will convince him of the need to add to that list of people. Of course, there will be rules and restrictions on when and for how long. And definitely no magic until you have been cleared by Abigail and Morghanna.'

'Of course. Of course. I will agree to anything if I can only help care for him. It will make my own magical convalescence so much easier to bear.'

'I bet it will.' His mouth quirked in a funny way she wasn't certain had anything to do with happiness or pleasure.

But she didn't care. She was allowed to keep working on more minor spells and potions and then she would, hopefully in the next day or so, be allowed to see Dougal and help to make him feel better, even if it was through simple nursing work.

It was almost like her own personal sun had taken to shining warmly inside her.

'I will go to Anna now and ask her,' Alistair said, turning to leave.

'No wait!' Alistair faced her, brow arched. 'Can you help me with this salve before you go? It will need some of your magic to combine the ingredients. It can then steep tonight and be ready for the second part tomorrow. If we can finish then, it will be ready to trial on Dougal when I see him—hopefully the day after next?'

'I cannot promise you will see him the day after next, but maybe the day after that.'

'That is fine. But if we can finish this potion, you or Morghanna can trial it on him until I am able to do it myself.'

Alistair shook his head at her, but he was smiling as he returned to the bench beside her. 'I will help as long as you promise not to get your hopes up too high.'

'I will try.'

Another sigh. 'I suppose that will have to do. Come on, let us make this salve. I would like to finish in time to walk Morghanna home from her rounds and talk to her about you seeing Dougal.'

Leanna almost bounced to the central table, grabbing the mortar and pestle and starting all over again. This time, she did not mind at all.

For she was going to see Dougal and everything would be right in her world after that.

12

ougal pulled at the covers that were piled over his legs. How many blasted furs and blankets did they think he needed? All he'd done was mutter he was cold a few hours ago before falling asleep and this was the result—so many coverings he was not only turning into a blazing inferno but he was afeared he'd be crushed by them all.

Not that he could feel the weight of them on his useless, wasted legs. It was more that he couldn't roll over with how weak he still was and it was both frustrating and infuriating.

But he'd be damned if he called out for help. He didn't want a single one of the Healers, Alistair or Cal—who had been helping now he was recovered from all but one of his injuries—coming in and seeing him wrestling with the Gods-damned covers like a newborn wriggling against its swaddling. It was bad enough having them do everything for him, let alone the way they constantly nattered at him about his future.

As if they truly thought a crippled Were could have any future.

It was maddening. As maddening as these blasted heavy coverings!

He was a sweat-covered mess by the time he'd managed to wrestle them off him and onto the floor—it was too much effort to move them to the foot of the bed.

And now his throat was raw with thirst. He looked around for the jug of water that was usually left for him on the bedside table, but it was a little out of reach. His arms were like jelly as he pulled and pushed himself closer to the edge of the bed so that he could reach it, but finally he managed to grasp the handle and drag it to him. It took him a moment of puffing and panting before he had the energy to raise it to his lips and gulp it down until it was all gone. Once done, he sank back into the pillows and closed his eyes.

Sleep immediately began to take him into its embrace. Blast it. He tried to fight it but he was as weak as a cub on the teat and could not hold it off for more than a few moments. The only compensation was he often dreamed of being with Le-le.

A soft knock on the door startled him to wakefulness sometime later. He opened his eyes to see the door opening.

Hells. He was sticky with sweat and knew he looked like haggis warmed over after his earlier efforts.

It was most likely Cal. Morghanna, before she'd left a few hours ago, had told him his friend would come in to carry him to the table to eat his evening meal because, 'It is time to get you out of that stinky bed for something other than to piss and shit.'

But he didn't want his friend to see him like this. Didn't want any of them to see him like this. And he didn't want to bloody-well be picked up and carted to the bloody table to eat a bloody meal he wasn't hungry for.

Temper roaring to the fore, poked by frustration and embarrassment, he shouted, 'Git out. I dinna want ye here.'

'Morghanna was right—you are in a filthy temper.'

His head snapped up. Leanna entered instead of Cal.

He was so shocked that he gaped at her as she walked across the room to place the tray of food she was holding on the table. What was she doing here? He had made it perfectly clear to Morghanna that he didn't want to see Le-le after he'd agreed to stop fighting her through the mating bond so she'd wake. He had simply wanted to ensure she was safe and well, but that didn't mean he accepted the mating bond. He was still looking for some way to break it, and to do that, he needed it weak. Not strengthened by her presence.

It was therefore essential she stay away. Far away.

Leanna seemed oblivious to his gaping as she walked to the table in the corner of the room and said, 'Would you like me to call Cal in to carry you to the table or would you prefer to eat in bed? I know Morghanna said it was time you moved around, but if you are not up for it, I do not wish to push. I know you are still in quite a bit of pain.'

Moving around? Was that what they called being carted around like a baby? It was mortifying. Especially being carried to the middens to relieve himself.

He crossed his arms over his chest and looked away to stare at the wall next to his bed. 'I dinna want aught.'

His stomach chose that moment to grumble loudly, giving the lie to his statement. Except, it hadn't completely been a lie because he hadn't been hungry at all until she'd entered. However, given he'd not eaten breakfast, the smell of whatever was in the bowl was suddenly very enticing and his wolf whimpered with the need to taste some.

Or maybe what it really wanted was to taste her. Like they did in their dreams. Despite himself, despite trying to make himself sink so far into his depression that he would cease to exist, as it always did, her presence made everything so much sharper and brighter. She smelled so enticing—her soft sun-warmed lavender with the sweet tang of a just-ripe apple scent, it made his mouth water.

Blast it!

She turned from what she was doing—was that a jar with heather and wildflowers that she was holding?—and smiled at him.

That smile ... it kicked him in the guts every time. It squeezed his heart. Made his balls ache. It made him long for things that were now impossible for him to have.

Things that were impossible to give her.

The only good thing in all this was that she still didn't know. She somehow hadn't remembered or even been aware she'd accepted the bond. And even if she was aware, it would make no difference because they would never fully complete it. They would need to share the intimacy of coital relations. Which he would never allow to happen. He wasn't even certain it could happen, but if it could, it wasn't going to. No matter how much he had longed for it ever since he'd first seen her. No matter how hot and sensual his dreams featuring her were.

His cock twitched at the thought.

Blasted traitor!

He tore his attention from her distracting smile to glare at the jar of flowers in her hands—he'd once told her they were his favourite flowers. He really needed her to go before he did or said anything to jeopardise the frayed rope he was hanging from. So he snapped at her, 'What are ye doing with those? I hope ye dinna bring them fer me. What use have I got fer yer weeds?'

She looked down at them, her smile slipping a little—Gods help him he was sorry to see it go even though it had been his intent—and placed them in the middle of the table. 'I thought something from nature in the room might be nice. I remember you saying you love heather and the wildflowers from the forest.'

Blast her memory! 'I dinna want them in here.'

'Well isn't it lucky I did not bring them in here simply for you, Dougal MacCrae. Morghanna happened to mention your room could do with an airing and brightness. I also thought she and your other nurses would appreciate something pretty to look at and smell.' She bent to bury her nose in the bouquet and took a deep breath, closing her eyes as if it would help her to appreciate the scent more.

'Ahh,' she said softly. Then the pink tip of her tongue nipped out to wet her lips. 'They are lovely. Although maybe not quite enough to counteract the staleness in here. I think I'll draw back the curtains and open the shutters. The warmth of the day is still in the air so you should not be cold. Abigail says we have to be careful about not allowing you to get chilled, so just tell me if you are feeling even a little cold.' She said all this as she bustled about the room opening the curtains and shutters and allowing the warm afternoon breeze and sunlight in, her skirts swaying enticingly around her long, slim legs and shapely bottom.

His wolf whined with longing and his balls tightened and ached as his cock stiffened and he suddenly wished he'd not pushed all the blasted blankets to the floor.

As if she knew something was wrong, she peered back over her shoulder at him as she pushed open the shutters nearest his bed. He clapped his hands over his stiffening cock, not wanting her to see the obvious proof of his desire. Of his unruly needs.

She smiled at him and turned back to her task.

By all that was holy, had she been placed on this Earth to torment him? What had he done to deserve this?

He sat there mulling over the past, sinking into his dark thoughts as she finished opening the shutters and returned to unload the tray of food.

'I brought some of your favourite rabbit stew,' she said cheerily.

What had gotten into her? She was usually so quiet you barely knew she was there, but suddenly here she was, talking to him like he'd always wished she would.

'And Jeremiah made some of that crusty bread you enjoy—so I brought you a loaf thinking you could wipe up the sauce with it. There is also fresh whipped butter. And some honeyed mead. And Abigail sent you this to help with the pain.' She turned, an earthenware mug in her hand. 'She said to tell you to drink it all up this time.' She walked over and held out the mug to him.

Steam curled from the surface, the scent making his nose wrinkle in distaste. 'I dinna want it. The scent curdles my stomach.'

'Both Abigail and Morghanna say you must drink it. It will help with your mending.'

He rolled his eyes. 'This foul-smelling concoction can give me back the use of my legs, can it?'

'No ... I ...'

He hated that his sarcasm made her flinch but she didn't skitter away like she would have mere weeks ago. Instead, she continued to stare at him. So he said, 'Then why would I force myself to drink such swill?'

'Because it is good for you and it will help with the pain that is currently making you as likeable as a bear with a sore head.'

'A bear with a …' He made a choking sound as his wolf growled deep in his chest. 'So ye think insulting me with comparisons to a lowly bear the best way to get me to drink this shite?'

'If the description fits,' she said simply.

His mouth opened then closed, his mind stuck on how proud of herself she looked. How pretty she was. Damn it! He had to stop this, make her go. 'What are ye doin' here? I said I dinna want ye here.'

'But … Did Morghanna not tell you? I am one of your nursing team now. I'm here to help. I was hoping to start using a new salve to massage into your lower back and legs today. It is supposed to—'

'I dinna want yer help.'

It was bad enough when the others came in to care for him, but when it was Le-le …

He did not want her to wait on him or care for him. He didn't even want her to see him like this, useless to the pack and its witches, a burden on everyone he was supposed to care for.

A burden to her, his mate.

Except the damned stubborn lass seemed to be determined to waste her time trying to make him better when that was not possible.

She put her hands on her hips again, chin tipped up, and said, 'Well, I am here and I am not going away, no matter how you snap and snarl at me.'

LEANNA COULDN'T BELIEVE she was standing up to him like this, but it felt good. And necessary.

With her hands on her hips, and her gaze firmly on his, she felt … alive. Time with him always made her feel better. Fuller. More whole. Capable of things she hadn't thought herself capable of. Which was why she'd pushed so hard over the last few days to make Morghanna agree to this. She'd even agreed readily to all of their rules because she had to see him. Had known she would feel better if she could.

Seeing him now made putting up with the frustration of recent weeks worthwhile. The moment she'd walked in the door, she'd felt so much stronger and more capable of doing anything.

She rather liked that feeling. And she didn't want it to stop, especially when it put that befuddled expression on his face.

She rather enjoyed that too.

His befuddled expression changed and he snapped his beautiful lips closed into a tight line before growling, 'I dinna need ye here coddling me. And I most certainly dinna need yer pity.'

'That is good. I have no intention of coddling you or pitying you. I am a Healer—as you and Morghanna and Abigail have been at great pains to make me believe since I arrived. And while I am still not allowed to properly fulfil those duties yet, I can help to nurse you. So I am here to do that regardless of how you feel about it.'

An expression crossed his face—rather like pride and respect were warring with annoyance—and she thought she heard a sound like growling. 'Did your wolf just growl at me?' She was rather surprised given his wolf had always seemed to like her.

He muttered something too low for her to hear. She leaned closer and said, 'I am sorry, I did not hear that.'

He looked like he wasn't going to answer but then he snapped out, 'He dinna growl at ye. It was me that growled.'

Her brows rose as she straightened. 'Why?'

'Why do ye think?' He shifted, wincing.

'Oh.' He was in pain and here she was dithering on at him. She held out the mug to him. 'You really need to drink this. It will make you feel better.'

'I doubt that,' he muttered again.

She pretended not to hear him and pushed the mug closer to him.

He curled his lip and turned his head. 'Please, Dougal. Try it. I can add some honey to make it taste better.' She leaned closer to place it in his hands.

As she did she saw his gaze shift to her chest. She looked down to see her blouse had gaped a little showing a hint of her cleavage—it was a hot enough day to have made her undo the neck ties of her blouse while she was going about her chores in the herbal stillroom, and she hadn't done them up before coming here given nobody was around to see her scars.

As she looked back up at him, he stiffened, his face tightening. She'd seen that look on others many times and knew what it was—disgust. Disgust at the scars that twisted down the side of her neck and ran over her chest and shoulder. He, like so many others were obviously sickened by the sight of them given his expression and the sound he made—as if struggling to keep from vomiting.

'Sorry,' she said, jerking upright, her hand closing the front of her blouse. 'I did not mean to upset you with the sight.'

'What? No! Leanna, what are ye talking about?'

'It is fine. I understand. I will … fetch your meal.' But she realised she was still holding the medicinal concoction so thrust it back at him. 'Oh, I should have … here take this. I will fetch the honey.'

He snatched the mug away and threw it across the room. It hit the wall with a crash and splash of liquid that, by the look of him, did nothing to alleviate the burning inferno of frustration and rage deep inside him. A rage she understood given what had happened to him. What she'd failed to do for him.

It was no wonder he didn't want her here.

'I am sorry, Dougal,' she said, voice shaking, all her earlier confidence rushing away in the face of her failure. 'I am so sorry.'

Then she turned and ran out of the room not stopping even when he roared her name, the sound of his wolf fully in his throat, making her ache and need in a way that confused and terrified her.

13

Leanna went to the kitchen to pick up Dougal's lunch tray. She was still so ashamed of how she'd run from him a few days ago but she was determined to get past it.

She didn't want to be the one who always ran away. She wanted to be the one who stayed and fought for what was important.

Who was important.

Even so, it had taken everything in her to go back the following day and every day since.

For his part, when Dougal wasn't ignoring her, he acted like nothing had happened. Which was good—even though the way he barely looked at her or spoke to her hurt, her heart squeezing every time, something inside feeling like it was a little broken.

Despite the hurt, all the acting like she hadn't behaved like a fool meant she could almost believe it hadn't happened at all. Which was good. Because she needed to put all her energies into helping him, not being worried that she'd embarrass herself in front of him again.

She really was quite proud of herself with the way she was facing things and pretending things were fine. Of course, they weren't fine.

She rubbed at the constant, nagging ache in her chest before plastering a smile on her face and entering the kitchen. The smell of rich stew tantalised her and her stomach growled. She clasped a hand over it and hoped nobody had heard. 'Hello, Jeremiah,' she said to the pack's head cook as she walked over to the kitchen bench he was working at.

He looked up. 'Ah, Leanna. I'm serving up his bowl now. And I have just pulled some crusty bread out o' the oven. I thought ye both might like it to sop up the gravy. But ye will have to wait a wee minute before I can take it from the tray to put with yer lunch. It is too hot right now.'

'I am happy to wait. The fresh hot bread sounds lovely,' she said, glad for the moment to sit down before tramping across the square carrying the heavy tray to the Healer Hall. She should be stronger and have more stamina by now but even the short walk here and then back across the square took its toll.

Not that she let anyone know that. She didn't want them to stop her from working in the stillroom with the herbs in the morning and then taking lunch to Dougal and spending time with him for a few hours before the afternoon shift arrived so she could have her mandated—and much needed—rest.

Alistair suddenly appeared out of the store room, carrying a tray of the triangle pastries he called *kipferls*. In one of those strange bursts of memory he had about his life before he came here, he said he'd learned how to make them in *Ostarrîchi*, although he had no idea when that was or why he had been there. Regardless of their origins, the flaky triangle pastries were fast becoming a favourite of the coven and the pack, almost to rival his tarts. His face lit up when he saw her. 'Le-Le! Is it that time already?'

'Yes. Are those for afternoon tea?'

'*Oui.*' He opened the door on the stone oven he'd helped the Pack Masons design and build—another memory was that he had worked with ones like this in big mansions in *Italia* not long before he journeyed here and fell in love with Morghanna. Morghanna said it fitted with what he'd told her of his life before the battle where he was so drained that he almost lost his life.

Alistair placed the tray in the oven with a smooth surety that spoke of practice and then turned to face her. 'I will ensure Dougal gets one with his dinner.'

'He is bound to enjoy that.'

Alistair leaned across the bench to take her hand in his. 'You look a little tired. If you need to rest, I can take Dougal's lunch to him and sit with him until Morghanna arrives for her shift.'

'No!' she barked so loudly both Alistair and Jeremiah stared at her. 'I mean, I know you have things to do and I do not want you to give them up for me. Besides, I am fine. I just got up from resting for an hour—' which was completely true, '—as you and Morghanna said I must, so I do not need more rest right now.'

He tipped his head and regarded her for a moment. She thought he was going to argue with her, but then he let go of her hand and tapped a rhythm on the wooden bench. 'Very well. I trust you know your own body and how bad it would be to push yourself.'

'I do.'

'*Très bien*. But let me at least carry the tray over there for you.'

She wanted to say yes—it would help her to save energy—but ... 'I do not want to be a bother.'

'No bother. I am going that way,' he said, smiling. 'Besides, it will be heavier than usual because Abigail sent word to say he needs a pitcher of fresh water as well as the special tea you created for Dougal, and I thought maybe a few slices of the berry pie I took out of the oven ten minutes ago might be just the thing to tempt his appetite. He has as big a sweet tooth as you.'

She was well aware of that. Which was why she always put something sweet on the tray for him every lunch. Despite Dougal's grumbling about her trying to make him fat, he always ate the sweets even if he didn't finish anything else.

Alistair pulled the pie from under the bench and cut two large slices then added a small jar of thick cream. He placed a pitcher on the tray with two mugs next to the bowl of stew, then managed to get the teapot into the small spot in the corner. Jeremiah added the loaf of bread on top of the plates and the tray was full. And looked incredibly heavy.

She possibly would never have been able to carry it all the way even when she was fit and healthy.

Alistair picked it up with no effort and walked to the door. 'Coming?'

She thanked Jeremiah, hopped off the stool and hurried out the door behind Alistair.

They chatted as they walked across the square and she was only a little out of breath as they ascended the stairs to the porch of the Healer Hall. Even so, she ran to open the door for him then followed him down the hall to the room that had been given over to Dougal. He stopped outside the door as if waiting for her to open it. But she didn't want him in there with her. Even for a little while. This was her time with Dougal and she didn't want to share it—not even with Alistair.

She reached for the tray. 'I can take it from here.'

'Are you sure? It is rather heavy.'

'I can manage to walk into the room and get to the table.'

His lips quirked. 'I have no doubt. Tell Dougal I will see him later. And if you need anything, I will be just down the hallway helping Abigail with a few things.'

'What of your *kipferls*?'

'Jeremiah knows when to take them out.'

'Oh. Thank you.'

He gave her a little salute then walked away, leaving her staring at the door, the weight of the heavy tray pulling at her arms.

As she always did, she stopped a moment to take a breath and pull herself together. It was necessary. And not just because of her exhaustion.

It was something she hadn't mentioned to anyone else, not even Alistair or Morghanna, because she didn't want to worry them or make them think she had to be kept away from Dougal. Because the closer she got to him, the more it seemed she could feel Dougal's pain. It had started the moment she woke, this feeling in her chest like the throb of an old broken bone complaining in the damp weather. A feeling she knew rather well given all the bones in her body that had been broken in the explosion that killed her parents and permanently scarred her.

Over the weeks since she'd failed Dougal, the feeling had become stronger.

She'd thought it an imagining at first, but since being allowed to care for him, she knew it wasn't. The feeling too closely matched the pain he was in—surging when it worsened for him, easing off when the pain medications they gave him took effect. She'd seen it with her own eyes, the reflection of it inside her.

Feeling his pain was bad enough—and might be the reason she was still struggling with her own energy levels and recovery—but it was also feeling the level of his frustration and anger that worried her the most.

Pain they—she—could deal with, but the emotional issues were something else entirely. Especially if the patient was too intractable and stubborn to admit to any of it let alone talk about it.

Which he wouldn't do with her or anyone else. Especially her.

It hurt her in a way she couldn't explain when he turned his head away like he did every day. But she wouldn't stop going to him. No matter what anyone said.

Taking a deep breath, she pushed the door open with her hip and entered.

'So, how is my favourite patient?' Leanna asked as the door swung shut behind her, a big smile on her face despite her worry over him. 'You are looking a little brighter today.'

'Ye ken ye are a terrible liar,' he rumbled.

She tried not to jump for joy at the fact that he actually spoke to her in an almost reasonable tone. Most days he either barked at her to go away or simply ignored her. But if he thought that would frighten her away he was greatly mistaken. She had grown up with a mother whose treatment of her was harsh—to toughen her up for a hard life, so she said—so she was used to being spoken to harshly by people she cared for. And as for the other, given she'd spent most of her time trying to vanish and be invisible since the accident that made her an orphan and scarred her so terribly, she was also used to being ignored. It might sting a little because this time, she didn't wish to be invisible, but she didn't need him to acknowledge her.

She just needed to help make him better.

So she hid her delight at his answering her and said, 'It is not a lie.' She began to cross the room to the table. 'You are sitting up today, although I had hoped to find you sitting in the chair by the window.'

The chair she'd prepared for him earlier in the week with the view out the window that overlooked the village.

She'd hoped that a seat at the window would be enticing to someone who had lived for the outdoors; where the perfumed breeze could blow the freshest air on his face and play in his shoulder-length black hair. She had also hoped that he might be drawn to show interest with the life of the pack if he could see some of the comings and goings from the window.

She'd made the large armed chair even more comfortable by bringing extra cushions—one of them the one he'd admired months ago when he'd seen her working on the tapestry used to cover it— and she'd pulled over a side table so he could easily reach his mug of special tea she brought him every day. The one that was supposed to help build his strength. She'd also moved another stand in to place just to the right of the chair to put blankets on within easy reach. If he got cold he could pull one over himself and not have to wait for someone else to get it for him. It was quite a cosy little nook now in front of the windows if she did say so herself.

But he hadn't used it once.

It did hurt a little. As did the way his face folded into a frown as she walked across the room to place his lunch on the table.

He was never happy to see her. In fact, it seemed like he'd be happiest if he never had to see her again. Where else it made her so incredibly happy to see him—like his presence lit up the sun inside her. She'd never known a sun like that was possible inside a person before meeting him, but now she did, she wanted to feel it's warmth all the time. She lived for seeing him every day.

She had to hope he was as grumpy with everyone as he was with her because of how unhappy he was since the accident.

Since she failed to use her Healer power to mend him fully.

She thrust that thought away and the darkness that came with it and smiled even more brightly at Dougal as she said, 'Hungry?'

'Not even a little.'

'I am sure I can entice your appetite with what I brought you today.'

A strange expression crossed his face—surprise mixed with something else far more heated. It made her stomach clench and tingles chase across her skin followed by blazing heat.

Her gaze met his for one, astonishing second.

He groaned.

'Are you in pain?'

'Nae. Aye. I …'

His voice … low, husky, full of something that sounded like the need inside her. She trembled. He groaned again, his hand moving as if to reach for her. She took a stumbling step forward.

'Dinna look at me like that!' he groaned.

'Like what?' she asked, her voice embarrassingly breathy.

'Agh! Ye dinna even ken.' He tore his gaze away and muttered so low that she wouldn't have heard if her entire being wasn't so totally focused on him, 'Control yerself. Nought can happen. Ye have to save her.'

'Save me from what?' she asked, not even wondering why she knew the muttered comment was about her.

'Leave.' The look he aimed her way was like a cold blast of icy winds straight down from the mountain peaks in winter.

'No.'

14

She wasn't sure where the defiance came from given she was still trembling—it was like she was in the sexy dreams, able to do and say things she never could in real life. But she was glad of the courage, for it warmed the ice in her veins caused by that look. 'It is my job as a Healer to look after you these next few hours.'

'Damn ye, Leanna. Damn ye. It would be better fer ye to go.'

'For whom?'

He glared at her for a long, long moment before making a sound that was both pained and annoyed as he turned his face to the wall.

Uncertain, uncomfortable, she quickly turned away from him. She now wished he had ignored her like he did most days because it was a lot easier to deal with than that confusing and turmoil-filled conversation. Not that you could really call it a conversation. A conversation was something a person took part in with another, and generally helped with mutual understanding. She was the one who did most of the talking and yet seemed to understand nothing about what was going on. Dougal on the other hand said very little and yet seemed to have no lack of understanding.

She clenched her hands, willing them to stop trembling and glanced back over her shoulder. She should ask him for an explanation, but he had that stubborn tilt to his chin as he looked intractably at the wall—as if the swirls in the whitewash were fascinating.

She stared at where he stared. No. Nothing very interesting there at all. Except maybe the fact the wall needed a fresh coat of whitewash. It looked dull.

She frowned. He sat or lay in that bed every day all day except when he was lifted out of it so they could change the bedding and for him to eat at the table—something that had only been happening since she'd taken over the lunch shift. It was no wonder he was so glum with only the boring ceiling or that wall to stare at. He was someone who loved to be outside, to observe and record the beauty he saw—he truly was a talented painter.

Her eyes widened as a thought hit her. She should put something on that wall. Maybe she'd ask one of the Maternals if she could have one of the paintings he'd done for the Youngling's Hall. She'd been so impressed when she'd found out that many of the murals that adorned the walls of the main hall, the dinner hall and some of the private spaces, were Dougal's work. He had a way of capturing the light on the landscapes and forests that he so loved.

But her favourites were the series of paintings he'd done of wolves and cubs, running, playing and at rest. She knew he was particularly pleased with them—not that he'd said, but she could see the way he looked at them, the light in his eyes and the slight smile he couldn't suppress. One of those would be perfect for that wall and might draw the smile out again.

She'd love to see that smile once more.

The one with the cubs at play would be the best option. Yes. She'd ask Sally, Jeremiah's wife. She was in charge of the Younglings Hall and would be sure to say yes.

She turned back to place their lunch out as she'd done every day. And as she did, she began to think of other things she could do to make him happier with his current state.

He loved painting, although his duties—taking on more than he should of Iain's job as well as giving him energy and power to help keep Iain in place as Alpha—meant he had little time anymore for the art that sang to his soul. He hadn't said as much to her—until Lachlan attacked, he never would have spoken against his Alpha even in so small a way because it was disloyal to the Alpha position—but she had read it in his emotions and energies every time he spoke of painting and drawing before the explosion. It was like he became a little lighter.

She should have thought of this before!

His art.

He could draw even sitting in bed. Painting was perhaps a little more difficult. But maybe she could talk to one of the carpenters about building an easel that could span across the bed so he could paint there. Yes.

It would mean talking to Were she'd never spoken to before, but for Dougal she would raise the courage to talk to males who had always intimidated her because of the sheer size of them—the carpenters' work making them wider across the chest and shoulders with bulging muscles that shouted of the kind of strength that could crush someone like her with barely any effort at all. She knew they were probably very nice but knowing that hadn't made her want to get close to any of them.

But she would. Today. If doing so would help to make Dougal's life better.

She would bring his drawing supplies to him first—maybe this very afternoon once she was finished here. Alistair would help her she was sure. Then she would spend some time over the next few days while the carpenters built the bed-easel, gathering various flowers and plants from the herbal stillroom, a mortar and pestle and the other supplies he would need to create new pigments for painting. It might take her more than a few days to collect everything he would need—energy still being an issue. But surely that would start to improve soon?

She was already feeling more energised just thinking about organising drawing and painting things for Dougal.

Oh. He'd also need different mediums to paint on—she remembered he'd spoken about enjoying working with different mediums.

She'd had to ask him what he'd meant but now she knew it was paper and parchment and different kinds of wood board as well as a range of materials to use as brushes to create different textures. He would also need some charcoal. Maybe there were other things he could draw and sketch with too. She'd have to ask the Pack Librarian and the artisans.

There were so many things about painting to learn so that she could engage him in something he loved. It was sure to make him more positive about his future.

It was—

'What are ye planning?'

She jumped at the sound of his voice—she had been pretty certain she wouldn't get another word from him today after the tenseness of earlier. 'I beg your pardon?' She spun around to face him, surprised to see he was staring right at her with a look on his face that was more curious amusement than anger, or the strange expression he'd had earlier.

'I asked what are ye planning?'

She wanted the painting idea to be a surprise, so she said. 'What makes you think I am planning anything?'

His gaze narrowed on her in a way that made her shiver. 'Ye hum when ye are planning something.' He tipped his head on the side. 'Ye were humming. Which means ye are planning.'

She blushed. She hadn't noticed that she hummed at all let alone when she planned. When she was young she used to sing all the time with her papa, but since his death, there hadn't been any reason to sing. In fact, music most often made her sad, so she avoided it. It was one of the reasons she rarely stayed long at any pack celebration.

'I am sorry. Was it out of tune?'

'I ... Nae. Yer voice is quite lovely. Ye should sing more often.'

Her blush deepened but she didn't stutter and rush away like she used to. No. She stood a little straighter, wanting to preen in his compliment. 'Papa said I had a voice like a nightingale. I always thought he was rather biased.'

'From what I just heard, I would say he was right.'

Had he just complimented her like he used to?

Good Goddess. Could her face get any hotter? 'I ... well ... thank you.' She turned back to the lunch—she was getting better at being more forthright but it was still difficult not to fall back into habits that were years in the making. She was still a far cry from the daughter her mother had always wanted her to be—outgoing and strong and capable of taking over leadership of their coven when it was time.

The thing was, she could feel his eyes on her which made her even more self-conscious, particularly after what happened earlier. Which was silly because why would he stare at her now when he'd made it perfectly clear every day that her presence annoyed him?

She peered over her shoulder. The heat in his eyes as their gazes met arrowed straight to her stomach and burned there with such force she gasped.

At the sound he tore his gaze away. His mouth was a thin line, the bones in his face suddenly more prominent as if he clenched his jaw, and red flags rode high on his cheekbones—as red as the ones heating her face.

Was he angry with her? Maybe. She could be annoying—her mother had told her often enough. But she didn't think that's what this was. It was more like what had occurred between them earlier. That needy, achy heat that burned through her body and centred tightly in her core.

She shifted, trying to ease the discomfit now. His eyes darted back to her as if he was aware of her every little move.

'Are ye okay?' His voice was so raw, so husky and scraped her nerves in a way she wanted to hold onto.

She shivered—the kind of delightful shiver she got when a potion worked out and exceeded her expectations—and shook her head. 'I am fine.'

'Ye dinna look fine. Ye look ... unsettled.'

She was but she wasn't about to admit to that. Not with him. Not right now. Not with how strange this was and how much she felt he knew things she didn't. 'I am fine. It is you I am worried for.'

'Dinna do that.'

'What?'

'Worry. About me. I am not worth an ounce of yer energy.'

She gaped at him for a moment, shocked he would think such a thing let alone say it out loud to her. 'You are worth everything, Dougal. You *are* everything.'

'Dinna say that.'

His voice. Oh the ache in it! It pulled at her, forced her to stand against his words. 'I *will* say that. Because it is true. You were the first one here who made me feel safe. You befriended me when I thought I was not worthy of being befriended. You saw something nobody but my papa had seen before.'

'I wasna the only one.'

'No. But it was your friendship that made me realise I was worthy of Morghanna and Abigail's time. You made me realise that my work was valued.'

'They said so too. Often. I heard them.'

'Yes, they did. But they were meant to say those things given I am their student and they my mentors.' Where on earth was this coming from? It was almost like she was possessed—not by something else but by the version of herself she'd always longed to be. And while it was shocking and frightening to be this vocal, this open, she couldn't seem to stop herself. Didn't want to. So the words kept spilling out. 'It is their role to find the positives and try to make me believe. That was not true for you. You simply believed. You believed even when I barely looked up at you from under my hair. You looked at that frightened, mouse of a girl who wanted to never be seen and you saw her. You saw something in her that was worthy of your time, your effort, your kindness.'

'I wasna being kind,' he said, his voice a gruff growl.

She shrugged. 'I know. You were being you. You were being a friend. A friend when I'd never had one before. Never thought I deserved one. I did not even realise at first because it was something I never thought to have and when I did, I was so shocked that it was hard to believe it was true. But it *was* true. You were my friend. You *are* my friend no matter how grumpy you have been lately. Because I treasure that friendship more than I can say. Which is why I am more than sorry for the fact I was not strong enough to complete your Healing. If I could find some way I—'

'Nae! Nae! Dinna think ye are to blame fer how I am.'

'But I know you hate it. I know you wish you were dead.' She took a stumbling step towards him, hands stretched out as if in supplication. 'I understand you can never forgive me for that. But I could not let you go. I could not. You are my only friend. More than that. I lo—'

'Leanna! Ye dinna want to say that.'

She blinked. She had been about to say she loved him. She had no idea why she would say such a thing—it was something she never meant to say out loud. Yet she had been about to speak those words.

But he did not want to hear them.

She closed her eyes against the pain of that. Not that she blamed him for feeling like he did. He was her *Sgàth*. And he had extended the hand of friendship only. She had been the one to take it and try to turn it into something it wasn't. She hadn't meant to, but then again, it wasn't surprising. He was the most amazing male she had ever met. Of course she would fall in love with him. But she couldn't have expectations of him. Had to let him know that.

So she pushed back the tears and clenched her hands in front of her. 'I know you can never feel the same. I do not expect you to. But my feelings are my feelings and I will own them. Do not worry though, I will not bother you with them. I promise.' She took a shuddering breath as he stared at her, mouth agape. 'But I will not go away. I need this, Dougal. To be here, helping you. So please, let me.'

He stared at her for a long moment—so long she braced for his denial. But then he nodded curtly and said, 'Very well.'

She beamed at him, then turned back to the table to hide her trembling. 'So I have rabbit stew, fresh bread and Alistair's berry pie. And some fresh water and the tea to wash it all down with.'

'Not more of that vile stuff Abigail keeps sending in fer me to drink?'

She almost laughed as she spun back to face him. 'No. A special blend of tea I created. It has anti-inflammatory properties so should help with the muscle cramps. And it tastes quite nice if I say so myself. Shall I call Alistair to carry you to the table or do you wish to eat in bed?'

He stared at her then past her at the table, then at her again. 'Maybe at the table today. And then maybe after I can be set in that armchair by the window.'

'Oh! Yes. Of course.' She had to stop from clapping her hands like a child. But it was just so thrilling. She hadn't expected that at all! Maybe her honesty had made a difference? She hoped so. Because maybe now he knew just how much he meant to her and the others, he would start to try to live with how things were, not continue to long for how it was before.

'I will go fetch him,' she said and rushed out of the room.

15

Leanna walked into Dougal's room, calling a cheery hello and not being upset he didn't respond. She could feel the pain he was in—it was a dull stabbing in her lower back—so didn't expect much from him today. She was pleased though to see him sitting in the armchair by the window again. It was only two days in a row, but it was progress where there had been none before. Maybe today was the day she could talk him into allowing her to try the massage potion on him. She didn't want to push him too far too fast so she hadn't braved bringing it up yet.

But still, they needed to start soon because Iain would be home for the next full moon and she would need as much time as possible for it to work.

As she set about preparing his lunch—which she would serve to him in his armchair—she noticed a strange grimoire sitting on the table beside the tray Alistair had brought in moments before her arrival. 'What is this?' she asked, holding it up so Dougal could see.

'Oh, Morghanna received it only this morn—it came with a larger package from Bridgette. She thought ye might want to look at it immediately. She said it felt promising.'

It did indeed feel promising, but she was here to spend time with

Dougal, not pour through a tantalising grimoire. She put it back on the table and finished making his plate of bread, meat and cheeses with the pickle chutney he liked. She took it over to him.

He looked up at her. 'Are you not eating?'

'I am.' She went back to fetch her smaller plate of food, pulled up a chair beside his and sat down to eat with him.

As she ate quietly beside him—he still barely said anything to her—she couldn't help glancing at him. And noting the paleness of his handsome face and the way his lips were pulled thin. He really was in pain. She should have dealt with that first.

She quickly finished her bread and cheese and got up to make a fresh pot of tea—the blend she'd made for him which he seemed to like. Today she would lace it with the milk of the poppy.

She didn't like using such a strong drug, but Dougal refused to allow Abigail or Morghanna to use their Healing on him to help with his pain any more—he said their energies were best spent elsewhere. And Sebastian was still away with the McVale Pack Healers learning how to best serve his own pack and nobody else in the pack knew how to take pain away.

And the Goddess only knew, she couldn't use her powers in that way yet. They were still barely a flutter inside her. So painkilling drugs it had to be.

As she set her plate on the table, her gaze was drawn immediately to the grimoire. She was suddenly filled with a certainty that she would find something helpful to Dougal's recovery in there. The urge to sit down and start to pour over it was so great, she almost gave in to it. But Dougal made a small sound of discomfort, which brought her attention back to what she had come to the table for.

The grimoire could wait until after she had seen to his needs and finished her shift with him today.

She felt a strange kind of stillness come over the room despite the breeze starting to rattle the windows, and turned to see Dougal giving her a strange look, apparent even through the pain so evident on his features.

She must have been standing there like a ninny as she stared at the grimoire. She shrugged off the need to open it and said brightly, 'I think I'll just put the kettle on.' She picked up the empty teapot from the sideboard and waggled it. 'I'll put extra honey in just for you.' The honey would help hide the bitterness of the milk of the poppy.

He grunted and returned to staring out the window. But that was as much of an ascent as she was likely to get given his mood.

He was not having a particularly good day. It made her ache on the inside. Yesterday had given her hope that he'd been getting better but today he seemed to have taken a step backwards.

She shivered as the breeze coming in through the windows freshened up even further—Brionne had said there was a storm coming and it seemed she was right. Leanna wouldn't be surprised to wake in the morning to see some very early snow on the craggy mountain peaks. She wanted to close the windows but didn't because she knew that, despite the fact he hadn't said it, he liked the cooler breeze.

She picked up a shawl she'd left here yesterday and pulling it around her shoulders, pushed the kettle on its swing arm back over the fire in the hearth. While she waited for it to boil, she busied herself with cleaning away their lunch dishes—and couldn't stop her gaze from continually going back to the grimoire. She really wanted to start reading it, but she still had another hour with Dougal and she wasn't about to give up any of that time. It was too precious to her.

The water began boiling just as she finished wiping down the table and she quickly made the special blend, letting it steep for a few minutes before pouring Dougal a mug. 'Here you go. This will warm you up.' He took the mug from her with a nod of thanks and sipped on the hot beverage straight away. She was pretty certain he knew there was a painkiller in it but when he was like this, he just took it and drank it without complaint.

'Enough honey?' she asked as he sipped.

'It is good. Thank ye.'

Feeling a little chuffed she had actually got a thank you despite his pain, she decided to freshen up his bed while he drank his tea. Once done, she stoked the fire, building it a little higher to ward off the chill being let in through the open windows. That feeling of success of any kind on this difficult day gave her a little boost of energy so she did a bit of extra cleaning and tidying to make the room nicer for him.

She noticed after a while that his mug was sitting on the side table, which usually meant he'd finished. Given the amount of pain he'd been in—the ache of it inside her had become like a sharp spear jabbing in her back—he could probably do with another mug.

'Would you like some more tea to warm you, Dougal?' He didn't answer. 'Dougal?' A soft sigh of sound was her only answer. She put the teapot down and edged forward as quietly as her tired legs would let her and peered around the armchair.

He was asleep.

She was both glad for him and glad for her. Glad for him because he needed the rest and was now not in pain. Glad for her because him falling asleep meant ...

She glanced over at the table.

In the last few days if Dougal had fallen asleep on her she would have been devastated—she was greedy with her time with him—but today ...

It meant she could start reading the old grimoire now rather than have to wait until after she'd finished her shift and then had her afternoon nap—more and more essential every day.

Before she could read it though, she had to make sure Dougal was comfortable and would stay warm while he slept.

She placed a blanket over his legs—one she'd brought from her own room that her grandmother had woven for her before she passed. It was the deep blue of the loch, very soft and warm without being heavy. Dougal seemed to prefer it—although maybe he wouldn't if he knew it was hers.

The breeze coming in the windows was so cold now she had to close both windows for fear of them both getting a chill. Then she adjusted the pillow behind his head so he wouldn't get a crook in his neck, and tiptoed back to the table.

Gingerly, she picked up the grimoire—old magic prickled her

fingertips, but not like a warning, more like a warm stroke up her arms and a gentle hug. Maybe it, like other spelled grimoires, recognised not only that she meant it no harm, but that her magic was familiar. Abigail had remarked the other day that she had a way with the grimoires from other places and she now began to wonder if her mentor was right.

The grimoires liked her. They trusted her. Even the darker ones behaved themselves for her.

This one was no exception.

It was so old though—the oldest she'd ever seen. An age she felt deep in her bones, humming a vibration of a time long past; a time long lost.

She placed it down gently, reverently in front of her chair then sat, took a few deep breaths to calm her excited mind, then looked at it properly.

The cover was a deep red, so dark in places it was almost black. It was cracking a little near the binding and the signature emblem on the front was so faded she couldn't make it out. She'd have to oil it when she got back to her room and do a little rejuvenation booster to the preservation spell she could sense on it—it was barely functioning anymore which explained the state of it. She ran her hand like a stroke across the cover and whispered, 'Do not worry. I will take good care of you. I will ensure your gifts are not lost and the beauty that was once yours is returned to you.'

The humming in her bones got a little louder, a little brighter, warming her in the still chilly room and she knew she had its permission. 'Thank you,' she whispered again.

Very gently, she lifted the front cover. The binding crackled as she opened it, the leather stiff and the threads tight with age.

As she opened it, a strong scent of aged parchment, lavender and sandalwood wafted around her. Mmm, quite lovely. There was also a slight hint of something sweet—like the night blooming flowers she'd once seen in a village when travelling with her parents. It made her think of health and times of joy.

Just the scent alone, what it gave to her, had her heart beating faster in her chest with excitement. 'Show me your secrets, my lovely one.'

The words written on the parchment that had been quite faint became a little brighter—bright enough for her to have no trouble reading them now despite the yellowness of the parchment and the lightness of the violet ink that had been used.

She read for ... she had no idea how long. The writing was dense and in Ancient Greek, with notes scrawled in the margins that she wanted to read too. But then she turned the page and ...

It spoke of a regimen of massage and movement of paralysed limbs that had helped certain patients with paralysis injuries, sometimes even getting them back to walking when added to certain potions and spells that focused on repair and muscle and spinal cord rejuvenation.

She'd never heard of anything like this being used, but it was revolutionary! This regimen, alongside the muscle enlivening salve that she'd finally managed to perfect thanks to Alistair's superior magic and was yet to try on Dougal, was exactly what she'd been looking for to get the injured Were's muscles ready for when she had her magic back and she could finish the Healing she'd started.

Despite what she'd promised Morghanna and Alistair, she wasn't giving up on that. There had to be a way that didn't require God-like power, and she would find it!

But this! This was an amazing discovery. 'Oh my Goddess!' Leanna snapped upright. She had to show this to Morghanna and Abigail. 'They will have to agree!'

'What? What is it, Le-le?'

She started at Dougal's husky, sleep-filled voice and warmed all over. She loved the sound of his nickname for her on his lips—the one he'd started calling her not long after she'd joined the coven here, that a few others like Morghanna and Alistair had started using too. She loved that nickname, but she loved it the most when he said it.

He'd barely used it at all since the accident. She hadn't realised until now how much she'd missed it.

'Le-le? Do I need to shout fer help?'

The panic in his voice had her snapping out of her meandering thoughts and turning to face him. 'Sorry, I did not mean to wake you.'

'I wasna ... it is fine. But are ye?'

'Oh yes!' she said, closing the grimoire carefully before getting up to stand where he could see her. Exhaustion pulled on her muscles but she ignored it—this was too important and she had to share the news with him. 'I think I have found something that is going to help you gain back feeling in your legs.'

'Ye mean it will allow me to walk again?' He pushed himself up straighter in the chair, his blue eyes—that were still taking on the electric blue colour of an Alpha despite his injury—pinned on her.

She bit her lip. She hadn't meant for him to think that. And she couldn't lie to him and raise false hope, but she hated to see the light go from his eyes. So she hedged. 'I am no expert.'

'Ye are more an expert at Healing than most others here.'

'Well ... I ...' She blushed and looked down at her feet. 'Morghanna and Abigail are the true experts. They need to look at what I found and give their educated opinion, but ... If I am right, along with the special balm I have created that I found in another old grimoire, I think we can improve things to a point where you will start to gain feeling where there currently is none.'

He stared at her, hope hovering in his eyes. 'If I regain feeling ... that would mean I might be able to walk again?' He smiled at her.

She nodded, his smile—his beautiful smile—was like the sun bursting into sunrise and lighting everything up inside her. It made her feel better than she'd felt for weeks—if ever!

So rather than douse his hope—and the brilliance of his smile— she returned it and said, 'I think you will. I really think you will.'

16

Alistair arrived soon after their conversation to move Dougal back to bed and take over the shift.

'Where's Morghanna? I thought she was doing the afternoon shift.'

'She is in the herbal stillroom doing something with Abigail. She will be in once they're done—hey where are you going in such a hurry?'

'I have to show Morghanna and Abigail something,' she said, grabbing up the grimoire and rushing out the door.

She was exhausted and her movements were stiff, her joints aching, but the excitement of what she'd found, the possibility it promised to truly help Dougal, gave her energy a boost so that she was able to push herself to keep going and not give in to the need to lie down and have a long sleep.

She was grateful though that the rain had passed. The heaviness of wet clothes would have dragged on her even more and not even the boost of excitement would have helped to allow her to last for as long as she needed it to.

The air held a definite chill though and she shivered as she ran, hunching over the grimoire as if it needed protecting from the cold.

Its thanks wound around her, warming her again, making her hurt a little less, giving her energy a boost. Her tired jerky running smoothed out, her stride lengthened, and suddenly she was moving faster.

'I found it,' she declared as soon as she burst through the door. Her two mentors looked up at her in surprise.

'Whoa, calm down, girl,' Abigail said from her perch on the stool at the end of the bench. 'What exactly do you think you have found?'

'The next step in Dougal's recovery. It is in here.' She tapped the grimoire she held against her chest. It responded by sending something through her, like a warm, encouraging hug. It felt so good, she couldn't help bouncing on her toes.

'What are you talking about?' Morghanna asked as she retook her seat opposite Abigail.

'This.' She held out the grimoire as she rounded the bench to Morghanna. 'The grimoire you left for me to have a look at. You were right. It does hold something special.'

Morghanna took the grimoire from her and placed it on the bench between her and Abigail, fingers trembling as they ran over the cover. 'It is older than anything previously found. I thought maybe it would show us what we have lost.'

'It did. It has. It is written by a master of all aspects of the Healing arts.'

'A very rare witch indeed,' Abigail said.

Morghanna angled her head to the side and closed her eyes. 'It is whispering to me.'

Leanna's eyes widened. 'It whispered to me too and welcomed me to open it.'

Morghanna opened her eyes and turned to Leanna. 'You felt this magic?'

Leanna nodded. 'My magic is not as damaged as we thought.'

'Hmm. Perhaps.' Furrows appeared on Morghanna's brow as she turned away, her gaze going to Abigail. 'Should she be able to feel this? To hear it speaking?'

'With what we have been feeling of how low her magic reserves are ... no.'

'I am standing right here,' Leanna said, putting her hands on her hips. 'You do not need to talk about me as if I cannot hear nor understand you.'

Their brows rose, eyes widening slightly, as they stared at her.

It was no wonder they were surprised. She was surprised too. Normally she would have backed down, stood there with her face lowered, hands clasped before her. But right now she had no intention of doing so. She wanted them to hear her, to read the grimoire, to agree with her about starting the treatments.

'Whether I should or should not be able to hear the grimoire because my magic is still too weak is beside the point. I can hear it. It allowed me to read it. And I found this.' She reached over and, despite her anger, opened the grimoire gently and turned it to the page she wanted. 'This Healer was a powerful practitioner in Ancient Greece and she made it her life's work to help those who had lost feeling and movement in their limbs. She called it *paralysis*—a disabling of the nerves of the spinal column—long before the word came of use here centuries ago. And I believe, given what she says about the technique she developed, that it will help Dougal.'

'Oh? How?' Abigail asked, reaching for the grimoire, but winced and grabbed her arm as she pulled it back in to cradle against her body.

'Abigail!' Leanna skirted the bench to her mentor.

'I am fine, my dear,' Abigail said, waving away her help. 'My joints do not think much of this weather today.'

Magic prickled on the air—magic Leanna should not have been able to feel as strongly as she did—as Morghanna sent Healing energy towards Abigail. While she relieved the elderly witch's pain, Leanna placed the grimoire in front of her elderly mentor.

'Thank you,' Abigail said, rubbing her elbow. 'Now, where is this entry?'

'Here,' Leanna said, pointing to where the passage began.

Abigail held her hand above the grimoire, hovering a few inches above the page, her eyes drifting closed. 'Its protective spells are obviously failing.'

'I will take care of it when I get back to my cottage.'

'You will do no such thing,' Morghanna said. 'You may oil the cover but I will teach Alistair the preservation spellwork and he can reset it so that it returns to what it should be.'

'I can manage magic as small as a preservation spell!'

'Can you?' Her gaze met Abigail's again. 'That should not be possible.'

'No, it should not.'

Leanna sighed in exasperation. 'You are concentrating on the wrong thing. Please, read the entry. Tell me that I am not misreading it or letting my hopes run away with me.'

Morghanna stared at her for a moment longer, assessing, then narrowed her eyes in a way that meant she was looking at her aura. She tensed as Morghanna's frown deepened, wondering what by the Holy Goddess she saw there. Given the quick look she shot Abigail, whatever it was surprised her and not in a good way.

She was tempted to ask except ... the grimoire and Dougal were far more important than what was going on with her. 'Please. Read the grimoire and let me know what you think.'

Abigail nodded at Morghanna and then bent her head to the grimoire. She worked a translation spell, then read it not once, but twice. Once done, she looked up, her dark honey-coloured eyes sparkling. 'I think you are on to something here.'

'I knew it. I felt it in here.' She pressed her hand against her chest over her heart.

Abigail lifted a finger, her gimlet gaze pinning Leanna to the spot, stopping her bouncing up and down. 'It is not a cure. This may not fully mend Dougal's injury.'

'I know,' Leanna said, nodding vigorously. 'She makes that clear. It does depend on the degree of severity of the break in the back and where the break is.' She leaned over to point at the specific passage. 'But the physical therapy and massage added to the muscle enlivening cream—which sounds very much like the salve I just created—should not only give him relief from the pain, but also help bring some sensation and movement back to the muscles by rejuvenating some part of the nerves. And any step forward while we continue to look for a way to fully mend the damage is a positive thing, right? I mean, the need to keep his spirits up.'

'That is paramount now, yes,' Abigail said, gaze returning to the grimoire. 'And I think this is the best solution we have right now. In more ways than one.' Her eyes darted to Morghanna, her brow raised.

Morghanna nodded as if in answer to a question, then said, 'It does sound like it is the most promising treatment we have come across.' She moved around the bench to Abigail's side. 'I think I should read the entire grimoire as soon as possible. It appears we have lost far more knowledge than any of us ever imagined. I will have to let Bridgette know so she and Malcolm can increase their efforts to find more of these lost grimoires, diaries and journals.'

'I would like to help with them when they come,' Leanna said, excitement at the thought blooming inside her. Because inside one of them could be the ultimate answer she was looking for.

Morghanna chuckled and held up her hand. 'Slow down. You are already busy enough and only have a limited amount of energy to give.'

'Besides which,' Abigail said. 'Given what I just read, we will need you to be a part of the schedule for this new therapy. He will require multiple sessions per day and one of those sessions will need to be when you are caring for him.'

'Really? I can help to give him his therapy?'

'Yes. Although we will have to monitor how it affects your recovery and there is to be absolutely no magic use.'

'But there is a small amount of magic tied in to part of the therapy. I will not be able to complete a session if I cannot use a little magic.'

'Alistair or one of the others with Healing abilities will be there to action that part of the therapy.'

'I am not a baby to be cosseted at every step.'

Morghanna gave her a regretful look but it was Abigail who spoke. 'No. You are not a babe. You are a powerful Healer witch who has damaged the access to her powers because you pulled on and used too much. It is like a bad break in the leg bone, one that can bear no weight or risk it mending improperly, which would impede function forever. If you use too much of your magic before your access pathway is properly restored, you will never have full access to it again.'

Leanna gaped at her as hopelessness washed away all the energy that excitement had given her. She suddenly felt weaker and more tired than she'd felt since waking after the explosion. She leaned against the stool beside her, worried that it wasn't enough support— that her legs would give way entirely in a moment and she'd end up in a heap on the floor. 'I ... I ... why is it still so bad? Why am I like this? Am I defective? It has been more than a month since the explosion. I should be better by now!'

'Yes, you should.' Morghanna put her arm around Leanna's shoulders and gave her a hug.

'Then why am I still like this?'

Morghanna glanced at Abigail before her sorrowful gaze came back to Leanna. She brushed Leanna's hair back from her face. 'We do not know. But we need you to understand how worried we are— especially now we know you are somehow feeling, and tapping, in to magic you should not be able to.'

'But it is only a little magic. Hardly worth noting.' She was so exhausted now she could barely sit upright.

Morghanna put her arm around her, giving her support and allowing Leanna to lean against her as Abigail said, 'It is more than worth noting. Because you should not be able to feel it, let alone use it.' The elderly witch glanced at Morghanna. 'We have never seen a magical access as raw and damaged as yours. We have no idea how long it will take to fully restore.'

Leanna gasped, but before she could respond, Morghanna said, 'Abigail is right. But that is not our only worry. The one thing we do know is that if you use the magic you are somehow able to access, that you will not only do more damage, but by the look of your aura, you will endanger your life.'

Leanna stared at her mentor. 'That is ...' She shook her head. 'Are you saying I will explode like ...' She swallowed hard, because even thinking the words was painful. But say it she must, so she pushed past the pain and said, '... like my papa did?'

Morghanna squeezed her as Abigail said, 'No, love. Not like that. We think you will just fade away until you are a wraith. A dangerous, soul-sucking wraith.'

Leanna's mouth dropped open. 'Surely you jest?' Wraiths were but a myth. A story told to frighten naughty coven children who would not heed their parents or their teachers. Her own mother had used stories of witches and warlocks becoming wraiths. It had frightened her so much that she was afraid to use her power at all, which only angered her mother further.

Morghanna and Abigail—and Dougal—had helped to undo some of the damage done by those stories that had horrified and traumatised her when she was young. They'd helped her to see that her mother had simply been trying to control her with stories that were but cruel faerie tales.

Yet now Abigail was saying ... that they were true? That she could become one of those creatures she hated and feared? 'You ... you are lying.'

Abigail shook her head sadly. 'I fear I am not. Our kind have, in the past, turned into those creatures of dread. Usually out of a need to suck more and more power in ways they should not, but occasionally because they use their power too much in the service of others. Healers have fallen prey to this mistake more than any others.'

'I ... that cannot be true.'

'It *is* true. All myths and legends have a basis in reality and the stories of the wraith most definitely come from stark truths our people have long not had to face. After the advent of the Darkness into our world, our powers more often went in the opposite direction of that needed to create a wraith. We exploded in fits of power too wild to be controlled. But now we are bound by the wonder of Bridgette's Pact with the Were, some of the old issues we once suffered from have the possibility of returning. And this includes the reality of wraiths being created once more.

'But I would not ... I would never ... I do not crave power so I could never become a wraith.' She looked from Abigail to Morghanna and back again. 'Your fears of that happening ... they are unfounded.' She meant it to be a statement, but it came out more like a question.

'As I said, Healers became wraiths as much as those who longed for power.'

'But, if the stories are correct, wraiths are made when a witch or warlock leeches too much power too often from others.'

'Yes. That is true. But that is precisely what a Healer does, is it not? We might not take power from other witches or warlocks in the traditional sense, but we do take power from the very nature that surrounds them, from the universe, to transmute into Healing power. We also use the energies from the one we seek to Heal to bind with our magic so it is accepted fully by the injured body. And then we give all of this to the injured. And now, because of the Pact, we have the power of the Were to pull on too. Usually, this process ends when the injured is fully mended.'

'I know how the Healing process works,' Leanna said shortly, frustration and fear making her close to snapping.

Abigail raised a gnarled finger, shaking it at Leanna as she would at a wayward student. 'Ah, but if you did know the entirety of it, you would not be doing what you are doing.'

'And what is that?'

'Making the same mistake those Healers did who gave too much and became wraiths. They thought they could keep up a Healing, kept the process I just described going, on and on and on until they had nothing left.'

'Then they would flame-out.'

'Yes, that should have been what happened,' Morghanna said,

placing her hand on Abigail's which was shaking as it lay on the table.

Leanna suddenly realised just how distressed the old Healer was. She felt badly for being the cause, but couldn't stop from asking, 'But you are telling me that did not happen.'

'Yes. It should have been the natural conclusion, but it was not,' Morghanna said quietly. 'Somehow they tapped into a greater well of energy—like we now have with the Were. And the upshot was that they became wraiths, determined to suck on the lifeforce and souls of the healthy to give to who they perceived as injured until even that little shred of good intent was twisted and the only injured ones they gave their stolen power to was themselves.'

'I ... I ...' It was too hard to believe this was true, but she could see by their expressions, the way they openly met her questioning, confused gaze, that they were telling her the truth. 'Why is this not part of the wraith legend?'

Morghanna shrugged. 'It is. If you know the right stories to read. However, the story that is most widely told is the one about witches and warlocks who let their lust for power control them and become wraiths as a consequence. Which of course is more useful to frighten wayward children into listening to their elders. But the other stories are just as true.' She sighed. 'What is not clear is the particulars.'

'What do you mean?'

'I mean, what exactly made those Healers turn when others flamed-out. We think it had to do with the kind of injury they were trying to Heal—usually one that had the patient close to death if the diaries are correct—and that they had access to a greater well of power which acted together in some way to create the tragedy and horror of the wraith.'

'So, it might have nothing to do with how I wish to help Dougal? Because we can help him. I know we can with this new therapy.'

'Possibly.' Morghanna sighed as she gestured at Leanna. 'However, your slow recovery gives us pause. As does the fact you have access to the pack's strength through me. A strength you pulled on when you brought Dougal back from the dead. For all we know, you might have already begun the process and your current weakness is part of that.'

She stared at her mentors, horrified, but managed to say, 'But you do not know. Not for certain.'

'No. Not for certain. But one thing we do know for certain is, every single one of those ancient Healers who became a wraith were determined to Heal someone who could not be Healed.'

'That is not Dougal! He can be Healed. Maybe not fully, but what we have found here says we can help him more than we thought we could.'

'And you see,' Abigail said, pointing her gnarled, arthritic finger at Leanna, 'that is the problem here. You should not need this as much as you do.'

Leanna's chin trembled, but she forced back the sting of tears that flooded her eyes. She would not cry! She was not the trembling, scared girl her mother and tragedy had made her be for too many years. 'But if we are to help him to believe in his greater worth to us all, then we need to give him something to hold to. We have to give him hope that he will not have to live his life being completely reliant on others. Because without that, we will never be able to make him see himself as we see him. As *I* see him.' She thumped her chest as she said the latter. 'And the only way we can do that is to find treatments that will help him to feel his lower body again and hopefully, be able to use those muscles once more. Even if he can never be fully returned to what he once was physically, he needs that much at least.' She stood, unable to stop her trembling, but hoping they would see it as passion rather than the exhaustion fast threatening to take her down. 'So, will you help me with this therapy I have found?'

The two witches looked at each other for a moment and she wondered if they could communicate in ways she was unaware of. Then they turned back to her and nodded.

'We will learn the treatment and take part. But only if you abide by certain rules until you are fully recovered.'

'I will not become a wraith like you fear.'

'Mayhap not, but your promise I will have,' Abigail said firmly.

'I promise to abide by whatever rules you put in place.'

Abigail extended her hand and they shook, her magic binding her to the promise. 'Done. Now it is time to begin.'

17

This was torture!

It wasn't simply the pain of the exercises they put him through three times a day. He could handle pain. What he couldn't handle was Leanna's hands on him, massaging and moving his legs in those absurd exercises they were certain were going to help him to be able to move again.

Not walk. Abigail and Morghanna were very careful not to promise that when they'd explained the process to him.

Leanna was the only one who thought there was still a chance he'd walk again. Her hope was a different kind of torture, one that was getting harder and harder to endure. Especially given it kept alive the barely flickering flame of hope he had that everything would turn out the way he wished it to and that Leanna could be his. That they could let the mating bond be completed.

But that was a fool's wish. A hope he could not let turn from flicker to fire.

He was never going to be a fully functioning member of the pack ever again. And when Iain returned, he would order his death.

Hopefully he would have figured out how to break the mating bond by then. But he was fast running out of time. Iain would most definitely be back before the next full moon. He couldn't keep the Hunters, lieutenants and soldiers he'd taken with him away from the pack for another full moon. They would need the comfort and strength that re-bonding with their packmates under the light of the full moon gave to the pack. Especially if they were to continue the hunt for such a dangerous enemy to the pack as Lachlan had proved himself to be.

Leanna pressed her thumbs down his spine to rub the cream-like potion she'd made into his lower back, bringing his thoughts arrowing straight back to the current torture. He groaned.

'I am sorry. Does that hurt?'

'Nae.' It didn't hurt. At least, not in the way she meant. In fact, it felt good—way too good. Which wouldn't be a problem if he could stay like he was. But when she was finished rubbing the cream into his back and legs, she'd help him roll over so she could rub it into the front of his legs.

When he did, she wouldn't be able to miss the raging cockstand currently pushing into the mattress.

Some might say that he should be happy he was capable of being aroused, and feeling all there was to feel with such a thing, but for him, it made this all so much worse. It would be easier to feel nothing rather than the constant tease of something he could never have.

'Are you sure I am not hurting you?'

'I am certain,' he said as evenly as possible.

'Good. Because this is the part that is supposed to help take away the pain. The leg exercises however ... I am sorry they hurt. But it is also good that they do. It is good that you are beginning to feel something in those muscles, even if it is pain.'

'Aye.' Although, there had always been pain. Not in his legs, but most definitely in his back. The entirety of it ached every day all day on the good days—on the bad days it alternated between feeling like he was being stabbed over and over, hit by lightning and burned alive. Not that he had experience of the latter two, but from what Lele had told him of her own experience a few months ago about being burned, he was fairly certain this was how it would feel.

And it made him admire Leanna even more.

He would do anything to be able to change what she'd been through. To have saved her from the agony of being struck by the uncontrolled lightning of her father's powers as they'd exploded, killing her mother and half their coven in a blaze of fire and lightning strikes. It was a wonder she'd survived.

Her father—who she had loved so deeply, who had understood her as no other had understood her, who had championed her against the expectations of her demanding mother as best he could. His loss had been the source of the greatest agony, the instigator of the greatest grief his precious Leanna had been forced to endure.

And endure it she had. In a way that showed just how precious and strong and special she was. Because how many people would have suffered and lost what she had and still remain so good, so full of a need to be of service, to be useful and help others in a way she could not help herself?

He gritted his teeth as her hands moved his loosened drawers down to expose the naked flesh of his buttocks.

Ah ye Gods! This was one of the worst parts! He'd long imagined —ever since he'd first seen her edging across the corner of the village square, trying to act like she was invisible, not knowing that he saw her, that he would always see her because he and his wolf instantly recognised her as their mate—what it would be like to have her hands on his body. He dreamed most nights of a time when she would run her hands over his back, cupping the globes of his arse as he did hers, then moving around the front to wrap those beautiful long, strong fingers around his co—

Hells! What was he doing? Losing himself to his imaginings was making it even worse.

By the Moon—could his cock get any harder? Thank the Moon the mattress—one they'd placed on the special table Morghanna had asked the carpenters to make for this treatment—was soft and dipped in various strategic places, otherwise his cock would be bent in two right now. Or mayhap it was so hard it would drill a hole right through the table.

The latter felt more probable as Leanna rubbed the cream over the globes of his buttocks, her fingers kneading into the muscle.

Thankfully he could barely feel most of it; there was not a lot of sensation from the lower part of his arse cheeks and down. It was more that the harder she kneaded, the more his body moved up and down and side-to-side, telling him exactly what she was doing. And the way his body pushed into the mattress told him exactly where those beautiful hands of hers were and that they were moving lower and lower.

Ahh ... fuck!

Had he thought his cock couldn't get any harder? He'd been wrong. So horribly wrong. And if she kept doing what she was doing, the friction of her movements rubbing him up and down against the softness of the sheet under him, rubbing against his over-sensitised flesh in a way that ...

Blast it all to hell! He was horribly afraid he was going to blow his load.

His wolf whimpered, the only sound he could make with how stressed he was. How much pain he was in. And he was in so much pain. Pain because he couldn't come out and help Heal them like he usually would with the change; pain because of the knowledge they'd never run again; pain because his mate was so close and he couldn't show himself to her, but most of all pain because he couldn't be with his mate.

He understood the reason just as surely as the human part of him did, but he ached so badly, so deeply, from it, he strained against it while bowing to the necessity of it.

They could never hold their mate to them when they were broken like this with no hope of recovery. She deserved so much more than what they could give her now. So rather than howling inside him, forcing him to tell her she was his mate as they'd always planned to do when she was ready, making her finish the mating she'd unwittingly started when she'd brought them back from death and done the second Healing on them, the wolf simply showed his distress by whimpering, unable to stay completely quiet.

Dougal wished he could do something more to comfort his other half than stroking him in his mind, but there was nothing to do. Except endure.

Until they died.

The pushing movement stopped and Dougal realised she had moved down to his legs, pulling his drawers back over his buttocks.

Thank the Moon! Maybe things would calm down with her not working in regions that were ... sensitive to her ministrations.

Sensitive in ways that they weren't when Morghanna or Alistair did the treatment on him.

He took in some deep breaths.

'Is everything fine?'

'Mmhmm,' he managed.

'Are you feeling anything while I do this?'

Oh, he was feeling something—just not the something she meant. 'Nae.'

'The Ancient Greek witch wrote that it could take up to a month of treatments before any change was truly felt. So do not lose hope.'

'Aye. Hope.' He had none but he couldn't tell her that. Even if it might make her stop this torture if she had no hope, tearing it away from her would cause her pain and he didn't want to do that. There would be pain enough in her future when Iain ordered his death. It wasn't something that could be avoided. Their fledgling mating bond made certain of that. But stopping it from forming any further would save her a lot of pain if he couldn't find a way to break it.

He never wanted to cause her pain.

She'd had too much of it in her life already.

'I hope Alistair will arrive soon to help turn you over as I am almost finished rubbing the potion into your back and legs.'

'Why do ye need Alistair fer that?'

There was a pause and he thought she might not answer, but then she said, 'I was worried that I was not helping you enough to turn over so I asked Alistair to come and help you.'

'You were helping fine, Le-le.' He did not have his strength back in his upper body yet, but it was better than it had been, especially since they had begun the treatments. He did need some help with moving his legs and hers had been fine for the first few days—although the last few days she'd seemed to struggle more and more and had excused herself afterwards, leaving the room for a quarter hour or so —which had allowed him to regain some control of his unruly cock.

He'd thought she'd excused herself to go to the privy, but maybe not. Maybe she had truly struggled and needed some time to recover.

He wished he could see her now to judge how she was doing. He'd barely looked at her for the last few weeks that she'd taken a shift to nursemaid for him. It had been self-preservation that had made him try his best to ignore her presence—although he hadn't been able to stop himself from responding to her and looking at her when she wasn't facing him. She'd caught him staring sometimes and those moments had been ...

He swallowed hard as his cock flexed at the memory.

But he had to admit that even in those moments, he'd been thinking more about what she did to him and how increasingly diffi-cult it was to keep her at arm's length. He'd not truly looked at her—at least not with eyes filmed over with love, lust and need.

So much need.

She was life. She was laughter. She was the very air he breathed.

She warmed him like the sun he loved to bask in and gave his soul beauty like the moon he bayed to in the wolf hour when nothing else but it could give him what he needed.

Nothing but her.

Because she had, since the moment he saw her, become his everything.

His cock flexed again just at the thought of how much he and his wolf needed her.

He suppressed another groan as she moved away from him. He lifted his head to see if he could catch a glimpse of her, to try to truly look at her and see if she was indeed struggling and he'd been too preoccupied with himself to see it.

His wolf growled at him—and at itself.

Aye. He deserved that. He was angry too. Angry with himself for not taking care of her. For not looking out for her. For being too caught up in himself and the agony of what he was going through, that he hadn't made certain she was recovered.

Unfortunately she was out of his line of sight. All he could see was the swish of her skirts as she collected more things from the bench against the far wall. His mind flashed to the shapely bottom and legs beneath those skirts that he'd had occasion to see the outline of when she'd been helping to harvest the lavender crop—unlike most of the females who simply tied their skirts into a knot on each side when harvesting to keep them from catching on the plants, his Le-le chose to wear long breeches. Some of the younger ones had begun to do the same seeing how much easier it was to work in that attire, but it had shown so much more of her shape and given him so much more to fantasise about.

Fantasies that had once tormented him with healthy longing and sexual desires he had thought would at some time be sated when his courting of her, his gaining of her trust, had come to fruition. But now those fantasies tortured him because they could never be.

His wolf growled at him again. *'Yes. You are right. No time to feel sorry for myself.'*

He shoved those distracting thoughts far away and concentrated on Le-le.

She'd turned his way and even though he couldn't see her face, he had the feeling she was listening to something.

'Is there a problem?' he asked softly, not wanting to startle her.

'I just ... I thought I heard growling.'

Before he could address the horrifying fact that she could hear his wolf so easily, Cal burst into the room. 'Soren just returned. Iain and the hunting party will return the week before the next full moon.'

Dougal stared at him. 'That is only fourteen days away.'

'Aye.'

He let his head thump back to the massage bench. He was running out of time. It no longer mattered if Leanna's treatment had given him back some sensation. It no longer mattered if some time in the future it might give him back even more.

Iain would only see the drain that he was in the present.

And he would order his death.

He had fourteen days to find some way to cut the bond. Fourteen days to separate himself from Leanna so she wouldn't follow him into death.

Fourteen days to make her hate him so much the bond would be nothing but a withered thing easily sliced away.

His wolf whimpered.

'Are you hurting?' Leanna asked.

'Yes. I need a break.'

'Oh. Sorry. I will just ... I will fetch some of the pain medication so we can continue. In the meantime, Cal, given Alistair has not arrived yet, would you be so kind as to turn Dougal over so I can continue his treatment after he has taken the medication?'

'Of course.'

'I will be back momentarily.'

'Fine,' Dougal grumped, wishing she would simply stay away forever. His wolf growled at him—she stumbled back a little, staring down at him.

'Oh the pain must be bad. I will be back as soon as I can.'

Cal moved out of her way as she left the room then turned back to stare at him. 'She can hear yer wolf?'

'Aye,' Dougal said. 'She sometimes heard him in the past but now she hears him every time.'

'That means the bond is stronger than what ye thought. What are ye going to do?'

'What I must. I canna still be bonded to the lass when Iain returns.'

'Ye will break the bond? Is that possible?'

'It is. If I make her hate me.'

'Can ye do that?'

'I have no choice. I canna make her suffer through that pain or have her die with me.'

'Mayhap Iain will see reason given ye are bonded and allow ye to live.'

Dougal glared at his friend. 'If ye think that, ye have rocks in yer head. Iain willna care she is mated to me. He will force Morghanna to bind her more tightly to the Packbond so she willna die with me—he will say if he stayed alive for the pack by doing so after his Mariah died, then my mate can stay alive. Especially given she isna even a Were.'

'Maybe she willna die. Maybe the fact she isna a Were will save her.'

Dougal's heart squeezed and his wolf whimpered again. 'I wish I could believe that may be so. But I canna trust that it will. And even if it is true, she is still bound to feel my death more keenly and for longer if she is mated to me when I die. I have to make her change her will or whatever made her bond to me the night I was injured. I have to make her hate me so much she will cut the tie herself. I canna allow anything bad to happen to Le-le. And I canna allow Iain to tie her more firmly to him. He will use her power and energy as he has used ours. That would be almost worse than her dying.'

'Ye are right.'

'I know. I have fourteen days to make her hate me and have the bond wither so much I can tear it asunder.'

Cal's expression was full of sorrow and his wolf howled along with Dougal's. 'I wish there was something I could do.'

'I wish that too. But there is nought. I must die. But first, my mating bond must break. It is the only way to save Le-le. And I must save her. If it is the last thing I do, I will ensure she is no longer mated to me. I will ensure she survives.'

18

Leanna plopped down on the stool at the bench, unable to continue to stand. She was only halfway through her work—she needed to get the batches of potion mixed before Alistair joined her to do the magic parts—and her body wasn't allowing her any more than twenty minutes at a time before she needed to rest again. She tried to stand but her legs wobbled and she sat with an 'oof' before she collapsed on the floor. 'Blast it all to hell!'

The swear words—learned by being around the Were—felt strange on her tongue. She'd never sworn before this, but it was the only thing that truly expressed her frustration and anger.

And yes. She was angry. So very angry. And desperate. Although she had no idea why she felt any of that.

It had been growing inside her for the last week. Ever since she'd left Dougal with Cal after he'd delivered the terrible news that Iain was returning a few days before the full moon. He and his Hunters hadn't found Lachlan, but they had to return because too many moons away from the pack created problems for many Were. After refilling themselves with what they needed, they would return to look for Lachlan.

Whether they found the murdering Were or not, Leanna didn't

really care. All she cared about was the fact that Iain was returning soon and she was running out of time to prove that she could Heal Dougal. That she could make him a valued member of the pack in Iain's eyes. Because if she could do that, Iain wouldn't demand Dougal's death and everything would be all right.

Of course, nothing was going how she wished it to because, since the news, her own recovery seemed to be going backwards. And now the only thing that made her life worth living was slowly being taken away from her.

Her ability to help Dougal.

It was no surprise anger and desperation were growing inside her like they were. Because with every day that passed her increasing weakness and dizzy spells were getting harder to hide no matter how much she rested.

And she was resting a lot.

Too much. More than she should need to rest for a witch who'd flamed-out over a month ago. Even one who had done something that shouldn't have been possible. She should be full of energy by now, in full control of her powers.

Instead she was this weak, powerless, wobbling, dizzy thing. Who couldn't even help the man she loved in the way she wanted to.

At least this meant she couldn't possibly be turning into the wraith that Abigail and Morghanna feared she could become. For nothing so powerful could come from something so horribly weak.

So weak that she wasn't sure she could still do even the small part she'd been doing. She'd thought it had been bad enough that she hadn't been able to do every treatment. Then she thought having to give up doing parts of the treatments she could do, handing it over to Alistair so she could have brief rests was the worst.

But now ...

Her eyes prickled with hot tears she didn't want to shed because it was just another sign of her weakness. She pushed her knuckles into her eyes, as if she could shove the tears back from whence they came. The pressure-pain worked, giving her thoughts more clarity—the fog of exhaustion could make it so difficult to think straight.

And exhaustion was becoming a constant in her world.

Over the last few days Dougal's therapy was taking more and more out of her. It wasn't helped by the fact he was increasingly grumpy and unhappy and snapped and sniped at her when he wasn't ignoring her existence. He had returned to treating her as he had before the day she'd thought was such a turning point when he'd agreed to sit in the armchair by the window. In fact, it was worse. Much worse. He was almost cruel.

Not that she blamed him for his behaviour given everything. But being on tenterhooks around him was sapping the meagre energy she had even faster and she barely made it through an hour of therapy before having to give over the rest of the treatment to Alistair or Morghanna and retire to her room.

Thankfully Alistair had suggested it might be a good idea if she were closer to Dougal while they were trialling the new therapies and potions. Morghanna had agreed with him and they'd moved her and all her things—including what she used in the herbal stillroom—to the large room next to Dougal's in the Healer Hall. She had to admit, while she would never have asked for it herself—she would never want to admit how bad things were getting because admitting it would make it truer—it was quite a relief not to have to make the walk across the village. It was also good to be closer to Dougal even though he didn't seem to want to see her at all.

Having a room next door had made a big difference for a few days but then she had continued to worsen. After a few days, she found that on returning to her room, she'd barely been able to stay awake long enough to read any of the grimoires or diaries as had been her routine. A few days after that, she needed to sleep as soon as she returned to her room—a sleep that went from an hour to two, to taking her right to the supper hour.

And now those rest periods weren't even proving to be enough to keep her going through the morning and afternoon. She was forced to stop constantly. And her mind was foggier and foggier, unable to concentrate for long periods—which was a serious problem for translating the potions and Healer theories she found in the grimoires, let alone creating them. Most potions took time. Consistent time. Not ten minutes here, twenty minutes there time.

She wasn't going to complete anything! Or help anyone! Especially Dougal.

She might be able to live with not being the one who actually made the potions to help him, but that added to her being unable to fully participate in his treatments ... 'Argh! It is bloody unfair!' She slammed her hands down on the bench, enjoying the sting because it brought clarity to her mind like pain always did.

But the pain was quickly followed by dizziness.

She grabbed a hold of the bench and closed her eyes, breathing deeply until the sensation passed. Cautiously, she opened one eye, then the other, so very grateful that Morghanna or Alistair hadn't come in to check on her yet as they had a wont to do before her shift with Dougal.

She was fairly certain they were ensuring she was well enough to take her shift. It was so frustrating that they were suspicious she wasn't as well as she was trying to make out. Even taking the potion she was currently trying to make another batch of—an energy regenerative tonic they made for the sentries and anyone who needed an energy boost for short periods—wasn't helping in the way it should. It helped her push through but she was even more exhausted after a session with Dougal than she'd been a week ago.

She was horribly afraid they'd soon see how bad she was becoming. Because if they did, they'd stop her from her work and worse—stop her from helping to look after Dougal even in the increasingly limited capacity she now had to endure.

Seeing him every day was what got her up and going in the morning—something that was increasingly more difficult.

Why was she getting worse?

She had never heard tell of, or read, about a witch or warlock taking so much time to recover from a flame-out. It was getting harder to believe Morghanna and Abigail's reason: that she'd used a huge amount of magic, unlike they'd ever seen before, in Healing Dougal, and it was going to take more time to recover than usual.

But she had passed 'more time' as well as 'even more time' and was now somewhere in the vicinity of 'would she ever feel normal again?' time.

She was horribly afraid that the answer to that was a resounding 'no'!

Her shoulders slumped and it was all she could do not to give in and collapse to the floor.

She lifted her chin and said, 'Stop it! Stop feeling sorry for yourself, Leanna. It will not help Dougal. And that is all that matters right now. Helping Dougal.'

She took some deep, steadying breaths, focusing on the fact it was almost time to see him.

Just the thought gave her a little boost in energy. Seeing him each day always did that. Not that it lasted long. The minute she started his treatment and he started grumping and saying those things that were filled with little barbs that hurt—even though she knew he didn't truly mean them—her energy started to wane. And the more she remained hopeful and positive in the face of his grumpiness, the worse he got.

And the worse she was when she finally gave in to her exhaustion and stumbled back into her room to collapse on her bed.

Now there were only seven days left before Iain's return. Seven days to improve Dougal to the point that Iain wouldn't demand he die.

Her heart began to beat faster, her chest squeezing a little, making her breath shudder. It wasn't right. She wasn't ready. Seven days wasn't enough. Fourteen days wasn't enough for the treatments to have had time to show significant enough change. The grimoire had said it could take a month but more likely longer before there was any sign of the kind of change she needed. But she'd thought maybe, if her powers had started to come back—the powers everyone said had brought Dougal back from the dead—then maybe she could speed that up. Maybe she could work a miracle.

But her powers hadn't come back. And there was no hope that the very minute Iain got back, he'd wouldn't ask why Dougal wasn't dead yet and then insist it be done immediately because he was a sap on pack energy.

And by pack energy she knew Iain would truly mean *his* energy given he'd been leeching power from the strongest in the pack, especially Dougal, for years. Because when pack members were injured, pack energy changed and was transferred in differing degrees through the Alpha—and from the Alpha—to the Pack Healers so they could speed up the Healing process and do things like what witch Healers did.

She knew this because after Lachlan's original attack, Iain had been weaker in the weeks afterwards because the young Pack Healer, Sebastian had to use the power and energy of his Alpha to help the injured Were. The strain on Dougal had been immense because he gave more power to Iain to keep his Alpha strong enough to do his job, while also giving to Sebastian and the Pack Healers from the McVale Pack who had come to help.

But now he had nothing to give as his wolf had cut them all off— as wolves did to protect themselves and their human side, or so Cal had explained to her. So Iain was not only cut off from sapping Dougal's energy—making him worthless to Iain—but he was taking some of what Iain had come to think of as his.

She became aware of how far the shadows had crawled across the floor. It was almost time to start her shift with Dougal. Which begged the question—where was Alistair or Morghanna?

She'd got so lost in the muddle that was her thoughts that she'd completely lost track of time.

Damn it!

No. Don't get distracted again! Concentrate on the now!

And in the now, Alistair and Morghanna weren't here. And one of them at least should be to help with the spells to finish the potions she was working on. But even more important, she needed them to carry in the bed-easel and paint supplies she meant to give to Dougal today. She certainly didn't have the energy to do so. So where were they?

She frowned, standing while holding on to the bench for stability.

Was something happening in the village she was unaware of?

Or ... Had something happened to Dougal? That would definitely keep them away.

Panic a live thing in her chest, giving her a boost of energy she desperately needed, she ran—well, walked in a tripping kind of fast pace—to the door and out into the hall. She was halfway to Dougal's door when she heard voices coming out of the room across the way.

A room Morghanna had taken as her office, so hearing voices from there wasn't unusual.

What was unusual was that the voices comprised of both her mentors, Alistair and another voice she'd thought to never hear again outside of her dreams.

Her dead papa's.

19

Leanna crept closer to the closed door. Her heart beat so loudly in her chest she was surprised no Were came running to see who was making so much noise.

But the Healer Hall was quiet—all patients except Dougal had been allowed to go home and came in for treatments when needed. And there were no visitors for Dougal because, aside from Cal, he refused to allow anyone but those involved in his treatments to see him. The only people here were Dougal, herself and the three people in the room on the other side of the door she now leaned against.

No not three people. Four.

Because there was most definitely a fourth voice in there who sounded like her papa.

She reached for the door handle, hand shaking so badly she didn't think she could grasp the knob to turn it. But she had to. She had to see who this person was who sounded like her dead papa.

She forced her trembling fingers to curl around the knob and was about to turn and push the door open, when the sound of her name stopped her.

'Leanna needs to be told!' That was definitely Alistair. And he sounded upset. In fact he was almost shouting.

She should open the door, find out why, but for some reason, she couldn't move her hand on the handle as her papa's voice sounded again.

'I tried to make her see this weeks ago when I visited her in the astral. I do not understand why she is still not aware of what is happening.'

The astral?

Her hand slipped off the door handle.

Her papa had visited her in the astral. She had thought it a dream.

In that dream he'd told her not to return to her body but to listen. To learn. And to heed.

Except, when she woke, she could barely remember any of it, which was why she'd thought it but a dream. A dream she hadn't really given much thought to because the dreams she thought about were the sexy ones with Dougal.

But if her papa had visited her in the astral, if it wasn't a dream, then what had he wanted her to hear?

She tried to grasp the memory now. At first it slipped from her grasp but then she grabbed a tendril, then another, piecing them together.

Abigail and Morghanna had been sitting by her bed. They'd been talking about her. About her and Dougal.

And their mating bond.

Her mind span as all the memories of what she'd heard came tumbling back. There was a roaring in her ears but in amidst that roaring, Abigail's voice chimed through.

'Cal tells me the bond is still incomplete. Partly because she seems unaware, but also because they have not completed the rites. Although, he said it is stronger than it should be given all that.'

'That is because she is feeding power into it.' Papa again, his strange, echoing voice sounding incensed. 'Power that is stopping her from recovering. The drain on her power is affecting her in every way. It is even affecting her memory.'

'What do you mean?' Morghanna asked.

'I did not know how to tell her she was mated and have her believe it, so I pulled her into the astral and sent her to listen to you all talk about the mating and your fears. I hoped she would listen and stop giving power through the bond. But she did not. In fact, she seemed not to remember any of what she heard at all. I do not know if it is because she cannot let herself believe that she could possibly be Dougal's mate, or if it is simply the power drain affecting certain memories. But whatever the reason, her response was to give more power, not less.'

Leanna's mind span with so many questions, but she had to push them aside to keep concentrating on what was being said.

'Maybe she does remember and that is why she is giving more power so freely,' Alistair suggested. 'Because she is actively trying to save her mate.'

'No,' her papa said immediately. 'I have gone to her a few times and told her things that should make an impact on her, but when she wakes, she seems to remember none of it.'

'You need to stop going to her in the astral,' Morghanna admonished. 'Spirits are not meant to be in the astral. I fear it will drain you to the point where you will never be able to move on.'

'How can I move on when my daughter is giving her life for another in this way?' He swore under his breath. 'I do not understand why you have not done something about it.'

'We did,' Alistair said, his French accent sounding more pronounced. 'We told Dougal to stop trying to block her and push her away given it was hurting her. But with Iain's imminent arrival, he is trying everything he can to break the bond because he does not want to drag Leanna down with him. And he will not listen to us.'

By the Goddess! This was ... she didn't ... how could it be true?

Their voices faded out again as her thoughts centred on one thing: Dougal was fighting their mating bond. He was trying to break it! As he had before.

Her mate did not want her. He had never wanted her.

Her knees buckled and she almost fell to the floor but managed to catch herself on the door jamb before she did.

She couldn't breathe. Her vision was fogging because she couldn't catch her breath. And her heart was beating so loud, so fast, she had to press her hand against her chest because she feared it was about to break out of her ribs.

This couldn't be right. She was mated to Dougal!

It should have been the most wonderful thing she'd ever heard and yet … it was horrible. Because she had failed to make the significant change in Dougal necessary to stop the death heading towards him. Despite apparently giving all of her power to him—no wonder she hadn't recovered!—he was still not significantly better than he'd been weeks ago. She simply wasn't strong enough.

She had failed him.

Was this what Morghanna and Abigail had been so worried about when they'd spoken of how a wraith was made? Did they still think that could happen?

Her mind span, blackness edging her vision. Her entire body began to tremble and she pushed against it, hard. Because she needed to hear more of what they were talking about. She couldn't pass out now.

The trembling retreated and she leaned her ear up against the door, trying to hear more. But for some reason now she could only hear snippets of the conversation.

If only she could do a spell that would enable her to hear more.

Although … maybe she could. There was a perfect one she'd read of recently—the witch had called it her 'bee on the wall' spell. She'd link herself to a bee, although any insect would do, and then send them into a room to be her eyes and ears.

It was a tiny spell using only the smallest amount of magic. Surely that wouldn't take too much away from Dougal—now she knew that's where her power was going, it made sense, but she didn't want to stop giving it to him if it was keeping him here. Even if it wasn't strong enough to truly make a difference. Which was why she wouldn't become a wraith. She simply wasn't powerful enough for that to take place.

If she pulled a little of the power she was feeding to him back though, she should be able to do this small spell so she could hear exactly what they were saying about her. And Dougal.

She closed her eyes and felt for her magic. It was there, pulsing unevenly under the surface and was heading out of her—why hadn't she noticed that before? Maybe it was because of what Dougal was doing to block her? By the Goddess that thought hurt enough to take the breath out of her, but she understood why he was doing it. He didn't want her. She wasn't good enough.

She shoved the pain of that aside and pulled on a strand of silvery magic that twined around the outside—it was steadier and surer than the rest. She willed the strand to work down her arms and into her fingers. It didn't feel as easy as usual—it fought her somewhat—but even so, it felt so good to be using magic again. On purpose.

When she'd pooled enough power so it was sparking on her fingers, she wrote the sigil in the air as she whispered the spell, calling an insect to her.

It took a moment—probably due to her weak magic—but after a minute an ant appeared from a crack in the floorboards. It ran up the wall to where it was even with where the sigil hung glowing in the air.

Her breath was coming in soft pants but she kept her fingers steady as she gestured with them to move the sigil to where the ant was and then flicked it into the ant.

It shuddered—so did she as the magic pulled energy from her— and then the small black insect ran back down the wall and under the door.

She whispered the final words of binding. There was a pop that made her sway unsteadily as more energy was pulled from her. She grasped for the door jamb again to steady herself as her conscious- ness split and suddenly she was running along the floor in the room and up the leg of the desk to the top where the best view of the group was.

They stood by the fire, gathered around Abigail who sat in the armchair in front of the hearth—she was having trouble staying warm these days, the cold making her joints ache more.

At first she couldn't see anyone else there except for Abigail, Alistair and Morghanna, so she scuttled along the desk to get a better view then up the stack of books on the corner.

When she stopped, she had a good view of all four people.

The fourth person wasn't her father. It was Stephen Samuel, a harvest mage. He was the coven representative of the Harvest Co-op. He had no talent in Healing. So what was he doing here? And why had she heard her papa?

Disappointment surged through her so strongly she almost lost the connection but managed to grasp it, aware at the same time her fingers were digging into the door jamb desperately trying to keep her body upright.

She wasn't going to last for much longer at this rate. But she had to because she needed to hear what they were saying. Papa had told her to listen and heed. She was only trying to do what he had bid. Maybe that's why she'd heard his voice—it was her subconscious making her remember.

This time, she was determined not to forget.

She couldn't forget.

Which meant she had to preserve energy—standing was taking too much out of her. And if she used up too much energy, she might pass out and not remember anything when she woke like she apparently had already done. So she turned and leaned against the wall and let herself slide down to the floor to save some energy. As her bottom hit the floor, she refocused on what was being said in the room.

'Iain truly is no Alpha at all,' Stephen said—except it wasn't Stephen's voice but her papa's. That's when she remembered that Stephen's secondary power was that of a Spirit-talker. Could her papa be speaking through him? There was an oddness about his features and expression that made her think of her papa. It was like Papa was inside Stephen.

Was that possible? She'd never heard of it before but ... he was most definitely talking like her father. It was his voice with his intonations and even his facial expressions.

She wished she could walk in there and ask but that would mean she'd lose the opportunities listening in afforded her. Not that she'd be able to walk right now. The spell was taking too much out of her. Still, it was hard not to be able go in there and talk to her papa given he seemed to be in Stephen, using his body like a puppet master did a puppet.

Blast it. She was letting herself be distracted by questions that didn't matter and was missing parts of the conversation again. With an effort that had sweat breaking out on her brow, she focused back on what she could see and hear through the ant.

Morghanna was pacing as she said, 'I know it is not ideal and I wish there was something I could do to change it, but the fact remains that Iain is Alpha and unless someone comes forward to challenge him, the pack will continue to follow him.'

'And the only one even remotely capable of making a challenge and winning,' Alistair explained to her papa, 'is Dougal. Was Dougal. But even before his injury, he was not ready to challenge Iain.'

'Pity,' Abigail said. 'He would be a wonderful Pack Alpha.'

Stephen-Papa made an impatient gesture with his hand. 'Why does he not see it is a stupid kind of loyalty?'

Morghanna sighed and rubbed her brow. She looked so strained. 'I do not think it is loyalty to Iain so much as loyalty to the position and to the pack. He will not do anything that affects the health and happiness and strength of the pack, and he believes that having the stability of a single Alpha through this difficult time of transition is what serves the pack best.'

'But Iain has been draining him and the others in the pack leadership,' Stephen-Papa said. 'From what I have observed from the Beyond, this is not something a good Alpha would do. At least, not for as long as Iain has. And certainly not as a way to cover for the transgressions and cruelties of his child. You need to talk to Dougal.'

'Do you not think I have tried?' Morghanna said. 'That we have all tried.' She waved her hands at the others. 'We might have been close to having him agree before but now ...' She shook her head. 'He will not even let us talk about it. The minute we bring it up he shuts down —and when he does that, Leanna becomes worse.'

'I know. I have seen how all this is affecting my daughter.'

Wait! What? She hung on the next words, hoping Morghanna or her papa would say more, but Alistair took over.

'We understand your concern and share it. But even if Dougal thought he should challenge Iain, a challenge is now impossible anyway, because he can no longer fight in the way the Were do in a challenge.'

'There were other ways to challenge,' Stephen-Papa said slowly. 'Ones that did not include a physical fight to the death. I have heard some of the ancient Were over here mention it.'

Abigail looked up at Morghanna as Alistair said, 'You were right!'

Morghanna's eyes were bright with hope as she went to Stephen-Papa and grabbed his arms. 'You have to tell me what these options are. I have been searching the diaries and found reference to challenges where power was wrested from the old Alpha without his death—particularly in cases where the old Alpha was rendered incapable of making decisions either through severe injury to the body or brain—but none of them say how. There was also mention of Were, who were not physically powerful, challenging their Alpha because they were not serving the pack as they should, and won by means other than a physical fight. There were female Alphas if I am reading things right—and they held and challenged males far stronger than them. And the pack followed them—their lack of physical power not an issue. However there is no mention of how any of this was done. Only that it *was* done. And none of the Pack Elders who will speak with me about such things are aware of anything like it. All they know is the violent path the Darkness had led them to, where power was wrested away from one Alpha and taken by the winner only through strength and death.'

'And Dougal is hardly capable of that kind of fight anymore,' Abigail said sadly.

'Even if we find a way to Heal him completely it will take too long for him to regain enough power to challenge Iain and win—especially with the others still feeding our Alpha their strength and power,' Alistair said.

'So what does that mean for my daughter? What do you need me to try to convince her of? Stop channelling her power into him? Because if I know my daughter—and I do—she will not cease doing that even if it means her death.'

'It means we need to find a way for the full mating to take place. We need to—'

She heard no more of the conversation because her entire body chose that moment to seize and with a gasp of pain, she lost control of the spell; lost control of her body. And as she crumpled to the floor, a howl, filled with grief and pain like she'd never heard before, split the air.

Before she could even fully register it, the blackness of unconsciousness engulfed her.

20

Dougal snarled at the fly buzzing around on the wall opposite his bed. A wall where Leanna had hung some of his favourite art the other day.

Art he was coming to hate because of the ache he got every time he looked at it. An ache that wasn't about the art itself—although they did remind him painfully of better days—but because of the thought behind the gesture. A thoughtful gesture that indicated just how well Le-le knew him. Just how much she cared for him when she shouldn't. Couldn't.

And it reminded him of just how much he longed for her and couldn't have her.

Reminded him just how badly he was failing at damaging the mating bond so he could break it. He'd been so unpleasant to her, very unpleasant, but it made no difference. In fact, if anything, it was making the bond stronger.

Which simply shouldn't be the case.

The fly flew close to his face and he swatted at it, growling because it wasn't the only thing annoying the fuck out of him!

She was late! She was meant to be here by now. It was time for her shift. So where was she?

Not that he wanted her here. It would be better if she didn't come at all. But given she was supposed to be here and wasn't …

He growled again, his wolf joining in.

Where was she?

She said she had a surprise for him today—something to do with those Gods-damned paintings. And bloody donkey's arsehole that he was, he wanted to know what it was.

But she wasn't here yet when she should be.

She was usually early. As if she couldn't wait to be with him. Which he hated.

And wanted more than his next breath.

Damn him! He had to be over this! Had to stop wanting her. Had to—

His wolf howled at the same time dizziness washed over him and blackness fogged the edges of his vision. It felt like he was about to pass out. Except, it wasn't him on the verge of losing consciousness, it was …

'Le-le!'

The sound of his yell rang around him as he flung the sheets back to hop out of bed.

But of course his lower half didn't respond. There was some buzzing in the muscles and nerves—he'd experienced it over the last few days, particularly when Le-le was around—but no proper movement. Nothing that would help him get up and leave this room to find out what had happened to his mate.

His mate.

No. He couldn't let himself think that. She couldn't be his mate. He wouldn't let it. He—

Pain spiked through his head as he heard yelling from the hallway outside his door. Before he could call out to get someone's attention and find out what was happening, everything went black.

Then flared to bright colours around him.

The rainbow brightness pulled at him. Pulled at him in a way that made him want to scream.

He fought against the sensation, against the pain. Then, just when he thought he could take it no more, he broke free, flying down a long tunnel flaming with the colours of his impossible bond with Leanna, and into a place that was like the moors in a twilight mist.

Except the misty moors at twilight were never this loud.

Running footsteps echoed around him—not crunching like they would across the grass and bracken in the moors but like someone running on floorboards. There was the sound of doors banging and voices shouting. All of it was loud and tumbled around him in confusing, never-fading echoes he could make no true sense of until he heard:

'Leanna! What did you do?'

That name, her name, brought everything into sharp focus. He looked around. He stood—no floated—in the main corridor of the Healer Hall just outside Morghanna's office. A number of people were milling around something on the floor.

No. Not something.

Someone.

Leanna!

She was lying there, limbs like a rag doll splayed across the floor, her head and shoulders at an odd angle against the corner between plaster and floorboard as if she'd slipped down the wall but hadn't made it all the way down.

Her face was so pale it was almost grey. And her eyes ... By the Moon, her eyes!

They were open and swirling with the colours that made up her part of the mating bond mixed with a silver so startling it was pearlescent grey-white.

It was an extraordinary sight and yet somehow incredibly wrong. And not just because that wasn't the normal colour of her eyes or the fact the swirling colour covered her entire eye and not just her irises.

It gave him the chills. The pearlescent glow had a feeling of otherness about it that was unnerving.

But he had no time to be unnerved. He had to help his Le-le. He tore his gaze away from the oddness of her eyes and yelled, 'Help her!'

The others milling around her—Morghanna, Alistair, Abigail—didn't hear him. But the fourth person there did. He turned to look right at Dougal. He was a man Dougal had never seen before—a thin man, over six foot tall judging by the fact he was just a little shorter than Alistair. His eyes and nose and generous mouth reminded him of someone, as did the light golden-red tint in his hair and close-cut beard.

However, he was certain he'd never seen the man before.

'Why are you here?' The man's voice wasn't familiar. But he was looking at Dougal, staring him down.

Morghanna glanced up at the man. 'I am trying to help Leanna, Johnathan.'

'I was not talking to you.'

'Then who are you talking to?'

'An unforeseen complication.' He glanced down at Morghanna. 'Please, do not worry. Just concentrate on helping my daughter.'

His daughter? Leanna was this man's daughter? But ... 'Ye are supposed to be dead.'

'I am,' Johnathan said. He gestured at his body which Dougal suddenly realised was slightly see-through.

'Ye are a ghost?'

'I am. It is interesting that you can see me as such and not the body I am inhabiting.' He frowned and looked down at his daughter. 'Hmm. I wonder ...'

He didn't continue, his face folding in to a deeper frown. Then his gaze snapped back to Dougal. 'You should be dead and yet you are not. Thanks to my daughter.'

Dougal's gaze returned to the witch he loved still sprawled on the floor, unconscious. 'She tried to Heal me.'

'She did more than that.'

'What do ye mean? Are ye talking about the mating bond?'

A sour look crossed the dead warlock's face. 'That and other foolishness.'

Dougal looked back at his love—she was as pale as death and still wasn't responding to anything Morghanna was doing. Abigail hovered next to her with Alistair. 'Why are they simply standing there? Why are they not doing anything?'

'They are. They are giving Morghanna their power.'

'Why is it not working?'

'It is ... slowly. You need to be less impatient. Something I would think you are very practiced in.'

'What do ye mean by that?'

The ghost turned slowly to pin him with a glare. 'If you need to ask, you are not the male I thought you were. And if that is the case, you will never be worthy of her.' He jabbed a ghostly finger towards Leanna.

'I ken that! Do ye not think I ken that I am not worthy of her now? It is why I have been trying to break the bond. For I must die.'

'It is too late for that.' The ghost winced. 'There is no more time.'

'What do ye mean?'

'I—' Johnathan cried out in pain and clutched his head.

'Are ye all right?'

The spirit bent over double. 'I cannot ... hold ... on. It ... is coming ... for me ... if I ... stay.'

'What is coming for ye? I dinna understand.'

Leanna's papa lifted his head and gasped out, 'You need ... to get back ... to your body ... You will be ... no use to her ... if it catches ... you here. You must go. I must ... go.'

'I dinna want to go. Not until I ken she is safe.'

'She will never be safe ... again. Not after ... what she did to ... save you,' Johnathan said as his form flickered and faded.

'What did she do?'

'Something ... remarkable ... Something Goddess-like ... Something you have to save her from.'

'I dinna understand.'

'It comes!' Johnathan yelled. Flinging his arms out towards Dougal, he shouted, 'Return!'

Then Dougal was flying back, flashes of rainbow-coloured light obscuring his vision and then he slammed into something so hard it stole his breath.

He tried to suck oxygen into his lungs but his chest, his entire body, felt like it was simultaneously on fire and being squeezed like an orange for its juice. Blackness started folding in on top of him as pain flooded through him. Just when he thought he could take no more, there was a loud pop and he was back in his body.

A body that was spasming in extreme agony.

He gritted his teeth against it, tried to push back, because he needed to yell. Needed to get someone's attention to find out what was happening to Le-le.

The bond to her flared, pulling at him, making him cry out with the need, the longing, to accept all that it offered. But he couldn't. He couldn't do that to her. He had to free her. Because they all needed her and he was dragging her down with him. He was certain that's what her father had been trying to tell him before he'd been stopped by ... whatever that was.

That he was no longer good enough he knew too well.

He tried to reach for the bond now, to try to pry it loose, but the pain was too strong and the blackness rushed in too fast, smothering him so he couldn't fight.

Unconsciousness beckoned.

But just before it did he heard a voice in the distance, so weak he could barely make out what it was saying.

But he thought it sounded like Le-le. Crying in pain.

Because of him.

Fuck!

He couldn't bear it. He had to let her go.

And then unconsciousness dragged him down, his final thought that he'd failed her.

DOUGAL STARED up at the ceiling, sweat beading his brow as he concentrated on trying to break the bond that Leanna had foolishly made stronger when she should have let him go.

And now she was dying. He could feel it through the bond. Felt it the moment he'd regained consciousness. He'd called out for someone and Alistair had arrived moments later, face tense and drawn, to find out if Dougal needed anything.

Bitter laughter almost choked in his throat at the question. Did he need anything? Yes. He needed to be able to walk, to run, so he could go to his Le-le and stop her from doing what she was doing.

Feeding her power into him as she'd been doing since she'd first Healed him. He'd thought—they'd all thought—that he'd been able to stop her from doing so when she had woken after that second Healing, but it seemed they'd been wrong.

Alistair confirmed his worst fears before he'd run back out, responding to Morghanna calling for him.

Nobody had been back in the hours since then.

And in those hours, he'd done everything he could to try to block Le-le's side of the bond or break his side.

But nothing he did seemed to make an ounce of difference. She was still there, glowing and strong inside him, feeding everything she was into him.

Killing herself in the process.

He fisted his hands at his sides, clenching the furs as if by gaining purchase on them, it would give him leverage to push against her need; a need that was fuelling the bond.

Digging deep inside, he pushed back against that need, ignoring his and his wolf's need for her.

Sweat slid down his face and bare chest, running down his ribs to dampen the furs beneath him. The feel of it, the realness of it, was a stark contrast to the nothing he felt below his hips and made the aching cavity inside him—a wailing emptiness where the hope for his future used to live—throb and grow. He rubbed at the wound with the bitterness that filled him; bitterness over everything that had been stolen from him by an insane Were that he should have taken down years earlier.

Bitterness he leaned into, hoping it would seep into the bond, make it brittle and easier to break.

If only he had a knife or sword, he could put an end to this right now. Le-le would survive his sudden death surely—Morghanna, Abigail and Alistair would hold her to life. And while it would hurt her, it was better than her dying to keep him alive.

But there was nothing close enough to reach with which he could hurt himself, so all he had was his will to destroy what he had always longed to possess.

He dug deeper, pushed harder into all the dark, lonely, bitter thoughts he had and flung them towards the mating bond.

'Dougal! What are you doing? You have to stop!'

21

Dougal started and opened his eyes, surprised to see Morghanna standing beside his bed. He'd been so deep inside his head, that he hadn't heard her or sensed her enter.

'What are ye doing here?' he asked her, the pain inside him making it difficult to think beyond what he must do. 'Ye should be with Le-le.'

'Of course I should be, but I had to stop you from doing what you are doing, you foolish Were.'

'I have to break it. I have to stop her.' He closed his eyes again and continued what he'd been doing.

'Dougal. Stop it!' Morghanna said, placing her hands on his chest. Immediately, the warmth of Healing energy began to filter into his skin.

'Nae!' he shouted, trying to edge sideways, but finding it difficult given how weak he was—he was expending a huge amount of energy in trying to break the mating bond. 'Nae, ye have to let me go! It is fer the good of everyone, especially Le-le.'

'No! It is not. You have to stop.'

'Ye dinna understand. I—'

'No. It is you who does not understand. What you are doing ... it is killing Leanna.'

'Nae. It will set her free. It will stop her from killing herself fer me. Although it would be faster if ye gave me a knife and let me take care of it once and fer all. Not only will it free the pack from the burden of me, but my death will irrevocably break the mating bond. It is the only way to save her.'

Morghanna cursed as she stared him down, her hands still on his chest, feeding more Healer energy into him than before. 'You are as stubborn as any Were I have ever met, but you need to listen to me.' She moved her hands to cup his face so he couldn't look away from her, her expression so fierce it almost stole his breath. 'You are truly an idiot if you think that your death will solve anything.'

'It will solve everything.'

'It will ensure everything is worse. For the pack. For us. For Leanna. Especially for Leanna. Because she will follow you in death. Or worse.'

'What is worse than death?'

'I do not have time to go into that with you right now. But she is fast on the path to becoming something none of us would survive. Unless you accept the bond.'

'I canna do that. I canna tie her to me like that.'

'Then at least stop trying to break the bond or kill yourself for now. She is dying faster because of it. Or ...'

'Or what?'

'Becoming something worse.'

'That makes no sense.'

She made a sound of aggravation. 'The more you push back against her, the more you try to break the bond or kill yourself, the more energy she gives to keep you here, to hold the bond intact.'

'Then stop her.'

'Do you not think we have been trying? We kept her away from you at first hoping that would work. When it did not, we wove shield spells around, then spells to retard the flow of magic, but nothing has worked. She has continued to become weaker and weaker as she gives more and more of her energy and power and soul to you.'

'I dinna want that.'

'We know. But please believe me that you fighting it is only making her give you more even faster than before. In fact, it is likely at this point that she will pass into the veil in the next few hours. Or, as I said, become something far worse.'

Panic gripped his chest and he blurted out, 'So what am I to do? Just lie here and allow her to give everything she is to me until she is dead?'

'No. All that is needed is for you to decide to live. Not just for Leanna, but for yourself. For the life you could build here with her. For her. For yourself. For the pack.'

'I will be of no use to the pack like this.'

'No. You will not if you stubbornly cling to wrong-headed thinking. Your strength is not contained in your lower limbs. It is so much greater than that. Leanna has been trying to make you see that. She is still trying to make you see. And she will die trying to make you see.' Morghanna leaned forward, hands clasped, eyes pleading. 'Do not let how you currently see your value to this pack take her life. See beyond. See yourself as we all see you. As your mate sees you. Live. Accept the bond. And take the new path that forms in front of you with your mate at your side.'

He stared at her for a long moment. Could it be that simple? 'What of Iain?'

'We are working on that.'

'He will return in seven days.'

'We will not let him kill you. He cannot kill you if you are fully mated to Leanna. Pack precedence is in our favour on this.'

'Fer a Were it is. But fer a witch? He will say it is different.'

'You know it is not different. Your behaviour has severely impacted Leanna. We will all make Iain see that was is true for a Were-mate is true for a witch-mate. But it will only work as long as you see reason and do the only thing that can be done right now. Accept your mating to Leanna. Embrace it. Pull her into your heart and soul and show her that she can do the same with you. For when you have done that, she will not need to expend all her energy and power on you. It is the only thing that can save her now. Do you understand?'

'I never wanted to tie her to me when I am like this—of little use to her.'

'She sees your use to her very differently. As do we all. What matters now is that you see it. That you not only do this to save her, but that you do it to save yourself. That you commit fully to this life that the Fates have given you and make the most of it.'

'Why is that important?'

'It is important because she is not only a Healer, she is an empath. She can feel, even in the slightest way, your misery and self-pity as much as she feels you wanting to die. Fight for yourself, for you own life, and she will fight for hers. Can you do that?'

He shrugged. 'I do not ken for certain. But ... I canna be the death of her. I thought I was saving her but ...' He choked on the stab of grief at the thought that he would lose her to death. 'I will give it my all. I promise.'

'Do not just promise. I need your vow.'

He nodded. A Were-vow was forever; an unfixed, unchanging thing that would mean the Were's death if they were to break the vow for anything other than to save their pack or coven members. 'I vow,' he said softly. 'I vow to make the best of things to save Leanna.'

'Good.' Morghanna clasped his hand and shook—a sensation like buzzing insects ran over him as the vow was sealed with magic.

He looked up at her and asked, 'How are we supposed to do this?' His wolf whimpered—he too had no idea how they were supposed to come to terms with living like this. But like him, he was resolved that they would. For if Leanna needed him so much to survive, then he would do everything he could to be worthy of that. Worthy of her.

For Le-le, he must turn weakness into a strength. He had no idea how, but that didn't matter right now. All that mattered was how he was to undo what he'd already done.

'Tell me what to do.'

'First, you need to open yourself to her and accept the mating in full.'

'How can I do that when we canna make love?' He gestured futilely at his lower half. 'I dinna ken how to fully complete the mating without joining with my Le-le in that way.'

'You Were are physical beings, which is why a physical act is what has always completed the mating. But now that is not the case for you and your wolf, so you will have to find another way to complete that part of the rite so the mating feels true to all of you. But that is a problem for later. For now, simply stop fighting her and be open and accept. It will be enough until we manage to move you to her bed.'

'You want me to lie with her in her sick bed?' By the Moon he needed that more than his next breath. Except ... 'Would she not do better alone?'

'Does any mate do better alone?'

'Nae.' A sick mate always got better faster with their mate beside them, touching them, loving them, feeding them energy through the bond with simply their presence. 'Then move me.'

She gave him a small smile. 'Alistair will be here in a moment—he and Abigail are taking Leanna to her bed. Then, when you are lying together, Abigail and I will send Healing energy into you while you concentrate on the bond and fill it with positivity and love. Can you do that?'

He nodded. He might not feel positive yet about his own circumstance, but he could feel positive about Le-le and what she meant to him. He could feel incredibly positive about the need for her to live. Or not turn into what Morghanna seemed so fearful of.

Hopefully that would be enough. For now.

Morghanna spoke true when she'd said he couldn't be false in his want to stay and live his life with Le-le. He would need to change a mindset that had been ingrained in him—in all the Were—through the generations.

But hadn't they already been doing that ever since the Pact brought the covens to them and joined them as one? He'd thought they'd come so far, but they apparently had so much further to go.

Not wanting to wait until he was lying next to his mate, he closed his eyes, concentrating on the Healing warmth Morghanna fed into him, the life and energy of it and her strength—a strength that had only grown stronger since Lachlan's attacks. Then he and his wolf opened their metaphorical arms to Leanna, to their bond, welcoming them finally.

A bolt of light shot through the bond and into them, pulsing through them, filling every fibre and pore of their being with joy and laughter.

Pure Le-le. That's what it was. He could almost hear her shout of triumph in his ears as she flew down the bond and wrapped him up in the essence of her heart and soul.

He cried out, surprise and elation wrapped into one as he truly felt her properly for the first time.

Everything he'd thought about her before was only a drop of water in the largest loch. She was sunshine after a cloudy day. Rain after a drying drought. Fire that renewed, not destroyed. Wind to blow the detritus away so that everything new could spring to life and grow anew.

She was everything and more.

And she was his.

Forever and always.

'Forever and always,' a voice intoned in his mind. Her voice. Still so weak, but echoing down the mating bond and filled with a certainty he now felt stupid for denying.

She had been his mate in truth since that first moment he'd seen her. It had simply taken this catastrophe for them both to know the truth of it.

As that realisation struck, so did another. The physical sex act would not be necessary for either of them to complete the mating—it was already done. Maybe through the sexual dreams he suddenly knew they'd been sharing. Maybe just simply because she was who she was and her acceptance and joy alongside his was all that was needed to make it complete.

He would endeavour though to find a way to bring her the kind of pleasure only two bodies joined together could bring. His cock certainly worked, so that was in his favour. It might be interesting to see, once she was recovered and the issue with Iain resolved, what they could discover together.

'What are you smiling at?' Morghanna asked softly.

He opened his eyes and looked up at her. He wasn't about to tell her exactly what he had just been thinking about, so he said, 'Le-le. She is truly mine.'

'Yes, she is. She always has been.' She closed her eyes and magic prickled against his skin again. When she opened them, her smile was wider, the tension in her body sliding away. 'Abigail says Leanna is already showing signs of recovery.'

He nodded. He didn't need her to tell him that. He could feel it. His mate wasn't conscious yet, but she would be, soon.

The door opened behind her and Alistair entered. 'Cal has rustled up some other Were to bring in a larger bed to Le-le's room, but for now, you will have to make do with sharing her single bed.'

'That is fine by me,' Dougal said. He didn't care how small the bed was as long as he got to share it with his mate.

Morghanna nodded. 'Are you ready?'

For the first time in weeks, Dougal managed a smile. 'Aye.'

22

Dougal's was the first face Leanna saw when she opened her eyes.

A wildly handsome yet scowling face glaring from where he was lying close beside her.

He wasn't pleased.

Or was he in pain?

'You're awake, finally!' His voice was tight with tension.

Definitely in pain. She had no idea what he was doing on the bed beside her—since when had her bed become big enough for her and a large Were to lie side by side with room enough between them?— or indeed how he came to be in her room, but she was glad he was, because at least she could do something about his pain without having to use up precious energy to go anywhere else.

She had to help him. It was a violent song of need in her heart.

She tried to sit upright, hands lifting to touch him, Healing power already warming in her hands.

'Do not even try,' a voice said from behind her.

Hands grasped her shoulders, pulling her gently onto her back, easily pushing her hands down to the bed.

Morghanna sat on the bed beside her. 'You cannot use your powers, Le-le. You are still too drained.'

Too drained from what? Not that it mattered right now because … 'He is in pain.'

Was that croaky, weak voice hers? It had to be. Her lips had moved and her throat had vibrated. And it was now throbbing and sore. She tried to ask again, but pain stabbed through her throat.

'Bloody buggering hell,' Dougal snarled. 'Le-le, please. I am not in pain any longer! Although I will be if ye dinna take care of yerself.'

She wanted to say she had been taking care of herself, but her throat seized and she clutched at her neck as she struggled to swallow.

'Le-le! What is wrong?'

'Dry. Thirsty.'

'By the Moon, Morghanna. Give the lass a drink.'

Morghanna didn't need Dougal's prompting. She was already lifting a cup to Leanna's lips, her other hand slipping under Leanna's head to lift it up so she could drink.

As the cool water slipped through her parched lips and across her dry tongue, she moaned. Water had never tasted so good. Cool and fresh with the hint of minerals and a hit of mint. It wet her dry, sore throat and all she could think of was, *more!*

She grasped the cup, trying to tip it up so she could gulp greedily, but Morghanna pulled it from her grasp easily—why was she so weak?

'Not too much. We do not want you to be ill.'

She wanted to grumble, but Morghanna was right. She should know better than to try to drink too much water all at once. If her weakness and dry mouth and throat was anything to go by, she'd been ill for a few days at least.

Had the weakness that had been plaguing her and getting worse finally got the better of her? It must have if this is where she'd ended up with both Dougal and Morghanna looking at her so worriedly and sternly.

But why could she remember nothing?

'You need water and food, but slowly,' Morghanna said as if to a recalcitrant child.

She suddenly understood why patients grumbled at her when she only allowed them to have small sips and bites. Because she was thirsty. And hungry. And wanted more.

Even so, she nodded her understanding and after a moment of staring at her, Morghanna put the cup back to Leanna's lips. She almost whimpered as she sipped slowly at the water, savouring it in her mouth before letting it slip down her throat.

Too soon Morghanna pulled the cup from her and gently laid her back on the cushioning pillows.

'Should she have some food? She has not eaten fer days. She is all but skin and bone.'

'Not yet,' Morghanna said. 'We need to see how she keeps the water down first.'

Dougal grumbled and then winced.

'Dougal,' Leanna said, trying to turn back over onto her side, to see him, to reach for him, to help in some way.

'Morghanna. She's doing it again!' Swearing from the bed beside her. 'I told ye this was a bad idea. Ye should have moved me back to my own bed when ye felt her waking.'

She frowned at that, rolling her head to the side taking in for the first time that Dougal was not lying on his back or sitting upright in the bed as was his preference, but was lying on his side, hand stretched out as if he had been touching her—or wanting to touch her. Although, given his scowl, she had to be wrong about both. He looked like he'd prefer to be very far away from her right now.

'Le-le, no!' Morghanna placed her hands on either side of Leanna's face, forcing her to look back at their powerful Coven Leader. 'You must stop.'

'Stop what?' She had no idea what they were talking about. Only that she suddenly felt tired and a little dizzy.

'Stop pushing your energy down the bond and into Dougal.'

'I am not giving any energy to the Packbond.'

'Not the Packbond. The mating bond.'

'What?' She went to sit up again. Morghanna moved to push her down but Dougal's hand grasped hers and she stilled. Then, as if time had slowed, she turned to meet his gaze.

The impact of it hit her like it always did, stealing her breath, immobilising her limbs. She flopped back on the bed the few inches she'd managed to rise, and with no conscious thought, rolled to face the male she loved so deeply. So truly.

And saw in his eyes ...

Hope caught in her throat on a gasp.

It couldn't be. Morghanna couldn't truly have meant what she'd said. Not in the way Leanna wanted.

Not in the way she desperately needed.

And yet ...

Whispers of memory fluttered through her mind, unsubstantial and yet, somehow, she knew she'd heard this before. More than once. Memories that illness and exhaustion—and something else?—had taken from her.

But she didn't need those memories to know her hand was clasped in the warm comfort of Dougal's hands. Because this feeling, it wasn't imagined no matter how impossible it was.

For it felt like he wasn't just lying on this big bed beside her, his thumb stroking across the back of her hand in a movement she was sure would be hypnotising if not for the fact his breath fluttered over her face, cooling the sudden heat in her skin, down her neck to the rise of her breasts, keeping her thoroughly grounded in this moment, in this feeling.

It felt like he was ... inside her?

Not in a sexual intercourse way.

No, this was deeper, more intimate—although what could be more deeply intimate than sexual intercourse with Dougal, she couldn't imagine.

But this was. It was a connection that defied all description.

Except for one.

The mating bond.

Morghanna had said it. The flutter of memories suggested she had known it before now.

And despite the fact it seemed like an impossibility, it felt right. It felt true.

It felt everything.

'We are to be mates?' She looked from him to Morghanna then back again.

'Nae,' Dougal said softly. 'We are already mated.'

'What? That is not possible.'

'Oh, but it is possible, Le-le,' Morghanna said, coming to stand on the other side of the bed so Leanna could see her without having to turn away from Dougal. 'Dougal knew you were his mate from the first moment he saw you. The first binds of the mating occurred then and only got stronger the more time you spent together and the closer you got.'

'But I ... Why did you not tell me?' Her gaze darted between them.

'It was not my news to tell,' Morghanna said.

Her gaze landed on Dougal, brow rising.

He looked down at their clasped hands and said, 'My wolf and I ... we did not want to force ye into anything ye were not ready fer. Ye had already had so much forced onto ye ... so many decisions taken from ye. We wanted ye to be sure before ye accepted us—my wolf and I—as yers. We wanted to make certain ye knew us ... truly knew us without the burden of being aware of what being our mate meant to us. So we became yer *Sgàth* and befriended ye. And courted ye.'

'Oh.'

'We were going to tell ye the night we went to place the sleep spell on Lachlan—after ye had seen how strong ye were and would have no doubt that ye could stand foot to foot with our strength and dominance. Ye needed to know as we did, that ye could never be secondary in our relationship or in the eyes of the pack. That they—and ye— would see ye as we always had: that ye are the stronger one in our mating. That I am the one who has to step up to match ye. But then the explosion happened and ...'

Yes. *And.* That 'and' encompassed so much. Including the fact that, if they were already mated, she had to have accepted the mating. But when? How?

Memories spiralled before focusing in on the moment she thought she had lost him. The moment she had reached out and pulled on the strongest most secure link to all the power she needed to pull him back to her. 'Oh,' she said. 'I did it. I accepted the mating bond when I saved you. Even though I did not register what it was at the time, I knew pouring everything I had into it, then using it as a conduit to all the power around me, was the only way I could save you.'

'Aye. I dinna really remember it happening but ...' He moved his head in a gesture towards Morghanna who stood behind him. 'They said that ye accepted it then without knowing truly what ye did. And then you bound yerself to me more tightly when ye did the second Healing. Which is what has been making ye so ill and weak.'

She shook her head. 'That is not possible. Mating bonds are supposed to strengthen those that share them, not make one mate weak.'

Shadows of pain and guilt dulled Dougal's eyes before he tore his gaze from hers. 'That was my fault. Because of my situation, I fought the bond. But I was unaware ye were feeding Healing power through it to keep me here, to help me improve beyond what I should have given my injuries.'

'But ... I have had very little power or energy. I could not have been feeding you anything.'

'You were,' Morghanna said. 'You were constantly feeding him your power from the moment you first brought him back. It was why we were so afraid you would become a wraith. But we thought we had stopped it, or halted it at least. We did not realise just how much you were still giving until you collapsed.'

Morghanna moved to sit on the bed at Dougal's hip, her gaze firmly on Leanna. 'You were going to drain yourself until you died or became a wraith. We could not seem to stop you by any magical means. So we ...' Her gaze went to Dougal and a strange look crossed her face as she said, 'We told Dougal what you were doing, that you had already accepted the bond and that fighting it was hurting you. The moment he understood that and accepted the fact the mating bond was already in place you improved. You improved further the moment we placed you together in this bed and you lay in his arms. The bond strengthened immediately as it always does with physical touch, and as it strengthened, so did you. It took days but now you are finally awake. And your mating bond is strong and healthy and very real.'

'Look inside yerself,' Dougal said softly, his breath brushing over her face, his words drawing her eyes back to him. 'Ye can feel it if ye concentrate, but ye can also see it if ye look inside yerself. Like ye can see the Packbond.'

'Really?'

'So Morghanna says.'

She tore her gaze from his only long enough to see Morghanna nod, but then returned to staring at his beautiful face—it seemed to hurt more when she wasn't looking at him. 'Where do I look for it?'

'Well I—' Morghanna began before cutting herself off. 'When I asked Bridgette, she said she could see hers and Malcolm's in her mind alongside the Packbond—but it is much brighter and stronger so you will not mistake it for stray threads of the bond with the pack.'

'I need to see it.'

Dougal's hands tightened on hers before she could close her eyes, holding her gaze with his even while he turned his head a little towards where Morghanna sat behind him. 'Is that safe?'

She patted his shoulder. 'It is fine. She doesn't need to use any power to see into that part of her mind.'

His gaze met Leanna's as he nodded for her to go ahead.

She closed her eyes even though she didn't want to look away from him, but the need to actually see the mating bond—hers and Dougal's mating bond—was too great right now.

The moment she'd accepted it was real, she realised she could feel it pulsing there with an overwhelming sensation of home, of strength, of belonging.

But right now it wasn't enough to feel it. She had to see it.

She sunk into her mind to where the Packbond sat, looked beyond it and ...

Gasped at the wonder that was their mating bond.

23

The mating bond ... it was so bright. So glorious.

Sun-bright and diamond hard it was twining strands of a green—Dougal—and sunset-coloured strands mixed with a brilliant silver—her—pulsing with life and energy and ... them. Her and Dougal. A living embodiment of the strengths they both held within, of all they could be and have as they grew together. Becoming more.

Becoming everything to each other.

Although how that was possible when he was already her everything, she wasn't sure.

But she felt it, deep in her heart. Deep in her soul. That as the years passed, they would grow—as individuals and as a unit—as their bond grew stronger and there was nothing on this Earth or in the Heavens that could ever break them apart.

She belonged to him and he belonged to her. Forever.

The joy of it filled her up, making the mating bond glow brighter as it flexed and pulsed, another strand weaving into place, making it even stronger.

Dougal made a sound of pleasure that had her opening her eyes to drink him in.

His gaze roved over her, already drinking her in, until finally, it met hers and clung.

'You are my mate,' she whispered as he stared into her eyes. 'You are truly my mate.'

'Aye.'

He sounded proud and happy, but ... there was more than happiness in that word—not all of it good.

Her joy stuttered as his previous words slammed through her mind like an axe through dry wood.

He had fought the mating. She had known that. Had heard it before. And yet, even remembering it, the fact slashed at her heart, at her soul, making her try to pull her hand from his grip.

But he held on. Not painfully so, but tight enough that she would have had to use more energy than she had right now to jerk her hand from his grasp. And Gods-damn her, she ached for his touch—even his unwilling touch fed the need inside her.

Her eyes burned and she bit her lip trying to stop the tears from falling.

'Le-le,' he whispered gently. 'What is it?'

She didn't want to say it. Didn't want the words to be spoken for fear that the answer would bring the final death-blow—for living, tied to a mate who did not want to be mated to you, it was like dying. But no matter she didn't want to utter them, the words were torn from her anyway. 'You do not wish to be my mate.'

So much pain and grief in those few words—it shattered her to say them, shattered her to hear them. She closed her eyes and screwed them shut so as not to see in his face, in his eyes, the answer she did not want to see, as if shutting out all sight of him could stop him from speaking the answer she did not want to hear.

His grip tightened, his breath speeding up—she fancied she could hear his heart beating faster too and some noise that sounded like a wolf howling.

'Hells, Le-le. Nae. Nae. How can ye think that?'

Without opening her eyes she took a steadying breath and forced the answer. 'Because you do not sound happy in the way Were are when they find their mates. Because you said ... you said ...' She swallowed hard, not wanting to repeat his words, hoping he would know what she was trying to say without her having to say it. But the words tore out of her anyway. 'You said you were not aware I had accepted it. That you fought it when you realised I had. Which means, you did not want this.'

The wolf howling sounded louder—it made her heart hurt to hear it.

Dougal's grip tightened on hers and he took her hand in both of his, thumbs sweeping over the sensitive skin at her wrist.

'Oh, nae, Le-le. Nae,' Dougal said, his voice strained, pained, his accent stronger as it always got when his emotions were heightened. 'I dinna wish fer ye to ... that's no' what I feel at all. Finding ye, feeling ye are my mate ... I long fer it more than I have ever longed fer anything. It has been excruciating to have to wait all these months since I first saw ye across the square in front of the Pack Hall when Morghanna welcomed ye and the others that came with ye and ye were bonded to the pack.'

Leanna's chin trembled and tears leaked out of the corners of her squeezed-shut eyes—damn them. She sucked in a shuddering breath and said, 'But that was ... before. You said you came to feel differently after I failed ...' She gulped in a breath that hurt like knives were being thrust into her chest, slashed down her throat. 'After I failed to ... to Heal you.'

'Hells, nae! Nae ... Le-le I ... Please open yer eyes. Look at me. Ye will ken I speak the truth when I say being mated to ye is the single most wonderful event of my life.'

She shook her head, squeezing her eyes tighter while holding on to his hand as if she feared he'd let her go. 'I know what I heard.'

'Ye canna be hearing the right thing if ye do.'

She nodded. 'I not only heard it. I saw it. On your face. In your eyes. There is a part of you that is not happy.'

'I ... that is ... That has nought to do with how I feel about ye. How much I truly wish to be mated with ye. To call ye mine and to have the world ken it as so.'

'But you said—'

'I ken what I said, but that is only because I am ... like this. Unable to be a true male. A true mate. A true Were.'

Her eyes flared open as she gripped his hand tighter. 'No. Do not think that! You are still alive and whole and everything I could ever want or need.'

He moved his shoulders, wiggling forward a little but then stopped with a grunt of annoyance. Breaking her gaze, he glared down at his body. 'Ye see! This is nae whole. I dinna want ye to be saddled with this. Weighed down with the burden of caring fer me when I am like this. Useless. Nothing. I canna even wiggle across the bed to ye and take ye in my arms and kiss ye and show ye how much ye mean to me!'

She gasped again, heat arrowing down to her womanhood even though she was still upset that he did not want the mating. 'You want to kiss me?'

His head jerked back up, his gaze colliding with hers once more. 'Out of all I just said, that is what ye heard? Do ye not ken what it means? Ye are so strong, so powerful. Ye deserve a mate who, if not equal to ye, is close. Who can support ye in a way that will only make ye stronger. Mated to me ye will forever be my carer. Forever be held back by my needs, the things required simply to get me through a day. I dinna want that fer ye. Ever.'

'I am a Healer. Caring for people is what I do.'

'But ye shouldna have to care fer me!'

Enlightenment was the key to happiness. Her papa always said that. She hadn't truly understood until right now. She began to smile.

This wasn't about her. It wasn't about not wanting her. About thinking she wasn't good enough or strong enough to be with a Were as powerful as him.

It was about his Were pride. His male pride. He truly thought her strong and powerful and wanted to be a match to that. But not only that, he needed to be able to care for her. To stand between her and anyone who might harm her in any way. To be her knight in shining armour and swoop in and save her from whatever she needed saving from—given her stubborn nature, would most likely be from herself. To make her dinner when she'd had a tough day or bring her flowers from the woods or heather from the moors just to brighten her day and let her know he was thinking of her always. To paint all the things she loved, all the things they did together and wanted a record of. In her mind flashed images of all the myriad things he had wanted to be able to do for and with her in the years to come. Things he saw as being impossible now.

But not only that, he had wanted to help her to believe about herself what he believed—that she was a supernova of bright light and strength in the dark.

Truthfully, knowing that was how he saw her was all she would ever need from him. She did not need him to become her knight in shining armour because he already was that in so many ways.

Just the fact of him being alive and in her life gave her strength she never thought to have. His friendship and gentle encouragement had opened her up to things she would never have opened up to. It had made her see that she could reach for more; be more.

And the fact that they were mated—no matter how incredible that seemed—meant that the Fates saw her as strong and powerful enough to match her to him.

She did believe that. Wanted to show how much she believed it. It was what made her say again, smiling knowingly, 'You want to kiss me.'

He swallowed, hard, eyes flaring with heat before they dipped to her lips. 'More than I want my next breath.'

'Good,' she said. Then using what little strength she had, she leaned forward and pressed her lips to his.

Such a simple thing and yet, the explosion of light and laughter, of love and pleasure—so much pleasure—that raced through her was extraordinary. Bigger, more profound than anything she'd ever experienced.

Except, she had experienced this before.

She gasped a little before the kiss sank deeper and pulled back, her gaze roving over his face.

'What?' he asked.

'Those dreams. They were real.'

'Ye remember the dreams?'

'Yes. How could I not? We made love, experienced all that joy and pleasure together.' She laughed, joyfully. 'I thought they were my dreams alone, that I was delusional to think that I could ever share anything like that with you.' Which was why she'd blocked out every time she'd heard they were mated. Her papa had been right about that being why she couldn't remember. She'd done that to herself because it just seemed impossible. But she remembered being in the astral with her papa, remembered hearing Morghanna, Alistair and Abigail talk about it, remembered what she'd overheard standing outside the door. All of it had been real.

Including the dreams with Dougal.

She laughed joyfully. 'They were real. Those dreams ... we shared them together.'

'Aye. Through the bond. It allowed us to share what needed to be shared even though neither of us was capable because we were both weak.' He frowned and broke their gaze.

'What? What is it, my love?'

His eyes flared and his gaze came back up to meet hers again. 'My love? I never imagined hearing that would sound so good.'

'Well, you don't need to imagine it because I will never stop saying it to you. My love.'

He smiled, but she could still feel the frown in him—the worry that was stopping him from returning her words of love. She knew he felt them. Could feel that emotion pulsing so hard through their bond, it was a wonder she hadn't felt it until now.

Probably had something to do with him fighting it because he thought he was saving her from pain. 'What worries you? And do not pretend you are not worried. I can feel it.' She pressed her fist against her chest over her heart. 'Like it is my own worry. I just cannot gather what the worry is.'

His frown deepened and he paled a little, his gaze dropping from hers once again.

She pulled her hand from his to cup his face, stroking her thumbs across his lips. 'What is it? You know you cannot keep it from me forever. Now we are mated I will get it out of you.'

'I ...' His gaze went past her.

'Are you worried that Morghanna will hear?'

'Nae. She left when you kissed me.'

Oh. Her eyes lifted to look behind him and sure enough, Morghanna was not there. Nor did she feel the other witch's presence in the room at all. 'I must have missed that.'

He was smiling at her when she looked back. 'I would have missed it too when you started kissing me except she touched my mind when she got up and told me she would be back later.'

'Really?' Leanna lifted one brow, her lip curling up on one side in what she hoped was a sexy, enticing smile. 'So we have time for some kissing and ... more than kissing.'

His face blanched and he looked away again.

She frowned as she moved her hands over his face, urging him to look back at her. 'What is it, my love? Now you have me truly worried.'

He hissed out a breath and then looked at her as she'd been urging him to do. Although, the grief and pain in his eyes made her wish he hadn't. 'I am worried ye will not wish to be mated to me.'

'What? That is ... No.' She shook her head. 'That could never be how I feel. Ever.'

'Not even when you discover I willna be able to give ye the "more" ye just spoke of?'

'What are you talking about?'

'The ... love making. What we shared in the dream ... That may never be something we can share in reality.'

'What are you talking about?' she repeated.

'Maybe ye dinna ken ... despite our dreams, ye are an innocent ... but my injury ... it may not allow me to ... give ye pleasure.'

Her gaze dropped down his body to the rather impressive bulge in his breeches. Without thinking, she reached out to cup it, enjoying the hiss that escaped his lips and the way the bulge flexed against her hand. 'I do not think that is something you need to worry about.'

A smile flickered on his lips, but the frown remained furrowing his brow. 'I … that is a recent thing. I started truly feeling in that part of me while ye were performing your damnable treatment on me. It became quite embarrassing, I can tell ye.'

'You should not have hidden it from me. If I had known …'

He breached the small gap between them—she had moved closer to him without realising it—and kissed her, stealing her breath. His tongue ran along her lower lip, making her tremble and glad she was lying down and not standing because she would have collapsed to the floor.

But then he pulled back a little, separating them, stopping the delicious sensation, making her moan in protest.

THAT MOAN, her reaction, it made Dougal smile. But he had to explain, had to make her understand what it meant to be mated to him, what they might never have, because, while he couldn't break the bond—and no longer wished to now that it was healthy and alive inside him—he needed her to know. Needed there only to be truth between them so they could build the best future they could together despite his limitations.

She had to be prepared.

So, despite the fact it hurt to even think it, let alone admit it, he said, 'I may be able to get an erection and, if ye sit on top of me, we will be able to make love that way. But I will never be able to … give ye the other things I gave ye in the dreams.'

She blushed—actually blushed—and by the Moon he loved her a little more because of it. 'Oh.'

'And I will never be able to taste ye in that way; will never be able to drive ye pleasure in more than that position. I will never—'

She put her fingers over his mouth. 'I am certain we can find all sorts of ways to give each other pleasure.' Her eyes danced and she blushed at the same time—she was magnificent, truly. He was the luckiest Were alive to be mated to her.

'But I—'

'I will research all the ways we can make love. It will not be staid and the same as you worry about.'

'Research?' Only she would think of turning to books for answers to this particular problem. His love for her grew and he said, 'Mayhap I can help ye with that.'

'It would be all the more pleasurable if you did.'

But then the laughter left him. There was still one more thing to bring up; one more thing she was not thinking of as he had over and over again in the days since they'd laid him down beside her to share her bed.

'You are still worried,' she said, her fingers caressing his furrowed brow.

'Aye.'

'What about?'

His wolf whined inside him as he said, 'I may never be able to give ye a *bairn*.'

She stared at him for so long, he worried the shock of his admission had been too much. Then finally, she lifted her hands to cup his face once more, moving a little closer. She kissed him softly before pulling back enough to look into his eyes, hers so full of love he felt drowned in the sensation. 'We shall not borrow trouble. If we are not to have children, then so be it. There are many children out there in need of a good home. We have enough love in us to open our hearts and home to them and adopt them as our own.' She tipped her head to the side. 'Maybe we can do that even if we can have our own children. If you are fine with that idea.'

He searched her eyes, seeing only her heart and her faith and trust there. She was remarkable. More remarkable than he ever deserved. He would spend his life trying to find ways to make certain he could be worthy of being by her side.

Filling the bond with all the love and trust he felt for her, he said, 'I would like that very much.' He leaned forward and kissed her, passionately, deeply. 'I would like that very much, *mo ghrádh*.'

'*Mo ghrádh?*' she asked against his lips.

'My love. Most definitely, my love.'

24

They kissed and kissed and kissed. Soft, lip only kisses to begin with, then opening to each other to explore with teeth and tongue.

By the Moon he loved the wild sun-warmed berries and lavender taste of her. And the way she cupped his face, her fingers digging into his hair a little then shifting back to hold his face again, made him heat and tingle in places he had feared not so long ago were dead. The heavy gathering sensation in his balls wasn't quite as full and intense as it had always been, but it was a start. And his cock was definitely feeling it, thickening and growing, flexing and twitching every time she licked into his mouth and made that moaning-groan when he sucked on her tongue.

He would have kissed his Le-le forever and done so much more except ...

Except he was still unable to move his legs and she was exhausted. He didn't need the bond to tell him that—he could feel it in the way she trembled against him. The trembling had been of the sexual excitement kind at first but was quickly becoming the uncoordinated twitching of muscles that needed rest and recuperation.

Despite the fact both he and his wolf wanted to kiss her for longer

—for eternity, there was never going to be enough of kissing his Le-le for them—he began to pull back.

She made a sound of protest and clung to his face with shaking hands.

He lifted his hands to hers, meaning to grasp them gently and move them away, suggest she close her eyes and get some sleep while he held her—something that had become his favourite thing to do since Alistair had carried him to her bed days ago.

He meant to be strong. Meant to take care of her in the only way he could.

But she chose that moment to play dirty, sweeping her tongue along his bottom lip before sucking it into her mouth in just the way that drove him wild.

His wolf hummed inside his chest, its fur brushing the inside of his skin, caressing the bond.

She gasped and pulled back a little. 'What was that?'

'My wolf,' he said roughly, his wolf clear in his voice.

'But I could feel something, not just hear him. It was like fur caressing my skin.'

He pulled back a little, delight filling him. 'The fact ye can feel him so strongly this early in our mating is extraordinary. Not that I should be surprised. Ye heard him often before I thought the mating bond strong enough to allow ye to do so.' He brushed her silken hair back from her face, enjoying the texture of her soft skin under his fingertips. 'My wolf ... he desperately wants ye to see him, to feel his love.'

'I do.' She touched his face, fingers tracing over his brow and down to the corner of his eyes. 'I can see him. Your eyes. They've changed.'

'Yes.' His wolf was pushing close to the surface, desperate to be seen in some way, any way, given he still could not truly show himself.

Morghanna, Abigail and the McVale Pack Healers still said that allowing the change would cause more damage at this point, not help fix it.

So they could not shift. He ached for it, especially now they were mated because being petted by their mate would help settle the wolf's need to escape, to run—a need that would now never be sated.

'*Shh,*' he said to it inside his mind. '*Soon. I promise.*'

'Are you speaking to him?' she asked, her head tipped to the side, expression awed, curious.

'Ye can hear that?'

'Not hear it. More that I am aware of it. It is like ... like whispers in the sunlight of the bond.'

'Aye, I like that. So does he.' His wolf was making a contented rumbling sound deep in his chest.

His Le-le smiled, trailing her trembling fingers down to his chest to press her palm over where his wolf's fur was brushing against the inside of his skin like it was about to burst out. The sensation of Le-le's warm palm against his chest and her breath caressing his chin and throat as she looked down at her hand was making his cock twitch and thicken.

'I can feel him in your chest over your heart the strongest.'

'Hmm.' It was all he could manage with her voice all low and breathy like that and her fingers flexing into his chest a little—in and out, in and out—the press of her nails making his head spin.

'Dougal?'

'Hmm?'

'This is so lovely. Knowing I can feel and hear your wolf. I cannot wait to see him and hug him and stroke him for real.'

Her hand pressed harder now, digging in to his pectorals in a way that made his breath catch and his wolf hum his pleasure more loudly.

'Do you not like that?' She pulled her hand away.

'What? Why do you think that?'

'Your wolf made a strange noise and so did you.'

'Oh. That was a good strange noise.' He grabbed her hand and put it back where it had been. 'Believe me. We both very much loved what ye were doing.'

'Oh. Good.' She blushed again, her head dipping a little but not before he saw her pleased smile.

'Aye. It is so good.'

She continued the action and then stretched up to kiss his neck. He moaned.

'Another good noise?'

'Oh, aye. The best. Let me show ye.'

He moved his hands up to her face, tipping her chin to give him access to her throat and then placed his lips on her soft, scented skin.

By the Moon she smelled good. He opened up his mouth and licked. Mmm. She tasted as good as she smelled. He licked again.

She made a moaning noise in her throat.

'A good noise?' he asked between kisses and licks.

'Yes,' she said breathlessly.

He worked his way to her pulse point then opened his mouth and suckled. She made a choked sound and her fingers clenched on his chest, hard. 'Good?'

'Mmmhmm,' was all she managed.

He nipped then licked then suckled again.

'Ohhh!' Her body jerked and twitched in his arms, the heavy scent of her arousal rising around them.

He thought he'd loved her scent before but this ... it was even better than he'd dreamed. His balls tightened, the heavy sensation increasing. There was a pooling sensation in his gut and a prickling in his upper arse cheeks and cock which said good things were going on.

'Dougal?'

'Hmm?'

'My turn?'

He lifted his head and found she'd raised up on her elbow and was staring down at him, her breath coming in pants, a look in her eyes he'd never seen before—hungry and needy and curious all at the same time.

'Do ye not want more?'

'Oh yes! But I wish to try the same on you. I need to. I cannot explain it.'

'I can. It is what happens when ye desire another. Ye want to give as well as take. But I think mayhap we should stop. Ye are exhausted.' Her trembling had worsened. He gripped her hands and tried to pull back.

'No, no. Please, Dougal. Please.' Her eyes met his and clung. 'I need this. Please. Let me do this. Then I will rest.'

He wanted to say no, to be the sensible one, to care for her in this way—one of the few ways he could. But that look in her eyes and the throb of need in her voice ... He lifted his head, giving her access to his neck.

He thought she'd be tentative but she bent to her task with anything but tentativeness. She kissed under his chin with an open, hot, hungry mouth, licking and nipping and sucking in a way that said she'd taken note exactly of what he'd done to her—and then embellished it. She swirled her tongue on his neck, dragged her teeth over his whiskered skin.

She made her way down his neck to the pulse point, slowly, so slowly. His wolf was almost purring in pleasure and so was he.

Then she latched on to his pulse and licked, nipped, then licked the sting away before suckling where his pulse was banging in his throat so hard she had to feel it deep in her mouth.

'Taste so good,' she said on a gasped in breath before she started the madness over again. 'I never ...' lick, 'want ...' nip, 'to ...' lick, 'stop.' Suck!

Oh fuck!

His voice echoed around them—had he shouted that out loud?— the shock of hearing it pulling him out of himself for a second. Long enough to realise she was trembling badly now.

He opened his eyes—he hadn't realised he'd closed them, giving over completely to the sensation of her so close, of what she was doing to him while doing so little. Goddess knew what she'd do to him with a little knowledge and some practice.

But that brought his thoughts careening back to the realisation that she could do so much to and for him, but he wouldn't be able to do the same for her. He wasn't even doing his best to care for her now.

He pulled back, managing to grasp her seeking hands again—one was still on his chest but the other had made its way down to his cock and was starting to do things that stole his breath and made stars explode in his eyes.

'Le-le,' he gasped. 'Ye have to stop.'

Her hands twisted weakly against his and she made a mewling sound of protest. He took both her hands in one of his, the other grasping her chin gently, lifting her face up.

She was so pale, despite the flush of passion colouring her high cheekbones. And her eyes were bright—too bright. Her breath came in shallow pants and now she'd stopped kissing his neck, her teeth began to chatter.

'*Mo ghrádh*, ye are beyond exhausted. I am a terrible mate fer not stopping ye before now.'

'No. No. I wanted to do this. I wanted to share this with you,' she managed between pants. 'I need to be close to you.'

'Ye are.' He pulled her closer. 'In more than flesh.' He put their hands between their chests. 'I feel ye through the bond, the same as ye feel me.'

She nodded.

'Ye canna get closer than what we already share.'

'But ... we have not made love. To fully strengthen ... the bond. I know we must do this ... to be truly bonded in the eyes ... of the pack. To fully secure against ... Iain.'

She could barely string a few words together between panted breaths and she was trembling both from exhaustion and worry he realised now. Because while they were bonded in every way, mated in heart and mind and soul, she knew the pack expected a physical union to solidify the bond. She was afraid that without it, an Alpha like Iain could use it as an excuse to say the bond wasn't complete and demand his death.

And yet ... 'We are fully bonded. If I didna already ken it, Cal confirmed he and everyone here could feel it through the Packbond.' He gripped her hand tighter against his chest. 'The bond is so strong already. It is unbreakable. Nobody could doubt it is fully formed. Not even Iain.'

She stared up at him. 'Are you certain?'

'I am. Can ye no feel it?'

'I ... I do not know what it is supposed to feel like. But it does feel strong. And sure.'

'So very sure.'

Her gaze searched his as she asked, 'Was it the dreams?'

'Aye. I think mayhap yer magic made it so we met in a way our bond accepted it as if we met on the physical plane.' He smiled down at her as he brushed his thumbs over her cheeks. 'Those dreams were quite spectacular. I believe that in our hearts, in our souls, we have experienced all the intimacy a mated pair shares in the physical. That it secured the strength of our bond the moment I stopped being such an idiot.'

'But ...' She frowned—he loved the way her brow furrowed when she was thinking something through. 'Those dreams ... they were ... before you accepted ... the bond. How could ... they ... secure the ... bond now?'

He shrugged. 'Mayhap it is because the only acceptance that truly mattered was yours at that point. The bond came from me, you accepted it, we shared those dreams and ... it fully stabilised and strengthened.'

He pressed a kiss to her frown and pulled back, loving the way she flushed again just from such a simple thing. 'All that matters is that it is so strong and secure. So ye dinna need to worry over this right now. We can take our time. Be physically able to do right by each other when we share this intimacy with our bodies and not just in our dreams. Right now though, ye need to rest. Ye are exhausted. Ye can barely take a breath and ye are trembling badly—and not entirely from what we were just doing.'

'I—'

'Please, Le-le. Let me hold ye in my arms while we sleep. We both need to rest. I need to rest.'

It was playing dirty to say the last, because he'd done nothing but rest and was not tired at all right now, but he could see that it was the only way she'd agree without arguing and trying to push herself more.

Her eyes flared wide and her fingers flexed against his. 'Oh, of course,' she said. 'You need ... to sleep.'

'Yes. So settle here,' he said pulling her body next to his and somehow managing to flop onto his back.

She rested her head on his chest, her hand pressed over his heart.

'Sleep now,' he whispered against her crown as she yawned against him. 'I am here.'

He tightened his arm around her and then began to stroke her hair. She mumbled something that sounded like, 'Mm nice,' then her body went soft against him as she fell into sleep.

Despite being vividly awake, he closed his eyes and breathed in this moment, holding it in his mind so it would be there forever more.

Because she was his. Forever.

He was never letting her go.

Leanna pulled away from Dougal's kiss with a groan. His fingers tightened on her hip and in her hair. 'Dougal,' she said breathily. 'If we do not cease now, I will not be able to stop myself from climbing on top of you and riding until this unbearable ache ceases.'

'Sounds good to me,' he whispered against her throat.

She groaned as his lips found that place just under her ear he had discovered yesterday that made her toes curl and shot sparks through her entire body. She wanted more than she could say for him to continue what he was doing. She longed to give in to the sensations rampaging through her. Longed to not only ride her mate to completion, but she wanted to try all the things they'd done in the dream—including sucking his impressive manhood.

They had almost got to that point yesterday morn, after she'd woken from sleeping through the night, when Morghanna had burst in to stop them. Apparently she and Abigail had read more of the grimoire while she'd been unconscious and it indicated that this kind of physical activity could undo the progress they'd made with Dougal's muscles and nerves.

Which was the last thing she wanted. Particularly with Iain's imminent arrival in the next day or so.

They also had concerns about her—they wanted to ensure she wouldn't give too much of herself during such an activity and deplete herself of power and energy once more.

She was less worried about that than she was about hurting Dougal.

So she pulled away—it took every last ounce of control that she had to force her body to obey—and somehow managed to avoid Dougal's clever hands as she rolled away and out of bed.

'So eager to leave me already?'

His tone was teasing but she turned with a jerk and said, 'Never. I never wish to leave you.'

His grin slipped. 'Sorry. I shouldna make light of such things.' He held out his hand.

She took it, gripping tight. 'I ... I know you meant nothing by it. But I never want you to doubt how much I want and need you, to be with you, always.'

'I do. And I want ye to ken the same. My wolf and I chose ye. Ye are our everything.' His eyes glistened with the depth of his emotion. 'I just wish I could truly show ye.'

'I know. I feel the same. But you know what Morghanna and Abigail said. That we need to be careful not to physically consummate our mating yet. Not until they are certain—'

'Of me,' he broke in. 'That my body can handle the ... activity.'

'And that I do not channel all my power through the bond to you once more. Do not forget that part.'

A grin flashed on his face. 'So fierce,' he said softly, proudly.

'So truthful,' she said, unable to stop her lips from curving in a return grin.

He nodded. 'Aye, that ye are. So it is on the both of us.'

'I will agree to that. As long as you agree not to take more blame than is yours to take—for this or anything else.'

He chuckled. 'A big ask for a stubborn Were. But for ye, I will try.'

She shook her head at him slowly then sighed dramatically. 'That will do ... for now.'

He laughed out loud and she couldn't help the smile of joy and pride that filled her from head to toe. That she could make him laugh like that despite the pain she knew he was still in—physically and mentally—was a gift she never thought would be hers to give and accept.

She let herself bask in it for a moment longer than she should but then had to break away because Morghanna would be there shortly and she was in nothing but her shift.

She went to the wash basin to give herself a quick wipe over with the soft cloth and the water from the wash pitcher that had been left last night. She'd stayed in bed too long to put the kettle over the fire to warm her wash water, but that didn't matter—having as much time with Dougal was what truly mattered to her. Icy wash water was something she would happily bear for an extra ten minutes in his arms each morning.

As she wiped herself with the cold cloth her mind wandered to thoughts of bathing in the hot springs in the hills above the forest. But she did not want to leave Dougal that long or be so far from him right now. Not because the bond was too new and might break—it was as strong as the strongest element on this Earth. Stronger. No distance or time could break it now. Not even death because it went deeper than their souls.

No. It was simply because she could not bear to be away from him.

But still, as the cold water brought goosebumps to her skin and made her shiver, she could not help but long for the bliss of the warm water of the springs, its minerals working in to her muscles as its bubbles fizzed and caressed her skin. It had been months since she had gone there for a proper bathe and to cleanse her aura and relax her muscles within the special properties of the water.

Oh!

Her eyes flared wide and the cloth dropped from her hand with a splash in the cold water of the basin.

The hot springs!

There had been an entry in one of the grimoires about the efficacy of hot, mineralised spring water on certain muscular injuries among other things. She hadn't paid it any heed at the time because there was no way they could have moved Dougal that far when moving him from the forest where he'd been injured and to the Healer Hall had almost killed him. It had been a miracle enough when he'd become strong enough to be moved from his bed to his chair or to the treatment table—but even that had tired him more than it should. So taking him to the hot springs was something that hadn't entered her mind.

But now ... it could be managed. It would help so much with his pain and was likely to help with his treatments. For with the muscles and ligaments soothed by the hot waters before and after his therapy, he would not be left in such pain and his recovery would be faster.

But how to get him there?

They could carry him through the forest and up the hill to the springs each day—he was so much stronger now the bond was in play. If she sent strength through the bond to him, and used her power to cushion him, then he would be able to manage the move there and back easily. Maybe even multiple times a day.

Except ... even when Iain comes back with the Hunters and his lieutenants, the pack and coven would still be pushed to their limits. The explosion had caused deaths and injuries and given they were still getting back on their feet after Lachlan and the Darkness's original attack, too many people were already covering jobs that used to be done by so many more. Alistair had already been covering so many roles to help fill the gaps and was helping her with her research and with Dougal—she really couldn't expect him to carry the injured Were to the springs a few times a day, especially given he was already taking Abigail up there.

He'd need help. And there truly was no one to spare given how many they'd lost. Maybe they could manage it a few times a week and even then, only once a day, but to work as it should, the water therapy was something he needed every morning and every afternoon.

Her shoulders sagged.

Although ... she tipped her head to the side as the thought fully manifested.

Yes.

There was an abandoned woodsman's cabin in the clearing just beyond the spring that Morghanna's sister, Morrigan, had discovered not long after they'd come here. Before she'd run from the pack and abandoned her sister and their coven, Morrigan had often gone there to escape her responsibilities to the pack, taking advantage of the fact it smelled terrible to the Were—being full of animal droppings and the carcasses of things that had gone there to die, they gave it a wide birth. Having gone there once with Morghanna when she was looking for Morrigan after she'd run away, Leanna didn't blame them. She had no idea how Morrigan had stood the stench of animal refuse and rotting things.

It would need a thorough cleaning and some patching up given the roof had rotted through on one corner. But if her memory served her well, it had a solid stone hearth and chimney—that would need a clean out given some bird or wild animal had probably made it home —so it could be kept warm when the weather turned cold and food could be cooked there. It had a small stable and a cool room to keep provisions in so they would be safe from both weather and animals. There was also a stream with fresh water from higher in the mountains that ran nearby. It even had two rooms—the main larger one they could use to live in and set up to be a therapy space for Dougal, and the smaller one could be a herbal stillroom where she could create her medicinals and tonics for the pack and coven and continue her research of the grimoires. Dougal could even help in her research of lost Healing arts by reading through the Pack Diaries—he could become a Pack Librarian, helping to store and carry the knowledge of the pack and coven.

It was perfect. They could move up there—her and Dougal—and Alistair could come up every day because he already went up there every morning with Morghanna, carrying Abigail so she could benefit from the properties of the water on her aching, swollen joints.

While Morghanna was tending to Abigail, he could carry Dougal to the springs and help with Dougal's therapy and then he could stay with her for their magic lessons with Abigail. Abigail could conduct some of her daily lessons there as all of the coven came up at varying times to take advantage of bathing in the warm waters. She could even have a second soak when Dougal was having his. Alistair wouldn't need to stay for that as there would be plenty of coven members strong enough to help carry Dougal back to the cabin and then help Abigail back down to the village.

It could work!

She had to make it work.

All she needed to do was bring the idea to Morghanna and Abigail and talk them in to agreeing with her. She was certain she could rope some of the able Were and coven youngsters in to helping clean up and prepare the cabin. It would save the Were from building them an entirely new cabin as they did for the newly mated.

It was an ideal solution on so many levels.

'Leanna!'

She jerked as Dougal's voice came through to her and she turned to him. 'Why are you shouting my name?'

'Because ye did not hear me the first ten times I spoke yer name.'

'I … sorry. I did not hear you.'

'Obviously,' he said, crossing his arms, the worried look on his face replaced by one of loving amusement. 'Where did ye go? Or are ye plotting again?'

'I do not plot.'

'Ah, so plotting it is. Fer good or evil?'

Her lips quirked. 'Silly Were. I only ever plot for good.'

'So ye do agree ye plot?'

'I would not call it plotting.'

'Ye just did!'

'I used your word so you would understand.'

He chuckled, his amusement a warm caress. 'So what is it I need to understand?'

'I have a thought about getting you to the hot springs to do your therapy up there.'

'Ooh, I would like a proper bathe. Being wiped over by a cloth and cooling water while lying in bed does not fully get rid of the sickbed stench.'

'I thought you would approve of the idea. Although there are some things I need to discuss with Morghanna, Abigail and some pack members first, so I will say no more until I am certain my plan can come to fruition.'

'I love that about ye, my mate.'

'What?'

'How there are times when ye throw yerself at something with nary a thought fer the consequences and other times ye like to make certain all the moving parts are in full working order before ye show the whole of yer creation to the world. Being with ye is like being in the eye of a storm one minute then tossed around on enormous storm-driven waves the next.'

'My mother used to say that was my worst quality. She spent her life trying to make me more like her.'

'What? Plodding and boring? Nae.' Dougal shook his head. 'Never listen to the ghost of yer mam again. She was wrong to try to make ye other than the glory of what ye are.'

'And what am I?'

'Chaos and serenity combined in one beautifully perfect package.' His smile was like a benediction as he looked at her with such love. 'Life with ye will never be dull, that is fer certain. And I wouldna wish it any other way, *mo ghrádh*.'

She blushed but didn't look away as she once would have done. 'I love you,' she said, her voice husky with emotion.

'Aye. I know,' he said, his smile smug and his voice full of wolf-growliness.

She chuckled as she turned back to pick up the cloth and finish her bathing. It took longer than it should because her hands were trembling with emotion and the need to go to him and kiss him and lose herself in him. But she couldn't do that for multiple reasons.

It didn't help though that she could feel her mate's eyes on her the entire time she bathed and dressed. It took far longer than it should to pull on her thick stockings—the weather was getting cooler as autumn marched towards winter—and skirts. Her hands trembled and her fingers felt like all thumbs as the weight and pull of Dougal's hungry gaze, not to mention his need, made itself known through the bond. She dropped and fumbled things too many times.

But finally she reached for her tunic to pull it on over her shift.

'Are ye sure ye are well enough to return to work today?'

She jerked at Dougal's voice as she pulled the tunic on. Reaching for the leather belt she used to pull the tunic in at her waist and to hang things from for ease of carrying her tools during the day, she turned and smiled—she couldn't stop herself from smiling whenever she looked at her mate. 'I am more than well enough, my beloved mate.'

Oh, how incredible that word sounded, but even more astonishing that it was true. And she knew it was, deep in her bones, in her heart, her soul. It had only been a few days since she'd awoken to find out she was mated, but it felt like her entire life had been lived in those two days. And she felt better than she'd ever felt before. She only wished she'd remembered the fact earlier.

'Are ye certain, *mo ghrádh*? It has been but a few days since ye awoke.'

She walked the few paces back to the bed, leaned over, cupped his face and gave in to the need to kiss him once more—although she pulled away quickly before she could lose herself to the taste and scent of him. She took in a too shaky breath and said, 'I feel better than I did before the explosion.'

Which she knew Dougal knew. He could feel all of her through the bond just as she felt all of him. And while he obviously wasn't feeling as good as she was—he wouldn't until he was back to what he had been before—he was far and away better than he had been. It was one of the reasons she was feeling better—because she didn't have to hold onto him to keep him with her. He wouldn't leave her now. At least not by his choice.

She tipped her head as she pulled back from him, gauging his expression and everything she could feel through the bond.

He was worried.

But his worry, his question wasn't truly about if she was well enough to go back to her duties.

It was because Iain was due back in the next few days.

And with his return came burdens both of them had been ignoring these last few days of bliss spent talking and kissing and cuddling and sleeping in each other's arms as they strengthened their bond and she recovered.

His return meant reality would come crashing back in because either Iain would be the Alpha he should always have been, or he would continue to disappoint them all.

If it was the latter, they would need to figure out a way ahead. Because living under the thumb of a leader like she thought Iain would always be, was no longer something she could do.

Dougal had to feel that inside her.

Just as she could feel how lost he was over what to do about it now he thought he could no longer be Alpha.

She hoped Morghanna and Abigail would find the solution in the old grimoires they were still pouring through to how he could challenge Iain and win. Because if they didn't, she wasn't certain how they were all going to deal with the consequences.

26

'I will not allow Iain to ruin this for us,' Leanna said in response to what she could feel coming from her mate. 'And I will not allow you to let him ruin it either.' She kneeled on the bed and grabbed his face, staring deeply into his eyes, trying to push all of her intent, her belief, her need, into him. 'It does not matter what he thinks or says. We are mated and there is nothing he can do about it. He will just have to accept it and move on.'

'So fierce. I wouldna want to be our Alpha facing up against ye fer the world.' His lips quirked. 'Although, I would love to see the stand-off.'

She kissed him fast and hard before letting go of him and hopping off the bed before she gave in to the ravaging hunger inside her.

A hunger for him.

She crossed her arms to stop herself from reaching for him and said, 'The stand-off I wish to see is between you and him. *You* should be our Alpha.'

Dougal broke her gaze for the first time and looked away. 'That horse has bolted and is lost in the forest forever.'

His voice—so achingly sad and intractable. It made her want to cry for all the things he thought he'd lost.

It was now her job to ensure he came to believe that was not true. Just as she believed. As Morghanna and Alistair, Cal and Abigail and many others in the pack believed too.

But first she had to get him away from the negative vibes that surrounded him and was coming at him from some of his packmates.

And key to that were her plans to get him into the cabin near the springs where they could make it a home of their own like a normal mated pair—the added bonus being that with the help of the curative properties of the hot springs, he would improve exponentially. Which of course would help him to come around to her way of thinking about him.

Which was that *he* was the answer to so many of Pack MacCrae's problems.

But it was pointless arguing with him about how he should be Alpha until after she'd proven to him he could get some function in his legs. He would just lift that stubborn chin, and there would be no talking to him. She knew him well enough to know that.

So she simply sighed and said, 'We will agree to disagree on that.' She smoothed down her tunic and then her hair. 'Do I look presentable? And healthy? I want Morghanna to allow me beyond the bounds of the Healer Hall so I can see some patients.'

'Kiss me.'

'No.'

'Kiss me,' he said with that roguish grin she had missed so much this last month.

Even though it was so enticing she took a step back and said, 'No.'

His grin widened as he said, 'So harsh.'

She raised her finger. 'You are enticing me to things I should not give in to.'

'Who said we shouldna give in to it?'

She tutted. 'You know exactly. We just spoke of this before I dragged myself away from you.'

'What if I promise not to entice ye too much?'

'That would be impossible. You entice me by simply being.'

He laughed, low and sexy. 'As ye do to me.'

'Then it would be an altogether bad idea to kiss you right now.'

'Not even a goodbye kiss to tide me over until ye return?'

Her lips twitched. 'Not even that. Besides, I am only going over there,' she pointed at her work bench, 'to make more of the tisane that has been doing you so much good until Morghanna arrives and hopefully allows me to do a little of what I was born to do. So there is no need to kiss you goodbye.'

'Ye are a cruel mate, my Le-le.'

'Given I will hold strong—even against you—when it is what is best for both of us, I think that makes me the best of mates.'

'It does indeed. I am a very lucky Were.'

She tipped her head to the side. 'You know your accent becomes thicker when you are in a playful mood—or a sexy one.'

'Does it, lassie? Do ye like it?'

'You know I do.'

'Then it is very lucky I am a Highland Were, isna it?'

She narrowed her eyes at him. 'Now you are doing it on purpose.'

'Am I, *mo ghrádh*?'

'You are. And if you think that is going to make me change my mind about kissing you, you have another think coming.'

'I am hoping to have a different type of coming, my beautiful lass.'

She screwed her face up to stop from laughing. 'I am going to work now.'

'Without kissing yer lonely, bedridden mate?'

'Agh!' She threw up her hands. 'You are impossible.'

'Ye love it.'

The smile she'd been trying to stop from showing—Goddess knew he didn't need encouragement in this—slipped through, becoming all mushy as she crossed back to the bed and leaned over to kiss him.

Then screamed as he grabbed her and pulled her to him so she collapsed against his chest. 'Dougal!' she protested weekly, fire shooting through her veins at the feel of his solid warmth beneath her.

'I love it when ye say my name, *mo ghrádh*.'

She melted into him—she couldn't help it when he called her that. 'You are my weakness.'

'And your strength.'

She pulled back enough to look down at him, surprised by the hint of question in his voice. Did he not know exactly how strong he made her feel? 'You make me feel stronger than I ever knew possible. Do you not know that?'

His arms tightened around her as he looked deeply, earnestly, into her eyes. 'I ken ye are my strength. Ye gave me the will to live, to carry on. With ye by my side I now am hopeful I will find purpose.'

'You will. We will.' She wished she could tell him all her plans now but the impulse to kiss those perfectly contoured lips that were so close was just too great. She leaned in and with a hum of pleasure in her throat, pressed her lips to his.

His hands splayed on her back then one brushed upwards, fingers spearing into her hair, to angle her head so he could take control of the kiss.

He opened his mouth to her, licking along the seams of her lips—which made her open to him on a gasp. He took advantage by running his tongue tip across the inside of her bottom lip before sucking it into his mouth.

She moaned and trembled, then trembled some more when his wolf made a satisfied rumbling sound. It came at her through the bond and in a vibration through his chest followed by the sensation of fur brushing against her skin.

She gasped again and pulled back far enough to say, 'I can feel your wolf's fur against me again.'

'He wants ye to see him so badly. But seeing as I canna shift, he wants to show his love fer ye. A love that is from here to eternity.'

'Dougal—the things you say.' Then she was kissing him again, her hands digging into his hair, her legs dropping either side of his hips so she could feel the hardness of his erection pressing against the part of her that was throbbing and hot and wet—so wet. She pushed down into it as her tongue tangled with his. He groaned into her mouth.

All she could think of was getting closer and feeling more. She reached for the buckle of the belt she'd just put on. She needed to lose the clothes and he needed to lose his and—

'*Mon Dieu!* That is a visual I did not need to start my morning with.'

The voice had her jerking back and twisting to the side to see Alistair and Morghanna standing in the doorway.

'Dougal! Leanna! I thought we told you it was not safe yet to—' Her hand waved, indicating what had been happening—or very nearly was about to happen—between her and her mate.

She looked back at Dougal, expecting to see as much chagrin and horror on his face as she was certain was on hers. Instead he simply looked proud—and adorably tousled. Then his gaze met hers and he began to chuckle.

The chuckle turned into a laugh and then she was laughing with her mate and it was glorious.

'What the ever loving fuck is going on here?'

The new voice stole her laughter—and Dougal's—as they both turned to stare at the male pushing past Morghanna and Alistair.

'Iain,' Dougal said, his wolf making a growling sound inside. 'Ye werena due back for another day or so.'

'Dougal,' Iain snarled as he prowled towards them across the room. 'Why the fuck are ye still alive?'

Leanna stared at the male who had just pushed his way into her room, shock at his sudden appearance holding her still—as it apparently had to Morghanna and Alistair who were still standing just inside the door, mouths slightly open.

He was back early. She thought she had another day or two. This was too soon.

Dougal was the only one not held frozen by shock because he moved swiftly—more swiftly than she thought him capable—pulled Leanna across him so that he was between her and the irate Alpha stalking across the room towards them. His wolf was growling loudly —at least to her it was loud—and her mate's need to protect was a scream inside her.

Iain's words—they were like a torch to kindling, firing the rage inside her that she had suppressed for her entire life.

Standing up for herself by tapping into that rage had never been something she'd thought to do—in the secret heart of her, her mother's opinion that she wasn't worth the effort had shaped her need to always hide away, even before she'd been scarred.

But for her mate …

She rolled away from behind him, leapt off the bed and rounded it in seconds to stand between her love and Iain.

'Le-le—nae!' Dougal said, reaching for her, but she moved just beyond his reach.

His cry seemed to mobilise Alistair and Morghanna. Morghanna's hands raised as she crossed the room—maybe to warn Leanna against any foolish reactions, or to prepare a shielding spell of some kind—Alistair at her side more obviously pulling on his magic.

The need for that raised the temperature on her rage even further.

Glaring at Iain she dug into her power and twisted it in a way she never had before. Magic flowed down her arms, sparking in her fingertips—visible orange and silver sparks that had Iain coming up short.

'Ye dare threaten yer Alpha?' Iain barked, looking more flabbergasted than angry.

She could practically hear him thinking, *That little mouse is standing up to me?*

Morghanna moved to stand in front of Iain, hands up, Alistair at her side. 'Now, Iain. There is no need for aggression.'

'Stand aside, witch. This is nought yer business.'

'Do not talk to your Coven Leader like that,' Alistair said, bristling in a way Leanna had never seen before.

'Get out of my way, Frenchie. This is none o' yer business either.'

He stepped around them so quickly, he left them staring at the space he'd been in while he moved towards Leanna and Dougal.

'Iain!' Dougal said from behind her. 'Dinna hurt her!'

'He will not hurt me! For I will not allow him close enough to do so.'

'More threats?' Iain roared as he came to an uncertain stop. His fear—despite his anger and the claws that had sliced through his fingertips—was a bitter frisson in the air.

It hurt her, that fear, because despite her anger with him right now, she was a Healer at heart and she never wished anyone any harm—physical or emotional. 'I am not threatening you,' she said through clenched teeth, trying hard not to cry in the wake of his fear.

'Ye would use magic agin me.' He made a jabbing motion towards the sparks on her fingertips. 'Tha' is a threat.'

'I am not using magic against you,' she said as evenly as she could. 'I am shielding my mate from you.' And so saying, she released the magic and created a shield that surrounded her and Dougal in a glowing orange and silver half sphere.

'Leanna!' Dougal said, his voice full of fear for her. 'What are ye doing?'

'Protecting you.'

'Dinna do that. Not if ye risk hurting yerself. Ye are barely recovered.'

'I am fully recovered. Besides, this is not hurting me.' She flexed her fingers, pushing the arc of the shield out, enjoying the orange and silver sparkles that glittered over its surface—it was quite pretty. She hadn't expected that when she'd created it.

Despite how pretty it was, Iain skittered back from it, his fear no longer masked by anger and bluster. 'What in the blazing hells is that?'

'It is a shield,' Morghanna said as she came up beside him.

'An incredibly strong one if my senses are correct.' Alistair walked past his lover, reaching out to the shield.

'Dinna touch it, yer mad Frenchie,' Iain shouted, taking a few more steps away from it.

'There is nothing to fear,' Alistair said, his hand playing along the surface of the shield, a smile blooming on his face as his gaze met Leanna's. 'Clever.'

Morghanna joined her mate, placing her hand beside his. Her eyes widened and then snapped to Leanna. 'Clever indeed. How are you doing that?'

'Doing what?' Iain spat.

'Come and feel this,' Alistair said.

'Ye are fetched in the head if ye think I will touch live magic. Or let it touch me.'

'Ye let it touch ye all the time through the Pact,' Dougal said.

'Not to mention the Healing magic you have let touch you often,' Alistair said, his smile widening further as he ran his hand over the sparkling shield.

'That is completely different,' he said, jabbing his finger towards the shield again.

'No, it is not,' Morghanna said, smiling blissfully as she ran both hands over the shield's surface.

'I would never mean harm to anyone,' Leanna said, her tone full of the hurt she'd been trying to push down since sensing Iain's fear. 'Not on purpose.'

'Maybe not,' Iain said, his eyes wary as he backed up another. 'But that does no' look friendly. And it pushed out at me. Aggressive.'

'It was not aggressive,' Leanna said at the same time Alistair snorted and Dougal said, 'Le-le is not aggressive.'

She loved the way Dougal backed her like that—like he always had—but she couldn't bask in that right now. And while she didn't want to take down her shield until she was certain Iain would listen to them and stop demanding her mate's death, she hated that anyone would view it as a threat. So she backed herself and said, 'I am not aggressive. And neither is my shield. It is purely meant to protect. It would never hurt you or anyone.'

'Of course it would not,' Morghanna said. She looked over her shoulder at where Iain stood glaring at all of them like they were insane. 'It is made from Healing magic. I am not certain how, but it is. And ahh,' she sighed joyfully. 'It is marvellous.'

'*Certainement*, you need to come and feel this,' Alistair said. 'It is filled with such goodness and hope and love.' His eyes went to Leanna again. 'It is you. Pure you.'

'I am no' going anywhere near that thing.'

'Well I am not taking it down until you stop threatening my mate,' Leanna declared.

Iain's eyes snapped to Leanna. 'Mate? Who is yer mate?'

'I am,' Dougal said as she turned to take his hand in hers. 'Which, if ye had taken a moment to think about the pack and link to the Packbond while ye were away, ye would have felt our mating come into being.'

Iain's nostrils flared. 'Tell me ye didna tie this Healer lass to ye when ye are nought but a useless cri—'

'Do not say that word!' Leanna yelled. And as she did her power lashed out, slipping from her control and whipping out towards Iain.

'Leanna!' three voices yelled at once, Morghanna and Alistair turning, raising their hands, their magic beginning to buzz in reaction to hers.

But it was too late because the tentacle of magic had already latched around the Alpha, pulling him forward and into the outside of the shield, catching him like a bug in amber.

27

'Leanna—what are you doing?'

Leanna stared at Iain who seemed to be caught in a bubble of her shield that had formed over him on the surface of it. 'I did not mean to,' she replied to Morghanna's question, her voice a horrified whisper. She didn't know what had happened—or what was happening now.

'Well, stop doing it!'

'I am unsure what it is I am doing.'

'He doesna look harmed by it,' Dougal said as he peered around Leanna. 'He looks peaceful.'

'Dougal is right,' Alistair said, moving around the arc to where he could see Iain's face. 'He is smiling.'

'That is more than a smile,' Dougal said, his awe over what she had done coming loud and clear through the bond. 'I have never seen him so blissful. Or peaceful. He is usually such a crabbity bawbag if truth be told.' Dougal chuckled, Alistair joining him.

'This is not funny!' Morghanna said.

'I think it is a little bit funny,' Alistair said.

Leanna started shaking her head. 'No. No. This is not funny at all.'

'Le-le?' Dougal said, his laughter dying. She could feel his frustration at not being able to reach for her, to turn her around so he could see what was going on with her, to pull her into his arms to comfort her. But he was stuck in the bed, unable to do any of what he thought was his responsibility as her mate.

His frustration made her want to cry, to go to him, to comfort him as he comforted her, but she couldn't do any of that. She could barely move—it was like she was stuck in the shield with Iain and couldn't move until she'd figured out how to fix this.

The problem was, she might have been responsible for this, but she had no idea what it was or how to undo it.

'I am fine,' she said in answer to Dougal—although she sounded far from fine. Because she was fairly certain she might have just made things so much worse for herself and Dougal.

Attacking the Alpha—and Iain would undoubtedly think of this as an attack after she'd figured out how to release him—was considered a challenge to the Alpha for the Alpha's position.

And no unsuccessful challenger walked away from their challenge alive. An Alpha couldn't allow it. And as far as she was aware, Morghanna and Abigail hadn't yet found out how the ancient Were made a successful challenge without using killing strength and violence.

And despite the fact he had been unwilling to challenge Iain for the good of the pack even when he had use of his legs, Dougal would want to fight the challenge in her place.

What had she done?

More importantly, what was she going to do? How could she fix this so Iain didn't take it as a challenge?

Was that even important when she still didn't know how to undo what she'd done?

By the Goddess this was bad. For the longer he was stuck there like that, the more likely one of his lieutenants would arrive to check on him—she was lucky one hadn't accompanied him into the room in the first place because they would have instantly attacked her for doing this to their Alpha. How long would she have before someone did come in? By the look of him he'd just arrived back in the village—

hadn't even stopped to wash or change his clothes before barging in here. Those Were who went with him would have headed straight to their families and loved ones, and to wash and change and have a meal so as to be ready when Iain called the Council—he would need to report what had happened on their hunt and to hear reports of the goings on here while he'd been gone.

She might have an hour or more before anyone came looking for him. But not much longer.

'Please talk to me, *mo ghrádh*. What are ye thinking?'

'Yes, Leanna. Talk to us,' Morghanna said.

'Let us help,' Alistair finished.

'But you cannot truly help,' she said softly, her gaze fixed firmly on Iain as her mind worked the problem.

'Why do ye think that, *mo ghrádh*?'

'Because I did this, so I am the one who has to fix it.' She flexed her fingers—they were stiff from clenching them at her sides. Maybe picking up the challenge she'd thrown down was the only option before her. Maybe with her magic she could—

A rustling sound followed by a grunt of frustration behind her— like Dougal had tried to move closer somehow—interrupted her thoughts and she turned to see her mate pulling himself across the bed to be closer to her.

'Please, *mo ghrádh*,' he said, voice full of suppressed frustration, fear and not a little pain. 'Please believe me when I say that thinking about challenging Iain isna canny. It is the worst choice ye can make.'

She wasn't even surprised he knew what she was thinking. 'I do not want to make that choice,' she said emphatically. 'I am no Alpha. That is your future.'

'Nae.' A thumping sound on the mattress as if he'd hit the bed. 'Not anymore. No Were would accept an Alpha who couldna' stand fer them in a fight.'

'There are other ways to fight,' she said, fingers curling into trembling fists. 'It is difficult to fathom how idiotic and backward the Were have allowed themselves to become.'

A sucked in breath behind her that she felt down to her toes, but now she'd started speaking, she couldn't stop the words from spilling out as she returned her attention to Iain. 'In the ancient Pack Diaries that Morghanna and Abigail and the Pack Librarian have been reading through, they discovered that your people in times past were extraordinary. They were a vibrant, creative, educated, cultured and intelligent people ruled by rationality and a tightly held loyalty to each other no matter what.

'This idea that you can only become Alpha by being the biggest and strongest and most violent is not who your people were. Alphas were the Were who were best able to lead—and they included females and males more suited to diplomacy than violence and fighting. They stood strong for their packs not through strength of body but strength of mind.'

'That … it canna be true.'

'It is,' Morghanna said. 'It is clear from what we have read so far that the best Alphas gained their positions because they proved themselves using reason and intelligence to solve issues between packs. They found solutions to every problem that came their way without using up their people in useless warring and power plays centred on violence. They held large swathes of land and led their packs to a kind of prosperity that we only dream of now. And not a single one of them gained their Alphaship through violence and death.'

'If this is in the diaries, why do we know nothing of them?'

'We found these ones only after your injury,' Alistair answered. 'The explosion opened a crack in a landslide that had covered caves your people must have used thousands of years ago by the looks of some of the paintings on the walls. Some of your cubs discovered the opening to these caves on a run. There were old chests in there, covered in dust with no enchantments on them to protect them from the elements. The diaries inside are very damaged, the parchment, or scraped bark they were written on, is tattered and torn, the ink so faded that without our spells they would be unreadable. Some are even written in ancient languages that need special spellwork to enable us to translate them.'

'We would not have begun to read them,' Morghanna said, 'if not for what we ourselves are finding in the ancient grimoires that Bridgette and Malcolm are sending to us. So much has been forgotten and lost to us ... we thought maybe it was the same for the packs. It has been a treasure trove of information about who the Were had been before the Darkness. They clearly show us who your people should be; who they would be if not for the Darkness and the way it infected the Were.'

'I canna believe it,' Dougal said, his voice fogged with wonder and confusion and an agony of hope.

'You do believe it,' Leanna said. 'I know you do.'

'As so many others do too,' Morghanna continued. 'It is what many of you wish to become again. And, like Le-le does, I know you are one of them. I know it was your influence that made Iain—despite his reticence and hesitancy to fully embrace our coven—agree to bond the MacCraes to the Pact, as Iain McVale and so many other Alphas and their packs had already done. They all wanted a better future for the Were—just as we want a better future for our covens. Your people ... they want more than the violence that has pushed them to retreat further and further from the world and their place in it. And so do you. You have believed this for years—have spent too much energy on Iain trying to get him to see it too.' She shrugged, shaking her head. 'Maybe once he could. But for too long now he has not been able to see beyond the loss of his mate and the insanity of his son and his needs. Which is why he cannot be our Alpha any longer. Why he *must* be challenged.'

'Exactly,' Leanna said firmly. 'If you believe there is another way, others will follow. Especially if the Pack Librarian and strong Were like Cal back you up.'

'Ye are all moon-touched if ye think I could win in a challenge now against Iain or anyone else fer that matter. Yer idea of a better future is a beautiful one—and aye, it is one I want—but that future is not yet here. Many of our people are still too lost in the way things have been done under the violent influence of the Darkness. They willna' accept a crippled Alpha, no matter how they may respect my other strengths.'

'You are right,' Alistair said solemnly.

'Ali! How can you say so?' Morghanna turned to stare at her love as he came to stand beside her.

'I say it because it is true for many of the Were.' He held up his hand to stop either of them protesting, his gaze going to Dougal on the bed in the middle of the protective shield. 'But Le-le is also right. There are many Were who are ready for such a change and would throw their support to you.'

'Not enough to win right now,' Dougal said evenly. 'Especially given so many strong Were are still feeding Iain their strength.'

'You are right—for now. But soon, if we all play our cards right, I think there will be enough.'

'I dinna wish to split the pack in half.'

'None of us want that,' Morghanna said. 'But challenging Iain for the Alphaship is something that will have to occur if he keeps going the way he is. His selfishness and mania about saving his son will destroy Pack MacCrae more certainly than any challenge that comes forth now. And while we will be able to hold him off from demanding your death for now by convincing him of your mating and its significance, I think we all know that he will not stop trying to be rid of you. Because you are a threat. The more the pack sees your strengths as you overcome and find ways around your inability to walk, the more the threat rises. Particularly as you are no longer letting him drain you of your strength. Your strength will grow exponentially now you are free of him, especially now you are mated. So, you have to face the fact that challenging him might be the only way out of this for both of you if nothing else. And if we can find out how it used to be done when physical strength wasn't the only thing prized in an Alpha, then you will succeed.'

'I canna put the pack at danger of the kind of fight that would ensue if I were to do that now just to save myself.'

'Not even to save your mate?' Alistair asked.

Dougal winced but Leanna cut off his response by saying, 'I would not ask such a thing from him.'

'Nor would he do it going by that torn look on his face. Pack comes first for both of you,' Morghanna said solemnly, touching the shield again. 'It is why you both would be such an amazing Alpha pair—one that could create a stronger and more prosperous pack and coven than has been seen in centuries. A pack that would inspire others and would last through the ages.'

Leanna could feel the intensity of her sincerity through her mentor's touch on the shield—it was somehow a part of Leanna as much as it was a construct outside of her. And as that intensity and sincerity settled into her, she began to see an image in her mind; a vision of an older Dougal with an older version of her sitting by her mate's side.

They were holding hands and smiling at each other, then she stood, still holding his hand, to gesture expansively to the table she could suddenly see in front of them. A round table like in the myths of an ancient king and his magical egalitarian kingdom where he ruled alongside his knights and advisers; for at that table nobody had more power or say than anyone else, no matter their position in the hierarchy. Her papa had told her about this king and his magical Camelot when she was but a child and even then she could see how he longed for such a thing to be a part of their world.

And here was a similar round table in this vision where she and Dougal sat.

As she stood at the table in the vision, other figures joined them —Were and coven and humans and a few other creatures besides that she did not recognise. It was a true representation of races and species of the area—she had no idea how she knew this, but she did —and they were all greeting each other as friends.

And the way they came to Dougal and her, the respect and love in their eyes ... it stole her breath and snapped her back from the vision all at once.

'No!' she cried, reaching out with her hands as if she could grab a hold of it and pull it back. But it was gone and she had no idea how to recall it or even what made her see it in the first place.

'Anna ... Le-le,' Alistair whispered. 'What did you see?'

28

Leanna blinked, her eyes slowly refocusing on Morghanna who wore a blissful, knowing smile. 'You saw that too?'

Morghanna nodded, her smile widening. 'Of course.' She stared at her hand on the surface of the shield. 'My touching this must have allowed you to see my vision of the future too.'

'So it was true?'

'It was a possible future—a likely future if our intent counts for anything.'

Hope filling with sunshine, she turned to Dougal. 'Oh, my love. It was so beautiful.'

'I felt it,' he said. 'Very strongly through you; the wonder, the happiness, the hope. And I fancy I saw something ... us and a ... round table?'

'Yes! Yes, you saw some of it. One of the most important parts. The parts that show what I have told you about the past could come true for us in the future.'

'What do ye mean?'

'In the future, you are a respected and beloved Alpha.'

His eyes brightened. 'Do ye mean to say I could walk again?'

She frowned. 'I ... I did not see you stand. You did not have to. Everyone came to you.'

The brightness fell from his eyes. 'So I dinna get use of my legs back.'

She jerked, his words shocking her enough that she was finally able to move. She crossed to him as she said, 'No. Do not presume that. I did not see enough.' She took his face in her hands, forcing him to look up at her. 'But do you not see? It does not matter if you can walk or not. You become the Alpha, that much was clear.'

'Was it?' he asked, gesturing to Morghanna. 'Morghanna made it clear no vision of the future is ever certain. We may choose badly today and send ourselves on a different path.'

Tears pricked her eyes as realisation hit. 'You mean whatever I choose now could change that future.'

'Nae. I said we and I meant *we*.' He gestured to encompass all of them. 'Even what Iain decides or how we respond to him could change things. Ye are not alone, Le-le. Never again will ye be alone.'

She swallowed hard. 'You will not be either. Not now we are mated.'

He nodded. 'Aye. We are together, forever. All that needs be done now is to put our heads together and figure out how to unstick Iain from that amber shield. And if he doesna try and kill us immediately, ye can bring me those diaries and we can research the answers together. After that we will see what we can do to make that glorious future ye saw come true.'

Iain had started making drunken noises that sounded like a mix of confusion and pleasure. Was he waking up? Or was it more like a stupor and he was now coming out of it?

'Oh Goddess, is he waking up?' Le-le said, shifting her weight.

Morghanna moved closer to Iain to study him. 'No. I do not think so. I do think, however, he is having the most wonderful dream.' He made a deep sound of pleasure. 'Perhaps too wonderful,' she said, shuddering and making a 'yuck!' face.

Alistair laughed and Dougal chuckled but Le-le just stood there, wringing her hands as she stared at Iain.

. . .

DOUGAL COULD FEEL his mate's consternation over what she had done, and it sobered him somewhat. She was right to be worried—although not about her ability to undo what she had done, more what Iain would remember of it when she did. And how he would react. Or even how quickly he would recover.

'So, what can ye do to get Iain out of there?' He was thankful his voice was calm and even despite the inner turmoil that simmered so close to the surface. He needed to remain calm because his mate needed him to be.

Because she was horrified at what she'd done—as a Healer her entire life was dedicated to helping people, not frightening the bejesus out of them. Not to mention the core of who she was—who she would always be regardless of what her power manifestation was —was kind and gentle and caring. It hurt her to think she might have hurt or frightened Iain.

She didn't show any of that deep-seated worry, fear and pain though—so fucking strong, his mate. She simply frowned deeply, her expression showing that she was seriously trying to figure it all out.

'I am not certain,' she said, her voice only a little shaky. 'As I said I do not even know how I did whatever this is.'

'What were you thinking when it happened?' Morghanna asked her, running her fingers around the edge of the part of the shield surrounding the Alpha.

Leanna tore her gaze from Dougal's—a pity because everything felt so much better when she was looking at him.

He could even believe in the future vision she'd seen through Morghanna's sight—even if he was fated never to walk again, he could believe they would be part of a ruling body like that of the fabled Camelot. When he looked deeply into her eyes he could believe that anything was possible.

Except him being able to walk again or become Alpha.

His wolf growled.

Le-le stopped saying what she'd just started saying, her head whipping around to him, her gaze clashing with his. 'What's wrong with our wolf?'

Our wolf. He couldn't help but smile, his wolf's growl turning into a pleased hum because of those two words.

'Dougal?'

He realised he was smiling stupidly at her, and gave himself a mental slap, answering her question. 'There is nought wrong. He is cranky with me.'

'What for?'

'Nothing that matters right now.' He nodded his head towards Iain. 'We all need to concentrate on the problem at hand. What were ye saying to Morghanna?'

Le-le didn't look completely happy with his answer, but she nodded briefly and turned her attention back to Iain.

'I was saying that I was angry that Iain was threatening you, and hurt that he would think I was threatening him by protecting you. I wished him to calm down and listen.'

'Ah, *mai oui*,' Alistair said. 'I think you have just put a finger on it.'

'On what?' Le-le asked as Dougal nodded, Alistair's point making complete sense.

'That you wished it, so it happened,' Morghanna said slowly.

'What happened?' Le-le's confusion sang loud and clear through the bond. Dougal pulled her down to sit on the bed beside him so he could wrap his arms around her, giving her the comfort and support she so clearly needed. And as he did, he said, 'Ye wanted him to calm down and so ye made it happen with yer powers.'

'What? I ... That is not how Healing magic works,' she said, twisting out of his arms to look at him.

'I would have said that was true before today,' Morghanna said, her gaze flicking to Alistair who looked equally confused but nodded anyway. 'I would also have said it was impossible for a Healer to do what you did, Le-le, when you brought Dougal back and then mended him far more than a Healer should have been able to. I think maybe we are just starting to see how different your powers are.'

Le-le's breathing had become fast and shallow as Morghanna

spoke, and now her chest was heaving as she tried to respond. 'I do not want to be different. I do not want to do things like this.' She jabbed a trembling hand towards Iain. 'I could be hurting him right now.'

'Ye would never harm anyone.'

'Not purposefully,' she said in a ragged voice. 'But I did not do this purposefully. It just … it just happened. Oh Goddess, I could hurt you without ever meaning to.' She skittered further away from him. 'I am out of control.' Her entire body trembled with her distress.

He needed to take her in his arms once more; hold her until she calmed down enough to listen to reason. But he couldn't do that, damn it, because he couldn't get to her like he should be able to if he was any kind of useful mate.

The shield about them started to pulse and shake.

'What is going on?' Alistair asked as Morghanna yelped and jerked her hands back from the shield.

'I hurt you,' Le-le cried. 'I hurt you.'

'No, you did not,' Morghanna said. 'I was overwhelmed by the flood of emotion pulsing through the shield. You simply need to calm down and control it.'

'I cannot. I told you, I cannot control what I am doing.'

'Le-le. *Mo ghrádh*,' Dougal said. 'Please calm down. Just come over to me and I will help you.'

'I cannot.' She was looking around wildly, eyes wide and frightened—so frightened. Of herself. 'I cannot. I cannot.'

Suddenly, strands whipped out from the shield and wrapped around Le-le's arms, writhing up them to wrap around her body. She cried out and Dougal roared, his wolf growling and howling inside him, lunging to get out and help their mate.

'Dougal. Help her.'

'I canna. I canna get to her.'

'You are her mate. Physically is not the only way you can help her!'

Le-le began to shudder and shake and make a noise that sounded like a banshee wail. He didn't know what he could do if he couldn't take her in his arms to calm her. Touch was essential to the Were and was the only way one of them could truly be calmed when upset.

And she was well beyond upset.

She was …

Not a Were!

She was a witch. A witch who had spent much of her life living very much in her mind. A witch who had spent much of her life shying away from touch. She touched people to Heal them, but even then, touch wasn't necessary. Mostly she held her hands a few fingers' width away from the person she was helping.

So, maybe Morghanna was right. He didn't have to physically touch her to get through to her.

There was the bond and the power threaded through it that he knew was not usual. Power that felt and smelled like her and yet wasn't her Healing power.

It was what the images he'd seen had come through, and the reason he could sometimes hear her thoughts so clearly in the last few days.

It was a conduit to her mind.

And he could use it now to reach her.

Closing his eyes, he dove deep inside himself to where the bond was. The silver thread was there alongside and winding around all the others, pulsing erratically.

There was no time to think about what he should do. He just reached out and grabbed the silver thread with everything in him and …

Fell into a wide maelstrom of panic and distress.

And in the middle of that, Le-le stood, arms flung out wide, threads of magic flying from her fingertips to attach to an invisible arc above them, moving out like some crazed spider web, surrounding them, cutting them off from everything.

Cutting her off from life.

'Le-le! Nae!' he cried, racing across the space separating them and grabbed her up into his arms, not caring about the magic flying everywhere out of her.

Her eyes snapped open and she looked up at him, face filled with terror. 'Dougal! What are you doing here?'

'I came fer ye. To help ye.'

'No. No. You have to go. I could hurt you.'

'Ye will only hurt me if ye hurt yerself. And that I willna allow.'

'No. No. You have to leave. You might die if you stay here with me.'

'Then I die. Fer I will never leave ye. Not now. Not in the future. Not even in death. Ye have to ken, *mo ghrádh*, that ye are never alone. I am always here fer ye no matter what.'

'But ... but ... I am dangerous.'

He smiled at her. 'I dinna think ye are, *mo ghrádh*. Ye just need to cease panicking about what ye think ye canna control and concentrate on what ye can.'

'And what is that?' she asked, blinking rapidly as tears filled her eyes.

'Healing. Take all that power and Heal with it.'

'But I do not know how,' she wailed, looking at the power that was still shooting out of her in threads that snaked around them and flew out to that invisible arc wall—but much slower than before. 'The power is so different.'

'It may be different, but it is yers. It belongs to ye. It is part of ye. And ye are good and kind and beautiful of heart and soul. Yer power is not bad—it is simply wild and bigger than ye are used to. It simply needs a firm hand and guidance. And ye can do that.'

'I am not certain I can,' she said, but she didn't sound so panicked.

'I am,' he said, wrapping his arms tighter around her. 'Use my certainty until it is yers. Take control. Tell that power who is in control. And above all, tell it that I willna let it or aught else hide ye away.' He glanced up at the spider web of the power that was slowly filling in to create a solid arc wall around them. 'Ye are too special to ever hide away. The world needs yer beauty and power too much. I need it too much. So dinna hide yerself, *mo ghrádh*. If ye do that fer me, I promise to do everything I can to bring what ye saw to fruition, whether I gain use of my legs again or no.'

'Promise!' she said on a shaky sob.

'More than that. I vow. And ye know a Were can never break a vow.'

She took in a jagged breath and nodded. 'Do not leave me.'

'Never. I will be with ye forever.'

She smiled up at him with tears in her eyes—tears that couldn't hide the hope and belief growing there. 'I will hold you to that.'

'Good.'

She took in another deep breath through her nose and then meeting his gaze, holding it, she said, 'Hold on.'

He did. Just in time.

The world dropped away as the power-filled arc exploded around them.

29

The world spun and tumbled, but he hung on to Le-le, not letting go despite the fact it felt like everything was trying to tear them apart. He would never let her go. He couldn't even if he wanted to—which he didn't. He'd been foolish to ever try. She was woven into his very soul. She was part of him in the way his wolf was part of him and he would die without her.

The tumbling stopped but the world still spun around and around.

He frowned. No. Actually, the world wasn't spinning. And neither were they. But something definitely was.

Silver threads of magic flew wildly through the air in a tangled mess that buzzed, hissed and shrieked, sparking with orange flares. It was beautiful and frightening at the same time.

'What is happening?' Dougal asked above the noise the magic created as it flipped and twisted around them like a pit of angry snakes.

'It is fighting me.'

'Why?'

'Because I am trying to stop it and it does not want me to.'

'Why would it not obey ye?'

'I do not know. I am trying but ... it is angry.' She looked up at it, brow creased with worry. 'It is trying to protect but it feels like ...'

'Feels like what?'

'That it hates me.' Her gaze snapped back to him, panic in her eyes. 'You have to leave. You have to get out. Get away from me. Or ... or ...'

He looked at her askance, jaw tightening. 'Ye dinna think I need protection from ye?'

'I did not think so ... I only ever wanted to help you, to Heal you. But this magic ... it is upset with me. And despite the fact I know it wants to protect you, I think, in its anger with me, it could end up hurting you. And a lot of other people beside. It is so ... so big. And wild. And ... I am afraid I am not enough to control it.' She looked down, away from him, as if she was ashamed.

He cupped her face and gently urged her to look up at him again. 'Ye are daft if ye think ye are not enough. Ye are more than enough. Ye are the strongest person I know.'

'Am I?' She blinked rapidly, her throat working hard for a moment before she whispered, 'How do you know?'

'Because ye saved me. And I dinna ken if ye realise it yet, but I am one stubborn Were. I had resolved to die—I wanted to die. I had resolved that I was not good enough fer ye injured as I am and I was ready to let go of our bond so as to give ye the life I thought ye deserved with someone who would not weigh ye down. But ye ... ye decided otherwise. Ye decided I was wrong. Ye decided to make our bond stronger. Ye decided I was not allowed to die no matter what I thought. Ye overrode, with yer strength and yer will, what I thought must be and created the future ye wanted. This future with us mated; our life together spread before us to shape in the way that best suits us. And I am certain ye have many ideas—far more than I can see—fer what that may be.' Her expression flickered and there was a sudden flare in her eyes so he knew he was right in everything he was saying. 'This magic might be strong, but ye are stronger.'

'I wish I was as sure as you are.' She looked around at the madness surrounding them. 'I think this is what I truly am on the inside. Dangerous. Unpredictable. It is what my mother always said I was. She told me I was too weak to be all I should be.' Her gaze slammed back to his. 'I am dangerous. So you have to go. You have to protect yourself. From me. You have to protect everything and everyone from me.'

'That doesna make sense.' He searched her gaze and could see she truly thought what she said was true. 'I dinna need protecting from ye. If anything, I need to protect *ye*. I want to protect ye. Yet I canna do it in the way I ought. The way a true Were should.'

She cupped his face, holding firm as she looked deeply in his eyes. 'No. No. You are wrong. You protect me all the time. You always have. You are doing it now. You are here, after all, protecting me from myself.'

'Protecting ye from yerself? That makes nae sense. Why would ye think that?'

'Because I have no idea what this is.' She gestured at the tangled mess of magic threads flying around them. 'Or how it works. It came to being with a call I did not even know I made.'

'But we agreed ye didna hurt anyone with it. Ye protected.'

'I protected myself and you, but I did not protect Iain. I have no idea what I have done to him.'

'Ye have not hurt him. Of that I am certain. Just as I am certain ye are no danger to anyone, not even yerself. Ye are too good, too kind-hearted to ever be a danger.'

'Then why can I not control it?'

Dougal frowned. 'I dinna understand. Ye made it stop doing what it was doing.'

She shrugged helplessly. 'Did I?'

'It is no longer building a wall.'

'No. It is now buzzing around us like a swarm of angry bees. It is still as effective a barrier as the wall it was creating.'

He glanced up at the magic swarming around them. 'I got through. It—you—let me in. So I dinna think it is trying to be a wall. I think it wants ... in.'

Her face creased in confusion. 'We are in my mind. It is already in.'

'Nae. I mean it wants acceptance. It wants ye to acknowledge it and love it. If ye were a Were, I would say it is akin to yer wolf.'

'What do you mean?'

He waved one hand at the wildly swirling magic above them. 'It is reacting like our wolves did when they were kept from being truly one with us by the Darkness. Wild and angry and grieving.' He looked back down at her, cupped her face. 'Ye are keeping it separate from yerself in some way.'

'How am I doing that when I did not even know it was there?'

'That perhaps makes it even worse.'

'What do you mean?'

He pursed his lips in that way he did when thinking deeply. Then he said slowly, 'If I ignore the needs of my wolf it hurts us both, but most especially my wolf. If I didna even recognise it was there ...' He sighed heavily and shook his head slowly. 'It would become horrifically violent in an effort to make itself known.' He pointed at the maelstrom of magic around them. 'Mayhap this is what this special magic ye never knew ye had is doing. It showed itself to ye when ye brought me back from death. And then it did all it could to try to maintain the mating bond by stopping me from tearing it apart.' He swallowed hard, shook his head, taking her hands from his face, holding them tightly. 'And none of us saw it. I didna see it. Ye didna see it. Morghanna, Alistair and Abigail didna see it. We didna see it and didna thank it fer helping ye to do the remarkable things ye have done. And it is hurt and grieving fer the wonder of that moment when ye did call on it and ye worked together to save me.'

'How?' She searched his gaze. 'How do you know all this when I do not?' She looked up at the magic around them. It vibrated and shook like an excited wolf pup's tail under her regard. In fact, it had done that every time she had acknowledged it in any way.

He said as much to her now. 'Look at it. It reacts excitedly every time ye so much as look at it. I think it simply longs fer ye to see it and love it as ye do yer Healing magic.'

LEANNA STARED UP AT HIM, mouth working for long seconds as her thoughts spun in her mind. A deep ache settled in her heart. For what she'd done to this magic she never knew she had. For ignoring all the signs it had sent her to show it was there. And for all she'd missed in not embracing it.

She'd hurt it so much.

She'd hurt herself.

And she could have hurt others as the Were did when their wolves turned wild. Because she'd not seen it. Not understood it. Not accepted it. 'How do I make amends?'

'Open yerself up to it now. Accept it in all its wild glory and love it, as we accept and love our wolves. I think that might be the only way.'

'But ... but how? I do not know how!'

He glanced around at the wild threads of power tangling and pulsing and thrashing around them and she looked up to see what he saw.

She drew in a sharp breath—it was quite beautiful. She'd hadn't noticed it before now. Had simply seen it as threatening and out of control. But now, after what her mate had said, likening it to his wolf, she could see it for what it truly was. Wild, yes. And so very strong and powerful. But beautiful in a way her Healing power wasn't.

The power threads seemed closer, like they'd drawn towards them as they'd been talking.

And as she stared at them, saw them, they drew even closer, flicking out as if longing to touch her, to be touched; to connect.

And suddenly she knew what to do.

She let go of his arms and reached towards a strand, not just acknowledging it or seeing it, but inviting it in.

Just as she'd done for the mating bond, she reached for it and welcomed it home.

The threads stopped in their swirling and thrashing for a breathless moment and then rushed towards her outstretched hands. They wound around her fingers, her wrists, writhing up her arms, doing the same around her body and legs.

'Come to me. Be one with me, my lovely friend,' she shouted.

The magic surged forward, pushing into her skin, entering her open mouth.

She screamed, the pain huge and exquisite.

In the distance she was aware of Dougal shouting her name. She thought maybe Morghanna and Alistair were too, but she couldn't answer, couldn't move, as the threads shoved through her skin, down her throat, entering through ears and eyes and nose. It filled her and filled her until she was certain she might explode.

Except she didn't.

And when she finally opened her eyes it was to see she was back in her room inside the shield. Morghanna and Alistair stood on the outside of it shouting at her, hands against the shield wall, their power sparking against it as they tried to get in. She turned her head to see that Dougal was in the bed behind her, roaring her name, his wolf howling and growling for her. And in front of her, Iain was still stuck in the shield, his eyes open wide as he shook and shuddered, the shield pulsing around him.

She hadn't known how to release him earlier but the knowledge was suddenly in her, whispering, telling her what she must do. She lifted her hand and said, 'Release!'

The shield disappeared and Iain dropped to the floor just as two Were barged in the door.

30

Dougal didn't even have a single moment to celebrate with Le-le over the fact she'd managed to be at one with these new-to-her powers because Callum and Bram came charging into the room, racing over to their fallen Alpha.

'Iain! My Alpha!' Bram cried. 'What did ye do?' he asked, his accusatory glare aimed squarely at Alistair.

Cal—always the calmer of the two—put his hand on his younger brother's shoulder. 'Wisht, Bram. We dinna ken what happened here.'

'I can see what happened. The French witch has attacked our Alpha. Iain was right to mistrust him when he arrived.'

'No, he was not!' Morghanna said, stepping in front of her husband. 'Ali has done nothing but help and protect our people. He almost died helping me face down the Darkness's Beast and extricate it from Lachlan. He even sacrificed his memory of who he was and where he was from so I could finish the battle. He might think Iain to blame for much of what happened—and he was,' she said loudly over Bram's instinctive and naive denial, '—but Ali has only ever stood at my side and helped keep this pack and coven together and protected. He did that while your Alpha chose to leave and search for his son with the Hunters and all of the lieutenants and senior soldiers who were well enough to go with him, leaving us virtually defenceless. You should be praising my husband, not accusing him.'

'It is well, my love,' Alistair said quietly, his calm demeanour impressing Dougal with just how extraordinary their Coven Leader's husband was.

'No. It is not well,' Morghanna said. 'It is far from well. I want him to apologise to you.'

Bram's head moved jerkily as he looked between the two witches. 'I ... but ...'

'Ye need to apologise,' Dougal said, the Alpha tone vibrating in his voice. 'He is one of our coven and they would no more attack the Alpha than one of us would. Ye are giving way to old ignorances we need to rid ourselves of if we are to be as strong as we once were.'

Bram looked for a moment like he would respond to the Alpha voice, but then his gaze skated down to Dougal's useless legs lying motionless under the bed coverings and he sneered—a sneer he'd learned from their Alpha when he looked down on those he thought beneath them. 'Ye dinna speak as my senior lieutenant any longer, not given ye are still here when ye should have done what is expected of ye and taken yer miserable, useless life. Ye are not who I thought ye were.'

'Bram!' Cal said. 'That is enough! Dougal deserves our respect after all he has given this pack and our Alpha. Ye need to apologise to him. Now. And to Alistair too.'

Bram looked down at Iain then up at his brother. 'I will not apologise to a dead man walking—or sitting as the case may be. And I will only apologise to the male witch when I know who attacked our Alpha and not before.'

'Bram, do not be so foolishly stubborn,' Cal said just as Le-le admitted, 'It was me.'

The two Were lieutenants stared dumbly at her, Bram being the first to break their stupor. 'Dinna be ridiculous! *Ye* couldna have taken down our Alpha.'

'Yet I tell you I did. I did not mean to, but I did.' Her back straightened and her chin went up. She was strength and determination, her power emanating from her so strongly he fancied he could see it.

Maybe he could actually see it, because Bram struck a defensive posture in front of the prostrate—and peacefully sleeping—Iain, as if he did believe her a threat to his Alpha.

Cal didn't move but his eyes widened as he looked anew at Le-le. 'What do ye mean ye did not mean to?'

She gestured at the power sparking like an aura around her but Cal just looked blankly at her, obviously unable to see what she was gesturing at—although, by the looks on Morghanna and Alistair's faces, they could see it. So the power was obviously visible to witches but not Were—then why could he see it?

When Cal and Bram kept looking quizzically at Le-le as she flapped her hand at power they couldn't see she sighed and said, 'This new power. It has come to me just recently and I did not know what it was or that it was even there. But without me meaning to, I used it to bring Dougal back and Heal most of his injuries and I used it just now as a shield to protect him from Iain.'

'Protect him from Iain?' Cal asked. 'Why would Dougal need protecting from Iain?'

'He was demanding Dougal's death.'

'As is his right!' Bram barked then blinked, his anger obviously flailing as his attention centred on Le-le. 'Ye say ye put up a shield to stop him? That canna be right. No shield ever knocked a male as strong as Iain out afore now. One of ye must have attacked him!' His glare moved to the others in the room.

Le-le took a step forward, bringing his attention swinging back to her. 'Nobody attacked him. He came barging towards Dougal saying he had to die,' she said, hands twisting before her, shifting from foot to foot. 'I wanted him to stop so I ... so I ... I just ... settled him.'

'Ye did what?'

'Bram!' Cal put his hand out to stop his brother from surging forward. 'What do ye mean by "settle"?' He looked down at Iain who was still on the floor, a blissful expression on his face as he slept.

'What does it matter?' Bram roared, pushing against Cal's firm hold. 'Our Alpha is on the floor, unconscious. And she admits to doin' the deed. She has to pay!'

'Do not put a hand on her!' Dougal roared so loudly the glasses on the shelf shook. 'Anna, Ali, stop him. He canna hurt my Le-le.'

'Yer Le-le?' Bram barked out.

'Aye, mine. She is my mate.'

'Yer mate?' Bram turned, his brows raised as he stared in shock from one to the other. 'By the Moon. Ye are mated?' he said on a ragged breath eyes widening further. 'That canna be true.'

'It is true,' Cal said softly. 'Can ye not feel her in the Packbond now?'

Bram's eyes flared wide. 'When did this happen?'

'The night Le-le saved my life she accepted it,' Dougal said.

Bram looked at him belligerently, as if he didn't believe him, then looked a question at his brother.

Cal nodded.

Bram seemed to sag. 'I-I thought I felt something that night but then it was chaos and Iain dragged us all off and given nobody announced anything and there was nothing clear through the Packbond, I thought I must have been mistaken. Especially given ye were fated to die. Why would ye take on a mate when ye are like ye are?' He tipped his head on the side, looking at Dougal in puzzlement.

Le-le hissed her aggravation. 'You Were and your outdated views about the ability challenged.'

'He canna walk,' Bram said, pointing at Dougal. 'Canna run with the pack. Canna fight. Canna hunt. If he canna do those things, how can he be a Were?'

'The Maternals do not do most of those things and do you think them lesser Were?'

'I-I ... They can walk and run.'

'He does not need to walk and run to prove his value. Those with sense enough would be able to see it.' Bram jerked a little at that hit, but didn't get a chance to say anything else because Le-le continued. 'And as to the mating, he did not want to mate to me at first, but I forced the matter. As my mate said, I had already accepted the mating when I Healed him. But then he refused me and ... well ...' She glanced back at Dougal, throwing him an apologetic look for bringing this up. 'I sickened the longer he denied me.'

'Ye were mated and denied it?' Bram asked, more astonished than before.

Shooting Le-le warmth and surety through the bond, he said, 'I didna realise she had accepted the mating. My side of the bond was dulled because I believed death my only future. I was determined to stop what I had started so she would not be affected when I died. But then she sickened and collapsed and Morghanna made me see the mistake I was making. So I accepted to save her life and it was ...' He took a deep breath, unable to fully explain the depth and breadth of wonder and joy that encompassed his entire being.

'We all felt it here,' Cal said. 'It was astonishing. We only had a glimpse of her power through the Packbond before then, but feeling it through our friendship bond like I did ...' He shook his head as he looked at his brother. 'She is truly a gift to us all.'

Bram's expression turned from shock to anger in an instant and he roared, 'Ye are all insane! She is no gift! Our Alpha is out cold! By her hand! She admitted as much. She needs to be taken under guard and ...' He made to move towards Le-le.

Cal rounded on his brother and used his entire body to stop the irate Were from laying hands on Le-le.

Dougal wanted so badly to leap out of this blasted bed and protect his mate but all he could do was roar his protest as Alistair raised his hands to weave magic and Le-le ... she just stood there as if she thought she deserved everything coming her way.

But surely she didn't? She hadn't even hurt Iain—he was sleeping peacefully. Couldn't Bram see that?

The younger Were kept pushing to get past his brother but Cal was a stone wall.

'Bram! Stop. Think. If indeed she has done wrong we will take her into custody and she will be judged by the Council of Elders fer her actions. But afore we take that step, we best make certain there is a crime here.'

Bram pointed down at their Alpha. 'What more proof do ye need than that?'

'That he has been harmed.' He looked over his shoulder to where Iain lay on the floor. 'He dinna look harmed at all. He looks like he is but asleep.'

'He is asleep. I think,' Le-le interrupted.

Bram growled and Cal shot her a 'not helping' look as he wrestled his brother back. 'Look at him, Bram. There are no marks on him or signs of attack.'

'She is a witch. She dinna need to lay hands on him to hurt him.'

'She is a Healer witch,' Morghanna said quietly. 'It would hurt her if she was to use her powers to hurt anyone.'

'Of course ye would say that,' he snarled. 'Yer lesser power is that of a Healer. It makes sense ye'd want us all to believe ye could do us no harm when the opposite may be true.'

'Are you calling my love, your Coven Leader, a liar?' Alistair said, stepping forward, an aura about him that shouted danger and authority in the same way an Alpha's aura did.

Bram stilled, his shoulders drooped and he couldn't seem to look up at Alistair.

Dougal was stunned. He'd always known the male witch was strong, but he wasn't a Were. He should not have the power only an Alpha could have over a Were as strong as Bram. But Bram was definitely acting like he'd been taken to task by a very strong Alpha— certainly stronger than the Were who was their Alpha. Even Dougal's wolf was shifting under his skin in the way it had only done when he'd met the Alpha of Pack McVale. Ioan McVale was the strongest Were Dougal had ever met. Ever since meeting him, Dougal had realised what an Alpha should be; what kind of Alpha he wanted to be when his pack was ready for him to step up and take it from Iain as was expected of him.

But suddenly he wasn't the one with the greatest power in the room.

Morghanna moved to stand in front of the now cowed Bram, an aura around her Dougal had only seen on the night she'd defeated

Lachlan and the Darkness. An aura that made him want to look away —and he had Alpha strength. At least, he had Alpha strength before he was injured. Now he wasn't so certain.

The purple magic of a powerful Spirit-talker flared around Morghanna. It prickled his skin, making him shiver—not only because of how it made him feel, but the very fact he could see it when he never had before.

The next moment, a rustling started up, followed by whispering in the air. Something brushed his face—like the cold caress of fog on the moors—and he shuddered.

'What in blazing hells is happening?' Bram said, head whipping from side-to-side.

'You forget, I am not simply a Healer,' Morghanna said, her voice echoing and strange. 'My major power is as a Spirit-talker. Would you like me to show you just what they feel about you calling me a liar and threatening one of their own?' She looked around her. 'Even the deceased Were who are here are very angered by your accusations. They feel you have been poisoned by the mutterings of someone who should not have had such sway over impressionable Were minds.'

She lifted her hands and the whispering got louder. The air around her simmered and Dougal could see shapes in the shimmering.

'She is very impressive, is she not,' a voice said from beside him. 'Although not quite as impressive as my Leanna is going to be.'

He whipped around to see a ghostly apparition sitting on the bed beside him.

'You!' he said as the handsome spirit smiled at him.

'Papa?'

31

Goosebumps prickled all over Leanna—although they weren't unpleasant. They'd begun when Morghanna called on her power and had increased as the spirits around them became visible.

Spirit-talking was not one of her skills—the fact she could see them now showed just how powerful Morghanna had become.

A curious tendril of her power curled out to touch her mentor. She stretched out her hand, about to call it back when she heard Dougal say, 'You!'

The way he said it made her spin around, her feet already moving to race over to him, to protect him from whatever made him sound like that.

She came to an abrupt halt. 'Papa?'

The spirit looked up at her, his eyes widening in delight. 'Rabbit! You can see me!'

'I can see you,' she repeated, wonderingly. Then a thought hit her. 'But why can Dougal see you?' A Were should not be able to see a spirit, no matter the power of the Spirit-talker drawing them into this realm. Were could sense them, but see them? Their minds didn't tend to work that way, physical-oriented beings that they were rather than spiritual.

Dougal was definitely looking at the spirit that was her papa though.

Her papa looked at Dougal quizzically, his mouth twisted to the side before he said, 'Yes, that is rather strange. Maybe it's because we met in the aether?'

'What? But ... how? Were do not travel the aether.'

'Your mate did. I expect that is why.'

Leanna blinked at her papa. 'What? Why? I mean, what do you mean "that is why"?'

''Cause we are mates,' Dougal said, still glowering at her papa—why was he glowering at him? 'It seems to allow me to access certain aspects of yer magics, *mo ghrádh*.'

Her papa's form flickered. 'Papa? Do not go.'

'I have little control over this, Rabbit.' He flickered again, his gaze going to the witch standing behind her.

'Morghanna?' She turned to her mentor. She wasn't prepared to lose sight of her papa yet. While she was confused about so much that was going on, she wasn't confused about the fact she missed him so much, and it was more than a blessing to see him once more. She didn't know how much longer Bram and Cal would be cowed like they currently were by all the ghosts whispering around them, or how much longer Iain would stay asleep, but when he woke and they stopped cowering, there would be no time for anything other than to defend what she had done and stop the Alpha from demanding her mate's death or exile.

'Please, Morghanna. Make him stay.'

'I am not the one who brought him here.'

'But it is you who is allowing us to see him.'

Morghanna frowned as she looked around at all the spirits that had come at her call—some mere wisps of movement in the room; others more fully formed but see-through; some, like her papa, which could clearly be seen as if they were still alive and standing in the room. If you didn't count the way they flickered.

Morghanna's frown deepened as she turned back to Leanna. 'I do not think all of these are here due to me. Something ... or someone else ... is drawing them here.' Her gaze roved over Leanna, assessing. 'Your aura ... there is something ... What are you doing?'

'I am not doing anything.'

'Oh, but you are. I can assure you, you are. I just cannot say what. It is unlike anything I have ever seen before.'

'She isna unwell again, is she?' Dougal asked, a note of panic in his voice. 'She isna channelling her energy into me again?'

Morghanna tipped her head as she assessed Leanna. 'No. It does not look like that.' She glanced at Alistair. 'What do you make of it?'

He was standing with Cal trying to get Bram to stop cowering, but he looked up at her for a moment, eyes flaring wide. 'I am not as practiced as you are in these things as yet, *mon coer*, but it does look strange. Not like before when she was giving her power. More like she is pulling it in.'

'From us?' Cal asked, body stiffening as he stood in front of Bram. 'Is she draining us?'

'No. I would not,' Leanna said.

'Nae. She wouldna do that,' Dougal said at the same time. 'I thought ye said the chance of her becoming a wraith had passed when I accepted the mating.'

Alistair and Morghanna looked piercingly at her.

'I ... Am I taking energy from you?' she asked breathlessly. She couldn't become a wraith. She couldn't. She would kill herself before becoming that.

'No, you are not taking energy from us,' Morghanna said slowly.

'There is definitely an energy transfer—slight though it is,' Alistair said. He glanced at Morghanna. 'It looks like ... the energy is being drawn from the spirits.'

'Yes.'

'What?' Leanna glanced back at her papa who was flickering more now—like a candle flame did when it was running out of wick. 'That is not me. I cannot do that.'

Morghanna frowned. 'I think you can. I think it is also why so many more spirits came at my call than I intended. I think your power linked with and boosted mine. And because you are mated to Dougal, the call also gathered in more Were spirits than I have ever had access to.'

'I did not ... I could not ...' Leanna shuddered. Was this something a wraith could do? They went after the power in human souls—still living souls. But the dead? She'd never heard of such a thing.

'Why would she do that?' Cal asked from where he kneeled now next to his brother, trying to comfort him as the flickering spirits floated around them, some of them gathering closer to the Were.

'She didna do that,' Dougal protested, his gaze fixing on Leanna.

'I think she did. There is no other reason for this to happen.' Morghanna gestured around them.

'But you have called many spirits before,' Leanna protested. 'As well as Were. You did it when we were fighting Lachlan's Beast.'

'Yes, I did. But it was a great drain on my power to do so and I had everyone plus the Goddess boosting me. This ... it has barely taken anything from me at all. In fact, I feel energised.'

'So she is channelling power into ye now?' Dougal asked, his tone horrified. 'Le-le. Ye canna do that again. Ye have to stop.'

'I am not doing anything!' she said her voice throbbing with worry and upset—because if she was, she had no idea how to stop it.

'You are not channelling, Le-le, but you are definitely doing something.' Alistair gestured to her. 'I can see it so clearly in your aura—it is brightening with every moment. And there are ... lines?' He glanced at Morghanna.

She nodded. 'Maybe cords are a better description.'

'*Oui*, cords. Like ribbons. They are coming from you to wrap around—maybe through?—the spirits and then back to you. It is quite beautiful. Not something I have seen before. Not that that is saying much as I can remember little of my life before coming here.'

Morghanna reached for his hand, smiling at him as she gazed into his eyes briefly. 'I have seen nothing like this either. And it *is* beautiful. But baffling. You do not feel any of it, Leanna?'

'I feel nothing except worried that you are seeing something in me that cannot be.' She took a step back, shaking her head. 'I am doing nothing.'

'Why would she do what ye sae she is doing, even if she could ken how?' Dougal said, reaching for her hand.

She was about to grasp his outstretched hand—she so needed the solidity and warmth of his touch especially in all this confusion—but she halted when her papa said, 'She would have. To see me.'

His voice was soft and glitched as he flickered.

'Papa? What do you mean?'

His gaze was piercing—he looked so solid when he wasn't flickering, like she could reach out and touch him. He looked at her for a long moment before turning his attention to Morghanna. 'She heard me when I took over the body of your man earlier. I have felt her longing to see me reaching out through the aether as she slept. When you called your power, Morghanna, gathering the spirits to you, I heard her call through you. To me. To those of our line who came before me. To those of his line—' he pointed at Dougal, '—who have passed into the great sleep.' He pointed around them. 'That is why there are so many here. And that is why some gather around the Were. They are hoping to be seen. Hoping to be heard.' He pointed at Bram. 'He hears their whispers. Do you not, boy?'

Bram lifted his head as if it was dragged up, gaze shooting from Johnathan to a spirit close by that shifted towards him. He whimpered, dropped his head and cowered closer to his brother mumbling, 'Make them stop. Make them stop.'

Cal leaned over him, gripping his shoulder tight, then glancing up at Morghanna pleaded, 'Please make them stop. He willna go after Leanna. He will listen to ye about what happened to Iain.' His gaze flickered down to their Alpha who was still unconscious but showing signs that he might wake soon—his eyelids flickered every now and then and the muscles in his face twitched. 'But not until the spirits are gone. They frighten him too much.'

'They do not frighten you?'

'Oh, aye, they do.' He glanced around and shuddered. 'But not so much as Bram. He has always been ... sensitive to them. Ever since he was a boy and was there when our grandfather passed. He never came to any pack death rites after that. He said he could feel them calling to him. It was fine as long as he stayed clear of places people had recently passed. Or stayed well clear of cemeteries. And he has had to stay away every time ye have called this particular magic fer fear of giving away he has this ability.' Bram whimpered as a spirit drew closer, clinging to Cal's leg. 'He sees it as weakness. That other Were will think he is insane, as they thought our grandmother was because she said she could not only feel them, but could see and talk to the spirits. She was taken away by our Alpha and we never saw her again. Bram fears that is his future.'

'It is not weakness,' Morghanna said. 'Nor is he insane. He is obviously a sensitive.'

'Can ye help him?'

'I am uncertain if our training will work for a Were, but I can try. It might help him to control what he feels.'

'I dinna mean that—although, mayhap he will want to do that after this—but now? Can ye stop them now? Make them go away.'

Morghanna glanced around her, then back to Leanna. 'It is the Were spirits that are gathering around him. I will ask the others to go given they did the job I wished them to in stopping Bram from hurting Leanna, but given they are not the ones bothering him, I do not think he will feel better.' She glanced at Leanna. 'He will only feel better if the Were go. Can you ask them to leave?'

'Me?' Leanna placed her trembling hand on her chest. 'You keep suggesting I am doing something but I assure you I am not.'

Morghanna sighed and gestured at the spirits flocking around the two Were. 'Well I am not the one who called the Were. And given I did not call them, I cannot ask them to go.'

'Could ye try?' Cal asked, bending to hold his terrified brother in his arms as the Were ghosts started circling them in a tighter formation. 'Please. Fer Bram. I ken ye might not think he deserves it after how he behaved. But he willna recover if this goes on fer too long.'

Morghanna looked torn. 'You do not understand. Because I was not the one to call them here, if I try to make them go, it could hurt them. Damage them. And—'

'And,' Alistair interrupted, 'she will feel their pain. So much so it could knock her unconscious if she has to be too forceful.'

'I am not worried about that,' Morghanna said, waving her love's concern away. 'I am concerned over what it could do to them. It could splice them; break them apart bit by bit. And they would be lost. You know the stories of evil spirits that haunt places?' Cal nodded and Bram made a sound of terror and clung even harder to his brother. 'Those are most often spirits that have been fragmented in some way and cannot move on. It is a torment. I cannot purposefully do that to any spirit.' She sighed deeply then looked pleadingly at Leanna. 'You are the only one who can make them leave without causing them harm.'

Leanna shook her head. 'But I cannot. I do not have that power.' She clenched her hands together in front of her. 'I did not do this! You know I could not. I do not have those powers.'

'I am not sure how you called them here either, other than what has already been suggested. All I know is that neither Alistair nor I called the greater majority of them to make themselves known on the physical plane. And the only other person in here who has magic is you, Le-le. No matter how it might terrify you when you are already grappling with new powers, it is true. It is the only reasonable answer.'

'But I did not do this!' She was trembling now, power gathering inside her, a hot burn under her skin. She tamped down on it but it pushed back and she let out a sound of distress.

'Leanna!' Dougal shouted, reaching for her. She stepped into his arms and it made her feel better, but not before she noticed the spirits that were circling Cal and Bram were flying closer and closer to them, looking almost aggressive. Some were beginning to do the same to Iain—one flew right past him, seeming to touch him. He jerked and mumbled in distress.

Bram began to shriek.

Cal's gaze shot to Leanna and over the noise he yelled, 'Please, dinna torment my brother like this. He may have meant ye harm but that was only in defence of our Alpha. He thought ye had hurt him.'

'I am not doing this,' she yelled back, her gaze flying from one to the other of those in the room, even her papa who had moved from his position on the bed to stand facing her. 'You are wrong,' she said to him. 'You are all wrong.' There was panic in her voice now and she edged further back into Dougal's embrace, needing to feel more of his touch to help stabilise the power that was roaring inside her suddenly, demanding to get out.

'Look at what you are doing to them!' Alistair yelled over Bram's shrieking, pointing to the spirits which were now spinning around them, flying in and out so fast that they were a blur.

Cal shouted something unintelligible as he bent over his brother, hands over his head as they were buffered by the spirits. Iain jerked, as if being punched by the spirits flying a wild pattern around him.

Dougal shouted, 'Alistair! Protect Iain from the spirits.' He pulled Leanna closer to him. 'If ye say ye dinna call them here, I believe ye. But can ye help Morghanna get rid of them?'

She shook, wide eyed, horrified by what was happening—and the dawning thought inside her that it was her. It was all her. That maybe this was because she was becoming a wraith. 'I do not know how.'

'Just concentrate,' Papa said from beside her, his presence a brush of cool air along her side. 'Close your eyes, touch your powers, and tell the spirits to be still. Or depart.'

'Will you go too?' He flickered so she almost missed his nod. 'I do not want you to go,' she said. 'I have not had time to talk to you.'

He moved his hand as if he was going to brush the hair back from her face like he always used to, but the movement glitched and he flickered again, this time not remaining so solid between flickers.

'I dinna ken ye have a choice,' Dougal said to her. 'It looks like whatever is affecting the others is affecting yer papa as well.'

'Dougal is right,' Morghanna said drawing up beside her papa. 'Johnathan could be hurt by what is happening.'

'No!' She moved to grab Papa, but her hands went through him and he began to flicker more violently.

Goddess no! This *was* her. She was doing this. But how? How? 'I do not know how to stop it!'

'Close your eyes, find your centre like you do when using your powers and feel your way to what you need to do,' Morghanna said.

'I do not have time!' she yelled as her papa flickered, a pained expression screwing up his face.

'Le-le. Ye can do this.' Dougal tugged her around to face him. He cupped her face, holding her steady with his touch and his gaze on hers. 'Ye are so strong. Ye can do anything ye put yer mind to. Help them. Help yer papa. Calm yerself. Then calm the spirits. Tell them to go.'

'I might be taking energy from them like a wraith does. Maybe a part of me does not want them to go.'

'The energy you are tapping into from them,' Morghanna shouted over the noise of the spirits, 'is not making them weaker. Can you not see that? You are no wraith.'

'How are you so sure?'

She didn't answer, but Dougal did. 'Because I feel it deep inside. Where I feel ye. Ye are no wraith. And I ken ye can let them go. I ken ye ken how. Ye just need to believe.' He kissed her softly. 'As I believe in ye, *mo ghrádh*.'

'You have to do it now,' Morghanna said urgently.

'I can do this?' she whispered as she stared into her mate's eyes.

'Aye, ye can.'

Closing her eyes, she held his trust and love to her and did as Morghanna said. She reached down and touched her power ...

Everything went black then grey and she was falling, falling into nothing.

32

Leanna screamed, calling for Dougal, but he didn't answer. She panicked, scrabbling for the bond but she couldn't touch it; couldn't even feel it.

No! No! What had she done? Where had she gone that she couldn't feel her mate?

Could he feel her? Did he think her dead?

Had she died?

Goddess no! Not that. Never that. Because if she died then Dougal would die too and she couldn't be responsible for that.

Couldn't continue to be whatever this was if she had killed him with her death.

She'd want to die ... truly die. Not be aware of anything. Just be gone. If she couldn't be with Dougal, she didn't want to be anything.

Except ... they were soulmates. If she had died and he had died then he would be here with her, wouldn't he? At least for a while until they were reincarnated into their next lives where they would ultimately find each other again as soulmates always did.

So where was he?

Maybe he hadn't died. Which meant ... maybe she wasn't dead.

So where was she? What was this place? And ...

Why was she no longer falling? At least, she didn't think she was falling. It was hard to tell surrounded by such a purple-grey nothingness.

She shuddered as it wrapped around her, holding her in place. It wasn't hot or cold but simply ... nothing.

It was the most unnerving sensation she'd ever experienced. Except for ... except for ...

She couldn't remember but she was certain she had experienced this before. Had been here before.

But when? How? Why?

She reached out to see if she could touch it.

She could see her arm—so she wasn't nothing—but it looked strange. A pearlescent sheen lit up the surface of her skin. It was unlike anything she'd seen, but quite beautiful in its strangeness. She turned her arm from side-to-side, watching the way the light moved across her skin, making it shine like sunlight on the loch.

Except, there was no sun here.

She looked around, wondering where the light came from but everything looked the same. There was no sense of up or down, no contours or distance or shadow. It was all just a misty purple-grey.

Scary in its nothingness and yet soothing at the same time.

At least it would be if she knew why she was here. Or how she got here. Or if Dougal was okay. The last thing she remembered was trying to reach for her power, the one they thought she was using to call Were spirits and her papa even though she had no idea how.

She'd closed her eyes and reached out for it and then ...

She fell in here.

Her eyes flared wide. No. She didn't just fall into this place. She was pulled in.

It had been like a hand had grasped her and yanked her away from where she was and into here. But that feeling had gone so quickly she hadn't registered it until now.

Now she had, it frightened her. And made her angry. Whatever had grabbed her had taken her away from helping those poor spirits who were stuck there because of her. And now she couldn't help them. Like she'd promised to.

She had to get back. She had to get out of here. She had to—

What? What could she do?

'*Fight,*' a voice whispered inside her mind. '*Fight to free yourself.*'

Yes! She could do that. She'd been fighting to free herself in some way all her life—first from what her mother thought of her and the weight of her expectations, then from the horror of her parents' death. She had then fought to escape the stigma of the burns that marked her face, neck and shoulder. After which she had spent so much of her time freeing herself from people's notice that she hadn't realised she was hiding and not free.

It wasn't until she'd come to be part of Morghanna's coven, and Abigail and Morghanna had noticed her and her talents and took her under their wing, that she realised what freedom actually looked like and had begun to step towards it, so tentatively at first that it was as if she'd escaped nothing.

But then she'd seen Dougal and something inside her shifted. Had changed. And that shift of change increased exponentially each day she spent with him guarding her, befriending her. He didn't just look at her, he *saw* her. He made her reach for something she had never thought she could have, and the strange thing was, she didn't even know she was reaching for it until she'd almost killed herself by pushing too far.

But he'd freed her from that too by accepting their mating, her love, and all they could and would be if they both stopped being so stupid in thinking they did not deserve the other.

She had fought for them without realising and then he had fought for them.

As she would fight now. To get back to her friends, to help the spirits.

To get back to Dougal.

She looked around, but there was nothing to give her a clue as to how she could get out of here. But she had to. She had to.

She started to move her legs, trying to run, but nothing happened

—either she wasn't moving at all or everything was so much the same that she could not tell if she was. There was no shift of air or feeling like she was pushing off anything, so she thought it most likely she wasn't moving at all.

She tried to swing her arms. Nothing happened. She reached forward trying to grasp at something, anything.

Nothing.

She began to move her arms and legs as if she were swimming and for a moment, it felt like something did shift in the purple-grey surrounding her. She swam faster until she was panting and sweat pricked her brow and between her breasts, dampening her blouse.

The feeling made her laugh and sob at once because it was the first time she'd felt anything external since coming here. Usually she hated the feeling of sweat running between her breasts because it was ugly and messy when it marked her clothing—and she felt ugly enough as it was. But now, here, she only felt pleasure in it. If she'd been here for much longer with no sensation around her telling her she was real, madness was certain to creep in.

She pulled more strongly with her arms, kicked harder with her legs, noting the strange sensation again like something shifting around her.

She was moving! She had no idea where she was going, but she was moving! She doubled her effort.

A curling kind of wave pushed out and away from her, like what happened when she was swimming fast through water. It was working! She wanted to shout with joy. Wanted to—

Something curled around her ankle, holding fast.

She shrieked and pulled against the thing holding her. It held tighter. She looked down—or up or across (who could tell in this place?)—to see what it was.

A tendril of purple-grey snaked around her ankle and halfway up her calf. What the hells? This stuff had tendrils? Or was it a tentacle? She bent down to tug at it, but another tentacle snaked around her wrist, stopping her from pulling it.

'Ugh! Get off!' She reached for that tentacle, but it tightened just as another one latched around her other leg. 'Ugh, no. Stop. Stop.' Another one wrapped around her free arm at the wrist, pulling it up and out, then another snaked around her waist, squeezing. 'No. No. Get off. Get off!' Pulling against them only made them squeeze tighter. Trying not to panic, she closed her eyes and did what she should have done in the first place—used her magic.

Reaching for her power, she began to incant an unbinding spell— a simple spell of unknotting that all novice witches were taught to practice, so it was second nature to call on it now.

Her magic leapt to her call, that strange strong power sparking just under it. She hesitated—should she use her magic when she wasn't certain what that new power was and what it could do aside from call spirits to her?

The tentacles tightened as she hesitated. If she didn't act now to free herself from them, she would not have the breath to try. Besides which, she had accepted her new magic and couldn't suppress it again as she'd previously been doing.

Grabbing the magic—threads of the newer power tangled along with the older, familiar magic—she opened her mouth to incant the spell.

'I wouldn't do that if I were you.'

She jerked against the tentacles, her magic slipping from her hold with a disappointed fizzle. 'What? Who said that?'

'A friend.'

Heart smashing against her ribs, she tried to turn to see who had spoken, but the tentacles held her in place, their grip now painful. All she could do was turn her head left then right, seeing nothing but the purple-grey. 'How do I know you are a friend?'

'I guess you don't, other than to take me at my word.'

'If you are a friend, you will help me to break free.'

'Oh, but why would I do that when it is holding you at my command?'

'What? You—' She pulled and twisted against the tentacles binding her.

'Do not struggle, dearest witch. It will only make them tighten. And I do not want to hurt you.'

'That is not how it seems,' she said, ceasing her struggles and reaching for her magic again.

'Honestly, I wouldn't call your magic here without listening to me first.'

'And why would I believe you?' she said through gritted teeth, her anger a bright thing in her chest, growing ever larger, wanting something to lash out at.

'Don't believe me if you wish. But if you call in your magic like that now, before you've heard what I have to say, I will not be able to help you.'

'I do not want the help of the person holding me against my will!'

'I simply did that to save you. You were swimming further into the inner space. You do not want to do that, surely?'

'If you are here to help me, then unbind me.'

'Certainly. If you promise to stop swimming and listen to why I brought you here.'

That stopped her thrashing. 'You brought me here?'

'I did.' The bodyless voice sounded so smug, like he'd done her a favour.

Her anger spiked, but she clamped down on it. 'You took me away from Dougal,' she said evenly, quietly—the sound of her voice threatening in a way she'd never known it could be. 'You cut me off from him so I cannot feel him. You stopped me from helping my pack-mates. Stopped me from releasing those spirits I had accidentally called. Including my papa. You—'

'Yes, I did do all of that to bring you here. It was necessary because I had to bring you here before you destroyed those spirits as you were about to do well before it is time to do so.'

'I—What? No. I would not do that! I do not have the power to destroy a spirit.'

'Oh, but you do. You have the most deliciously destructive power I have come across in an age. I didn't think the Fates would ever create more of you after their last attempt because of how powerful you can be. But then here you are.'

'What are you talking about?' she shouted. 'I am a Healer. I cannot destroy anything. If I did I would lose my magic. I would lose my mind.'

'Oh, but you can destroy as easily as you Heal. There are two sides to every magical gift. You witches think in term of good and evil, light and dark. But that is the wrong way to view it.'

'What do you mean?' He made no sense but at the same time, she had a horrible feeling that she would need his help to get out of here. So she held off using her magic for now and kept engaging him—he might give something away. He seemed quite eager to 'school' her. 'How do you view it?' she asked, pleased her voice sounded so calm.

'I am glad you asked,' he said superciliously. 'Think of it like a river. It has a surface—that which is seen and known and entices with the glittering flow of it—but the greater, stronger part lies under the surface. Let's call it the beneath. You witches are only taught the magic that flows along the surface, ignoring what flows beneath. You scare your children with tales of the consequences of turning to the magic beneath the surface, calling it dark magic and saying there is a terrible price to using it. But there is a price for using any magic, as you of all people, would know.'

A sensation shivered down her scarred cheek, akin to a caress—if the caress was with an icy cold finger. She stopped herself from flinching and asked, 'What does any of that have to do with my magic?'

'It has everything to do with your magic. Healing magic is all surface magic—running along the current of life, utilising the power of it as you Heal. But if you were to dive under the surface, you would not only be dealing in magic that can pull on what lies beyond life— the spirits let's say—you can use their energy in the same way you use life energy. The magic below the surface gives you power not only over life but of death as well. This is what you did when you saved your Were.'

'You know about that?'

'Anyone with a hint of magical ability would have sensed what you did. It shook the aether.'

'I did not know.'

'Of course you didn't. There hasn't been one like you in an age. You are running on pure instinct. Which is good.'

'What do you mean? If I could hurt someone with it as you say is possible, how is that good?'

'Instinct is always a good thing if you act on it. Especially with your gifts. Instinct is at the heart of the beauty of your hidden gift. The thing that allows you to use it with such efficiency.'

'I have no idea what you are talking about.'

'I know.' He sighed sadly. 'It is a crime you do not know who you are; what you can do.'

'Given you are so knowledgeable, tell me, what am I?'

'A Soul-wraith.'

'A what?' She'd never heard of such a thing, but it did not sound good.

'A Soul-wraith. The only one in existence. You balance between life and death. With the right encouragement, you could bring loved ones back to life—or destroy everything in existence.'

33

Leanna couldn't speak for long seconds as his words spun around and around in her head chasing everything out of it except for horror.

And fear.

It couldn't be right. It couldn't be true. She wouldn't do that. Couldn't be that.

And yet, the worry that she could become a wraith had been there ever since she'd been told of the possibility. She'd thought maybe what she'd been doing to the spirits was somehow connected with that, but then had dismissed it because Morghanna said she wasn't taking power in that way. Which was easier to believe than that she was a wraith.

Or a Soul-wraith, whatever that was. She'd never heard of such a thing. The voice was tormenting her with her own worries, obviously. 'You are lying!' she shouted, her power arcing up, fizzing just under the surface.

A chuckle and then, 'So feisty!'

'Do not laugh at me!' Power exploded out of her, tearing the tentacles to shreds and rippling the purple-grey around her, turning it a deep lilac and causing striations to snake out from where she stood, like cracks appearing in a glacier.

'Whoa-whoa-whoa! I told you not to use your power in here. Not until everything is ready at least.'

Shock at what she'd done had her power snapping back to her, hitting her like a gut punch. Air exploded out of her and she tumbled over and over until a tentacle grabbed her leg, stopping her uncontrolled movement.

'Let go!' she shouted as the tentacle pulled tight, trapping her again. 'Let go!' She thrashed against it, pulling at the tentacle, tearing at it with her nails. 'Let go!' Her power was there again, pushing to get out, hissing and spitting, lashing at her, demanding she release it to show this bodyless voice what it could truly do. It frightened her with its raw intensity. It wasn't like her at all. Afraid of what it might do, she grasped it, shoved it down, putting a mental cage around it before it had a chance to push back. She didn't want to cage it, but she needed it to listen. To work with her.

It snarled at her, banging against its cage as Dougal said his wolf had done between full moons when the Darkness was in control.

'Please, I am not trying to cage you like I did before,' she said to it in her mind. *'I simply need you to calm down and let me figure out what is going on. I do not want to play into his game, whatever it is. Do you understand? We need to be careful. Can you be careful with me? Please. I promise, once we know what is going on, I will let you out to do what you will.'*

She held her breath, waiting, expecting it to lash out again, but instead, it settled inside her, still a seething mass of incredible promise and danger, but controlled and content to wait. For now.

'Well, that is impressive. And super unexpected. I didn't think you had it in you yet.'

She turned her attention back to the tentacle holding her in place. Lifting her head to stare into the direction the voice came from she demanded evenly, 'Let me go!'

'I will. But not while you are still so angry. While I enjoy a good burst of anger—comes in handy nine confrontations out of ten—it won't serve either of us well in this instance. You need to calm down first.'

'Why? Why can I not be angry with you given what you have done to me so far ... given what you have said?'

'Because while you are angry you will not listen. And it is essential that you listen. But first you must remain calm—because neither of us can afford for you to destroy this place. At least, not yet.'

'Why should I remain calm when all you do is talk strangely with your "can't" and "won't" and similar words—'

'They're called contractions. Everyone will use them in the future.'

'And you laugh at me,' she said, more frustrated than she'd been with anyone in her life. 'And annoy me and say things that are not ... that cannot possibly be true. You are a liar! I cannot calm down and listen to a liar. I cannot trust a liar.'

A snort and then he said, 'That is some simplistic logic you are spouting there. Well I'll meet your logic and raise it with more logic by saying this: I told you the truth about the fact you shouldn't use your power in here, didn't I?'

He paused as if waiting for her response.

She remained silent, not wanting to admit he was right.

'You can't deny it, no matter how much I can see you want to. I told you the truth.'

He paused again and this time it was impossible not to respond as if the answer was drawn from her. And despite the fact she did want to deny it, she wasn't a liar. 'Yes. I suppose you did.'

'So generous,' he drawled. 'But now that you have agreed I told the truth, why do you think I haven't spoken truth about everything else I've said?'

She gestured at the tentacle wrapped around her leg. 'Holding a person captive does not engender trust.'

'Perhaps. However, it does not indicate that a person is a liar. Just that they're not averse to a little bondage.'

'Bon-what?'

A chuckle. 'So naive and vanilla. I shouldn't be surprised given the goodie-two-shoes company you've been keeping.'

'I have no idea what your words mean or what you are talking about, other than it does not sound complimentary. Which makes me trust you less.'

'Why? Because I speak in a dialect more in line with future times—'

'Future times?'

'Yes. Travelling through this space, which I have had occasion to do often, opens the mind in ways that pick up on the fact that in here, the issue is not that there is no time, but every time. And if you listen very carefully, look very carefully, you can hear things filter through from other times. For myself, I rather like the crude expedience of how speech evolves and have come to mimic it somewhat. But all of this, while interesting, is by-the-by. I was saying that part of your problem with me is that you find my speech strange. And you are letting that affect how you perceive me.'

What he said, it made her mind spin. She tried to steady it, to concentrate on the parts she could understand. 'Yes, your speech is strange—more than strange. But it is only partly why I do not trust you. Mostly I think you are talking like that to make me think I am lacking in intelligence or knowledge. So it feels very much like you are laughing at my expense.'

A light chuckle. 'Clever girl. Cleverer than I thought. Okay. Since you have impressed me with your wits, I promise you that I will cease to play with you as a mouse does a cat.'

'Do you not mean a cat does a mouse?'

'No. I meant what I said. Because in this place, things are not what they seem. And the mouse can be far more powerful than the cat.'

'Who am I in this scenario?'

'The mouse. You are always the mouse.'

'But you just said that you would stop playing with me as a mouse does a cat.'

'Yes.'

'Which insinuates you are the mouse and I am the cat.'

'Do you think of yourself like a cat or a mouse?'

She hesitated in answering. She'd like to say cat but the truth was she'd always been the mouse. She'd made herself as small and insignificant as one could to try to avoid the attentions of her mother and then, after the accident, of everyone who might look at her and see the scarred, ugly and useless thing she was. All she'd ever been good at was running. Scurrying away as fast as she could.

Things had begun to change since coming to this coven, finding friends, finding the true power of her magic in helping others. It had all been so empowering. Without realising it, it had allowed her to tap into something more that had always been hidden inside her. Something huge and astonishing. Something that allowed her to gift life, rather than death.

And yet, the mouse had reared its head again and made her not trust the gift that was hers. Had made her doubt her ability to wield it. Had wanted to scurry away from what confronted them.

'Ah, but if that is the case, how did you manage to keep yourself together enough that you actually managed to move around in here? And how is it that, if you truly are the frightened mouse, you managed to lash out with power in here and create true change to a place without concept or ability for such things?'

She didn't even question how he knew what she'd been thinking, just answered him. 'Because mice are not just frightened, scurrying things.'

'Yes. And?'

'They can be curious. They explore. They care for their families.'

'And?'

'They fight to survive.'

'Yes. The mouse is all of these things. It is clever and resourceful and a fighter and lo betide the world when the mouse learns to roar —because the change that will occur will be world-changing, universe-making, realm-shifting.'

'That does not sound good.'

'Why not?'

'It sounds like chaos.'

'Yes, it does.' The voice sounded gleeful. 'Nothing wrong with a little chaos.'

'That sounds like more than a little chaos.'

'Yes, it does. But everything was chaos in the beginning. Life and light and everything was born out of it. Is it destructive? Yes. But out of chaos dawns new, brighter things with endless possibilities. Isn't that exciting? Isn't that something to reach for? To be the instigator of such change? To be the mouse who plays with the cat rather than the other way around? To be the mouse who roared a new existence into being?'

'You are insane!'

'No. I am the sanest being you will ever meet. I am the only one who acknowledges and embraces truth: that in madness there is sanity. That out of chaos dawns new beginnings. That there is no light without darkness to define it.'

She gasped. She knew what this was!

Panic gripped her. She wanted to back away, but there was nowhere to go that wasn't him. He seemed to be all around.

The Darkness.

Was this where he lived? Was this entire place ... him?

'By my father, no. Things other than me created this little place of nothing that lies between the realms and the aether; between the awake and the sleeping; between space and time. A dreamer dreamed it into existence, so it could not be mine as I never dream. I plan. I plot. I fight. I win.'

'You have not won. We got rid of you—twice!'

'Bits of me, yes. Minor victories in a larger war that's been raging on for millennia ever since my traitor lover betrayed me and favoured her little world over me and my well-being. I am prepared to lose the smaller battles because I have already won an equal number. And ultimately, I will win this war.'

'And what do you think you will win?'

'Everything. And nothing. It does not matter. All that matters is that I win.'

'That sounds ... empty.'

A loud snort right near her ear—her hair shifted from the force. Without thinking she whacked at the area near her ear ... and hit something almost solid.

She spun to face it—him—in time to see a wisp of something like black smoke sink back into the purple-grey that surrounded her.

He was as corporeal as she was in this place. Well, as corporeal as a wisp-of-smoke-entity could be. She could strike him. Perhaps hurt him with her magic. She'd accidentally done damage to this place after all. So it was possible.

It went against everything she believed in though; everything her magic stood for. And even if she could make herself do it, what good would that do? Would it get her out of here?

She looked at the cracks she'd created, the faint light that had begun to seep through. Maybe if she could widen those cracks that would be a way out. Or maybe she could make him let her go if she caused him enough pain.

Maybe. So many maybes.

The biggest maybe though was whether she could do it. Could she push herself that far?

'Be the mouse that roared. I know you can be if you try.'

The voice came from all around her, like it was embedded in the purple-grey. Not fully a part of it but more like butter that has melted into toasted bread. She spun around, trying to find a central point but there was no change she could see that would indicate where he was gathered—or if he was gathered at all.

'You won't find me by looking with your eyes.'

'What else can I look with other than my eyes?'

'You're a smart witch. Think about it.'

She frowned. Could she see him with the magic that allowed her to see a patient's aura?

'No. That's not it.'

'Then what is it?'

'Come on. I know you can do it. I know you are intelligent enough, and strong enough, to find me.'

Leanna narrowed her eyes, pulling on the threads of magic that allowed her to see not only an aura, but into a patient to see what was wrong. And as she did, she saw a small curl of smoke slipping in and out of the purple-grey.

He was showing her where he was before slipping away. Tempting her. Taunting her.

Sucking in a breath she asked, 'Why do you suddenly want me to use my magic when you didn't only moments ago? Why do you want me to come after you?'

34

'Because I want you to become what you are meant to become in the way that will help me the best,' the Darkness said as if it was the simplest thing in the world.

She was not a plaything. She was a powerful witch—more powerful than anyone, including her, had ever realised. She didn't need to play his game. And she certainly was never going to become the wraith he wanted her to be. Needed her to be for obvious nefarious reasons.

She straightened her spine, squaring her chin and said, 'No.'

'No what?'

'No to you. No to whatever you want from me. No to whatever you want me to do.'

'But you don't know what that is.'

'I can guess, given who you are. And it is nothing good.'

'Depends on the perspective.'

The purple-grey in front of her wavered, like water when a stone was dropped into it. 'What is happening? What are you doing?'

'Look and see. Then you will begin to understand.'

Something like a mirror appeared before her in the purple-grey. An image formed in the mirror, wispy and translucent like smoke to begin with, but slowly it solidified until she could see the village clearly.

At first glance it didn't look like there was anything wrong.

Until she saw the shadowed figure slipping through the edges of the village, making its way towards one building: the Healer Hall.

She leaned closer trying to see who it was, but the shadows concealed his features. There was something horribly familiar about him though. 'Who is that?'

'Someone obviously up to no good, I'd wager. Nobody using the shadows to conceal themselves like that could be a friend—or do you think otherwise?'

'No.' She didn't. The shadowed person looked like they were avoiding being seen and somehow they were also avoiding being scented—almost an impossibility in a Were village. 'What is he intending?'

'Revenge.'

She hadn't expected him to answer, so it took her a moment to take in what he'd said, and when she did it made her suck in a shaky breath. She peered at the figure again more closely, suddenly understanding why she'd found him so familiar—the certain cocky swagger despite the stealthiness of his movements; the way he held his head as if he was looking down his nose at everything. He was skinnier, his clothing ill-fitting—obviously stolen from washing lines when he was on the run and trying to rid himself of the fullness of his scent that would be embedded in his own clothing. His hair was shaggier, a beard helping to hide the features of his face along with the shadows.

All of these changes were why she'd not guessed immediately who he was, but now she did, she couldn't unsee it. 'Lachlan! But why is he here?'

'I told you—revenge.'

'But ... but, it is madness, him coming back.' It wasn't like the coward he was at all. He always targeted the women he was attracted to when stronger Were weren't around to stop him. He did the same with those he tormented and picked on—those he saw as weaker than him. Leanna had mostly escaped being one of his regular targets because Dougal had so quickly become her *Sgàth* and was around nearly all the time. And when he wasn't, Morghanna always protected her—which meant her mentor had endured his slithering sexual attention more than she needed to, no matter that it upset her so much. 'It makes no sense that he is here. He can no longer become the Beast. He is completely outnumbered and outmatched.' He'd never had an Alpha's strength, no matter what he thought.

'Is he? He may not have his Beast anymore, but he still has me.'

'You?' Her gaze snapped to where she had seen the dark smoke show itself earlier. 'But we banished you from him in a way that would make it impossible for you to get back in and use him like you did.'

'Yes. Very clever. But not clever enough.'

The urge to ask him what he meant was great, but she had vowed not to play his game. And he had to be trying to trick her. Because there was no way he could be back inside Lachlan. So she asked instead, 'What does he plan to do? He cannot win against the entire pack, especially with the Alpha and his lieutenants and Hunters back again.'

'Pfsh. Your Alpha is no protection against him—he has always given in to his son. And he has made many of the pack lieutenants and leadership culpable because not only did they never stand up to him, they gave him their power to help him. They are all weaker because of it. The only one truly capable of standing up to him is now bedridden because you have not been able to tap into the part of you capable of Healing him.'

Oh, that stabbed, and she couldn't help snapping, 'I have done everything I can.'

'Not everything. If you became the wraith and embraced the power it would give you, you could not only Heal your mate but make him the most powerful Were alive.'

'And I suppose I would have to kill to do that?'

'Of course. But so what? If you need to feel better about it, you could kill only bad people. Like Lachlan.'

'You helped make him bad.'

'Did I? What does that matter now?'

'It matters.'

'Really? You do know killing him is the only way you can stop him. Especially after I have finished filling him with all the power you have been feeding me while in here with you.'

'What do you mean?'

The Darkness's laughter rang around her, making her shiver. 'It's a peculiar specialty of this place. It transfers power through emotional channels—and you have been emoting so beautifully. Your emotions are filled with so much power and they're spilling out of you like water does from a geyser. It's like manna to me!'

Shock and fury vibrated inside her. 'Is that why you brought me here? To feed from me?'

'In part—you are unexpectedly yummy—but mostly to make you realise you have to become the wraith if you don't want to lose absolutely everything right now.'

'I will never become the wraith.'

'Not even when it is the only way to win against me? The only way to get out of here? The only way to defeat Lachlan?'

'You cannot help him—we made that impossible.'

'No. You made it impossible for the piece of me that had been made weaker by being in the Were and on your Earth for so long. That part was destroyed. But you did not take into account that I am far more than that small piece. I am not simply one being. I split myself into many parts millennia ago, each part autonomous but working towards the same goal. Domination of the world my betrayer so loves.'

She was horrified by what she was hearing, because it sounded like it just might be true. That he was doing exactly what he said he was. That he was feeding Lachlan power that would truly make him a threat to everyone she loved. Panic swirled inside her, rising, and she said desperately, 'You will not win. I will not let you.'

'That is rather the point!' He laughed. 'I want you to try to stop me.'

She opened her mouth to retort but snapped it shut. She had to think this through. 'I will not try to stop you,' she said slowly. 'I will stay here.'

'Then you will be the cause of the deaths of everyone you love.'

Her heart twisted and squeezed at the thought but she still lifted her chin and said, 'No. I will not. You will be. If you follow through with your threat then you will be responsible for the deaths.'

'You may say that but I know you won't think the same when the massacre occurs. I may be the one to wield the instrument of death but you are the one who directs me where to place the blow—and on how many—by your lack of gumption.'

'You would try to kill them anyway.'

'Maybe. Maybe not. Maybe I'd prefer to look elsewhere to help enact my wrath. Maybe there is another pack and coven I could beleaguer and decimate. Yours is not the only one that would suffice to be an avenue through which I can return. The choice is yours.'

'It is not much of a choice.'

'How so? I think it a marvellous choice.'

'That I point you either towards my pack and coven to destroy or another in its turn? Either way I am a monster.'

'You are already a monster. You will simply be showing the world your true face.'

'That is ... I am not ...' She placed her hand over the scars on the side of her face. 'You are wrong!'

His chuckle rang all around her. 'The inside is represented by the outside, it seems.'

It shouldn't hurt—especially given it was the Darkness who said it—but it did. Just as every stare and pointing finger, whispers as she walked past and cut off conversations when she entered a room hurt. Each and every single one was like a stinging cut that by themselves probably wouldn't have been more than a momentary unpleasantness, but when added together, layered on top of one another, she had come to feel like she was nothing but a mass of bleeding, tortured flesh only being held together by something inside her that would not let go of the very little she had. The thing that had never allowed another Healer to rid her of the scars she so hated. For Healers had tried and had always failed and nobody knew why.

Was this why? Because this evil thing inside her needed to show itself in some way? Why else had she allowed herself to be beaten down by the whispers and looks and mean things people said?

'No. No. It is not true.' She yelled it into the purple-greyness around her, but the yell was as much for herself as it was for him. Because she wasn't evil. She couldn't be. She'd always done good. Loved doing good no matter what anyone else around her did or said. And if she wasn't good, then how could she have gained her papa's love and Morghanna's and Alistair's friendship and trust too?

How could she have become Dougal's mate? His wolf would never have wanted to be mated to someone who carried such evil inside her. She knew this as certainly as she knew Dougal loved her. She might not be able to feel it now, cut off from their bond as she was, but their love was a living thing inside her feeding the strength and courage that had always been inside her, helping it to grow and flourish.

It didn't matter what the Darkness or anyone said about her. What mattered was how she felt. And she no longer felt small, ugly and useless.

She felt ... strong. Powerful even. Loved—and worthy of that love. She was everything she thought she could be; everything she aspired to be.

She didn't have to be what the Darkness saw in her.

She'd held onto her scars, not because they represented evil inside her, but because they were a mark of the strength that had always lived within her. A strength that told her she was not this wraith he said she was. Wraiths sucked the life energy out of living beings, killing them or, if they didn't complete their feed, taking so much the victim was left nothing but a wasted husk of a person in both body and mind. There was no way she could become such a creature. Not only because she was a Healer, but because of who she was in the heart of her—a person who, despite what had happened to her and how she'd been treated before she came to live with Pack

MacCrae, was not bitter and twisted. She cared about people; had deep empathy for them and only wanted the best for them.

Not that she couldn't do bad things sometimes. Everyone had the capacity for evil within them—she wasn't so naive as to not understand that. But to become a wraith ... it truly wasn't possible. Not for her.

As if he knew what she was thinking he said, 'You are right, you are not evil. But the wraith isn't inherently evil, no more than a wolf that hunts down prey is evil for the death it brings. You've done a beautiful job suppressing the great power inside you all these years, but now you are finally becoming the mouse that roars, you will find it much harder to keep being untrue to yourself. And if you don't face this now, with me here to push you into using the beautiful, dark chaos inside you, then you will be lost as your parents were. But worse than when your father exploded, you will take half the country with you before the power is done. You will be responsible for more loss of life than anything that has come before you. It will, of course, be spectacular and I will enjoy it even though it will be a waste of potential. But I will content myself with the fact your soul will be destroyed and will never recover to be with your soulmate ever again. So whatever you decide works for me.'

Maybe she'd spent too long around the Were but she couldn't stop the snarl that curled in her chest and throat. She shouldn't let him get to her like this especially as she knew he was being cruel because he could. He was just trying to get a rise out of her because he wanted to make her react emotionally. Because he was apparently feeding from her emotions, becoming stronger, and sending that power and strength through to Lachlan somehow.

She had to stop feeling so strongly. So she took a steadying breath, reining in all the negative emotions and asked evenly, 'Why do you say I am supposed to be a wraith?'

'Not just a simple wraith. A Soul-wraith. And I don't say you're supposed to be one, I am saying you *are* one. It was what was stopping you from remembering that you were mated. It wants you for itself. It's there just waiting inside you for the right opportunity to come out.'

'Because I am a Healer.'

'No. You are not any run of the mill Healer. It's because you are a Soul Healer.'

A Soul Healer? She had never heard of such a thing before. 'What does that me—'

'Ooh look, Lachlan has got to the Healer Hall. I wonder what he's going to do when he gets inside?' He laughed, the sound echoing around her. 'You need to become the Soul-wraith now because it's the only way you can get out of here and stop him. Or you can hide away in here forever and never become what you are afraid of being. But then you must stand here and watch everyone you love being massacred by Lachlan who is now powered by the part of me that I've been able to shove into him thanks to you and your delicious emotion-driven power. Decisions, decisions. I wonder what you will choose.'

35

Every spirit in the room shrieked then vanished at the exact moment Leanna did.

Dougal shouted, 'Leanna!'

'What happened?' Cal asked at the same time.

Dougal turned to Morghanna who was peering around as if she could find Leanna in the air. 'Where is she? Where has she gone?' he yelled, every ounce of him wanting to move, to hunt for his mate. Desperation, fear, rage raced over him like a flame on a dry log. Muscles in his legs twitched, making them jump under the blankets, but despite the unexpected movement he had no control. He couldn't do more than roll his legs towards the edge of the bed. But he kept trying. He had to get up. Had to search for his love. Had to go after her wherever she was.

Because he could feel that something was dreadfully wrong.

Fear. Panic. Rage. They hit him through the bond, swamping the relief he felt at the fact he could still feel her there, deep inside him.

'Morghanna! Morghanna! We have to get to her. We have to go now.'

Morghanna looked at him, confusion in her eyes. 'I ... I cannot feel where she has gone.'

'She is in the place between here and the astral,' a voice whispered to him.

He whipped around, trying to see who had spoken. Beside the bed was an amorphous shape that looked like Leanna's papa, but was too faded to be certain. 'Johnathan? Ye are still here?'

'I am, but I can hold on no longer. I am being pulled away. Go to my girl.'

'How?'

'Follow the bond. You have done it before. Do so again now.'

Dougal wasn't certain how he'd done it the first time but he would do his best to go to her now. 'I will try.'

'Do better than trying. You must get to her. Now. Or we will lose her.'

Fear was like a wave crashing through him at those words. 'What do you mean?'

'The Da—'

The door slammed open. A figure charged in, eyes blazing red, canines extended, claws out. His hair was long and shaggy and a matted beard covered his face. The clothes he wore were too big for his thin frame, but there was no mistaking who it was.

'Lachlan,' Cal and Alistair shouted, both turning to face him as Morghanna raised her hands to draw wards in the air between all of them and the outcast Were.

Bram stumbled to his feet, a snarl on his lips, a wildness in his eyes that indicated he was acting on instinct rather than thought. Given he was still recovering from the presence of the spirits he was as likely to attack any one of them on this side of the shield as he was to defend them from Lachlan.

'Cal. Yer brother,' Dougal cried out.

But his cry was drowned out by Lachlan screaming, 'Ye will die fer what ye did.' His voice was filled with a thousand horrified echoing screams that had all the Were in the room snarling and the hairs on Dougal's body rising.

Lachlan surged forward.

Cal and Alistair lunged to meet him. Bram turned, looking like he was going to attack one of them as they ran past him.

Morghanna shouted, 'Stay behind the shields!'

'No!' Dougal shouted, managing to get his legs off the bed, his muscles twitching and jumping with the adrenaline and need chasing through him. He had to get up. Had to help.

'No. Go to Leanna!' the ghostly figure behind him yelled. 'She needs you now!'

'They need help.'

'Morghanna has it. See?'

As he said that, Lachlan hit the warding shield Morghanna had raised. The attacking Were flew backwards, crashing into the side table next to the door.

'Ignore what is happening here,' Johnathan yelled. 'None of that will matter unless you get to Leanna.'

'Do what he says,' Morghanna shouted back at him over her shoulder as Lachlan scrambled to his feet and threw himself back at the shield. He hit it with a loud smack, but this time only got thrown back halfway across the room.

'I cannot bring her back here with him trying to kill us,' he shouted, jabbing his finger at Lachlan who had quickly scrambled to his feet and tried again, hitting the invisible wall harder, bouncing back half the distance and staying on his feet.

'You must,' Jonathan said, his voice closer to a distant echo than something coming from right beside Dougal. 'It is the only way to get her out of the Darkness's clutches.'

'The Darkness? The Darkness has her?'

'Yes. It is why you can barely feel her.'

'But why is it going after Le-le?'

'Because she is a Soul Healer but could become a Soul Eater if twisted towards it. You must stop this. You are the only one who can.'

'Ye canna change what my master wills,' Lachlan screeched. 'He will have her, just as I will have ye, my beloved.' His gaze was pinned to Morghanna as he threw himself against the shield again, bouncing back half the distance he had before and then threw himself against it again and again and again.

Morghanna let out a grunt of exertion, her raised hands shaking.

So it was true. Lachlan still somehow had a part of the Darkness in him and that evil being had its clutches on his Le-le! Her papa was right. He had to get to her. But how could he concentrate enough to go to his mate with all this going on?

He closed his eyes to try, but the noise of Lachlan throwing himself madly against Morghanna's shield, and the sound of increasing agony in her grunts and groans each time he hit it, pulled at his concentration, at the protective part of him that would have been an Alpha if not for his injury.

His eyes flared open at a particularly loud thump and Morghanna's subsequent cry of pain. What was he doing to her? How was he doing it?

'Anna,' Alistair said, glancing her way but obviously not wanting to take his eyes off the Were attacking them.

'I may need help. He is abnormally strong.'

'Of course I am, my beloved. I have another part of the Darkness within me, lending me strength,' Lachlan said. 'And it is so much stronger than before, thanks to what his—' a jerk of his head towards Dougal, '—scarred bitch is giving him.'

'Leanna would give him nothing,' Morghanna, Alistair and Dougal shouted together.

'How little ye ken, my beloved,' Lachlan said, his face splitting in a voracious smile as he threw himself against the shield again, making Morghanna grunt once more.

'We defeated the Darkness and your Beast before,' Alistair said as he dropped his defensive posture and reached for her hand, grasping it tightly.

Something like electricity shivered through the air and the shield between them and Lachlan became visible, rippling like the water in the loch on a windy day.

'My beloved. Dinna stop me from freeing ye. We want the same thing.'

'She is not your beloved,' Alistair snarled at the same time Morghanna said, 'We want none of the same things, Lachlan. You have made a mistake coming back here.'

'The mistake will be yers fer denying me.'

His eyes focused behind them, pinned to Dougal. 'But first, ye will pay fer taking that which is no' yers to take.'

'Nobody took anything from you,' Morghanna yelled. 'You took from us. From Dougal.'

'If ye mean his legs, that was a pleasure,' Lachlan sneered, eyes gleaming.

'No, I mean Le-le.'

'Where is she?' Dougal demanded, everything in him wanting to answer to Lachlan's insult and his unwelcome presence with violence.

A sly smile slid over his face. 'Wouldna ye like to know.'

'Ye better not have done anything to her.'

'What are ye going to do about it? Quiver at me?' He laughed nastily.

'It will not be him doing the violence,' Alistair said, his voice cutting over the laughter. 'Morghanna and I are more than capable of taking care of you.'

Lachlan sneered at him, his laughter dying as abruptly as it had come. 'Ye canna do aught about me. Fer the Darkness is with me once more. I called to him and he came. Just as he did when yer precious Le-le called to him to save ye.'

'Ye are lying!' Dougal barked out. 'Le-le would never go over to the Darkness.' And yet, what the spirit of her papa had said only moments ago flashed into his mind, sewing a seed of worry—because why would her papa say it was possible she became this Soul Eater thing if there wasn't some truth in it?

Lachlan sniggered. 'There is no need fer her to go o'er. She already had the capacity within her. The Darkness has her now. And very soon, she will be here, his avenging angel, and she will suck the souls right out of ye all until there is nought left. Ye will be more useless than my ex-packmates there.'

He gestured at Cal, then at Bram, who seemed to have gathered some composure and were standing in defensive postures in front of Iain who was still lying on the floor, quivering and groaning occasionally.

Lachlan gestured at his father. 'I see my papa is as weak and useless as ever.'

'Ye dare insult our Alpha!' Bram growled.

'I do more than dare!' Lachlan yelled, his voice taking on an edge of hysteria. 'He should have given way to me years ago and yet selfishly he held on to the mantle, denying me my birthright!'

'Being Alpha is not a birthright,' Dougal said fiercely. 'It is earned through hard work on behalf of yer pack, loyalty, honesty and an ability to put those under yer care first every single day. Something ye have always failed in cause of the lack in yer soul.'

'Ye dinna deserve to be Alpha,' Cal said as Lachlan visibly trembled from anger on the other side of the shield. 'Ye deserve nothing other than what ye have ... nought.' He pointed at Dougal sitting on the side of the bed. 'If anyone deserves to be Alpha, it is Dougal.'

'That cripple!' Lachlan spat.

'Not a cripple,' Alistair said through gritted teeth—he had to be giving a lot of power to Morghanna to look like that. What the hells was she doing? It had to be more than holding that shield in place for her to be taking that much from her mate.

'Of course he's a cripple. He canna even stand.'

'We assure you, he can stand,' Morghanna said archly.

'What?' Dougal said under his breath. He felt stronger now than he had since his accident, his muscles bunching and twitching in his legs as if getting ready to be used, and there was more sensation than there had ever been before, yet he wasn't certain he could stand even for a second let alone maintain one for long enough to fool Lachlan.

'Stop being distracted by all this,' Johnathan whispered in his ear. 'Go to your mate. She needs you desperately or it will be too late.'

Somehow, Lachlan heard what the spirit said because he laughed and said, 'It is already too late!' Then threw himself at the shield once more.

Morghanna screamed, Alistair called her name as he put his arms around her, but he too looked like he was about to fall to the floor. Cal leapt forward to help hold them both up but she waved him back, somehow managing to remain upright.

She turned to Dougal and said in a strange voice, 'Now it is up to you!'

She threw her hand out, power streamed towards him, whacking him in the chest, but instead of falling backwards, it yanked him forward and up until he was standing on aching legs. Muscles in his back, bottom and thighs screamed in pain at the sudden movement into a position they had not been in in too long.

Yet he only noticed it with one part of his mind, because with most of his mind he was caught in a sensation of being ripped up and out of his body spinning and falling towards ... towards ...

'Dougal!' Le-le's scream tore through the air.

The whisper of a spirit figure that was far below flickered violently, his mouth—what Dougal thought was his mouth—opened wide on a scream as Leanna's cry rang through the air, tearing through the aether. It was high pitched and loud enough to pierce the eardrums of every Were in the room, snapping him back down and into his body in a way that punched the air from his lungs and flattened him to the floor despite Morghanna's magic holding him upright. As he hit the floorboards, Dougal automatically clapped his hands over his ears, the sticky warmth of his blood dripping down his neck and between his fingers as he groaned his pain, fighting with everything in him not to pass out from the pain caused by the scream peeling through the room.

Had the others passed out?

Dougal lifted his head and looked through hazy eyes to see Cal, Bram and Iain lying on the floor unconscious, blood pouring out of their ears and nose from the sonic attack. They were so still, hardly breathing, but they *were* breathing. For now.

But if Lachlan, and Le-le's papa, were to be believed—and that unearthly scream pushed him closer to accepting it was real—they wouldn't be alive for long.

'Son. You have to go to her now!'

The voice came from the foot of the bed, barely an echo, heard more in his head than with his damaged and bleeding ears.

He tried to make out the figure but it was only there like a faded reflection in water.

He went to answer, but the scream started up again, this time louder, driving him to the point of unconsciousness. But just before he slipped away, Johnathan's spirit shoved into him, knocking his astral spirit from his body and pushing it up and away.

As he flew away from where his body was, he heard clearly in his head, 'Follow the bond. Help my Rabbit save the day!'

And then there was nothing but blackness.

No. There was something more than blackness. In the distance was a speck of purple-grey that became larger and larger as he was pulled towards it, following the mating bond that now vibrated and pulsed in a way it never had before. It allowed him to see it shining so brightly, every thread illuminated as it pulled him along.

But suddenly the bond began to shake so violently that it looked like the edges were starting to fray.

By the Moon, no! He couldn't lose his Le-le. Not now he could finally call her his. Not now when he had just begun to think they could have a good future together. Not now when they had only just begun.

'Le-le! *Mo ghrádh!*' he cried out, voice and mind, shoving the words, the feelings, down the mating bond, hoping she would hear it or sense it. 'Wait fer me. I am coming.'

All he heard in return was another scream—but somehow, deep in the scream, his name fluttered, both plea and promise—and it drew him forward faster than ever before.

36

Dougal followed the pull of the bond, flying faster and faster towards the purple-grey. It soon turned from a dot-like smudge to the size of the sun in the sky. It kept getting larger and larger until he lost sight of the edges.

The closer he got the less it looked like a smudge and more like a solid shape—impregnable. The bond entered it and then disappeared. Worse, there seemed to be no space around the bond that he could slip through.

How was he supposed to get in? There was no door or anything that looked like an entrance.

He was getting closer and closer, moving faster and faster. Any moment he would smack into it and ... A rumbling sound made it shake violently then cracks appeared on its surface, lighter striations among the purple-grey, crazing along the surface, pulling it apart in sections so that he thought he could see within. And one of those sections was right where the mating bond disappeared into it.

Was this a way in for him? The cracks didn't look that big but he had no idea how far from it he still was, so they could be big enough for a Were his size to fly through.

He hoped so, otherwise he might just go splat against the surface if it was indeed as solid as it looked.

The thing vibrated more violently and the rumbling grew louder as he flew closer. The cracks got bigger and bigger so he did begin to believe that he could do this. He could fly in there and get to his mate before it was too late.

If indeed it already wasn't too late because whatever was going on in there couldn't be anything good.

Was Le-le getting hurt by whatever was causing the rumbling, vibrating and cracking? No, she couldn't be. The emotion coming through the bond wasn't fear or pain or panic.

It was fury and outrage. Pure and simple. And huge.

He'd never known anyone could feel anger that strongly, let alone his mate. Yet he couldn't deny that was exactly what he felt from her.

What in all the hells was the Darkness doing to her to make her respond like that? At least he hoped her fury was aimed at him. He hoped it wasn't aimed at anyone else—like him or any of her coven who she would expect to help protect her and have her back. Even though she would have every right to be furious given the fact none of them had stopped this happening; none of them had stopped her being taken.

The fact they hadn't known she was in danger from anyone aside from Iain and Bram was beside the point. They should have protected her. Should have realised, given how powerful she'd proven to be, that she would be in danger from those who might seek to use that kind of power—especially the Darkness.

Even though her power was good—was used for good; should only ever be good—he knew, better than most, how there was a dark side to everything, even the light. The best of intentions didn't always save you, or save you from doing something less than good. He'd thought he was doing the right thing when he'd agreed to let Iain channel his and the other lieutenants and senior soldiers' powers to help him keep control over his grief and over Lachlan, but look what that had led to.

And now this ...

Le-le was in danger and he could do nothing to truly help except travel through the aether to this place he knew nothing about and didn't even know if he could get in.

Not to mention he had no idea what he was supposed to do to help her when he was there. He had no magic. Nothing to stop her with if she was turning into this dangerous thing Lachlan said she was. It wasn't like he would hurt her. Could never hurt her.

So all he had was himself. And his love for her.

Given the depth and strength of her fury that was vibrating through the bond, increasing with every breath, he wasn't certain that would be enough. That he, how he was now, would ever be enough.

But he wasn't going to let that or anything else stop him from trying. Because Le-le deserved everything he had and more.

So he kept going. Kept following the bond towards the cracks in the purple-grey thing before him.

It seemed to be taking far longer than it should—why had he come into this place so far away from her? His wolf howled and snarled at how long it was taking, but there was no way to go faster than he already was.

Through the bond he said over and over, '*Hold on*, mo ghrádh. *I am coming. Hold on.*'

THE RAGE and fury were like a furnace inside Leanna. She held onto it with everything in her, trying hard to find a way not to let it drive her to be the thing the Darkness said she would become. But it was a losing battle as she watched Lachlan attack those she loved most.

She wanted to go to them, but she didn't know how to escape this place without giving in to the violent, dangerous thing inside her.

It was pushing up and up inside her and had screamed like a banshee upon seeing Lachlan attack. It wanted to get out, to take revenge for what had been done to her people; for what the Darkness and his minions would continue to do to her pack and coven, to witches and Were. For what it was getting Lachlan to do to them right now. It wanted her to see that using it was the only way forward.

She was horribly afraid it was right as she watched Morghanna and Alistair fighting to keep Lachlan back with a shield. The strength the Darkness gave to him ... he'd break that shield down soon, maybe even break them. Then who would be there to stop him from getting to the rest of the coven and pack?

Not Dougal—he had somehow been standing only to fall back on the bed and now seemed unconscious. What had happened to him? She had to get back to him to see. Had to Heal him. Had to save him.

He needed her and she wasn't there.

'Let me out. Let me take us to him!'

She wanted to. Oh Goddess, how much she wanted to.

'Ah-ha-ha! Yes.' Maniacal laughter and what sounded like clapping followed the outburst and pulled her spiralling thoughts back to where she was.

All around her the purple-grey place she was in shook and rumbled and more huge fissures had appeared, so wide she could see the cracks had broken right through to show the black of whatever lay beyond this place.

Was this her? Had she done this?

'Yes! Yes, you have. Yes, you are. No! Don't stop. Keep going. Show me what you're made of! Go save your mate. He's in terrible danger. As are all of them.'

She ground her teeth together. She couldn't do what the Darkness wanted. She couldn't. And yet ... She stared at the pool in the purple-grey in front of her. Her friends, her coven, her pack were all in danger. Dougal was in danger. Because of her. And she wasn't there to help. To stop it when she could stop it.

She was the only one who could. The Darkness said so.

But she shouldn't believe that evil entity. She couldn't.

And yet ...

There was a knowing stronger than any knowing she'd ever had, that told her he was telling the unvarnished truth this time.

She had the power and ability to save them. To save everyone.

But only if she let go of whatever was holding back the true heart of her power and just let it ... be.

She wanted to. She really did. This new power she'd caged should be let out to do what it did. Only then would all the pain she'd held inside her all her life be released.

But ... he'd called her a mouse. He'd called her that because he assumed she was weak. That she would give in. But she wasn't the mouse any longer. She wasn't weak and insignificant, she was everything that Dougal and Morghanna and Abigail had always seen in her.

She was strong in spirit and in body. And she was powerful.

So terribly powerful.

She wouldn't let the Darkness use her to destroy everything she treasured; everyone she loved. She wouldn't let him win.

She would show him he was wrong about her. She would show him that she could have the power but not use it in the way he said she must.

She was good.

She wanted to be good.

She wanted to be worthy of a mate as good as Dougal.

And she would be. She could be.

'But we have to break out of here and get back to him. Let me do it for us. Let me take us to him.'

'Yes! That's it! Become everything I know you will be!'

The Darkness's voice shrieked around her, a cackling, sharp sound that made shivers shudder up and down her spine and her ears feel like they were going to bleed. But she closed her eyes, squeezing them shut and shoved aside the discomfort with the steely will she was only just beginning to understand was hers and always had been, and concentrated on the power bubbling and roiling inside her, pushing to get free.

The power was telling her the truth. It could do what it said. But did it have to do it in the way the Darkness wanted her to? Did she need to let it take over who and what she was?

No. There was another way.

She had to find it if she was going to help those she loved most without being the thing that would also destroy them. She had to be able to let the power out and not cage it—because the pain of doing that was hurting her deep inside in ways she knew she would not recover from if she didn't figure this out soon.

If Dougal was here, he'd tell her to trust herself. He'd believe in her—as he had since the first moment. He'd tell her not be afraid of herself. His trust and belief in her ... it was everything. And it would always be hers. She could feel it through the bond even—

The bond! She could feel the bond! Not only that ...

She could feel Dougal!

Actually, she could hear his voice calling to her from a distance. It was getting louder and louder as if—

Her eyes snapped open as she turned towards the glorious sound of his beautiful, deep, warm voice. A voice that had always made her feel like she was being wrapped in warm furs and the softest silks every time he spoke to her.

But it wasn't just his voice that was here. *He* was here. Flying through a crack she'd widened with her cascading, uncontrolled powers, coming closer and closer as he yelled out her name.

'*Hold on*, mo ghrádh. *I am coming. Hold on.*'

And he was! He really was. Not his body. His body was still back in the real world collapsed on the edge of the bed. She could see it there out of the corner of her eye in the vision portal the Darkness had been torturing her with. And what was flying towards her had a slight translucent look to it—she gasped.

His astral spirit! He was travelling astrally.

How was he doing that? Only witches could astral travel through the aether and yet there he was, his astral spirit flying towards her, the gossamer thread of the link with his body stretching out into the dark of the aether behind him, a brilliantly glowing steel blue thread tinged with the colours of the rainbow. That same glow surrounded his astral body too, lighting up the handsome planes of his face, accentuating the breadth of his chest and shoulders.

Beautiful. So beautiful. Just like his Earthly body.

'Dougal!' she called out. She couldn't believe he was here—but of course he was because she needed him so. He had always been there every time she needed him. Why would now be any different? Especially given they were mated.

She wanted to cry. Wanted to shout her joy at the sight of him flying towards her, the glow around him intensifying as he drew closer. His face was folded in lines of worry, but his eyes glowed with joy and love.

For her. Always for her. So strong to see right there but to also feel down the bond that was now so firmly seated inside her where it was supposed to be.

'Dougal,' she said again, the sound a sob.

'Leanna!'

She held her hands out and jolted. The pearlescent glow that she'd noticed on her skin when she'd first arrived here was now like staring into the bright heart of a fire. And it was pulsing like a heartbeat with zaps of tiny lightning—brilliant white tinged with orange and amethyst—cascading down her arms.

Her power. This was her power about to explode out of her like witch lightning—a powerful and often deadly force.

She tried to pull it back, to get a grip on it but it was too late.

The lightning flew down her outstretched arms. It outlined the fineness of her hands and fingers—and the scars on the back of the right one—and then dove into her hands, making them flex violently before it burst out of her fingertips, heading straight towards Dougal.

He was now only half a dozen yards away. Too close to dive sideways and avoid the deathly strike of magic coming his way.

'Dougal!' she screamed as laughter lit the air around her, sickening and cruel.

Then as the lightning hit Dougal square in the chest, lighting him up in an explosion of pearlescent white, orange and amethyst, the Darkness cried out in a voice full of maniacal joy, 'I said you'd be the death of your mate!'

He was right! He was right. By the Goddess, he was right.

She screamed her horror and grief and the world exploded around them.

37

Dougal saw the witch lightning coming at him but could do nothing to move out of the way. He braced for the hit, expecting to be blasted into oblivion, at the same time, agonisingly aware that his Le-le would blame herself for his death. So, in the split second before the hit, he shouted down the bond, 'It isna yer fault. The Darkness did this to ye. It isna yer fault. I love ye. Forever and always will I love ye.'

He got no further.

The power hit him and ...

It was like nothing he'd ever experienced before—certainly not what he expected.

It wrapped around him, squeezing, pulling, then it was inside him too, expanding. It felt like his Le-le but was something else as well. Something huge. Something brighter than the sun and hotter than the bonfires on Beltane. And yet there was coldness there too, creeping into his bones, into the part of him that was the wolf.

The closest comparison he had was being huddled in blankets in front of a fire in the middle of a blizzard. With the cold and the fire fighting for pre-eminence, he knew one thing with certainty: he wasn't going to die.

His Le-le was fighting even now to gain control and not kill him with her extraordinary power. It was a close fight—white witch lightning, like black warlock lightning, most definitely could kill.

Although he had seen it used by Morghanna to fight the Darkness that had created Lachlan's Beast. She had drained the evil from the Beast, leaving only weak and mewling Lachlan, and had sent the Darkness to oblivion—at least, that's what they'd thought at the time. It appeared the Darkness was a many tentacled beast.

But if Morghanna's witch lightning hadn't killed Lachlan, there was no reason why Le-le's would kill him now.

Except ... except ...

His wolf began to howl in panic as the intense cold crept through it, draining it of energy, of strength, of all that it was.

No! No! It couldn't be.

The wraith.

This is what Lachlan had crowed about—the destruction Leanna could wreak because her Soul Healing could be channelled both ways. She could take as easily as she could give.

And with the Were, she could do both in one being because they had two souls.

She could suck on all the power of their wolves' souls, stealing their change, stealing half of who they were by killing the wolf. Even if the human side survived the process, they would most likely die from shock and grief over the days following. Any that might survive would be nothing more than husks that could barely function without help.

It would mean the death of the Were.

This was what Johnathan had tried to warn them about, why he'd been so determined to get Dougal here. He thought Dougal could stop her.

But how could he stop her? He was just the astral representation of his body. Even if he was fully Healed and in possession of the strength and power of his Were self, the Alpha in him bubbling under the surface ready to be called on, he couldn't stop her. She was too strong. Her power too vast.

She was remarkable; one of a kind. And he knew nobody could stop her when she truly gave over to this side of her power.

But ... Johnathan had to have known all this. So, what he must want from Dougal was for him to be the thing to stop Leanna from truly becoming. Because he could be the lesson nobody else would be for her. The thing she destroyed that would show her exactly what she was capable of—for if she could take his wolf from him, killing him, she could do it to anyone. The shock of it would stop her power from growing and growing, eating up all the wolf souls it had connection through the Packbond before reaching out to seek more elsewhere.

And, when the shock stopped her, it would show her how to rope it in.

That had to be why Johnathan wanted him here rather than Morghanna or Alistair—both incredibly powerful. Because he knew she would lose control and that she could never forgive herself for it. That she would never use the power again, no matter what happened.

But her papa had forgotten one thing in that scenario—or didn't truly understand it: his daughter was mated, heart and soul, to wolf and man; and if she killed her mate, she would follow him into death. Even worse, her soul would be forever tormented by it. She would never rest. Never find peace. Never be reborn to be with him in the next life.

She would roam as a spirit, eternally lost. And because of her power, she would truly become the wraith of legend that sucked life from everything it touched just to keep going in its eternal existence of misery.

Horrifying did not even begin to describe what would happen if he didn't stop her witch lightning from sucking the soul of his wolf from him.

But he didn't know how to stop her. Other than to kill her, which he could never do.

Fuck! He had to do something, anything, to try to break her free of whatever had pushed her into going this far. And the only thing he could think of was to say through the bond, *'I love ye, my Le-le. I know who ye are. Remember that now. Remember ye are beautiful and strong. Remem—'* The pain increased and his wolf howled. Yet despite the burning, searing pain, his wolf continued to fight hard to push the love for their mate, his trust in her, his belief in her, down the bond, doubling the intensity of what he was sending to her.

He wasn't sure it was working though—the pain was so intense as the power wrapped more tightly around them, pulling, sucking, tearing. Even so, they bore down against it, holding it back with everything in them so they could keep repeating the words and feelings of love and trust to their Le-le.

'Le-le. Remember ye know yerself. Remember to be you and only you, not what other people say ye are or could be or should be. I know ye think this act means that ye are evil, but I know better. Ye are not evil. Ye could never be evil. Ye are good. In yer soul and heart there is only kindness, empathy and goodness. One like ye could never be evil. If that is what he is making ye believe, dinna listen. Dinna believe. Ye are good. And ye are loved. Forever and always. I love ye for all of whom ye are, mo ghrádh. I love ye. I love ye.'

SHE WAS KILLING HIM. She was killing him!

Her power—this vast hungry power that had been inside her all this time had wrapped around Dougal and his wolf and was sucking on the wolf's soul.

Without his wolf, Dougal would die.

She was killing him!

Her heart was sobbing, her soul torn asunder. She couldn't breathe or think.

And yet she had to. Had to figure out how to stop it, even though she was horribly afraid she couldn't. Because she knew why she was doing it even if she didn't know how.

It was because she needed it. Needed to take the power from a living soul so she could use it to get out of here and save her coven, her pack, all the people who were supposed to be under her care. She had to save them from Lachlan and the bit of Darkness inside him, pushing him to do things a Were would never, could never, normally do. And this time, she was the only one who could stop him. Morghanna and Alistair, while powerful, couldn't pull on the strength of the Goddess again to help them fight this piece of the Darkness and oust it from Lachlan—the Goddess had specifically told Morghanna she couldn't help her so openly again without terrible repercussions.

And given nobody had ever been able to extract the Darkness without the Goddess's help, no regular witch or warlock, no matter how powerful, could handle it without a Godly kind of magic.

But she was no regular witch. She was something else, with a power inside her that had the touch of a Goddess.

The Darkness had been right. She was the thing he said she was —a wraith, a Soul Eater; taking the enormous power of a soul to use for herself.

And right now that poor soul was Dougal and his wolf.

No! No! It wasn't right. She couldn't do this. She loved him. She loved him! Surely that meant she couldn't be his death. The Fates couldn't be so cruel as to give them to each other and then make her the architect of his death.

Her thoughts wailed inside her. So loudly at first that she didn't understand the sound she was hearing. But then slowly, through the mists of her milling, turbulent, tortured thoughts, she heard it.

Dougal's voice. Telling her to remember herself. To remember her goodness. To not believe in the apparent evil of this act. Because he believed it couldn't be evil if it was coming from her.

He loved her. He trusted in her and her goodness. Forever and always.

Her heart throbbed but her soul ... her soul pulled itself back together, no longer rent and torn asunder. Because ... he was right.

She *was* good. It was the centre of everything she was. She had been telling herself just that before he'd appeared in this place.

So how could this power—no matter how huge, terrifying and unwieldy—be evil?

It couldn't.

Yes, it could be used like the Darkness said she had to use it—but that was his twisted soul talking. He couldn't see anything but evil being done by a power this strong and vast.

But he was wrong. Because while it could be evil, it could also be good. It all depended on her.

This power ... It had a purpose—to use the energy it pulled on for the benefit of others, not just because she needed it to survive.

Which she didn't. She didn't need the power from another person's soul to feed herself. That wasn't what this was supposed to be at all. Which meant ...

She dug deeply into the power, looking at it this way and that, feeling along its edges before shoving down and diving into the core of it.

Yes! She was right. She didn't need to completely use a soul up like the Darkness said she must. She just had to tap into it, link into the extra strength it gave her—like a second fire would give extra energy and warmth—so it could help her be the best witch she could be. So she could do extraordinary things.

So she could save people.

Not kill them.

She wasn't a killer. She was a Healer.

She wasn't evil. She was good.

Her entire reason for being was to save and to serve.

This power, this extra energy, could simply let her do this in ways no one else could.

Dougal saw that because he knew her in a way nobody else did. He saw her in a way that nobody ever had.

Just like she knew him. Just like she saw him.

And it was why she had instinctively linked the power into his wolf's soul. Because, for them, it was where the source of their bond could be found. It was where they essentially became one person. It was where the Fates had touched them, decreeing them mates and soul-bonded. That sparkle of Goddessly power, that gift of Goddessly touch, was what she was after. It was what she needed. Because it would let her tap in to the true source of her power where she only ever had to touch another soul as a channel to access all she was; all she could be.

There was no need to suck on the power of the soul and take it into herself. All she needed to do was touch it to switch into a state of being the likes of which nobody had ever seen.

And she could only do it because she was part of this soul-bond. She was one of the two who had become one.

They were not just Witch and Alpha in waiting.

They were the binary Alpha-Healer. Separate and yet forever together.

And they could destroy this bit of the Darkness.

More ... they could possibly one day save the world!

Dougal's words ... his words were everything. His faith was everything.

His love was everything.

But all of it wrapped together with her faith and love and trust in what they were and could be together was even more. It wasn't just the sun and the moon, it was the universe.

And it helped her to truly understand that if she always remained true to herself, she would never be what the Darkness said she was.

She would be the opposite. She would be an ante-Wraith. A life giver, not a life taker.

She would be something never seen before.

No—*they* would be something never seen before. Because she couldn't do this or be this without Dougal; couldn't do it without their mating and soul-bond.

She was like Airmed—the Goddess of life-giving and resurrection —and Danu—the Goddess of nurturing—rolled into one. But she was also something new and as gloriously bright as the heart of the sun.

With a laugh of joy she dove inside that brightness, pulling

Dougal and his wolf with her, wrapping them in the protection of her love and the glory of their bonds, and gave herself up to the power.

It wrapped around her, filled all the places that doubt had lived and exploded out of her in waves of brilliant love and harmony and warmth.

It was Dougal; it was her.

And it was more power than one witch should ever be able to carry—a thousand times greater than the explosions of power that had caused so much destruction and pain among her people, including the deaths of her parents. But she wasn't afraid because she wasn't a single witch. She was Dougal and he was her.

In this instant, they were truly one.

They were power. They were glory. They were the shining heart of love.

The power flew out of them in streams and waves.

And as it did, the Darkness screamed, 'No, no. What are you doing? What have you done? You can't do this to me. Not again. Not agai—'

His screamed words cut short as the power, having chased him out of his hiding place in the purple-grey, wrapped around him and burned away all the evil until there was nothing but the tiniest speck of light that had somehow hidden within. The Light whimpered to her and she enfolded it in to the being that was her and Dougal. And when she was done, she pushed them and the power out, slipping through one of the cracks she'd created earlier when she'd lost control.

Not wanting to leave destruction in her wake, she let a trail of power spread out behind her, repairing what she had damaged. Because despite what the Darkness had insinuated, he hadn't created that place to bring her to. No, it was older than him; as old as the universe. And while it wasn't a sentient being as she understood such things, she knew somehow that it did think and feel.

So she wasn't surprised that, as she Healed it, a wave of relief and thankfulness spread over her, coming from the purple-grey. Not only for Healing it after unintentionally hurting it, but it was thanking her for ridding it of the Darkness that had been using it. That evil being's presence had been like a canker and it was so thankful she had cut it out.

As she finished Healing it with the tendril of her magic, she sent love and support towards it and a promise to always help it when it was in need. Then she carried on, the power inside her throbbing with bliss at what they had done; what they had managed, all three souls together.

They flew through the aether, following the thread of Dougal's soul that anchored him to his body and led back to the realm of the living. They moved so fast she could see nothing but a blur of images that moved through the astral as they were pulled back. They were arrowing down through the astral plane and into the living plane and the blur became a single image.

The village lay below them, like seeing it through the eyes of an eagle soaring through the clouds. They rushed down towards it, speeding faster and faster—exhilarating.

Then, they were flying through the roof of the Healer Hall, into her room, and, with a final pull and a pop, they were back in his body.

His body? She was in Dougal's body! Not in hers. Hers had come with her when the Darkness had pulled her through space and time to imprison her inside the purple-grey entity. But it hadn't re-corporealised when they came back out of there.

In fact, her body was nowhere to be seen.

She was still the being of pure power she had transformed into when she realised who and what she was. And she was still twined with Dougal's souls—wolf and human—and was now inside his body like his wolf was. Part of him.

Forever?

She pushed the thought away, too big to encompass right now given the fight she could hear going on. She needed to see what was happening.

Suddenly, Dougal's eyes were on the fight.

Had she done that? Controlled him?

She recoiled from the thought. She could deal with being a part of him, locked inside him with no corporeal body of her own so that they could help people, but if that meant she controlled him? No. She didn't want that. Didn't want to be nothing but a puppet master like the Darkness had controlled Lachlan.

Was still controlling him even though she had destroyed the part of it that had been in the purple-grey. She could see its influence clearly in his aura as he smashed against the shield Morghanna and Alistair were holding in place.

Holy Goddess. Please don't let me be a monster like that.

'*Ye dinna need to fash yerself about that,* mo ghrádh.' Dougal's voice rang in her mind, clear and strong and sure.

'*Dougal! You are able to talk to me?*'

'*Always. Ye are in my body, alongside me and my wolf. Not in control as ye fear but equal. Together. Surely ye feel that, same as me. It is extraordinary.*'

As she let his words fill her, pushing out the fear that still seemed to touch her in some small way that she was a monster, she let her senses take in this new state of being.

Her mate was right. Threads of control spread between them, bounded by their bond, existing because of it. The control flowed both ways, indicating not one or the other was more in control of his body in this situation—they stood together, their thoughts and wills equal and moving as one.

What's more, the power inside her wasn't just her power, it was his.

They were linked in every way possible, closer and more intimate than she'd ever hoped for or thought could ever occur.

In the space in their combined minds, she suddenly saw him and his wolf standing beside her. He held out his hand. She twined her fingers with his as the wolf came to her side so she could twine her fingers through his silky fur. Their love and warmth wound around her, through her, as hers wound around and through them.

'*Look.*' Dougal's voice was clear in her mind, a warm, all-encompassing hug full of the eternal love that was the core of who they were.

It was also urgent and pulled her attention back to see through his eyes.

Colours she didn't even know were on the light spectrum appeared before her lighting up the auras of every living being in the room. And inside those auras, she could also see different shades and colours of what she suddenly knew were the soul-auras of everyone there.

'Do you see colours like this all the time?'

'Aye. Although it is a little more ... vibrant than what I can see through my wolf's eyes, but dinna let it distract ye. Look at Lachlan.'

He was right. She couldn't lose herself to what this new state of being was showing her. Fighting against all the distractions that kept pulling her attention this way and that, she centred herself and looked.

What she saw chilled her to the bone.

Lachlan's attack on the shield had become more than simply throwing himself against it and bashing it down by force. Every time he hit it, curls of darkened shadow hooked into parts of the shield's glistening surface, marring it, denting it, as they continued to lash at it and chisel through. More and more tendrils spiralled out of Lachlan's chest every second until almost all she could see of him was the tentacles she assumed came from the Darkness—using the power he'd leached from her in the purple-grey.

And yet, she could see clearly that Lachlan's aura was barely clinging to him; his wolf's soul-aura was so damaged that it looked like torn shreds of blackened cheesecloth hanging off him. And with every bit of the Darkness that shot out of him, his wolf's soul was damaged a little more.

Despite everything he'd done, despite all he was doing and obviously intended to do, despite the danger he posed, she couldn't help her heart throbbing in pain for him. She knew, from the stories she'd been told by others when she'd come here, and in the whispers that the loyal Were never meant for outside ears, that there had always been something not right about him. They'd assumed a certain damage or lack in his human soul, thinking this had been what the Darkness used to keep its hooks in him after Bridgette had cast it out of the Were when she'd cast the spells of the Pact.

But ... she could see no sign of a human soul within him—it seemed it was already gone or perhaps had never been there. She couldn't get distracted though by his lack of soul, not when the damage to his wolf's soul was something far worse than anything she'd ever seen. Had he done this himself with his hatred, jealousy and fury? Or was this entirely the Darkness at fault?

'I love yer heart fer the empathy ye feel, mo ghrádh, *but it doesna matter why or how he came to be the poor bastard he is. We need to help Morghanna and Alistair—fer if I am reading this right with this sight I share with ye, they are losing the battle.'*

He was right. So right. Ever the protective Alpha thinking of his people.

By the Goddess, it was a struggle to keep her mind and thoughts from flying all over the place in the vastness of the being she currently was. But she had to because Dougal needed her to focus with him; to help him figure out how to help those currently protecting them.

'What can we do?' she asked even as her mind spun over the problem.

'I dinna ken. I was hoping ye might.' His voice was tight and she suddenly realised that something else was going on inside them.

His wolf was pushing to the fore, trying to get out to defend the witches and attack the insane Were before them as its nature meant it to do. But rather than the symbiotic agreement that was supposed to go on between the human and wolf sides of a Were for the change to manifest, their wolf was trying to force the change. And Dougal was resisting. As he should. As he'd been told to do so as not to do more damage to his broken back.

She had to help Dougal stop the wolf from doing something so foolhardy—but she also had to figure out how to stop Lachlan, because a quick glance told her that things were going from bad to far, far worse.

She tried to talk to the wolf, to calm him down, to encourage him to abide right now while they dealt with the danger before them, but creature of instinct that he was, all he could see was the danger to his mate, his human side, and the other witches and Were he loved and wanted under his protection. And he kept pushing. Kept insisting. Kept trying to make the human give in. Make *her* give in. Kept reaching for the power to use—

Realisation struck like a lightning bolt, holding her still for one breathless moment as she saw what the wolf intended.

He was right. They had to let him come forth. It was the only way to win against the thing Lachlan had become. Because like the Darkness had originally created the Beast and had called it forth in Lachlan, this power of light and life that was her and Dougal and their wolf combined, was calling forth the wolf to be them; to represent them.

To be the Light's version of the Beast: the Werewitch.

'You clever wolf,' she said to him before turning to Dougal in this mind-space. Squeezing his hand more tightly, filling their bond with love, trust and hope, she said, *'Let go, Dougal. Let our wolf take us where we need to be.'*

'Nae. Nae. I canna,' he said, the effort in his voice so great, so full of the pain of holding back the other side of himself—something no Were ever wanted to have to do again now the Darkness wasn't tainting them all, keeping their wolves suppressed to come out only on the full moon as it had done for centuries beyond memory.

She imagined taking his face, pressing her lips to his in a gentle, assuring kiss, then leaning back and looking into his glorious eyes. *'He is right. Our wolf ... he knows what to do. He knows what to do better than us it seems. Trust me. Trust him.'*

She expected him to question, to speak his worries again—for it was not a little worry—but all he did was say, *'I do,'* and then he let go.

The wolf howled its acceptance of the trust and love given over to him, and then he exploded outwards in a glorious riot of rainbow light the brightness of the sun.

It filled the entire room in an instant, before sucking back in with a whump to the body they were in, finishing the transformation.

Changing the transformation.

They rose up, on two legs, part wolf, part human, part witch with the full extent of this ancient yet brand new power. And in this new form of wolf and human and witch and Light, they leaped forward to stand next to Morghanna and Alistair, claws and fangs extended, a glow like sun-filled amber emanating from the pale golden fur which covered their entire body—a body with the breadth and strength of Dougal and his wolf combined.

'I am walking! I am walking!'

Dougal's excited exclamation rang through her mind and with one part of her, she celebrated with him. But with the greater part of her she was all power and wolf, ready to protect those she loved and beat this thing in front of them streaming with the Darkness's shadow.

Dougal quickly pulled his focus back to what was in front of them, but his excitement, passion and determination thrummed through them. And as it did, the glow emanated back out into the room brighter and more forcefully than before, reaching to touch every living thing.

As that glow touched Morghanna and Alistair—who were staring at them in wide-eyed wonder—it seemed to soak into them, filling them with energy and strength and extra power. It touched their souls, wound around them, then added the power of those souls into their own. But they didn't take that power for their own—no, that wasn't who they were. It sent that power on an endless loop, taking it and feeding it back to those it had enfolded into the power, increasing in intensity with every loop. Strengthening them all.

When it was done with the witches, it touched the other Were in the room—Cal and Bram, even Iain. It filled all of them with the Healing power, fixing their exploded eardrums and filling them with the energy and wild strength that was the essential heart of the Were.

Their soul-energy was added into the loop, making it stronger and stronger as they strengthened.

Cal and Bram rose to their feet, howling with joy, transforming as they did, their rainbow glow adding to the light coming from them, the Werewitch, making it almost too bright to see.

But they could see. And feel.

Everything.

Everywhere.

Each and every soul of each and every living thing in the village and loch and mountains around them.

They could have pulled on that soul-energy too, but it was unnecessary to have that much power to complete their task here.

With clear intent, they took down the shield and engaged with the piece of Darkness streaming out of its puppet.

39

Lachlan shrieked as the shield came down, a sound of rage and exhilaration that shuddered through the air, making the room tremble. Dust fell from the rafters and some of the white-washed daub fell from the walls in chunks. The sound was so loud and long and piercing, it should have exploded the eardrums of every Were in the room again, including them.

But they—the Werewitch—stood tall against it, their Healing glow still emanating from them, touching those who stood with them, stopping them from being hurt again.

As Lachlan shrieked, the ribbons of Darkness waved around him like tentacles in the water. The sight of them made her shudder inside the Werewitch, and bile rose into her mouth. Those tentacles were so full of a hate and fury that pulsed at her, pulled at her, almost felt like they were trying to stroke her skin. She shuddered again.

'That is enough of that,' the Dougal part of them said out loud, lashing out with the Light power that was the heart of them.

The Light pulsed across the room in a wave and the moment it touched Lachlan and the Darkness, he screamed. The tentacles of Darkness curled back in on themselves as if they were going to bury themselves back inside him.

'*No,*' their wolf barked into their mind.

'*Grab them,*' the Dougal part said.

She sent out a Light-tentacle of their own, wrapping it around Lachlan, then over and around the Dark-tentacles, pulling them tight together into one mass. They shrieked and fought, lashing out at anything in the room they could touch, trying to make it to the other Were there, to Morghanna.

'Get away from them,' she cried out with the Werewitch voice, pulling the Light-tentacle tighter and tighter as Dougal and their wolf sent another one out to cut down the mass of Darkness that had been pulled together.

And every time they cut a Dark-tentacle, it crumbled and disappeared.

It was working! It was working!

A tentacle of Darkness thrust out of Lachlan's shoulder, above where they had bound him with their Light-tentacle, and flew towards Iain.

Without thinking, they sent out another ribbon of Light to fight it off. But this time, the Darkness didn't shrink from their touch but fought to get past them and to the Alpha as another and another burst from Lachlan, trying to do the same.

Of course it was trying to get to the Alpha. He was the weakest link because of his inability to do the right thing about his son.

As the tentacles flew towards him, they sent out more of their own to fight them off, parrying with them like it was a sword fight.

But more and more tentacles of Darkness were thrusting out of Lachlan and soon there was a mass of them and a mass of Light-tentacles, slashing, cutting, stopping them from getting to Iain.

The Alpha didn't move except to throw his arms up over his head as the powers clashed above him. He cried out Lachlan's name as a Dark-tentacle snapped right in front of him, about to touch him—but he made no move to fight it off. No. He looked more like he would cower from it—or worse, step into it and let it take him.

They were having none of that. Iain may be a bad Alpha, but he was their Alpha and it would do the pack no good to have their Alpha taken in this way. Showing his true weakness. His unfitness to be in charge and lead.

Dougal sent another, larger strand of Light his way to fight it off. He managed to get it there just in time, slicing it in half just before it touched Iain. The Darkness shrieked, the remaining part shuddering and flapping about, smacking into the ceiling, the wall, making more chunks of wood and daub fly.

'Look out!'

Bram dived forward, tackling Iain to the floor as parts of the ceiling rained down.

All the tentacles withdrew towards Lachlan, but then as one, the ones that were free of the restraint they still had on him, lashed back out again, all heading towards Iain, merging as they went into one giant ribbon of power.

Their wolf snarled and leapt them forward, slashing at the thing with their long, Light-filled claws, slicing it into pieces. The sliced-off bits crumbled then disappeared like smoke on the wind, but what remained became separate threads, each lashing out, aiming right for their heart.

They leapt out of the way of its strike, sending out another thread of Light to parry with it as they did.

Multiple Light threads were now fighting with multiple tentacles of Darkness, and still more were coming.

'*This isna working,*' Dougal said.

'*I think we need to go for the whole,*' Leanna replied.

Their wolf howled his agreement.

They sent out another pulsing wave of Light. It hit all of the bits of the Darkness, lighting up the blackness in the heart of the shadow, and then obliterating them.

Lachlan screamed and fell to his knees, head bowed.

Had they won? Had they—

Lachlan lifted his head, eyes swimming with the Darkness that was still somehow inside him, and pinned them on Iain who was rising from the floor with Bram's help. 'Father, help me!' he cried as another tentacle burst out of him. 'They're trying to take my wolf. They're trying to kill me.'

'Lachlan!' Iain shouted, taking a stumbling step towards his son, towards the Dark-tentacles that were coming out of his son once more. How could he still have so much inside him? The Darkness had said she'd empowered him in the purple-grey and he'd sent that power to Lachlan—but this much?

They gathered their power, ready to hit out again, but before they could let it go, another, faster ribbon of Darkness shot out of Lachlan and arrowed right towards his father.

'No!' Morghanna threw up a shield between him and the tentacle heading right towards him. It hit the shield and Morghanna grunted and went down on her knees at the impact.

'Anna!' Alistair cried, joining his power to hers just in time as it struck again, stopping it from punching through. More ribbons of Darkness were shooting out of Lachlan to batter against the shield.

They sent out another Light wave to deal with them, but as fast as they cut them down, they seemed to reappear, even stronger.

They sent another tentacle of power towards Lachlan, wrapping it around him again, then another and another, trying to cover him to cut off the source.

'Father! Help!' Lachlan screamed as they sent more ribbons of Light to blanket Lachlan's entire body and stop the Darkness from getting out. 'They're hurting me! They're killing me!'

'Stop hurting my boy!' Iain cried, surging forward. He came up against the shield Morghanna and Alistair were holding in place, bouncing off it and stumbling back a few steps. Turning, a vicious expression on his face, he snarled, 'Take it down. Let me go to him. I can reason with him. There isna a need to hurt him.'

'Ye canna,' Bram said, coming to his side. 'Canna ye see, he is too far gone. The Darkness has him again. He let it in. It couldna get him like that if he hadna.'

'Nae, Nae,' Iain said, pushing Bram aside. 'Ye dinna ken what ye are saying. My Lachie wouldna do that. Not again.'

'He did,' Cal said, joining his brother beside their Alpha. 'Bram is right. It could only get in like that if he had let it. He let it in then brought it here to hurt us. To hurt the pack. Yer pack. Ye canna give in to him again.'

Bram nodded. 'We didna hunt him down all this time to bring him back alive.'

'I niver gave ye permission to kill him.'

'That is what Hunters do when faced with a Packmate who endangers the pack.'

'Ye canna kill my son. Ye canna do it. I dinna give ye permission. I willna allow it.'

'Ye are a weak Alpha!' the Dougal part of them yelled at him. 'Ye would destroy us all with yer weakness.'

Iain's eyes flared wide as he turned and truly looked at them, taking in all they were. But then, as if aware everyone was watching, he squared his shoulders, lifted his chin and asked, 'Is that a challenge?'

'Nae. We have much more important issues right now than fighting ye,' the Dougal part snarled. They pointed at Lachlan and the Darkness. 'But if ye let him get those Darkness tentacles on ye, ye willna survive. Surely ye see that?'

'Dougal is right,' Cal said. 'Ye canna let him destroy us by taking the Pack Alpha away like this.'

'He wouldna hurt me. I am his father.'

Cal jabbed his hand towards the tentacle of Darkness trying to break through the shield Morghanna and Alistair were just managing to keep up. 'That is no friendly thing. It wants to get inside ye too. It wants to turn ye. To take ye. To take the entire pack down with ye. Just like he did when he was the Beast and Morghanna and Alistair fought it and won. Yer precious son hurt ye then and he is goin' to hurt ye now. There is no good inside Lachlan. There hasna been fer a long time, Iain, if there ever was. Just open yer blasted eyes and see.'

'Ye canna talk to me like that!' Iain yelled, shoving both of them back—his Alpha strength, buoyed by the strength he took from his lieutenants and senior soldiers, still strong enough to make them stumble back a few paces. Giving him enough to turn and strike out at Alistair—who was closest to him and whose attention was solely on helping Morghanna keep the shield in place.

His blow to Alistair's head felled him, knocking him instantly unconscious. Morghanna screamed as Alistair's power was torn from her. The shield shuddered and fell as she went down beside her love, leaving Iain free to step forward into the tentacles of Darkness.

'No!' The Werewitch managed to block the tentacles trying to get to Iain with a thrust of multiple Light tentacles, slicing at them, parrying with them, each blow shuddering back along their threads of light, causing pain to ripple inside them. But they didn't give up. Couldn't give up. Because if Lachlan and the Darkness won, if they managed to get to Iain and kill him—or worse, take him and hold him in their thrall, using him and his Alpha strength for their dark purposes—then more would be lost than their pack.

They blocked another tentacle that Lachlan-Darkness sent at Iain, slicing it in half. Lachlan screamed; the Darkness inside him roared.

'Nae. Nae. Dinna hurt him. Stop hurting my boy.' Iain went to strike at them with a sharp claw, but Bram leapt in the way, taking the strike for them.

'Argh!' he cried out, the scent of blood strong in the air as Cal yelled, 'Bram!'

Bram hit the floor hard, screaming in agony, his back shredded by his Alpha's claws.

'Help him, someone. Help him.'

They wanted to but couldn't take their attention from the danger in front of them, or from Iain who, seemingly oblivious—or uncaring —for what he'd done to one of his senior soldiers, turned back to his son and took another step towards him, hands out.

'Lachlan. My laddie. Let go of this Darkness. Come back to me. Be my son again. I promise, all will be forgiven. Ye just have to give up this madness. Lachie. My Lachie.' His voice was almost a sob as he took another step forward.

His son looked at him with what could only be described as

hatred and disgust in his eyes. 'I dinna want *ye*. I want all of what ye have. What is rightfully mine!'

'And ye can have it once I step down. Only after I train ye up and ye prove to the pack that ye are not this dangerous thing I see before me.'

'I dinna trust ye!' Lachlan screamed as he sent out more Dark-tentacles to stab at his father—they only just managed to cut the seeking things down before they reached Iain.

'I am the only one ye can trust. I love ye, son. I vowed to ye mother I would always look after ye. And ye ken a Were canna go back on a vow. I will make sure ye are safe. And when ye are rid of this infernal thing inside ye, I will start to train ye so ye can take yer place as my heir, as is rightfully yers.'

'Nae! He can never be Alpha,' the Dougal part of them cried out as they continued to keep the dark-tentacles away from Iain. 'It is not a hereditary office. It has to be earned and he will never be able to earn it. He is rotten to the core, as ye well ken, Iain.'

'Aye,' Cal said from his place next to Bram on the floor. 'The pack will never trust him. They will never give the right of power over to him.'

'They will! They will,' Iain shouted. 'If I train him properly. If I show him—'

'Ye have tried fer years to set him right, to train him in the Alpha ways, but he never listened. Could only think of himself.'

'That is the Darkness within him. Once it is gone, he will be different.'

'No,' Morghanna said, rising from where she'd gone down next to Alistair, stumbling a little, her face pale with pain and exhaustion. 'We rid him of the Darkness when we got rid of the Beast. And yet he still chose to do evil, still chose to hurt and maim. Then he ran and welcomed the Darkness back in to take this new form. And it worked because he has no soul. We did not realise; did not think. But the Darkness can get in, will always be able to get in, because he is broken beyond redemption. He has never even treated his wolf in the way he should. Look at it now. Its aura is barely recognisable—a twisted thing with barely a spark of life in it. No Were would ever do that to their wolf if they had a care for anything other than themselves. If they had a soul. He is a soulless thing and he always will be. There is nought you can do to change it, no matter how much you try.'

'Nae. Nae. Ye are wrong,' Iain screamed, his face screwing up, reddened with fury and yet his eyes were full of fear because he knew. He knew that what Morghanna said was true. Had always known. It was why he'd got Dougal and the other lieutenants to channel their power and strength to him. He had used others to help him cover up for his son. Would always use others to cover up for his son. As he would use them now, not caring who was hurt in his efforts to try to save him.

The human and wolf parts of them howled as realisation finally struck. He was not worthy to be their Alpha. He was not worthy to lead them at all not even for a second longer.

He most definitely was not worthy to be responsible for what happened to Lachlan, because he would always choose his son over everyone else. That was now all too clear. They hadn't allowed themselves to truly see it before even though they'd known. Known their Alpha was a useless piece of shit who would destroy the pack to save his son.

It couldn't be allowed. Lachlan could never get his hands on Iain. And Iain must never be allowed near Lachlan again. Because either thing would mean the end of everything and everyone they loved. Look at what he'd done to Bram with nary a thought for his suffering.

With a roar, the wolf part of the Werewitch, incensed by this betrayal, lashed out with all the power inside them, sending out shock wave after shock wave of the Light power. It disintegrated the tentacles about to take hold of Iain as he moved towards his son, his arms open wide to receive whatever came his way.

Seeing what the wolf was doing, the Dougal and Leanna parts added their wills to his intent, tripling his effort and strengthening the power against whatever the Darkness sent their way.

All the tentacles disintegrated as Light shock wave after Light shock wave hit Lachlan, driving the evil inside him back, back, until the Darkness receded inside the vessel it had chosen to work through.

The wolf part of them howled again, and they moved forward, hands outstretched to wind the shock waves around Lachlan and squeeze.

The Darkness and Lachlan screamed in agony as the Light power surrounded him, lifting him up, squeezing tight as it pushed to get inside.

Out of the corner of their eye, they saw Iain cry out, fighting against Cal's grip as he stopped the Alpha from leaping towards them, killing fury in his eyes. The Leanna part of them reached out and touched Iain with Healing power, binding him with the spell of sleep. He fell silent and limp in Cal's arms. The Were promptly dropped his Alpha on the floor and returned to trying to help his brother who was still writhing in agony, his back shredded by his Alpha's claws.

'Morghanna, can you help him?' they shouted above the noise of Lachlan and the Darkness's screams. They were relieved to see her helping her now conscious mate to his feet. Even though blood ran down Alistair's face from the blow he took, and despite the fact Morghanna looked like she shared his pain, they both nodded and headed towards Bram.

Knowing their friends would only be safe once they had taken care of the danger before them once and for all, they returned their full attention to the evil in front of them.

They had to ensure this time that Lachlan could never be a vessel for the Darkness ever again.

40

Lachlan—seemingly impervious to the pain he must be feeling—sneered at them and continued fighting against the power entrapping him. He shoved against the waves that cascaded from them and into him, screaming his outrage, spittle foaming at the edges of his mouth. His claws clicked out and he slashed at the air.

It made no difference. The Light power they used could not be touched by something as mundane as his claws.

He called on the Darkness, swore at them, swore to get to his father, to seek his revenge on them all, but his struggling was in vain. His words nothing but pointless puffs of air that disappeared as soon as he spoke them.

He was nothing without the Darkness, his soul gone, his wolf's soul a shattered thing.

It made her feel so sad, and not a little helpless. For surely helping someone like Lachlan was something she should be able to do given she was a Soul Healer? If she had only known what she could do before he became the Beast, then—

'Ye canna take that on yerself, just as ye canna Heal what isna there, mo ghrádh.'

'*That makes me even sadder.*'

'*And I love ye fer that. But yer empathy cannot stop us from doing what must be done.*'

Their wolf growled, wanting to get on with what he saw as their duty. But she wrapped her mental arms around his neck as she reached out to Dougal to hold him still and stop him from acting as nature and instinct dictated.

'*We cannot kill him,*' she said.

'*That is the pack's way of dealing with a rabid Were.*'

'*I know it would be the simplest way to deal with him, but it cannot be our way. We are the Werewitch. We have to be more than the sum of our parts. We have to do things better than our forebears. We have to be different. Or else, we will be no better than the Darkness who sees nothing but weakness and pain and uses it for evil.*'

The wolf stopped growling and was still as he took in her words, while in the part of the mind that they shared, Dougal embraced her, his lips pressing against her brow. '*Ye are right,* mo ghrádh. *We must be better. We canna fall into the same path our Alpha took. We must be more like Ioan McVale and his cohorts.*'

'*But different from them too. Because we are different.*'

'*Aye. I ken ye are right.*' He sighed deeply as the wolf harrumphed its agreement. '*But what are we to do? Lachlan will never cease his actions to take control of the pack and kill those in his way.*'

Her brow furrowed as she thought about what could be done, but could think of nothing. They had rid the damaged Were of the Darkness, were endeavouring to keep him bound with their Light, but they could not do that forever. '*We will have to put him in the sleep,*' she said.

'*That did not work last time,*' Dougal said bitterly. '*What makes you think it will work this time?*'

He was right. Something about what the Darkness had done to Lachlan had enabled him to fight off the spell she'd tried to bind him with, calling on Dark powers for those lightning blasts as he did so. They could not try the same thing again for fear of a repeat—or worse—occurring. She shook her head slowly. *'I do not know. But we must find something.'*

It was the wolf who came up with the answer.

As Lachlan made another attempt to escape from the Light threads that bound him, the wolf sent out another wave of power, but this time, he pushed it in a slightly different way, changing the vibrancy of it. The Light wrapped around Lachlan, lighting up not only his body, but his auras and the only soul still within him—his wolf.

And as that soul was lit up, they saw the true extent of the damage done to the animal part of him.

'Oh, his wolf!' Leanna gasped. *'I knew from the look of his aura it was bad, but this?'*

'It is a wonder he could even change,' Dougal said, his tone horrified. Because it wasn't only the wolf soul that was damaged. Lachlan's wolf was a ruined, tortured thing, shying away from everything in a way a wolf never should. A way none of their wolves had, even when they had the Darkness driving them to violence. It was pitiful and agonising to witness. *'How could Lachlan have treated his wolf in such a way?'*

'I do not know,' Leanna answered her horrified mate. *'But it seems our wolf is acting accordingly.'*

'What is he doing?'

'He is giving the wolf what he has never had—a say over who and what they are.'

The Light from their wolf side reached out and caressed the cowering wolf that was supposed to be a treasured partner of Lachlan's but had obviously been treated as the opposite. Their wolf wrapped the Light around the cowering Lachlan-wolf, caressing it, gifting it strength, comfort, trust and calmness—things it had been lacking for so long—and then, gently, pulled it to the fore.

'Nae! Nae! It is my wolf. Ye canna make it do what I dinna want it to do!' Lachlan screamed, trying to fight against what their wolf was doing, using the ruined husk of where his soul should be in a way that should be impossible. A normal Were's human soul would be

linked to their wolf, working as one, but Lachlan didn't have a soul. What was there in its place though ...

It was a writhing evil husk of nothingness that had tortured the wolf into submission with its evil thoughts and lack of empathy or caring. The wolf had been destroyed first by what Lachlan had done to the female members of his pack and coven when he'd preyed on them, breaking their trust—a sacred covenant between packmates; and then had been tortured further when it was used to meld with the human in a way never intended to create the Beast. While Lachlan could never again turn into the Beast, the evil of it in him was unabating. The wolf was terrified of it and him, and that terror, especially of its human side, had caged it. He was ruined by it, cowering away, unable to fight his human side anymore.

'*He needs our help,*' Dougal said, taking Leanna's hand in their mental bond, and then bound them more firmly into the wolf part of them.

Leanna gave herself over to them both, trusting they knew what to do with all the power at their fingertips. The greater part of the magic might come from her, but she no longer thought about it as hers because they had made it more. They'd made it sing within her. She'd been so afraid to let go because of what had happened to her parents, but now ... now she was ready to fly.

'*Not fly. Run.*'

She laughed at the thought she knew came from both Dougal and their wolf. '*Yes. Run. We will run wildly and freely. Run, my loves. Run. Do what needs to be done. Set that wolf free.*'

The power surged through her and out of her as they did exactly what she bid. They poured everything they had, every part of her Healer magic directly into Lachlan's wolf, bypassing the Packbond that would have to go through Iain, creating their own.

And it was everything the MacCrae Packbond should have been if Iain had been the Alpha they all needed. The Alpha they all deserved.

The Alpha they did deserve stood beside her within the Werewitch. Dougal was an Alpha any Were or coven would be proud to call their own. And she was going to make certain he realised that when they were done here.

The amount of power they were using to Heal the Lachlan-wolf was extraordinary. Normally using this much power would exhaust a witch or head them towards losing control and exploding. But she didn't feel weakened at all or even close to losing control. In fact, she felt stronger and more in control than she'd ever felt. Because while they were still fighting, they were fighting in the way that suited her powers the most. They were Healing—the body and the soul. They were making the wolf whole.

And her powers were basking in it. They wanted to win this fight in a way they'd never wanted to win before.

They wrapped the power around the Lachlan-wolf despite Lachlan-human's struggles, the fight he was putting on, trying to use the incredible power that was inside him that shouldn't be there. A soul was the most powerful thing in the universe—if it could truly be tapped into, the power would be greater than a thousand suns—but Lachlan didn't have one. He had something else and it was strong. It was giving Dougal and their wolf problems they hadn't thought to have. Dougal had always seen Lachlan as weak, but now he was fighting for his life, he was showing just how much desperation could strengthen a being.

And he was desperate. Incredibly so. She had never felt such a strength of desperation in anything before. If only he put this kind of strength into something good, he would have been the Alpha he'd always wanted to be.

That strange strength—had this come from the power the Darkness had taken from her in the purple-grey, or had it always been there—made her worry about what would happen to the wolf after they gave it dominance over the human side. Because it, along with his desperation, would surely mean that eventually the human would push its way to the fore and return the wolf to the pathetic state they'd found it in.

It was a pity they couldn't use their powers to keep the wolf whole. Once the wolf was Healed, they would give it the power to take over and not only make the change, but hold it, keeping the human locked inside in the way the wolf had once been. It was the wolf's choice though. Their wolf had asked it what it wanted and this had been what it had decided.

Maybe it was cruel to Lachlan, but she could read in Dougal and their wolf that it was just punishment, because it was exactly what Lachlan had been doing to his wolf. The main negative was that the human side of Lachlan—that twisted and empathy-less thing—would be inside the wolf doing what it had always done. Even if it never got control again, such evil was sure to leak out and affect the wolf.

She hurt at the thought.

Maybe they would need to do this regularly. Maybe they would need to create a spell—a powerful spell unlike anything created before—to ensure Lachlan-human could do nothing to his wolf again. Maybe—

Oh!

The power fluctuated, showing her the answer.

She stepped to the fore in the Werewitch, still letting Dougal and their wolf continue to fight Lachlan-human off—not simply by wrapping their power around him tight to hold him still but pushing it inside him and covering the blackness that was where his soul should be, stopping it from getting to Lachlan-wolf. And while they did that they still Healed his wolf. It was incredible, but it meant that they didn't see what she saw.

They also didn't know this power like she knew it. They didn't understand what that pulsing-pull of magic was that folded around the wolf. Didn't know what it wanted to do if only they understood how to use it.

She suddenly did. Suddenly understood the true gift of what they were.

She'd heard it before—that she was a Soul Healer—but she hadn't taken in fully what that truly meant. Now she did.

To Heal a soul wasn't just about doing what they'd done for Lachlan-wolf, it was giving it its soul's desire.

And she saw that soul's desire now, pulsing within the wolf, a thing it didn't even let itself believe in, but it was there in the deepest part of it in a way it was not in other Were. A Were's wolf wanted the partnership with the human, needed it, but because of what Lachlan had done, because of how he'd used his wolf, Lachlan-wolf wanted freedom.

True freedom.

And she could give it exactly that.

She wrapped the power around her hand, pouring her soul's wish for freedom into it, and sent it out towards the wolf.

It stiffened at first when she wrapped that thread of power around it. As any Healer would with a conscious patient, she said into his mind what she wanted to do and asked for approval.

The wolf howled its need, its longing, its 'yes'.

Smiling, she wrapped her power around it and pulled.

41

'**W**hat are ye doing?' Dougal asked her as he stood beside her in their combined minds.

'*What the wolf truly wants. What he needs.*'

She pulled harder.

Lachlan screamed, the sound full of terror and pain. She hesitated. He screamed again, but this time, there was an echo of pleasure in it, of knowledge that her empathy might stop her from doing what she intended to do.

He continued to scream.

But the pleasure she'd heard, his certainty that empathy weakened her, strengthened her resolve. As did Lachlan-wolf's pleading in her mind—not words, but a whining sound that was both pleading and trust combined.

She hooked into that trust and kept pulling.

Lachlan's screams cut off, his surprise evident in his widened eyes. He didn't think she would do it.

But he was wrong.

She pulled harder, the wolf lunging into her pull, trying to help her. And with the other sense that allowed her to see beyond the aura, to see the glow of the soul, she saw the wolf splitting from the human.

But Lachlan wasn't about to let his wolf go so easily. He reached out with every ounce of determination and desperation in him and tried to force a change—which showed how desperate he was because if he changed into the wolf right now, they could easily lock the human inside it and ensure it did not come back out again. However, it would also allow him to embed himself within the wolf, making it impossible for her to separate them. He'd obviously decided that was the best scenario for him now. Because if he was inside, he might never be able to take his human form again, but he could gain control. However, if they took his wolf from him ...

There was no way back once his wolf was gone. Once they were separated, that was it as far as she knew. And her knowledge of things was so much greater than it had been before she'd melded with Dougal and his wolf to become the Werewitch. She had access to what she could only describe as all Were and coven memory. It wasn't in her mind all at once, but more like if she thought about something, the memory was there for her to access.

She would have thought there had never been a separation of human and wolf before, but there had been. It had been done only once, and recently too. The whispers in her mind told her it was because the wolf was dying and he gave up life and agreed to be separated to save his human. She wasn't sure if it had worked—she would have thought, for a normal Were, living without their other half would be a grief they would never survive—but she was certain the excision had occurred. And it was final.

She'd have to start writing her own coven diary with the new information that came to her. Others needed to be able to access what she was now able to access.

But first she would have to succeed in this most difficult of tasks. More difficult than she'd at first thought—because the knowledge she had in her mind now told her that this had only been managed that one time with the help of the Goddess.

And while she wasn't a Goddess, she was something similar in this form. Something equally as powerful if in a different way.

So she could do this. She just had to want it enough.

She did want it. For the wolf that had been so ill-treated. For the pack that had suffered because of Lachlan-human's machinations and Iain's weakness where his son was concerned. And for Dougal who had given too much of himself to keep Lachlan under control.

Without his wolf, the human would not be such a threat. At least, she hoped not. She still didn't know where he was gaining his incredible power from.

Lachlan screamed again, fighting her, trying to hold onto his wolf in any way he could—not because he loved his wolf but because …

She gasped. He'd been using the wolf and its soul as a source of power!

Horror and disgust filled her. How a Were could ever do such a thing was beyond her. It was beyond Dougal and their wolf too. They were equally disgusted and horrified—and grieved. Because they'd had no idea this was what the human-Lachlan had been doing. Had he always done this or was it a more recent thing due to the Darkness's greater influence?

She couldn't know that right now. Couldn't let the thought overwhelm her that the wolf had endured this all its life. It was too horrible, too painful. But rather than her empathy being overcome by this, it resolved her determination to continue, to help the wolf escape the terrible hand that Fate had made it endure. She would give it a chance at a new fate.

What she, and only she, could do in this form was a gift.

And she was more than happy to use that gift to give the wolf its freedom from the human that had used and abused it.

But she had to do it quicker. Except … Lachlan was causing his wolf incredible pain in his efforts to hold on. There would of course be pain, but this much? She looked closer and gasped when she saw what he was doing.

The black, twisted thing at Lachlan-human's centre had hooks in the wolf's soul. Hooks he was using to hold it in place. Hooks that were tearing into the wolf's soul every time she pulled—and would rip the wolf's skin during the change if Lachlan was successful in forcing it. If that happened, the wolf would be weakened to the point that it would be far easier for the human to surge forward and take control.

It was hideous, grotesque and calculating. Her mind reeled from the horror of such a thing for a moment before it centred on the one thing she needed to do: she had to slice those hooks away if she was to free him.

But how could she do that without hurting Lachlan-wolf further?

'What do you need from us?' Dougal asked.

She thought for a moment before saying, *'Hold him still.'*

'What about the wolf? He is being injured again. Do we need to continue to Heal him?'

'No. Do not give your energy to that right now.' Lachlan-human probably intended to try to weaken them by assuming they would continue to try to Heal the wolf as he was injured over and over again by those hooks. *'Just hold the human body as still as you can. And then channel the rest of your strength into me.'*

'We will give you every bit we have.'

Tears pricked her eyes at the trust and love in his voice. *'Thank you. That is more than enough. I will do the rest.'*

She waited a second while Dougal and his wolf secured Lachlan's human body, holding it completely still. Their efforts did what she'd hoped—made Lachlan put part of his attention and strength back into fighting them.

It didn't make him let go of his wolf, but the hooks stopped digging in deeper and pulling the wolf back into the tiny space it had been given.

She jumped on that distraction and did what her knowledge told her to do.

She split the tendril she'd wound around the wolf into a dozen thin threads. Then she envisioned them as sharp as the sharpest athamé. Once she was certain they could cut through anything, she sent them out to just above where the hooks cut into it. Then she sliced down, cutting through those horrific threads that tied the wolf to the human in a way that was evil incarnate.

As her knife-threads cut through Lachlan's dark ones, he screamed anew, but this time there was no sound of satisfaction. There was only the sound of desperation and a rage so big it vibrated through her, reaching towards her soul, trying to stop her.

But she wouldn't be stopped. She had to save this wolf. She had to save them all.

So, despite the emotions whirling inside her, the scream playing on them like mistuned lute strings, she dug down deep and kept slicing, her threads sharper than ever before. They cut through the hook-threads over and over—there were so many of them. But without the Darkness behind him, Lachlan couldn't keep producing them. There was only what had been there before they started this fight.

She was going to win! She was going to do this. She was—

The wolf screamed, the sound breaking her heart and tearing at her soul. But she pushed past her reaction to the wolf's pain—helped by Dougal and their wolf, their strength and support the rock she stood on—and looked at the wolf with all her senses to try to figure out what was causing it such distress and pain.

It didn't take long.

Now most of the hooks Lachlan had sunk into his wolf were cut away, she could clearly see the one that was the issue.

Lachlan had done what no Were human should ever do to the wildness inside them that was their wolf—he'd chained his wolf by sinking a hook into his heart. He had locked his wolf to him with no chance of escape. No chance of asserting his will over the complete being that they were. No chance of even enjoying the kind of partnership as all Were did. This explained why the wolf had never been able to assert any dominance at all. For if the wolf ever disagreed or baulked against what his human side did, he was punished in the cruellest way.

She'd thought Lachlan-human was cruel before, now she knew he was completely without feeling or remorse. His lack of soul was more of a horror than she'd ever imagined it could be. She'd thought she knew all of what he'd done to his wolf but this … this …

She couldn't find words or emotion to express what she felt about what she saw. She wanted to scream. Wanted to crawl into a corner and hide from it. She wanted desperately to go back to a time before she knew such horror, such terror, such cruelty was possible.

Because rather than let his wolf go and be free of him, Lachlan was willing to kill his wolf. Killing his wolf was unlikely to kill him like it would other Were—he did not have the kind of emotional connection that would make that a surety. He would survive the murder of the other side of himself. And it would probably affect him no more than a toy being taken away from a toddler who had too many other toys to play with. Maybe a little more than that because he would be denied access to the very thing he stole strength from. But his loss would be about selfish things, not true, grief-ridden loss.

He was a monster.

And she couldn't let him win.

Except …

She had no idea how to undo what he'd done without killing the wolf he'd caged.

'It would rather die than keep living the way it has been living,' Dougal said. *'Any wolf would.'* Their wolf howled his agreement and sent out power to hold Lachlan a little tighter, squeezing him.

Lachlan laughed and yelled, 'I have won. Ye canna take my wolf from me. Ye will kill him if ye do and ye canna do that. The little mousy witch wouldna allow such a thing. I won!' His laughter was wild but didn't hide the pain-laden whines of his wolf.

'Ye have won nought,' Dougal said firmly, his Alpha power blazing through his voice, reverberating around the room.

Lachlan-wolf responded to that sound, that power, stopped whining and straightened from where it had curled around the intensity of the pain the human part of him was causing. He howled his plea that they keep going; he wanted to be free no matter the cost.

But Leanna wouldn't let him die.

'Ye will find a way.'

She nodded. Dougal's faith wasn't misplaced. She *would* find a way. It was the only answer she could live with.

'*Hold still,*' she said to Lachlan-wolf through the power thread she sent to him with a pulse of Healing warmth. It whimpered happily at the touch and did as she bid.

It enabled her to look at what Lachlan-human had done in a clinical fashion.

The hook he'd sunk into his wolf's heart was bigger and nastier than any of the other hooks he'd had in its soul. It was barbed along the thread as well as at the head. It had also been there for longer than any other barb, scarred flesh growing around the barbs so that it was part of the structure of the heart now—like a human body threaded more bone structure around a broken bone. Or could grow flesh and muscle around a thorn it couldn't push out.

It basically meant that if she tried to slice through the bit that attached to Lachlan-human, the movement would cause the barbs to slice through the wolf's heart causing a painful death.

It was horrific.

And yet, she had to find a way around the problem.

She looked deeper.

The barbs were touched by a darkness unlike any she'd seen before. These ones had probably been there since Lachlan was a baby. Maybe even from the womb. More proof he'd never had a soul.

But while the age of this barb was a horror for the wolf, it might just be its salvation now. Scar tissue wasn't delicate like other tissue. If the scars were thick enough, they would protect the heart from any movement caused by the cut or Lachlan-human pulling on the thread at the last moment if he realised what she was doing.

She just wasn't sure how thick they were though.

'*Just cut it,*' Dougal said simply as she agonised over what decision to make, Lachlan-human's laughter ringing around them.

'*I cannot. The human is right. I could hurt the wolf more. Or kill him.*'

'*Ye willna kill him. For we will Heal him no matter what happens when you cut him from the evil of his human.*'

'But what if we cannot? What if I cannot? Lachlan-human could lash out and the damage could be more than I can fix.'

'Ye feel it. The wolf would prefer death over continuing to be caged. But I dinna think we need fash ourselves over such a thing coming to pass.' Dougal's arms went around her, holding her to his warmth, folding her into the enormity of his love. 'Trust yerself, mo ghrádh. Trust me. Trust our wolf. Trust Lachlan-wolf. We are pack and Lachlan-human is alone. Together, we canna lose. Together we will find a way to keep the wolf alive even if his heart is torn in twain. Ye are the witch, after all, who brought this ruined Were back to life and Healed me so I can move my upper body. Together we can Heal whatever Lachlan-human tears asunder. Evil like he is can never win against something as pure and astonishing as ye.'

'As us.'

The hug firmed, the imprint of his lips against her brow. 'Yes. Us. Always us.'

'Then let us do this.'

'I go where ye lead. Show us the way; our wolf and I will follow.'

'Let Lachlan-wolf know to be prepared.'

'He already is. He trusts ye to save him, whatever that may be.'

'He will live,' she said firmly.

'Yes, he will.'

Then, before Lachlan-human could pick up what she might be doing, she lashed out with her sharpest blades, pouring every bit of energy she had into the magical thread she was using, and sliced through the last hook-thread with one blow.

Lachlan-human screamed his shock and outrage—she took comfort in the fact there was no grief in that sound, only self-interest —and tried to grab at the wolf. But Dougal and their wolf had grasped the magic she'd already wound around Lachlan-wolf and pulled him away from his tormentor.

There was a burst of rainbow glory, like a Were going through a change, and then a wolf stood before them next to the human they held still with their magic.

'Nae. Nae. Nae!' Lachlan screamed, spittle flying out of his mouth as he struggled against their hold, his face brilliantly scarlet, lips twisted. 'It is my wolf. *My* wolf! Ye canna take it from me. Give it back. Give it back!'

But it was too late to do that even if they wanted to. The wolf stood before them—a beautiful silver-grey wolf with black and white shot through his fur. His eyes were a glowing amber, showing his health if the lustre of his coat didn't already give that away. He was not a large wolf, middling in height with fine bones. His ribs showed in a way they shouldn't, and he trembled as if the effort of standing was almost too much. Shock widened his glorious eyes before joy lit them. He shook, as if to ensure he was completely free of everything that had been caging him for years, and at the end of the shake, lifted his head to the heavens and howled his joy.

That sound ... it filled the Werewitch with so much joy to know that they had helped to bring Lachlan-wolf to this moment of pure joy. A joy that would never have been if not for the extraordinary combining of their powers; of who they were.

There was sadness here for Leanna though—because the wolf should never have had to long for this freedom from his human side or feel this joy once released. The bonding should have been the joy, and yet it had been a living hell for the wolf.

It was a crime of nature she wanted to ensure never occurred for any wolf or human again.

In their mind-sharing space, she turned to Dougal who stood strong and tall beside her, and he nodded, understanding her wish, her concern.

'We will ensure no other bonding is like this or will ever be like this again.'

She leaned up and kissed him softly, their wolf humming his assent and his joy at their bond. *'I love you,'* she said to them both.

'We love you too,' Dougal said, the wolf in his voice.

'Alistair, can you please help me put Lachlan to sleep and stop that noise?' Morghanna had stood up and was rubbing her head, Alistair at her side doing the same.

'Here, allow me,' Cal said, and promptly knocked Lachlan across the back of the head then watched as the human fell limp in the magical hold the Werewitch had him in.

'I did not mean like that,' Morghanna said, too tired to truly sound admonishing. Then she shrugged, 'But I suppose it will do.' She looked over at them. 'You might as well let him go. No need to use magic on him now. He's not going to be waking up for a while given he doesn't have his wolf to help mend the bump Cal just gave him.'

'We should check to ensure there is no lasting damage,' Leanna said.

'I will do it,' Alistair said with a sigh.

'I dinna ken why ye'd bother,' Cal said as he helped his brother up from the floor.

Bram stumbled away from them as he reached his feet, shoving his brother's help aside. His nostrils flared as he gestured at the Were-witch, eyes going wide as if he hadn't seen them—fought with them—earlier. 'Ye ... are ye to stay like th-that then?' Bram asked softly. 'Ye are ... not natural.'

'We are of nature,' Leanna said through the Werewitch's voice. 'Of the universe. There is nothing more natural.'

'Not to mention we saved yer skinny ball sack, ye ungrateful wretch,' Dougal growled.

Bram took another step back, his body stiff, hands out like he was ready to fend them off.

In their mind-place, Leanna nudged Dougal chidingly. *You are scaring him.*

The ungrateful Were needs a bit of scare in him if ye ask me. He is happy enough to let us save his arse but then afterwards he acts like this? It is insulting.

We do not know what is causing his reaction. Before we react, perhaps we can ascertain that—something we will not be able to do if he is afraid of us.

Very well, Dougal said. *I bow to yer better instincts on this matter.*

He subsided within her and she tried to make their outer self less intimidating as she said to Bram, 'Please, do not fear us.' She took a step forward, hands out. 'We will not hurt you, Bram. We will not hurt any of you.'

'Of course you will not,' Morghanna said gently. 'We can see clearly what you are.'

'Ye can?' Bram asked, expression incredulous.

'Of course,' Morghanna said. 'We can see it in their aura, in the Healing glow that surrounds them. In the glorious white-gold of their fur and the kindness in their eyes.'

'They are here to Heal and help those in need that others cannot help,' Alistair added. 'As they did here.' He gestured towards Lachlan and his now freed wolf. Then he gestured at Bram and Cal. 'As they did in Healing you from damage to your ears. And in helping you overcome your fear of the spirits Bram.'

'The fear is still there,' Bram said, lip curling.

'Aye, but you overcame it, brother. Enough to help in the fight against Lachlan and the Darkness that was within him.'

Lachlan-wolf whimpered at the reminder of that, and sidled over to the Werewitch to lean against their side. They reached down and stroked his head, their claw-tipped fingers sliding gently through the soft fur, feeling the too prominent bones underneath. The wolf hummed his pleasure, pressing up into their touch. 'See, the wolf knows. We mean no harm. We will never mean any harm.'

'I think Iain and Lachlan might disagree,' Bram grumbled, taking another step away from them, claws sliding out of his fingertips as if he thought at any moment they might attack. 'Dinna be waving those magic-tinged arms at me. I canna trust what ye will do after what ye just did.'

'Bram! Do not be ungrateful to our true Alpha,' Cal admonished, his face flushing with anger. 'They stopped Lachlan and the Darkness from hurting us all and from destroying the pack.'

'I dinna ken that ... thing ... is my Alpha. It looks like the monstrous Beast that Lachlan turned into when he first attacked us.'

'That is not true,' Morghanna said, coming forward to place her hand over their chest as she looked up into their face. 'The form might be similar in that it is a mix of wolf and human, but look at the softness of the fur, the empathy shining out of the amber of their eyes, the way their claws and teeth are not swirling with black oily evil but are glowing with something akin to stardust. All the signs of evil are absent. Not to mention the aura is one of pure joy. There is only goodness here.'

'And they are glowing with Healing power and something more besides.'

'It is that "something" that is making me and my wolf uneasy,' Bram said, still sidling away from them and Cal, who had walked closer as if drawn to them.

Alistair shook his head at the worried Were. 'It is a wonderful something, not a bad something. You can feel it, *sûrement*? It is coming off them like pulsing waves.'

'I can feel nothing,' Bram said, backing up another step, 'except horror of what I just saw them do.'

Alistair shook his head harder. '*Non*. You are closing yourself off if you cannot feel what the rest of us feel.' He made a move towards Bram, but the Were's claws slid out further and he growled.

Cal took a small step towards his brother, waving Alistair back. 'Do ye trust me, brother?'

'I do,' he said, not sounding fully certain of that as he looked between Cal and the Werewitch.

'Then believe me when I tell ye there is nought to fear here. They are made to help, not to destroy like the Beast was.' He sucked in a big breath as he looked back at them before closing his eyes in obvious bliss.

'What is wrong with ye?' Bram asked, horror and disgust still in his voice.

'Can you not feel that?' Cal asked as he opened his eyes.

'What?'

'The love, the togetherness, the ... welcoming they exude. They are a miracle. They are a wonder sent from the Goddess to set us on a path for the future.'

'Ye can feel all that from them?' Bram said, gesturing at them as if they were a bug he'd found in his mead.

'Come closer, Bram,' Cal said, joining Alistair and Morghanna who now stood at the Werewitch's side. He reached out one hand to his brother, touching the Werewitch with his other. 'We have witnessed a miracle here today. Can ye nae see that?'

'I see nought but the monster that knocked out my Alpha and then split human from wolf.'

'Because that human was keeping his wolf suppressed and using its strength and power in a way it was never meant to be used,' Alistair said, eyes narrowing as he stared at the Were who stood on the other side of the room, still edging away.

'Not to mention they also defeated the Darkness. Without the Goddess's help. It is a miracle,' Morghanna added.

'Do ye not see that is part of the problem?' Bram said, mouth curling as he stood protectively in front of his still unconscious Alpha.

'That they saved us?' Cal asked.

'Nae. That they have so much power they dinna even need the Goddess's help. What does that make them? What does that make us in the face of them? Can we trust that they willna want us subservient to them in the future?'

'Why would we want that?' Leanna asked just before Dougal asked, 'Are ye comparing us to the Darkness?'

'Who is to say the Darkness did not start out like ye? Who is to say the Darkness didna come to the Were with promises of helping and making us stronger? Who is to say our forebears didna open themselves to the Darkness's sweet whispers only to find themselves trapped in ways they couldna comprehend?'

'Nobody can say,' Cal said, shaking his head. 'The knowledge of how the Darkness came to us is lost in time as ye well ken. And the Spirit-talkers like Morghanna are yet to find a spirit old enough to tell us.'

'Exactly,' Bram said, pointing at his brother then jabbing a finger at them. 'We canna be certain it didna come to us like they are, seeming to be the avenging angel but truly a devil incarnate.'

Leanna jerked inside their form, his words a punch to her chest.

'Dinna call my beloved a devil,' Dougal roared. 'She has always been goodness incarnate.'

'Aye, I agree Leanna is everything good. But how can I be certain she has a voice within that thing ye have become?'

'I am here,' Leanna said, the voice changing into something that sounded more like her. 'A third of who we are is me.'

'More than a third, mo ghrádh,' Dougal said softly, affectionately inside their mind-link.

'Ye can clearly see that is true in its glorious form,' Cal argued. 'Why would ye accuse them of being from the devil when ye can see with yer own eyes that they are closer to a God or Goddess?' Cal asked.

'Which dinna mean they are good. Gods and Goddesses have oft done evil things in the name of their own glory.'

'But look at what they have just done!'

'Aye,' Bram said, gesturing jerkily towards an unconscious Lachlan-human lying on the floor and then the Lachlan-wolf leaning against their side. 'Look at what they did. They did what shouldna be done. They did a thing of horror for all Were—they separated a Were, human from wolf, without their consent.'

'We had the wolf's consent,' Leanna said, their hand continuing to stroke the wolf's head who was looking up at them with love and trust in his eyes. 'And we had the wolf's interests at heart. He was clearly a victim of his human side.'

'So ye say,' Bram said.

'No. So says the wolf. Just look at how thin he is,' Morghanna said crossly. 'The human side must have been feeding from his power somehow for him to look like that. But even if you do not consider that, look at how he is towards them. If they had done a terrible thing to him, would he now be leaning against them like he is?'

'Open up the wolf nature in yourself and ye will feel it,' Dougal said. 'Open up to the Packbond, fer ye will feel him there. The wolf is still attached to the pack.'

'Nae, he isna,' Cal said. 'He is bonded to ye both. Like ye both are his Alpha.' He looked up at them, confusion furrowing his brow. 'How are ye both the Alpha?'

'I am not the Alpha,' Leanna said. 'Dougal is. You are simply sensing that side of him when we are in this form.'

'Nae,' Cal said, shaking his head slowly. 'That is not it. What I am sensing, it is more like what I felt when our Alpha was in the same space as Ioan McVale. Except this is even stronger than that. It is something truly wondrous. And my wolf wants to bond to it immediately.'

'Nae. Nae. Ye canna do that,' Bram said. 'We have an Alpha and there has been no Alpha challenge.' He glared at the Werewitch. 'Do ye intend to challenge Iain to be Alpha?'

'I dinna intend any such thing,' Dougal said. 'At least not now he is weakened by confusion and grief and will be overwhelmed by what to do with his son now he is no longer Were. I willna strike a male while he is down, especially one I once respected and had some affection fer.' He took a deep breath and let it out slowly. 'But I canna stay under his rule. Neither of us can. He isna fit to be Alpha any longer and if he willna step down—which I fear he will never do—then we must go.'

'Ye will leave?' Bram asked cautiously. 'Ye will not challenge Iain to be Alpha?'

'Aye. I willna challenge him,' Dougal said.

'What about Leanna?' Cal asked. 'She is Alpha too. I dinna care what she says about that fact. I can feel it.'

'I will not challenge either,' she said, laughter in her voice because it was a ridiculous thought. 'It is not for a witch to challenge for the Alpha position.'

'Maybe for a normal witch. But ye are no normal witch. Especially when in this form.'

'We will not stay in this form now the need is gone.'

'Ye will change?'

'Aye,' Dougal said, his wolf rumbling his agreement. 'It is natural to be what we are as individuals as much as it is natural to be in this form. Just like it is for Were with the human and wolf sides of themselves. When there is need we will be like this. When there is not, we will be ourselves.'

'And when I am myself,' Leanna said, 'you will see that Dougal alone is the Alpha you wish to follow.'

'I disagree, my Lady Alpha,' Cal said firmly. 'But I guess we will see who is right about that when ye change back into yer individual forms.'

'I think Cal is right,' Morghanna said, Alistair nodding his agreement. 'I see something in your aura that indicates the Alpha part of Dougal has worked its way into your soul and form, Le-le. When you are yourself again, you will find there is Alpha within you too.'

43

'That cannot be right,' Leanna said, turning to the representation of Dougal inside her mind. *'I never wished to take anything from you, my love.'*

'Ye dinna take ought from me, mo ghrádh. Ye only give and make me more than I could ever have imagined being. As I hope I do fer ye in return.'

'You do. I am more than I ever thought I could be, more than I would have been if not for your trust and love and support.'

'The same is true fer me.'

'I dinna care if ye are Alpha or no', Bram snapped, interrupting their discussion. 'Ye dinna belong here among us. I want yer assurance ye will leave. That ye willna challenge our Alpha and tear our pack apart.'

'Iain has already done that with how he has treated his lieutenants to succour his son,' Cal responded. 'He has done that with how he let his son's wants and needs be more important than the wants and needs of the pack. He sent many of our young women away to other packs to keep them quiet about what Lachlan had done to them and forced us to keep quiet about it. Fer myself, I am ashamed of my part in all of this and I will take part in it no longer.' He turned to the Werewitch. 'Where ye go, hither I will follow. Ye are my Alpha now in reality as ye always have been in my heart.'

'Nae. Nae. Ye canna do that,' Bram shouted. 'Ye canna leave me.'

'Come with me,' Cal said calmly, turning back to his brother and holding out his hand. 'Come and be a part of a pack we will be proud to serve because our Alpha, this ...' He waved his hand at them, obviously uncertain what to call them.

'We think of ourselves as the Werewitch.'

'Perfect,' Morghanna said, clapping her hands together. 'We will write you into the diaries and you will be forever known.'

'We dinna seek claim. Just our own place in this world,' Dougal insisted.

'And we will make that, together,' Leanna said.

'I dinna care what ye choose to call yerself,' Bram said. 'I willna follow such uncertainty. I willna leave my pack to take up with something I canna trust. And I think ye are foolish to do so,' he said to Cal, lips curling. 'I canna believe ye would leave me, leave the place we were born, the place our ancestors dwell.'

'These are times of change,' Cal said. 'If ye dinna choose to change with them, ye will be swept away by the tide that comes along with it.'

Leanna shivered inside their form at those words that seemed to have an element of kenning about them. She wondered if perhaps there had been a witch somewhere in Cal's ancestry before the Darkness came into the Were and destroyed much of their society and history. It would explain how sometimes he just knew things. And would explain Bram's ability to see the spirits.

They had to do more to uncover their lost histories and use them to help shape their future.

'We will not force anyone to come with us,' she said. 'We do not seek to split the pack. But if Cal wishes to come, we welcome him to create a new home with us. We welcome anyone who wishes to come.' She said the latter to Morghanna and Alistair, a question in her tone.

Morghanna shook her head sadly. 'I am bonded to Iain and

unless you challenge him and win to be Alpha, I cannot break that bond without terrible repercussions. I also cannot leave behind those who will need to stay—like Abigail. Her health is too precarious to survive another move and big change, and I will not cause her death by forcing her to move with us all, especially given we do not know where you will go or how long it will take you to find a new home for your pack. But I will help you in whatever way I can and will happily allow any who wish to strike out with you to do so with my blessing.'

'Thank you.' Leanna nodded, her voice too clogged with tears to say anything more.

Morghanna waved her hand, obviously fighting tears too. 'We will sort things out in the next few days. I do not think you will have to leave right away.'

Leanna nodded and Dougal said, 'I think we need some time to talk things through and figure out what comes next. And we need some privacy to change back.'

'I am uncertain you will get that privacy right now,' Alistair said as he pointed to the window where a crowd could be seen peering in. 'By the looks on their faces, I think you are going to have to go out and show yourself to them. And we need to tell them what has happened here.'

'Better that ye simply leave,' Bram said. 'We dinna need ye stealing any other pack member from us when ye go.'

'I think the time for them to slink away without anyone knowing is long past,' Morghanna said. 'All of the coven has felt what happened here and from what I am feeling through the Packbond, the Were have too. You will cause more mistrust and division if you do not allow them to know exactly what happened here and give them the choice to go or stay.'

'That is Iain's choice. Ye have to wait for him to awaken afore ye make any more decisions about his pack.'

'It is not just *his* pack,' Dougal said with the Werewitch voice.

'And the attitude that it is owned by him is part of the reason we have such an unsettled feeling in the pack and coven,' Cal added.

'That is because of all the changes!'

'Nae, brother. Ye ken that is not true. Many in the pack are upset with Iain and are unhappy with his leadership. They should be given the choice to leave with us if they wish.'

'Ye will tear the pack in twain!'

'Nae. We will strengthen the pack by taking those who are unhappy. Ye ken this to be true even if ye dinna wish to admit it right now.'

'Iain will not be happy ye are making these decisions fer him. They are decisions only an Alpha can make.'

'And an Alpha is making them,' Cal said, turning to the Were-witch. 'I ken Alistair is right. We need to go outside and show them what ye are.' He gestured at the wolf leaning against their leg. 'We need to show them what ye did and tell them why ye did it. Many will feel as Bram, I am certain, but there will be others who will feel as I do. I am certain we will leave with a following.'

'We do not need a following,' Dougal said. 'We need those who will work alongside us. We need those who believe that being respon-sible to pack is as important as what we each receive from being a part of pack.'

'And we need those who are willing to embrace difference,' Leanna said. 'Because we are most definitely different, singularly and together.'

'That you are,' Morghanna said.

'In the best way,' Alistair agreed.

How Leanna loved those two. Such special people to have in her life and to help bring her to the point she was now—confident within herself and capable of not only loving, but allowing love in. Before coming here and being taken under their wings—and Dougal's of course—she would never have been able to do what she'd done in these last months. And she certainly wouldn't have had the strength to so completely bond with Dougal and his wolf that they would become a new kind of being.

But she had and she wasn't going to step back from it. Not even if it meant saying goodbye—for now—to these two witches who meant so much to her.

'*And to me,*' Dougal said.

She nodded at that. Yes, they had made a difference for him too in so many ways. They could never repay what these two had given them, but they would try to do their generosity and understanding justice by going out and creating the kind of pack they all deserved to be a part of.

'I think we need to go out now,' Dougal noted, turning their head towards the window where half the pack and coven could be seen, with more coming to join them. 'We dinna want them to be squashed against the wall.'

'We need to ensure Lachlan is secure and that Iain will recover. I do not wish to leave him unwell.'

'I will take care of any Healing that might need to be done,' Alistair said. 'You must go outside and see to that crowd.'

'I will secure Lachlan,' Bram said. His gaze flickered to Alistair and then to his Alpha and they understood he was also staying to ensure the French warlock didn't do anything untoward to Iain—as if he would!

'*Wisht,*' Dougal said to her. '*Alistair can stand up fer himself.*' She nodded and he put his arm around her in their mind-space and pulled her into his side as together, with their wolf, they walked outside as the Werewitch, Morghanna and Cal following in their wake.

As they walked outside, the witches, warlocks and most of the Were now gathered at the front of the Healer Hall began to cheer.

Morghanna leaned in and said, 'Our coven mates felt what you did. They have been telling the Were gathered here already.'

While it would be easy to bask in the glow of the cheering, they were aware of the Were who were standing back, obviously unhappy and uncertain about what had happened, some even emitting fear as the Werewitch walked into full view.

There was an audible gasp as Lachlan-wolf came to stand beside them.

A few of those who initially cheered, stopped as they saw the wolf. Others cheered harder. More fear arose from those who hadn't cheered at all.

That fear hurt Leanna, but she understood it. They had done something that, in the wrong hands, could end the Were as a people. It was a huge responsibility to hold such a power within them, one they would always be cognisant of and careful with.

'*It will take time fer all of them to truly trust we willna do to them what the Darkness did fer so long,*' Dougal said softly.

'*We must work hard to gain that trust. And the trust of those who will join our pack.*'

'*Aye, as well as the trust of other packs. Because, fer this to truly work, we will need to have affiliations and ties with other packs, so building good, trusting relationships will be a must.*'

She nodded her agreement and then had to turn from their discussion because many of those gathered were starting to yell questions at them that they needed to answer.

Thankfully Morghanna stepped forward to act as moderator so they could answer one question at a time.

The questions were petering out when one of the crowd yelled, 'Iain.'

They turned to see Iain being led out of the Healer Hall by Bram. He did not seem happy at all to see the crowd there, nor to witness the miracle of them standing there so strong and sure.

His eyes slid from them quickly though to land on the wolf at their side.

'Lachlan's wolf,' he whispered. It whimpered in answer, but he didn't go up to it or embrace it like she had hoped he would. Instead, his eyes slid away from it and he said, 'I wish ye two gone as soon as possible. I dinna need ye here telling me how things should be or making others turn agin me. And take that animal with ye. I dinna need to see any of ye afore ye leave.' So saying, he had Bram help him away.

Half of the crowd followed but half stayed—a surprising number of Were as well as most of the coven who wanted to know more about the magic they had felt being performed.

It was many hours later when they finally returned to Leanna's room in the Healer Hall, the wolf following them—he seemed to want to be nowhere else.

Lachlan had been removed from where he'd been left lying on the floor and the room had been tidied, the only indication there had been a magical fight the fact that some furniture had been removed, there were missing bits of plaster from the ceiling and walls, not to mention lash-like marks and burns on the walls where magical threads and tentacles had struck.

Tired, they sat upon the bed still in the Werewitch form.

'*So many of them are afraid of us,*' Leanna sighed wearily. '*More than I thought there would be given what some of them felt and saw, and what Morghanna, Cal and Alistair told them.*'

'*Ye are right. The smell of their fear is still in my nose. But it is little wonder. What we did is frightening to many of them. We need to show them they can trust we will never use such a thing against them.*'

'*I know. We will never stop having to build trust, I think.*'

'*I ken ye may be right. But there is nobody else I would wish to do that with,* mo ghrádh.'

She snuggled into him in their mind-place and they sat there for some time, enjoying the peace and quiet and the comfort of being so incredibly close to each other and their wolf—who was humming as he sat in that place snuggled up next to them.

But eventually Dougal broke that comforting silence to say, '*I think it is time. We must change back.*'

'*Now?*'

'*Aye, now.*'

The wolf made a grumbling sound—he was enjoying being this close to both his humans—but he understood that they could not stay in this form forever.

Leanna swallowed hard before saying, '*I do not know if you will still be able to walk once we separate. I do not know if the magic we have wielded today would have been enough to complete the Healing.*'

Dougal was silent for some time before saying, '*It doesna matter. To walk again would be wonderful, but if it is not to be my lot, I will be fine with that outcome as long as I have ye to stand at my side.'*

She squeezed his hand. *'You will always have me. And I will do everything I can to find a way to help you walk again.'*

'I think if we concentrate on designing ways for me to get around without someone having to carry me constantly, that would be my first priority.'

'I have some ideas about that. There were references to wheeled chairs in some of the very ancient diaries that came from Greece. And if we can get some form of movement and feeling into your legs, there were some suggestions for contraptions to strap to legs and to help with balance and movement too. I will take the entries to the carpenters and see if they can make sense of them and work up some prototypes to trial.'

Dougal laughed. *'Whoa. Whoa. We dinna yet ken if any of the carpenters might come with us. And we have to first concentrate on leaving as soon as we can. Iain wasna joking when he said we must leave in a few days. There will be trouble if we dinna heed him—and I dinna want trouble with those I once called pack.'*

'I do not either. But we do need time to talk about where we might go with those who wish to come with us.'

'Aye. We will figure it all out. Even if we dinna ken exactly where we are to head when we leave, we will figure it out soon after. Let us concentrate on packing and figuring out how to transport me.'

'We can travel in the Werewitch form.'

'Some of the time, aye, we can. But I think it is a mistake to take this form too often. We dinna want people to expect it or to think we are only strong when together. Also, I think the power we have in this form is something that should not be used simply to help me move around. Speaking of which, let us change now. It is little point talking about the whys and wherefores of travelling with a cripple if I have indeed been Healed.'

'You think you might have been? Do you feel something different?'

He tipped his head to the side then shook it. *'Nae. I dinna ken it has made much difference at all. But we will see.'*

She squeezed his hand. *'I wish I could ensure you could walk again. I wish I had that power within me.'*

'*Being like this with you has shown me there are many more ways to show strength and power than being able to walk and run and physically fight to get it. You have helped me understand there are many paths through which I can be useful to my pack.*'

'*You are the true Alpha,*' Leanna said stubbornly. '*Those who follow need you to be what you have always been to them.*'

He kissed her lightly on the lips before leaning back, his arms slung around her waist in a way she treasured. '*I am not Alpha alone. Ye heard what Cal and the others said. We are Alpha. Together and individually.*'

'*It is not possible.*'

'*Ye will see,*' he said with a knowing smile.

44

S he frowned. *'I will say to you what I said to them: I cannot be Alpha with you. Apart from the fact I am a witch and not a Were, there is only one Alpha for each pack.'*

He tipped his head to the side considering. *'Maybe that is the way it has always been but that is not the way it needs to be. Not fer us. Not fer the pack we need to build.'* He slipped his hands down to hers. *'This power that is yers, it is now in us: human, wolf and witch alike. It is our power. So too is my Alpha power. We are the Alpha now—as the Werewitch but also individually, in the same way the power we now share will continue to be in my wolf and me. Because we are Alpha, ye too are the Alpha. I canna explain it more simply than that. All I can say is I ken it to be true in the same way Cal saw it to be true. Ye ken it in yer heart too. Dinna say ye do not.'*

She nodded slowly. She could feel it, as he said, now she was open to it. Her eyes widened as the full realisation of it struck. *'We can be the Alpha of a new kind of pack. A pack that opens itself to anyone in need of our strength and guidance and love.'*

'Aye. And the first members of our pack are Cal and Lachlan-wolf.'

She turned to look at the wolf who had settled on the floor at the foot of the bed. It had been such a horrible thing to hear Iain refuse the wolf that was as much his son as the human side was; such a horrible thing to witness. She had hoped Iain would make up to the wolf by embracing him now. Instead he chose to cast him out, knowing he could never be a part of another pack nor could he be a part of a wild wolf pack. The wild wolves would never accept him as one of theirs because there was something about him that would set him apart.

He now didn't belong anywhere.

Unless they made a place for him to belong.

Which of course they would. The wolf, and any being like him, would be accepted into their pack in a way they would never be accepted elsewhere. Leanna had a sudden kenning, as the Scottish Were called it, that the Werewitch would need to come out often to help those who needed helping—the Alpha-ness of them would draw many others to their side, to come under their protection and strength and be accepted in a way they had never been elsewhere.

The Alpha in them would gather them all in and hold them safe and dear. As all Alpha's should do to those who looked to them for safety, comfort and strength.

Alpha. She was thinking like an Alpha. Dougal and Cal were right. They were both Alpha, singularly and together. Leanna saw that now. She didn't know why she had struggled to accept it.

Not that any of her struggle mattered now. All that did matter was that she fully embraced the fact she was a Soul Healer, and even better, could become the Werewitch with her beloved Dougal.

They had such a bright future together, it was almost too difficult to look towards it. But she would look forward and walk towards that which was theirs.

She gasped as the idea of walking forward brought a kenning to her.

'*What is it,* mo ghrádh?'

'*I see that we will head north,*' she said firmly. '*There is a place for us up there where we can create a new pack for those who need shelter, who need help, who need support and Healing—physically, mentally or in their souls.*'

He looked towards where she looked, seeing the vision that she saw because they shared this place in their minds. He nodded slowly and said, *'And we willna rule like Iain did.'*

'Certainly not.'

Dougal chuckled at her tone and she smiled with him but he said seriously, *'We willna use our people for our benefit. We will rule to benefit our people.'*

'And we will truly listen to our Council—Were, coven, Wiccan, shifter and others—and we will ensure all voices are spoken for, all voices are heard. We can never let what happened here with Lachlan and Iain to happen again. No soul should ever be treated like Lachlan treated his wolf. And no person should be sacrificed to lift up another.'

'And if any of our people want to leave, they will be free to do so with no punishment or penalty.'

'And they will be free to return at any time with no repercussions either.'

'Aye. Lone wolf-types will not be made to feel like outcasts, but valued members of the pack who have a job to do the same as others.'

Leanna nodded. *'Yes. They will each have a role to play, a job to do that will most suit who they are. And the Werewitch can help them figure that out by helping them be in touch with who they are in their soul and figure out what will make them the happiest.'*

'Aye. We will do that. We will do all that. We will take the best things from the best packs we know and we will look to the past fer inspiration and fer warning.'

'Yes, because if these past months have taught me anything it is that we have forgotten too much of our pasts and forsaken old knowledge that could help us now. We cannot let that continue. We must learn from the spirits too. They can be part of our pack in a way they never have been before. I will have to talk to Morghanna about this, but I am certain it can work. It will work.'

'If ye are at the helm of it, I am certain it will.'

She beamed under his love and trust. *'And we will be Alphas like there has never been before.'*

'We will.'

'*Together.*'

'*Forever.*'

And as they kissed, they changed, the glow of the change brightening the room around them until they were individuals once more, Dougal's wolf solely within his body and Leanna corporeal as she'd been before the Darkness had stolen her away into the purple-grey entity.

Leanna drew back as the change finished, her single focus on Dougal. 'Well? Can you feel your legs? Or move them?'

He tipped his head and frowned as if concentrating hard. He made a little sound of effort and his left leg shifted slightly, but no more than that. Shoulders slumping a little he shook his head slowly. 'I can feel a little more than I did before, but that is all the movement I can manage.'

Leanna swallowed hard, pushing back the tears that burned in her eyes—she didn't want to show Dougal her upset or disappointment. But of course he knew.

He cupped her face in his warm hands and leaned in to kiss her deeply and thoroughly before pulling back enough to say, 'As long as ye are with me, I will be fine.' He raised his brows suggestively. 'I will be even more fine if ye do something about the tent in my breeches. It has been aching fer ye every day since I awoke.'

'As I have ached for you too.'

'Ye have?'

'Can you not scent my desire?'

Aye, he could now that she mentioned it. He'd scented it many times before but just hadn't allowed himself to believe it could possibly be for him. But now he knew it was, there was no denying it. No refusing it. He would play the martyr no longer. He knew now with more certainty than he'd ever known anything that he wasn't less because he was unable to walk or prove his strength as a Were normally would. He was *more* because now he wasn't blinded by the path he thought had been set before him.

Now he could see all that had been missing from their way of doing things and was determined to make the changes that would benefit so many. He could be strong in other ways, be the type of Alpha—with Le-le—not seen before. And now, as the Werewitch, he could also defend what they planned for their pack and their future against those who would continue to use violence and fear to ensure things went their way, as Iain always had.

With Leanna, he had a beautiful future; one like he'd never imagined.

With his Le-le by his side, he would always be whole.

She had given him his entire world. She *was* his entire world. And now he wanted to show her just what that meant.

He lay back on the bed, pulling her down with him. Then cupping her face, he kissed her deeply, tongues and teeth and lips, sipping, sucking, nipping. Their groans of pleasure filled the air as hands raced over, then under, clothing, slowly removing everything they wore until there was nothing between them.

Skin stroked against skin, the sweetest of frictions. Still filled with the energy and strength of the Werewitch, Dougal lifted Leanna up so he could first take one nipple then the other into his mouth, lavishing them with the attention he'd longed to give them—and from the sounds she was making, she'd longed to receive. Then he lifted her up further, wanting to ensure she was truly ready—but also longing to taste her. She helped him, completely compliant until she was positioned so that he could use his tongue on her slit. He twirled it around her clit as he slid his hand from her hip to between her legs, his thumb sliding through her glorious wetness to press deep inside her.

She moaned and undulated against him as he licked and plunged two fingers deep inside her, ensuring she was wet enough and ready enough to take all of him inside her. He plunged those fingers into her over and over as he licked, teaching her the rhythm that would best suit them with her on top of him, riding him as he had long imagined her doing.

Her body went rigid and she arched her back, crying out his

name in a long undulation like a war cry. Her internal muscles clenched around his fingers, clamping down so hard it was difficult to keep moving and yet he did, lapping up her sweet fluids as she came hard against his fingers and tongue.

Just as he felt her soften, he pulled her back down his body so he could pay attention to her breasts once more. She whimpered then moved, wriggling down his body.

'I want your mouth on mine,' she whispered shakily. 'And I want you inside me like in our dreams.'

'Aye.' He wanted that too. More than he could express, his mouth suddenly dry and his cock harder than ever before. He waited, in agony, his hands drifting over her as she wriggled down his body, her hands caressing his chest, his stomach, his hips. She went to grip his aching cock, but he quickly grabbed her hand. 'Ah, nae. If ye want me to perform, ye will have to wait to do that later.'

She pouted her disappointment, but then her eyes glistened with a wickedness he loved to see and she leaned in close and whispered, 'My turn next time.'

'Aye, please.'

'Now it is our time.'

'Oh aye. But every time together is our time.'

She raised her brows in query as her hands wandered over his body. 'Do not tell me you gained as much pleasure from what you just did as I.'

'Aye, I did. Are ye not gaining pleasure from touching me?'

'Oh yes. I love touching you. So much.'

'It is driving yer pleasure higher, is it not?'

'Yes. Very much so.'

'As every bit of your pleasure does the same fer me. As with everything else, yer pleasure is my pleasure. I love making ye come.'

'Is that what I did?'

'Oh aye. And very prettily too. And fiercely. Ye are like a warrior princess. My warrior princess.'

She glowed—quite literally, her skin lighting up—under his praise. Then she asked, 'Will it be the same for you?'

'Shall I be a warrior princess?'

She laughed and pushed at his chest a little. 'No. I mean, will you feel the pleasure I did?'

'I hope so. Shall we see?'

Her eyes glistened with challenge as she smiled down at him. 'Oh yes. Show me how.'

He guided her down to place her wet core right over his aching cock. She bent her head to watch—somehow, her watching made it all the more pleasurable and drove his passion higher. He placed his cock at her entrance and said, 'Now, lower yerself down on me.'

She did so, so slowly it was torturous pleasure, but he understood. He was thick and long and he stretched her in a way she'd never been stretched before. It was an agony not to press on her hips, to make her drive down faster, but he held still, giving her the lead. He wished he could see her face, but she was arched so she could watch their joining.

By the Moon he loved that she wanted to see. She was so curious and needed to know how everything worked. It was one of the things he loved about her; one of the things that was going to make them the best kind of Alphas.

When she was fully seated, her wetness warm and silky against his balls, she looked up at him, her brow arched. 'That feels amazing.'

Fuck! The husky pleasure in her tone ... it drove his desire for her even higher. His cock flexed inside her and her brows rose at the sensation, her face flushing.

'Ye like that?'

'Oh, I do.'

'It will feel even better when ye move like I moved my fingers in ye earlier.'

Her eyes widened, and she smiled. 'Like this?' She rose up slowly, then came down slowly and as she did, her eyelids fluttered. 'Ohh.'

'Aye. Oh,' he managed to say. The sensation of her tight wetness gliding against him was incredible and he wanted more of it. So much more. 'Again,' he rasped out.

She repeated the movement again, slowly up, slowly down, over and over until he felt his balls tighten and his eyes were about to roll into the back of his head. Her breath had sped up in time with his and without his prompting, she began to speed up the movement, adding a little undulation that made him moan. Then, without breaking rhythm, she bent over to take his lips in a lush kiss.

He loved the fact she took the lead, learning what he liked by listening to his breaths, the sounds he made, the way his muscles twitched under her hands, the fastening beat of his heart. She licked his lips and then bit the lower one in a way that made him growl, his wolf right there with him in the sound he made. She raked her fingers over his chest, across his nipples as her tongue did wild things against his.

He thought he might explode, but he managed to hold on to his control because he did not want this to be over. This, their first time in the physical plane, needed to last for as long as she needed it to last and he wasn't going to be the one who ended it first. He wanted to get lost with her; partners in every way possible.

So he held on, muscles tight, as she moved on him, her hands exploring everywhere they could reach, her mouth wild on his.

He couldn't stop himself from exploring her more too, his hands moving from her hips now she had that movement down, to trace over her back, into her hair, the silky strands glorious against his fingers. He pressed against her scalp, loving the noises she made when he did so, but he wanted to feel her breasts as she moved, so he let go of her hair and traced down her arms then back up, across her shoulders to draw spirals on her silken skin. Skin that emitted a special perfume that wove around him like a delicious drug. Then he brushed the back of his hands over her nipples.

She jerked, making a surprised sound, breaking the rhythm to look down at what he was doing.

He stilled.

She grabbed his hand and encouraged him to brush over her nipple again. 'Ahhh yesss,' she moaned. Then continued to move as he repeated the movement.

She didn't return to his mouth, but sucked and nipped on his neck; his balls tightened and drew up in a way that meant he couldn't hold off for much longer. But he would. For her. And it was going to be so good when he finally let go.

He turned his hands over to cup her breasts and squeeze. She made a sound that indicated she loved that too, so he did it again, using his palms to brush her nipples at the same time.

Her pace quickened and she bit down into his neck just over his pulse. He leaned up to do the same to her, wanting to mark her as much as she obviously wanted to mark him. His wolf howled his approval and he bit down a little harder as her pace quickened, quickened, her breasts pushing against his hands and her pulse pounding against his tongue.

Just when he thought he could not hold on any longer, she made a tight sound, her body stiffened and her internal muscles squeezed hard around him. Then they released, moving in waves against his cock as she came, his name a shout against his neck.

He let go and came with her, shouting her name against her neck as he shot up and up and up into the stratosphere, into the universe twined with her. The sensation was so intense, so all-encompassing, it was something he never wanted to come down from; something he never wanted to let go.

And then he realised he didn't need to. He would always have this with Leanna.

For they were more than mates.

They were soul mates.

They were one.

And they would have this forever more.

45

It took three days of planning and organisation before they were ready to go—thankfully Iain did not make a fuss that they did not go immediately.

The craftsmen had got together and come up with an ingenious set of straps that would enable Dougal to sit astride a horse. He wasn't certain how long he could sustain that position, but it would at least allow him a semblance of self-automation. Le-le would use her Healing ability to aid the muscles in his shoulders, torso and arms to increase their strength more quickly so he could maintain an upright position for longer without strain.

Other craftsmen worked on the contraptions that Le-le and Alistair had found reference to in the old coven diaries—a wheeled chair that he could more easily be moved around in, and, if he managed to gain some movement and sensation in his legs, there was a set of leg braces and walking sticks designed to go under the arms that would allow him to swing his legs forward with practice so that he could move around without others helping him. Both were ingenious and he couldn't wait to try them out along the way—which was possible now as those craftsmen had elected to come with them.

More of the pack and coven than he thought had elected to leave

Pack MacCrae and come with them to set up a new pack and claim new Packlands. About a third of the pack and half of the coven were now part of their new pack. It was a blow for Pack MacCrae, but they were already the biggest pack in Britannia and would not suffer from the loss.

As to their new pack, it still didn't have a name as neither he nor Leanna wanted the pack named for them. They wanted a name that was representative of who they all were, so they were holding off on making a decision until they'd got to where Leanna had seen they needed to go. They would have others by then—Leanna was certain of it—and that would help them decide what they should be called.

As it had turned out, it had been easy to avoid Iain as they planned their leaving. The Alpha had not come anywhere near the Healer Hall where they stayed most of the time. Bram told Cal that he remained by Lachlan's side as he recovered from the blow to his head and from losing his wolf. Not that there was much for him to recover from with the latter—he was just outraged at the fact his wolf had wanted to leave him and Morghanna reported that he showed no signs of grief at all. Leanna knew he wasn't capable of it, so it shouldn't be something they expected of him, but for a Were not to grieve the loss of their wolf, or fade into death because of it, was a shocking thing. And just proved that they had done the right thing to remove the wolf from his soulless human.

Lachlan had been taken to a cave in the mountains that had been secured and set up for a long stay for the pack's prisoner. It had been set up quite comfortably for him, which was far more than the man deserved as far as Dougal was concerned. Cal said it was no longer his problem. 'Morghanna and Alistair are more than capable of dealing with Iain and keeping those under their care as safe as possible.'

He knew Cal was right, but still he and Leanna worried in those few moments they had to spare. A great deal of their focus was on leaving and on their new pack. It was paramount they take care of those who looked to them for leadership and strength and left them in no doubt that was so.

It was lucky though that Leanna would be able to keep in constant contact with Morghanna, Alistair and Abigail and they would both do what they could to help their friends and former packmates in any way they could.

And if Iain didn't stand down soon, he just hoped that he would learn from his mistakes and do better.

A sinking feeling inside him though told him it was a useless hope.

He sighed and pushed away that thought to worry over another day. Because now it was time to leave and he had to show a confident front; that he was an Alpha with an eye on a positive and bright future for his new pack. He owed those who followed them that much at the very least.

Sitting astride his horse, having already said his goodbyes to those he cared for, he watched as the pack and coven came out to say goodbye to those who were leaving. There were tears and sorrow—and some anger from those who viewed it as a betrayal—but the feeling from those leaving was one of hope that overrode any negativity. Which he was grateful for because his mate was too attuned to the feelings of others and he could see how overwhelmed she had been before that sense of hope had calmed her.

She stood beside him and his horse, watching as Morghanna, Alistair and Abigail said goodbye to their coven mates. They might be bonded to a new Alpha pair, but the ties to those they were leaving behind were still strong and they would not lose contact.

Finally, Morghanna, Alistair and Abigail turned to them.

Eyes full of tears and pride, Morghanna approached with her arms held wide. She folded Leanna into her arms and for long moments, they just held on to each other. He could feel Leanna's desperation not to give in to sobbing tears, her face buried into the taller witch's shoulder as she clung tightly to her. But finally, they drew apart, both of their faces damp but smiling as their gazes met.

'I will miss you horribly,' Leanna said, tears in her voice. 'How will I manage without you and Alistair and Abigail?'

Morghanna moved her hands up Leanna's shoulders and

squeezed. 'You have not truly needed us these last months. It is us who need you. But none of us would hold you back from your destiny. Which is what this is. You are meant to go now and create something new. Something never seen before. I for one will look on with pride as you do. And as you show us a new way, I promise I will try to bring some of what you are doing into the packs and covens who cling too tightly to the old ways much to our detriment.'

'I do not feel worthy of such praise,' Leanna said softly.

'You make us proud as you have always done. We cannot wait to see you shine. Both of you.' She looked up at Dougal to include him in her words. 'Look after our girl.'

'Always.'

She nodded and hugged Leanna again—more briefly this time—before giving over her place to first Alistair and then Abigail as they said their goodbyes to his mate and then to him.

Finally, all the goodbyes done, Leanna mounted her horse and, with the other horses and wagons ranged behind them, they headed out.

Iain had not come out to see them off—he hadn't expected him to —although Bram and the lieutenants and soldiers who were staying were there. At first he thought it was to ensure they left as promised, but as they wound their way out of the village, they ran ahead to line up on either side of the road in a guard of honour, their swords— more ceremonial than useful given they mostly fought in their wolf forms—held high.

It was a touching, unexpected tribute to the creation of a new pack and the forging of a new beginning for them all.

Riding beside him, Leanna reached for his hand. He took it in his and held tight. And together they rode out ahead of their new pack, heads held high, hope for a bright future so great he felt like it glowed between them and lit their way.

Leanna turned and smiled at him and he smiled back. Then they both looked forward.

To their future, excited for what it would bring.

He couldn't wait!

. . .

THE END ...

OF THIS INSTALMENT THAT IS. There is a lot more to discover with Dougal and Leanna and their new pack as they forge ahead into an exciting new chapter for the Were and their covens.

The next book in the Dawn of the Curse Series, *Hunter Bound*, will be coming in late 2025.

If you want to be advised when this is about to be released (along with other new releases and book related information), just sign up to my newsletter. I will share the sign up link (and details about a FREE book you get when you sign up) after I've shared with you the opening chapters of *Pack Bound: Book 1 Pack Bound Series*, which is set in the Dawn of the Curse world 500 years after the events of *Alpha Bound*.

If you've read *Pack Bound* already, just skip the next chapter, if not, then turn the page to read more ...

PACK BOUND

PACK BOUND SERIES: BOOK 1

THE CURSE OF
MORGHANNA CANTRAE

I curse you, my pack, to a life without magic. May the right to change be taken from you, your animals gaoled and tortured inside your flesh as I have been gaoled and tortured inside mine. I curse you to the eternal damnation of your kind. And I curse all others who let this insanity befall one in their care. Take warning, from these, my last words, all you who would come after: Look to the wellbeing of your Pack Witch or suffer the fate of the MacCraes.

I tie my curse unto my death,
I curse you all with dying breath
Three times three times three times three
My will be done, so mote it be.

Curse as transcribed by Father Luke as Morghanna was burned at the stake for witchcraft, 1502, Edinburgh, Scotland.

1

Skye stopped at the crest of the ski run and took a moment to appreciate the beauty of the Victorian Alps laid out before her. A breeze, full of the scent of eucalypts and the cool freshness of snow, blew a lock of red hair into her eyes. She swept it back under her ski hat and took a deep breath.

'What a beautiful day.' She'd skied in Austria and Canada, but even though the ski season was so much shorter in Australia and the snow not nearly as good, there was nothing like the stark beauty of the blue-tinged mountains of the Great Dividing Range. The other ski resorts were breathtaking too, but these mountains were home. They sang to her soul in a way the others couldn't.

Taking another deep breath, she pushed off over the crest and, with a wild 'Yahoo!', flew down the slope, her knees moving like rubber pistons as she attacked the moguls.

She ignored the swish and slide of other skiers around her, enjoying this moment of freedom on her last day, before she had to go back and face the real world. She wished she had an extra few days to gird her loins—as her grandpa used to say—against the responsibilities awaiting her at home, but it wasn't to be.

Instead, she was determined just to be happy with the now. It was a rare clear day at Mt Buller, and she was going to enjoy it to her fill.

She was just getting into a rhythm on the moguls when a strange chill crept down her spine—the kind of chill you got when someone was watching you surreptitiously. She'd been having that feeling off and on all day. She slowed, turning to see if she could catch them at it.

'Whoa!' she heard. Then something hard and heavy smashed into her. The sky tipped and an *oof* of breath exploded out of her as she hit the snow. A large body landed on top of her and then they were sliding, smashing over and through the moguls, until they finally slowed and came to a stop.

Head spinning, she lay with her arms flung out wide, crushed under the hot weight of a man. She moaned.

'Are you okay?' the man's husky voice murmured in Skye's ear.

'Only if I don't breathe,' she managed, surprised she wasn't winded. Snow inched into the collar of her parka. She shivered.

He shifted, pushing up onto his elbows to look down at her.

Despite the pain sparking through her body—damn, she was going to have some impressive bruises for show-and-tell on Monday —she became uncomfortably aware of the way their hips pressed together, legs tangled. She hadn't been this close to a man in way too long. This wasn't the way she'd imagined it happening again, though.

She tried to move. The action made his board—amazingly still attached to his feet—cut into her leg. She winced. 'Well, this is a very charming way to meet and all, but can you get off, please? You're crushing my legs.'

'Sorry.' He scrambled back.

'Oh, fudgy-duck!' She gasped as his board scraped over the bruise.

'Are you hurt?' He ran his hand over her leg, checking for injury.

Shivers chased across her skin that had nothing to do with the snow melting inside her jacket. Skye pulled away. 'No. I'm fine. Just let me stretch it out.'

He shifted back. But instead of getting up and skiing off like most other people would, he stayed, kneeling beside her as she stretched out her leg.

'I'm so sorry. I usually ski, but my brother talked me into trying out a snowboard this year.'

Her temper spiked at his words. Rubbing her aching leg, she snapped, 'Are you kidding me? What the hell are you doing on Federation? It's a black run—or didn't you notice all the signs up the top, you irresponsible arse?'

His eyebrows rose above his sunglasses. 'Wow. That thing about redheads and tempers is true.'

She bristled. 'You could have killed yourself, or someone else. Namely me!'

He brushed snow from his hair. 'For your information, I was doing okay until I hit that goddamned icy patch. I don't know why I agreed to try a board,' he grumbled.

He sounded so much like her twin, River, when he was pouting, that her flare of anger disappeared and she had to hide her grin. 'So why did you go over to the dark side?'

'My trickster of a brother said it would be a rush, but I think he just wanted to see me fall on my arse.'

Her lips twitched. 'That would be okay, except for the fact that you fell on mine.'

'It looked softer than mine.'

She choked on a laugh. 'Are you saying I have a fat arse?'

Rather than trying to back-pedal, his mouth curled into a lopsided smile—such a lovely mouth. 'No. In fact, I was thinking how nice it looked before I smacked into you.'

Skye dragged her eyes from his mouth. 'Is that why you took me for a toboggan ride, with me as the toboggan? To meet me and my nice arse?'

'That, and the fact you stopped so suddenly.'

She snorted. 'I thought you said there was an icy patch.'

'Yeah.' He laughed. 'I did. Didn't I?' He pushed his sunglasses off his face to look down at her.

She gaped.

He had the most startling eyes. They were deeply blue on the edge, almost black, but lightened to an icy blue at their centre. Lightning-bolt striations crazed through the iris, making it seem as if his eyes glowed. They reminded her of a picture of a wolf River had put on his bedroom wall when they were young. She'd asked him to take it down. He'd thought it was because she was frightened of big dogs, but it hadn't just been that. The wolf's eyes had haunted her in a way that confused her ten-year-old soul.

This man's eyes were even more dangerous to her equilibrium. They pulled her in. Her chest ached like she'd been winded.

He broke eye contact and pushed to his feet, allowing her to catch her breath. 'Here, let me help you up.' He put out his hand.

Don't touch him!

Skye hesitated as her inner voice barked at her; it was part of a spell her grandpa had woven to stop her from using her magic and to warn of any other magic users around. It usually sounded like her grandpa, calm and kind and supportive, but now her grandpa's voice held a tone like that of her grandmother, Morrigan Cantrae, at her commanding best.

Her first instinct was to do the opposite of anything Morrigan commanded. But she was no longer a child and instead of fighting it, she hesitated as she thought it through.

Her inner voice, changed or not, was only supposed to react so forcefully if she tried to use her magic—something that could never be allowed—or if an equally powerful witch or warlock was around or she was in danger.

Well, she hadn't used her magic and there was nothing about this man that suggested

he was a warlock; no tingling under her skin that warned her a true magic user stood before her. No sense of impending disaster.

And the chance of him being an axe murderer was pretty well zip.

So, if he wasn't a warlock or an axe murderer, there was no reason not to accept his offer of help.

She put her hand in his.

His fingers were strong as they wrapped around hers, and so warm the heat of him soaked into her, even through her gloves.

'Thanks,' she choked out as that warmth slid through her, doing something entirely untoward to her nerves. Overwhelmed, she pulled her hand from his grip.

He stepped back.

Perversely, now that he'd moved away, she wanted to get closer, beg him to touch her again. What the hell?

'Are you sure I can't do anything for you?'

Looking up into his face and those remarkable eyes, his voice a melting tenor in her ears, she forgot all about the pain in her leg and ankle. 'I'm pretty certain there are many and various things you could do for me.' Oh God! Had she said that out loud? She slapped her hand over her mouth, eyes wide. The look on his face told her she had. 'I'm sorry,' she muttered through her fingers. 'I don't know why I said that.'

He moved closer. 'I don't mind that you did.'

She swallowed hard, forced herself to answer. 'But I do. I don't know what's wrong with me.'

His brow furrowed again. 'Maybe you knocked your head.'

'I don't think so.' She tried to look away but couldn't. It was those eyes. And his voice. That was why she was behaving like such a weirdo. There was one room in the house where eyes and a voice like that really came into their own—and it wasn't the kitchen.

He was so gorgeous, with sinfully long dark lashes, the chiselled features of a male model and a dimple in his left cheek. The only thing that marred his perfect good looks was the scar that ran through his top lip—but that just made him look rugged and tough rather than pretty.

She sighed, wanting to touch his dimple, run her fingers across the stubborn jut of his jaw and linger on that scar. She wanted to flirt and have some fun. This was her holiday, after all. But she was vastly out of practice with flirting. She hadn't been on a date for years. What was the point when she could never get serious with anyone? Instead, she'd concentrated on building her business and spending time with River. Not that she minded: it was her fault her twin was housebound. She owed it to him to always be there.

The man stepped closer bringing her attention snapping back to him. 'Are you sure you're okay?'

The more he spoke, the more she thought of a good bottle of red, low seductive music and a plush fur rug before a fire. It was difficult not to reach for him, push her fingers through his silky brown hair and bring her lips to his.

But the way he looked at her indicated he didn't have the same inclination, regardless of his comments about her nice arse. He looked more confused than interested.

Disappointed when she knew she shouldn't be, she said, 'I'm fine, really.' She put weight on her sore foot and took a few hobbling steps. 'Almost as good as new.'

He looked unconvinced. 'Perhaps you should call it a day. You're limping.'

She shook her head. 'Are you kidding? It's not often you get days like this at Buller.'

She gestured at the blue sky, the snow-laden trees lining the run, the mountains of the Victorian Alps marching into the distance, covered in the blue haze of thousands of eucalypts. 'You would have to chop my leg off with your snowboard to stop me from skiing on such a beautiful day.' She cocked her head to the side, considering. 'Nah. Maybe not even then.'

He laughed, the sound washing over her like warm water lapping at her skin. 'Let me see you down to the bottom at least, make sure you get to the lift.'

Skye's gaze raked over his face, her vision blurring. The way he looked at her reminded her of something ... someone.

'Hello!' He waved his hand in front of her face. 'Don't tell me I gave you a concussion.'

She squeezed her eyes shut and shook her head. 'No. I'm fine. Just a bit of snow blindness.' Pathetic excuse, but with him standing so close, she couldn't seem to do better. Opening her eyes, she squinted. 'It's a bit bright with the sun. I should have worn my goggles.'

'Are you sure?'

His voice was hypnotic. She couldn't stop herself leaning forward, breathing in his scent. The need to give in to the temptation to touch, to kiss, to lick, was overwhelming. It was like she'd been bewitched.

She snapped upright. Panic clawed at her throat. Could she be? Bewitched?

No. Bron had said she had stronger shields than anyone she'd ever met, thanks to her grandpa's spell, and there was no reason not to trust her best friend in this matter. She was Wiccan after all. Not a true magic user like her family had been, but she did know about this stuff.

So what was happening to her?

Lust.

Yes. That was it. Mr Too-Gorgeous-For-Sanity was a fantasy come to life. She had to ignore the sensations shooting through her body. Force herself to be sensible. He was just being friendly because he'd knocked her over. And she'd made enough of a fool of herself for one day.

Biting her lip, trying to shelve her disappointment, she nodded. 'I'm sure. Go and kill your brother for making you snowboard and then enjoy the day.'

He chuckled. 'I might just do that. Adam needs a good killing.'

'Excellent. So, off you go. I'll be fine by myself.' Before he could say anything else, she hobbled down the hill to her skis. She clicked into the bindings, swallowing a gasp as pain sliced up from her ankle. Clenching her jaw, she endeavoured to ignore it. After all, she'd put up with worse.

There was the slide of board on snow behind her and she looked up to see the Adonis making his way down the slope towards her.

'How about I shout you a hot chocolate at Koflers just to make sure you're fine?'

Surprisingly pleased by his perseverance, Skye opened her mouth to say yes.

Don't say it! her inner voice snapped.

Taken aback, she blinked. *Why?*

He may not stink of magic, but there's something about him that's affecting you. Think about River. Think about what your magic did to him.

Even though the voice still didn't sound like it usually did, Skye knew it was right. This man might not have the magic to bewitch her, but he *was* making her behave strangely, almost to the point of acting without thinking—which she never did. She could never afford to lose control—her magic had only ever brought pain. She swallowed hard, knowing that despite the fact this was a holiday and she should be able to flirt and have fun, she couldn't do it with this man.

Taking herself in hand, she said, 'Thanks, but no thanks. I still want to get a few runs in before I call it a day.'

'What about a drink after? I feel I need to say sorry in some way.'

The wish to say yes was almost a pain inside her; but that in itself was reason to say no. 'I can't. I've got a prior engagement with friends.'

'I'm sorry to hear that.' He flashed a grin so charming it made her breath catch. 'I'll just have to hope we'll meet another time and your answer will be different.' He leaned forward, his astonishing warmth radiating towards her, and took a deep breath as if trying to breathe her in.

It was weird and yet ... unbelievably sexy.

'Okay,' she squeaked. Unable to stand his closeness for another moment and not give in to his invitation, she pushed off with her good leg and took off down the slope. Pain stabbed up her leg from her wounded ankle. A little whimper escaped from her lips.

What are you? A lion or a mouse?

A lion.

So ignore it. You have to get away from him.

She took in a shuddering breath—duck-it, she could still smell the warm male scent of him; earthy and yet clear and fresh, like the mountain air, yet so very different in how it affected her. Mountain air was cooling, refreshing; this was ... hot and made need simmer under her skin. She took in another breath as she created more distance between them; but the scent stayed with her as if it was imprinted on her senses.

A tingle started down her spine. Was he watching her? Were his eyes caressing her arse the way he said they had been before he crashed into her? She almost groaned at the memory of the way they'd come to a stop, his body spread on top of hers, chest to chest, legs tangled. Skye bit her lip as muscles well below her abdomen clenched and quivered.

It was a sensation she'd not felt for a long time—too long. Hell, she'd almost become a nun with the length of time she'd been celibate, and she'd been content with that. But coming face to face with that Adonis would make even a nun change her habits. It wasn't so unusual that he'd had such an impact on her.

Or was it?

She stopped herself from glancing back over her shoulder. It didn't matter what she felt. All that mattered was it couldn't be. Her life was like this by necessity. There was no choice. She'd come to terms with that a long time ago.

Lifting her face to the sun, she decided to luxuriate in the rare spring day and not worry about could-have-beens.

The sapphire blue sky was glorious.

And reminded her of his eyes.

She stared at the choppy snow in front of her. Yes, that was better. Nothing about the snow reminded her of him. It did remind her that she needed to thank Shelley and Bron once again for agreeing to change their plans for a Noosa holiday and had come with her to Mt Buller instead for the last of the season. Good snow in spring was a rarity, so she hadn't been able to pass up the opportunity when a few days before they were due to leave for Noosa, a huge dump was reported. Fresh powder, the blue skies of spring and the freedom she only felt in the mountains was a siren call she couldn't ignore. Thankfully her friends agreed, even though they weren't as keen to get on the slopes as she was and stay there all day. They were more into staying at the lodge or enjoying a cocktail or two at one of the bars that was still open at this time of the year.

Which was where she'd left them to come out and get in a few more runs before the lifts closed for the day.

They had planned to go out again tonight for their last night here and she'd been looking forward to it, but the pain in her ankle was beginning to make her doubt if she'd be able to. By the feel of it, she might have done some serious damage. Duck-it! Bron was bound to fuss and Shelley to lecture.

Her spine tingled again. Was Mr Too-Gorgeous-For-Sanity still watching her? She turned her head to sneak a peek and lost her rhythm. Her ski slid down the side of a mogul and pain jagged up her leg. She groaned.

'Are you okay?' he yelled, his voice winding around her like a feather stroke even at this distance.

She didn't look back again, only waved, hiding her red face, not wanting him to ski after her.

A moment later, she pulled up at the end of the queue of skiers and boarders waiting to get on the lift. She chanced a glance back up the slope. He stood right where she'd left him and something about the way he stood made her certain he was still looking right at her. She shivered, the sensation far too pleasurable for her own—or anyone's—good.

She shuffled forward, glad the queue was fast moving, but still she couldn't help breathing out a sigh of relief as she hopped on a chair and it climbed into the air through shielding trees.

Adonis might not be a warlock, but his combination of good looks, charm and velvety voice was just as dangerous. He'd not only made her want to change her nun-like habits, he made her feel like a horny teenager. He'd even made her consider, for a split second, turning her back on her obligations and the promises she'd made to her grandpa and to River.

She could never do that. Ever.

Those promises kept them all safe.

As the lift rose over the crest of the slope, she shivered. This time it wasn't the feeling of being watched that made that strange tingle race up and down her spine; thoughts of what happened all those years ago always did this. Her magic pushed at her, fighting to get out. She swore, pushing it back down. That man's presence had addled her brain, made her shields weak. Closing her eyes, she repeated the mantra she'd been taught.

Her magic was dangerous. To protect River and everyone she loved, it was something she could never set free.

2

'Was that her?'

With a slide of board on snow, Adam came to a halt. Jason didn't turn to look at his brother, his gaze still on the place where the lithe redhead had disappeared as the chair she was on rose over the crest of the hill. Unexpected warmth still fired through his body.

'If that was her, why's she running away?' Adam clapped his brother on the shoulder.

'Did you try your charm on her?'

Jason didn't answer. His mind was too full of the woman: those green eyes like spring pools, glistening with hidden depths in the sun; her hair, licks of flame on her shoulders; her generous mouth full of laughter and mischief. Even that spike of temper and the funny way she'd had of swearing had been sexy.

Despite himself, he was engaged. He hadn't expected that. And her scent—his wolf had growled at her scent. Familiar, yet there was also something strange about it.

'Aren't you going to follow her?'

Jason shook his head and brushed the snow off his pants. 'No. Something's wrong. She didn't recognise what I am.'

'Maybe she isn't our Pack Witch.'

Jason clicked his boot onto the snowboard and balanced for a moment, shifting his weight back and forth. 'I'm pretty sure she is. But there's something ...' He shook his head. 'She should have expelled some magic when she saw me, but she didn't.'

Adam frowned and sniffed. 'But I can smell that zip in the air, like the electrical build-up before lightning. Doesn't that denote magic?'

Jason thought about the last time they'd encountered the scent of magic—the night their parents, two older brothers and their mates had been murdered in their never-ending quest to find their kidnapped Pack Witch. The scent in the air now, a scent that lingered in his nostrils like a teasing perfume, was nothing like that acrid scent. 'It is magic. But she didn't expel it when she saw me. It's around her all the time, like a cloak, but muted or something.' That was definitely wrong. Yet he was sure it was her. He'd seen her in his dreams; dreams he'd always had of her; dreams that had been nebulous things until the Calling had caught up with him after his father's murder and he'd become Alpha.

'How can you be certain it's her then?'

'Because of the dreams. I saw her skiing here with her friends.'

'You dragged us here to chase down a woman who doesn't even smell like she has the magic of a Pack Witch all because of some dreams?'

'They're not just dreams. It's the link.'

'What link?'

'The link between the Alpha and the Pack Witch. Dad was linked to Paul Collins—'

'As Iris Collins was linked to Grandpa before him.'

'Yes.' It was the only way the magic worked. The Pack Witch fed it into the Alpha and the pack syphoned it from the Alpha through the Packbond—the ultimate form of synergy.

'But how are you linked to Paul's daughter?'

The question was understandable. A bonding wasn't supposed to be undertaken until a Pack Witch or Warlock was of age, after they'd imbibed the Bond Wine. But in this case ...

Jason looked out at the distant mountains. The moment he'd clapped eyes on her, he'd realised that Paul Collins had linked them all those years ago—the future Alpha and the future Pack Witch. It's why he'd had the dreams. It made sense of something that had always seemed nonsensical to him. Something he'd spent years denying because he'd been too young to understand the significance of what had been done to him. The proof was irrefutable though.

The link was the reason he'd found her when nobody else could.

'Paul linked us when Skylar was a few months old.'

'What?' Adam gripped his arm, his voice bitter. 'Did you keep this from me because I'm nothing but the Trickster?'

'No.' Jason clasped Adam's shoulder. 'And don't talk like that about yourself. From what I've been reading in the Pack Witch Diaries, the Trickster is far more essential to a pack than we remember. Besides, I have named you my second. I wouldn't keep anything from you. It's just ... I've only now realised what Paul did.'

He remembered standing in the dark room looking down at her crib, Paul lighting candles that had smelled like jasmine and cinnamon and honey. He'd muttered words Jason hadn't understood and in the quiet hush that followed, a sizzle had shot along Jason's skin, sinking into his nerve-ends and sparking in his brain. The baby had cried out, holding out her chubby little arms to him. Despite being a boy who thought babies were smelly, noisy things, he'd picked her up, bouncing her until she giggled. That giggle had fizzled inside him like popping candy, leaving him with the same sense of warmth and sweet aftertaste.

'It is done. You will keep my daughter safe,' Paul had whispered.

Jason hadn't realised the significance. He'd just been a small boy holding a pretty baby who smelled of powder and her mother's sweet milk.

'Why would he do that when it goes against pack law?'

Jason was brought out of his reverie by his brother's question. He understood the horror in Adam's tone. The pack's greatest duty was to look after their children. They would never do anything to hurt or place unnecessary burden on a child. But Paul had done exactly that when he'd linked Skylar to Jason.

'He was prescient. Maybe he'd seen this future. Maybe he knew I would become

Alpha and that I would have to find her.'

Adam shook his head. 'I always thought Paul looked sad. It's no wonder if this is what he saw.'

Jason glanced at his brother and sighed at the look of devastation on his face. Nobody would have looked at Paul and thought him sad, yet Adam had seen beyond the facade Paul showed to the world, to the grief of a man who saw things he shouldn't. It was remarkable sometimes, the things the Trickster saw. Things none of them had realised the significance of until it was almost too late. Now he knew that without Adam pushing fun and laughter into the Packbond, the pack would already have succumbed to the Curse. He'd maintained positivity when there was nothing to be positive about.

And it was taking a toll. As Alpha, linked to his brother in ways he'd never been linked before, Jason could feel the pressure of pack wellbeing tear at Adam. He wished he could take some of that burden but it wasn't possible. Not until they had their Pack Witch back safe and sound and the Curse averted. Because, more than anything, he knew that what Adam was doing for the pack was helping to keep him from slipping into deadly insanity.

Gripping his brother's shoulder, Jason whispered, 'I know. I know the burden that knowledge places on you.'

Adam swallowed hard. 'I know you do.' He gripped Jason's shoulder in turn. 'That's why you make one fucking great Alpha.'

Jason smiled and slapped his brother on the arm. Even when torn apart by a pain that wasn't his, Adam couldn't help but see the bright side. 'I think you're right about Paul. He saw at least some part of the future. That's why he linked Skylar and me at an age when it would normally be forbidden.'

'Did Mum and Dad know?'

Jason frowned. 'I think perhaps they did, after the fact. Why else would they have given me such freedom?'

'Because they were sick of listening to you whinge and whine about wanting choice,' Adam said. He managed to keep a straight face when Jason glared at him, then burst out laughing.

Jason chuckled 'You can't help yourself can you?'

'Comes with the burden of being the funny one.'

'You're funny, all right,' Jason said, twirling his finger beside his head.

'You can talk. I'm not the one following strange dreams.'

'You're right.' Jason sighed, all levity dying as his thoughts turned darker. 'I just wish the link had activated properly before Mum and Dad, Seamus and Sian, and Josef and Marianne were killed.'

'But that's not how it works.'

'No. Dad had to die for me to find her.' He ground his board into the snow, fingers clenched, the wolf desperate to break through and claw at something.

'You can't blame yourself for that. You didn't kill them.'

Jason's lips curled into a snarl. 'No. I didn't. But I swear by the Dark Moon, I will find who did.'

It all came down to the woman he'd just smashed into: Skylar Collins.

She was their hope of a future without madness. She was also the only hope he had of finding those responsible for causing the Curse to touch his pack, bringing them to near extinction.

'So, if that is Skylar, why didn't she use her magic when she saw you?'

Jason took in a deep breath of clear, cool air, trying to calm himself. 'I don't know. But I have no doubt that the reason why Cordelia or the old McClune Pack Witch could never scry for her is at the heart of it. Whoever took her hid her by changing more than her name.'

'So, what's the plan?'

'I'm going to bump into her again at the lodge and when the time's right, I'm going to share some wine with her.'

Adam's eyes glittered with understanding. 'Do you think crashing into her was the best way of meeting her then? I don't know if she'll want to share the Bond Wine with an accident-prone idiot.'

As was the Trickster way, Adam was trying to lighten his mood. It worked. Jason's lips split into a grin. 'I didn't think she'd stop short like that, but in retrospect it was a stroke of genius. Because if she heals herself, we'll know there isn't anything wrong with her magic. Besides, I got so close, I filled myself with her fresh scent. I can track her anywhere now.'

'Will that be necessary?'

'We'll see. But at least we know she can't disappear again. It's taken too long to track her down. I don't want to waste any more time.'

'I'm with you there. I'm sick of this.'

The growl in his brother's tone had Jason's gaze sliding to Adam. There was a red tinge in the amber of his eyes. The darkness Adam had banished moments ago had returned. Ultimately, breaking the Curse would cure that, but for now ... 'You need to hunt.'

'Later. Let's race.'

With a whoop, Adam took off down the slope, his motions balletic as he controlled the board. Jason's smile widened into a thoroughly wolfish grin as he caught Skylar's scent; still clear even though she'd was gone. His wolf wanted to hunt her down right now—it didn't like that she had run from them.

Soon, he promised, stroking his wolf with a mental hand. *For now, let's go chase Adam.*

The wolf growled its agreement.

Pushing forward, he followed Adam down the slope, catching air as he flew over a snow-capped boulder and cut Adam off. He heard Adam's bark of laughter as his brother tried to push past him; a sound he echoed as he passed the Trickster in a few quick movements, beating him to the queue by a hairsbreadth.

Adam might have been doing this longer, but nobody beat Jason in the chase. And Skylar Collins was about to find out that running only served to sweeten the hunt.

3

Skye hopped off the bus with an exhausted sigh. Limping to the back, she pulled her skis out of the rack. Just as she stepped away, that same strange crawling sensation she'd felt all day crept down her spine. She'd say it was her sixth sense, except her sixth sense was blocked by the repression spell.

She glanced around, trying to find the source.

People were beginning to clear from the bus, trudging through the snow to their lodges, but there was nothing out of the ordinary about that. Nothing to explain why she felt like she was being watched, as she had all day—except for when Adonis had knocked her off her feet. She'd forgotten all about being followed when she'd stared into his incredible blue eyes. Combined with his smoky-chocolate voice, they'd made her forget a hell of a lot. She'd been making her way back to the bus stop at the village when the feeling of being watched had come over her again. But apart from a couple of young guys who were ogling all the girls, nobody was watching her. Must be her imagination.

She shuddered, wishing her imagination would just shut up.

The bus moved off with a puff of exhaust and she headed across the road. Out of the corner of her eye, she saw a man standing in the shadow of the trees, staring at her.

She swung around, her skis clattering together at the suddenness of the motion and peered directly at the spot where she'd seen the figure.

Nobody was there.

What the hell? She was certain she'd seen someone standing there.

'Where did he go?'

'Did you say something?'

She jumped and looked up to see a man smiling down at her curiously. 'No. Just talking to myself.' There was something oddly familiar about him, but Skye was certain she'd never seen him before. He held a snowboard under one arm and a small set of skis over the other shoulder. A young boy, locks of sandy hair poking out from under a black helmet, hung off the man's leg, his forest green eyes watching her with suspicion that seemed out of place for someone his age. He began to pull at the man's leg, making him stumble sideways.

She knew she probably shouldn't engage with the boy, but she couldn't help it. She smiled at him. 'I think someone wants to get out of the cold. Hot chocolate coming your way?' she whispered conspiratorially.

The boy flashed a nervy smile. 'With marshmallows.'

Skye nodded. 'Mmm. My favourites are the pink ones. I love when they start to melt in the chocolate.'

The little boy's eyes screwed up. 'Pink is for girls.'

Skye laughed. 'Must be why I like them then.'

The little boy turned a pleading face up to the man. 'Do we have marshmallows, Uncle A?'

'I'm pretty sure I managed to pack some, Tombo.'

'You're the best, Uncle A.' He hugged his uncle's leg again. A deep ache settled inside Skye for the things she would never have. She turned her head to surreptitiously wipe at her damp eyes and froze. Her heart thumped in her chest as she fought against mind-numbing fear.

A big, grey, wolf-like dog trotted across where she thought she'd seen the man standing before. Her skis dropped to the ground with a loud clatter. The world swam in front of her eyes as the dog turned to stare at her with yellow eyes.

Back away. Now.

She didn't need the internal voice to tell her that, but she couldn't move.

A shiver ran down her spine—much worse than that sensation people blamed on someone walking over their grave. This felt as if death had marked her and was standing behind her with an outstretched hand, waiting to push her into her grave.

She couldn't breathe. The world began to spin.

'Are you okay?' A hand under her elbow stopped her from crashing to the snow. She looked up and saw the man—he and his nephew hadn't moved away.

'Did you see that?'

'See what?'

'That wolf-like dog. Over there. It was huge.' She pointed into the deepening gloom.

Nothing was there. There was a faint rustle of movement among the bushes to the left of where the wolf-dog had stood only seconds ago, but the bushes weren't big enough to hide it.

'There's nothing there now.' He picked up her skis. 'It must have run away.'

Skye nodded, trying to swallow. Trying to breathe past the constriction of fear in her chest. 'You're right. It just gave me a fright. I don't like dogs very much.' She shivered again, but made herself let go of the man's arm, realising she was clutching at it like a crazy person.

'Here.' He handed her skis to her. 'Are you sure you're fine?'

'Yes. I just got a fright.' She took her skis from him. 'I think I need a big drink.'

'That sounds like a great idea.' He looked at her, expectantly.

Was he asking her for a drink? It was nice of him, but even though he was rather nice looking, she certainly didn't feel the pull towards him she'd felt when Adonis had asked her for a drink an hour or so earlier. There was no temptation to say yes.

She took a step back, wondering how to let him down kindly, when she noticed the little boy jiggling on the spot behind him. 'You look like you've got a little one who's about to bust.'

He glanced down. 'Damn, I think you're right. Come on, Tom.' He took his nephew's hand and began to run to the lodge—the same one she was staying at. Maybe that's where she'd seen him—maybe they'd arrived last night and she'd seen him fleetingly before she and Shelley and Bron had gone out.

Skye threw her skis over her shoulder and crossed the road towards the lodge, limping as her ankle protested the movement. As she passed the bushes where the wolf-dog had disappeared, she peered into them. Nothing was there.

She was definitely going quietly insane. Maybe two drinks would be the thing.

'Skye!'

She turned. Shelley was racing across the road, having just got off another bus.

'Hi, Shells. Where's Bron?'

'She was chatting up our instructor in the bar.' She rolled her eyes. 'Felt a bit like a third wheel, so I decided to come home and have a nice cup of tea.' Piercing Skye with a look, she asked, 'Why are you limping?'

'I'm not limping.'

'Oh, really? So one of your legs has got mysteriously shorter, has it?'

Skye laughed. 'Okay. I got knocked over on Federation and twisted my ankle a bit.'

'You had a spill?'

'No. I got knocked over by a snowboarder. There's a difference.'

Shelley snorted. 'Is the offender still alive?'

'Ha ha. Very funny. He's fine, by the way. Boarded away and everything, legs still intact.'

'Yeah. But was his manhood?'

'I'm not that bad!'

'You keep telling yourself that.' Her laughter died. 'So, when did this happen?'

'On my last run of Federation. Just past the crest.'

Her friend's eyebrows disappeared under her bright green woollen ski cap. 'And I suppose you skied the rest of the way down and then all the way back to the bottom of Burke Street?'

'What? You wanted me to make a fuss and call ski patrol to come and get me?'

'That's exactly what I would have done if it had been me. But then, I'm sensible.'

'I'm sensible.' Shelley angled her a look that had Skye shrugging sheepishly. 'What?'

'Might as well hit my head against a brick wall as try to get you to look after yourself properly,' Shelley mumbled.

'I look after myself. I came home instead of continuing to ski, didn't I?'

Shelley rolled her eyes then said, 'Fine. You're the best at looking after yourself.'

'Too right.'

She chuckled. 'Come on. Let's see the damage.' Before Skye could protest, she took her skis and trudged ahead to the steps of the lodge. Skye limped after her. By the time she got there, Shelley had gone inside, put the skis away and was back at the door, holding it open.

Skye shook her head. 'You don't need to baby me.'

'I need to do something to you. Now, come in out of the cold and we'll see what needs to be done with your ankle.'

'Yes ma'am.' She snapped a salute.

Shelley laughed. 'Come on, you idiot.'

Icy fingers crawled up Skye's spine as she walked into the foyer. She shuddered and turned to look behind her once more.

'What is it?' Shelley asked, leaning to look around her.

'Nothing. I've just had a strange feeling all day that someone's been watching me.' Shrugging off the crawling sensation, she headed into the drying room, instantly enveloped in the dry heat and the smell of wax, waterproofer and sweat.

'Maybe your grandmother is scrying for you like my mum used to do to me.'

'That would be impossible.' Skye tore her hat from her head and threw it onto the bench. 'Grandpa was the magic user. Morrigan hates it as much as I do, especially after what happened to Papa.'

Shelley narrowed her eyes. 'I know I don't have any magic of my own, but I am Wiccan. I know magic when I feel it. And your grandmother uses magic. Not much. Just a little, but magic all the same—like you do.'

'Impossible.' Skye crossed her arms.

Shelley looked up and clenched her hands together before letting them drop with a slap to her side. 'All right. If you won't believe that, then could she have sent someone to keep an eye on you?' Shelley pulled her hat from her head and flipped her long blonde ponytail over her shoulder. 'I was kind of surprised she let you go away for two weeks without so much as a whimper of protest.'

Skye rolled her eyes at the ceiling and plopped down on the bench. 'Fudge it all to hell. You're right. Morrigan just can't keep her perfect Cantrae nose out of my life. I don't know what she thinks I might do if she stopped interfering for five minutes.'

'She's probably afraid you're going to hurt yourself.' Shelley looked pointedly at her ankle.

'Yeah, right.'

Her friend hung up her jacket, flipping her heavy blonde plait over her shoulder with a dull thump. 'Stop worrying about your grandmother and let's get your boots off. I want to see the damage.' She stood there, hands on hips, her height, flawless skin, hair the colour of golden wheat and eyes the colour of the ocean—so deeply blue they were almost violet—making her look like a Norse goddess.

Sighing at her own inadequacies in the face of such perfection, Skye bent to undo the buckles on her boots with a jerk, the loud snap not enough to assuage the anger seething inside.

The very idea that Morrigan had sent someone to watch her! She yanked off one boot and dropped it with a loud clatter on the floor. But when she tried to jerk the other boot off, she yelped. 'Shoot and fudge. That hurts.' Shelley chuckled. 'What?'

'I love your way of swearing. It's all so Disney. You used to swear like a trooper.'

'Yeah, well, I can hardly swear around the kids. I had to come up with alternatives. And even then I only let rip around you and Bron. Or when I'm angry.' She looked down at her ankle. 'Or when I'm hurt. So right now, I'm three for three.' She tried to pull the boot off again and winced at the stab of pain that shot through her ankle.

'Let me help.'

Shelley knelt in front of her and slowly edged the boot off her foot. Her ankle throbbed, and not the usual throb of relief after having been strapped into a tight boot all day. She bit her lip as she stood, careful to keep her weight balanced on her other foot as she took off her jacket, hat and gloves, and hung them up. She went to grab her boots, but Shelley had already put them on the boot rack. 'You don't have to baby me,' she said again.

'And you don't have to take your anger at Morrigan out on me.'

Skye grimaced an apology. 'I'm sorry. She just makes me so angry.' She clenched her hands at her sides, a hot ball tightening in her chest, fingers tingling. 'I mean, why does she persist in treating me like a child?' She hobbled out of the drying room and down the stairs, Shelley following close behind. 'No. *Worse.* Like I am nothing more than a possession.'

'I'm sure she doesn't think that.'

Skye laughed bitterly. 'You don't know Morrigan. It's easy to get charmed by her and miss the fact she can be a right royal bitch.'

Skye shoved the key in the lock of their bunk-room door and pushed it open. She hobbled through, angry that her ankle was so sore, because she sure felt like kicking something. 'I mean, why have me followed? It's like she doesn't think I can be trusted. She makes me so mad.' Her fingers were burning but she ignored the sensation, too caught up in trying to find a way to explain how her grandmother made her feel.

'Um, Skye.'

'I don't know why she bothers. I mean, she hates me. She always has. Thankfully, she cares about River, but me ...' She shook her head. 'I'm like the dirt she scrapes off her boots in winter—annoying and easily discarded. Yet even though she hates me, she won't keep her perfect nose out of my life. Always there. Always harping about my wrong decisions and the fact I should do so much better than I am.' She wanted to pace but could only manage a pathetic sort of limping hop, which made her temper spike higher. The burn in her fingers got hotter, but that didn't matter. All that mattered was the flame of anger in her mind, cauterising her heart at the thought of how little her grandmother truly cared for her. 'I'm so frustrated and hurt and angry—I feel like I'm going to explode.'

'Skye. You need to calm down,' Shelley said forcefully. 'You need to calm down *now*.'

'I don't want to calm down. I want to go back home and ask Morrigan who the hell she thinks she is. I want her to look at me. To really look at me and—' Skye turned and for the first time registered the look on Shelley's face—fear and awe. She glanced down to see what Shelley was staring at.

There was blue flame on her fingertips.

'No! No, no, no, no, no.' Fear gripped her throat, cutting off the words tumbling out of her mouth. She hadn't seen that blue flame erupt from her hands since the night she hurt River when they were ten.

No. This couldn't happen.

I HOPE you enjoyed that excerpt from *Pack Bound*. If you're interested in reading more, you can find the download links here:

https://books2read.com/u/3n8X55

As I mentioned earlier, if you don't want to miss out on news about *Hunter Bound,* the next book in the **Dawn of the Curse Series,** as well as special giveaways, sales, book signings and information on my other books, then sign up to my newsletter.

As an added bonus, when you join, you will get a FREE ebook copy of **Witch Bound,** a novella set 40 years before *Pack Bound.* Just keep reading to find out more:

LOVE A FREE BOOK?

YOUR FREE BOOK IS WAITING

One Fate, one mate, a bond too strong to deny ...

Paul Collins, duty-bound Pack Warlock and seer, must marry a strong witch for the good of Pack McVale. But his hidden feelings for his best-friend's sister, maternal wolf Ivy McVale, make this a more difficult pill to swallow every day. Especially when they begin to mate.

Then Paul has a vision: If they mate, Ivy will die. Desperate, Paul uses his powers to change destiny and make Ivy think she's always hated him. He can deal with any punishment the Fates make him pay for tampering with destiny, as long as Ivy lives.

After recovering from a bewildering month-long illness, Ivy notices her nemesis, Paul, is tormented by something. And strangely, she is the only one who can feel it. Unable to endure such unhappiness—even if he does call her Poison Ivy—she is determined to help him, no matter the cost. Because Pack McVale cannot survive without him, and curiously, neither can she ...

Simply sign up to my newsletter and I will email your free copy of Witch Bound to you. You will also receive the latest on upcoming books, sales, giveaways and relevant bookish news.

Get My Free Copy of Witch Bound Here:

But wait! There's more ...

If you're not into newsletters but think you might be into subscriptions that give you serialised content, exclusive chapters to new books, exclusive bonus content, signed print books and much more, then turn the page to find out about **Leisl's Legends** ...

JOIN LEISL'S LEGENDS

Subscribe to (or follow) me (via the QR code) at my Leisl's Legends page on REAM—a new subscription app like Patreon except it's designed especially for readers and authors for an amazing reading experience—and you will get early access to *The Huntress and the Vampire King*, my hot enemies to lovers, witch-and-vampire-licious urban fantasy romance that readers over there are already in love with. It's the prequel novel to the first book in the Blood-Rites Series - *The Blood of the Seer*.

Be the first to find out where it all began with Anita and Hei's love story.
BECOME A LEGEND NOW!
https://reamstories.com/leislleightonauthor

You will also find serialised chapters of the next book in my popular **Gods Cursed Series** there and can comment on the story as I write it! Not to mention you will also get extra bonuses like exclusive NSFW Bonus Epilogues, Bonus Prologues and cut scenes and chapters from all of my books.

Be part of creating the stories you love AND get exclusive access to a whole range of goodies including other WIPs, bonus content, voting rights, signed books and more.

Read on to find out more about The Huntress and the Vampire King PLUS read the opening chapters …

The Huntress and the Vampire King

She hates the vampire who saved her; he holds the key to her fate …

Hunter-witch Anita Middleton wants revenge against the violent vampire cults that murdered her father and has worked hard to become one of the best vampire hunters there is. But on a difficult hunt she is caught in an ambush and is mortally wounded … only to be saved by a mysterious warrior. A warrior with brilliant blue eyes and long silver-blonde hair who fights with a grace and violence like nothing she's seen. It is only after she wakes in the heart of his palazzo that she realises her saviour is a vampire - and according to her brother and mentor, this vampire king is their ally.

Lord Hei rules over an empire of witches, humans and vampires who have been trying to keep the vicious vampire cults, the Wild and Dark Brethren, at bay for centuries. Then he saves Anita and knows with one look she is the prophecied Huntress who could be his downfall or his salvation - and she is also his fated mate. But she struggles to trust him as her hatred of vampires is deep-seated. And she *needs* to trust him because only he can offer the specialised training a Huntress needs so her power won't overwhelm her.

But with the Dark Brethren mysteriously amassing, he has little time to win her over. And Anita must go on a crash course to learn how to control her Huntress magic ... or go slowly and violently insane.

The Huntress and the Vampire King is the exciting action-packed prequel novel to *The Blood of the Seer.*

If you love your vampires hot with a bit of The Witcher thrown in and your heroines as kick-arse as Buffy and even more tortured, if you love fated mates, enemies to lovers, chosen ones and epically hot romance mixed with action and mystery, then *The Huntress and the Vampire King* is what you've been waiting for.

Sign up to Leisl's Legends and start reading exclusive early release chapters of it now!

BECOME A LEGEND NOW!
https://reamstories.com/leislleightonauthor

ALSO BY LEISL LEIGHTON

PACK BOUND SERIES

Pack Bound

Moon Bound

Shifter Bound

Wolf Bound

Witch Bound

(A Pack Bound Series Prequel Novella -

FREE ebook copy to Newsletter Subscribers)

BOX SET

Pack Bound Series Collection Books 1-4

DAWN OF THE CURSE

A PACK BOUND PREQUEL SERIES

Soul Bound

Alpha Bound

Hunter Bound

Fae Bound

(Coming in 2027)

GODS CURSED SERIES

A Love Cursed Christmas Wish

Love Cursed

Soul Cursed

Blood Cursed

Hearts Cursed

Fates Cursed

Witch Cursed

Dragon Cursed

(Coming 2026)

BLOOD-RITES SERIES

The Blood of the Seer

The Blood of the Sire

The Blood of the Son

(Coming 2027)

BLOOD-RITES PREQUEL AND BONUS MATERIAL

The Huntress and the Vampire King

The Middleton Manifesto

(Available now via Leisl's Legends subscription)

ANTHOLOGIES

A Perfectly Paranormal Valentine

A Perfectly Paranormal Halloween

A Perfectly Paranormal Easter

A Perfectly Paranormal Christmas

A Perfectly Paranormal Prophecy

(Coming in 2027)

As well as writing sexy, epic and romantic paranormal novels, I write mysterious and emotional romantic suspense novels too. Check out the following titles for amazing, suspenseful reads:

STORM HAVEN SERIES

Need You Tonight

The Devil Inside

COALCLIFF STUD SERIES

Climbing Fear: Book 1

Blazing Fear: Book 2

ECHO SPRINGS SERIES

Dangerous Echoes: Book 1

Books 2-4 in this series, (written by Daniel deLorne, TJ Hamilton and Shannon Curtis) are also available now at all ebook retailers.

You can find all the buy links for Leisl's Books at her website:

ABOUT LEISL

Leisl Leighton is a tall red head with an overly large imagination. As a child, she identified strongly with Anne of Green Gables, and like Anne, is a voracious reader and born performer.

It came as no surprise when she went on to a career as a performer, script writer, script doctor, stage manager and musical director for cabaret and theatre restaurants.

After starting a family, Leisl stopped performing and began writing the stories plaguing her dreams. She now writes emotional stories mixed with mystery and a little bit of what goes bump in the night.

Her novels have won and placed in writing contests here and overseas. She is a passionate advocate for the romance genre, was President of Romance Writers of Australia from 2014-2017 and when she's not writing romantic stories of redemption, she is helping other authors reach their dreams with her Author Services.

You can contact Leisl through her website via the QR Code above or here: https://www.leislleighton.com

And if you want to stay in touch and be the first to find out about new releases, appearances, special deals and exclusive content and give-

aways, sign up to her Newsletter and pick up your free copy of *Witch Bound* via the QR code.

Or sign up to *Leisl's Legends* via this QR code to get *Witch Cursed* plus serialised early access stories and bonus content including a bonus

NSFW ending for Love Cursed.

You can also follow her on social media:

facebook.com/LeislLeightonAuthor
instagram.com/leislleightonauthor
bookbub.com/authors/leisl-leighton
amazon.com/stores/Leisl-Leighton/author/BooDBYRGZY

ACKNOWLEDGMENTS

Writing this book was such a joy and yet the path to publication was fraught with many interruptions - at the start of the year when I usually get a good amount of writing done, there was the OS trip to Japan with the family to celebrate us all finishing the school journey (especially through the last four difficult years of Covid times and my car accident), then upon returning my migraines played up big time, then there were health worries with my parents and my hubby's parents and then two hospital visits for me after a few silly kitchen accidents just to name a few!

But those interruptions were only part of the long journey of writing this book. Leanna and Dougal's story proved to be challenging to write in more ways than one. to you. They go through so much and it emotionally exhausting at times to find the right way to express all that was happening, but they needed their story to be told and pushed me on. I'm super proud of me and them for persisting and getting it done and I love how their story has shaped up.

So many people, both family and friends, helped out during this time and filled me with love and the encouragement I needed to keep pushing on. Thanks to all of you - you are superstars!

Of course, special thanks have to go out to my hubby, Mark, and my two beautiful boys, Jacob and Nathaniel, and to my parents, Kerrie and Jim, whose support has never wavered and whose love I could never do without. Love you all.

Aside from great family and friends, a writer needs a Coven of writing peeps all their own. Thanks need to go to these special people for encouraging me in this endeavour and giving me the strength to push on through all the highs and lows of doing this crazy writing thing—Anita and Marnie (my writing retreat buddies), Samantha and Helen (my fellow lovers of sparkly unicorns), Laura, Chris and finally Frana. I couldn't have gotten here without you.

Thanks once again to the insanely talented Samantha Marshall for her brilliant covers. Every day I thank the universe for bringing us together and for being able to count you friend.

A big thank you to to my editor on this one, Brooke Halliwell, who took on this project at the last minute and did a beautiful job of helping me get it to the finish line. I work with Brooke on the novels I have published with Escape, and she edited Witch Bound as well, so it was lovely to be able to work with her again on this new part of the series.

Thoughts and thanks also to my bestie, Helen, who is always with me and forever in my thoughts, and to the first writing friend I ever had, Liz—a part of you will always live on in my writing because I would never have got published without your helpful feedback and constant cheering support. Both of you will always be a part of my stories.

And a big shout out to all my friends in Romance Writers of Australia—you are inspiration and mentor rolled into a big ball of supportive writerly love. Thank you.

The final person I have to thank is my agent, Alex Adsett, for believing in me and my work and always backing every decision I make. Your confidence in me helps me believe I can actually do this writing thing no matter the path I take. Eternal thanks.